SPIRALS

A novel by
Ruby Standing Deer

FIRST EDITION SOFTCOVER
ISBN: 1622539540
ISBN-13: 978-1-62253-954-3

Edited by Megan Harris and Lane Diamond

Printed in the U.S.A.

www.EvolvedPub.com
Evolved Publishing LLC
Cartersville, Georgia

Printed in Book Antiqua font.

DEDICATION:

To Aya Walksfar,
For all your words of encouragement,
and for the hours spent making Spirals *possible.*

Introduction

As in Circles, the first book, I had to use words that would not have appeared in the language of the First Peoples to make it easier for today's readers to understand. Much does not translate into English.

The "hairy faces," the Conquistadors, did invade and push the Peoples from their lands, but some joined these bands and became dedicated members. You will meet one in *Spirals*. Evil lies in the hearts of many humans, but that does not mean it lives there forever.

Many of these characters are from *Circles* and not strangers to this next book. There are only a few you will not recognize.

Shining Light – Young Holy Man, family man with much yet to learn

Animal Speaks Woman - "Speaks" (heart name), Shining Light's woman

Turtle Dove – Daughter of Shining Light and Animal Speaks Woman

Gentle Wisdom – Shining Light's cousin

Tall Smiling Warrior – A hairy-face man (white man)

Flying Raven Who Dreams and **Makes Baskets** – Shining Light's parents

Soft Breeze – Shining Light's sister

Sparrow Hawk – Shining Light's brother

Hawk Soaring and Bright Sun Flower – Shining Light's grandparents

Wanderer – Unusual Holy Man

Falling Rainbow – Young woman whom Wanderer rescues

Night Hunter – Man who pursues Falling Rainbow

Sparkling Star – Pregnant runaway slave

Thunder – Mustang with her own mind

And of course - **White Paws and Moon Face** – The wolves

Chapter 1

Falling Rainbow's ceremony, a joyous celebration, turned sour when Night Hunter came to her parent's lodge with three mustangs as an offering for her. Elk Dreaming, her father, refused. Night Hunter could do nothing but walk away and promise to return with his last mustang, the prized male. He gave her father an angry glare as he left.

Falling Rainbow knew her father did not want his only daughter to go to a man whose face was etched in anger; he'd told her so days before when the man entered their camp. He'd told Night Hunter that his daughter was worth more than mustangs.

She hoped her father would come up with an impossible request for another gift.

She backed away into the darkness of their lodge and curled into her mother's arms. Her mother held her, cooing and rocking her as she had done since Falling Rainbow was a child.

Tears fell from both women, and the new woman pulled away. "Mother, I will never be Night Hunter's woman. I will leave the band first. Night Hunter is four winters older and I hold no desire in my heart for him. I do not understand why he wants me as his mate. I heard him speaking to his brother about Power. I do not understand."

"I know, Daughter, more that you think I do. But you must also know a man changes with the right woman, and four winters is not so much. Your father is eight winters older than I am. You must not judge a man by his age."

Her mother reached behind her for a pack. "Here. You will find food, a knife, and an extra humpback robe to keep you warm. I knew you would want to go into the canyons, after you ducked into one of the lodges of your friends when he showed up with his brother. Night Hunter will leave soon. I know your father will tell him you have other men who ask for you, and that he must allow each one to speak to him. It is not a lie, Daughter, not really. I have watched young men follow you with their eyes. Come back after maybe two sunrises. I smell snow even this late in the season, so you must walk with care. You can take one of your father's mustangs."

Her mother reached out and ran her hands over Falling Rainbow's face as if memorizing it. "Be safe. If the snow starts to fall, you turn around and come home, you understand?"

She nodded and hugged her mother. Taking a mustang would mean hoof prints to follow. She intended to walk where she would leave few footprints, but did not want her mother to worry, so she said nothing.

She slipped out under the lodge's edging, and disappeared into the coming darkness.

***

Falling Rainbow did not know which way to go. After two days of walking, the snow, a light fluff at sunrise, had turned into a fierce, howling blizzard. Sleeping on the ground with her robes would leave her shivering too much.

I should have listened to Mother about the mustang! The snow whisked around in deep circles, and her steps became more labored. Soon darkness would take the land.

Of all nights, this had to be the one when Sister Moon chooses to hide. I am sure he waits for me still, and I have no more food! Shelter now became more important than finding the paintings in the canyons.

Many times, she had searched for the paintings. Her parents knew, but no longer worried. The hairy faces had long ago stopped coming this way to hunt for the yellow stone. This is why her people had settled here this last time. The band moved to the new campsite four moons ago, just after the leaves fell, to escape the raids on their old camp.

Why do they steal our women when they have their own? And why my closest friend? Had I not gone home when I did, I would have been captured along with her.

She shook the memory from her mind and tightened her light ceremony robe, and the humpback one with the hair on the inside, around herself. She kept her arms inside, her fingers clinging to the outside edges. Neither robe did much to cover her ice-crusted hair.

"Why do these things happen?" She stared up searching for blue sky, but found only thick, grey clouds.

Are the Spirits angry with me? Do they wish me to be Night Hunter's woman? No, they sent me the dream vision! A vision of the paintings, so they must have plans for me that I do not yet understand.

"I am freezing! Why do you torment me?" she yelled, raising her fist to the darkening clouds, but quickly put her hands over her mouth and let her robes fall.

Angry Spirits might make the storm worse. She just needed shelter, but had no idea where to go. Father Sun had already lowered, and she could not see that well.

She scooped up both her ceremony robe and the one her mother had made her, and flung them back over herself. Beautiful tinkling shells and quillwork across the bottom of the ceremonial elk hide did little to keep the new woman of fourteen winters warm. Every turn she took looked the same. With so much blowing snow, she could barely keep her eyes open. Her teeth hurt from chattering, and her fingers ached, burning from the cold. She blew into cupped hands, her breath barely warm, and touched her round face, but her numbed cold skin felt little. She shoved her hands back inside and pulled what robe she could over her head.

I am lost! Lost! How can this be? Many times, I have followed these canyons on one-day rides or two-day walks. Stupid! Why did you walk? Where was your mind?

And where was your mind when you let Night Hunter take you that night, moons ago? You were lucky a baby was not made. Did he use some kind of trick to draw me to him? Why did he take me knowing I was not yet a woman? Why did I allow him to dishonor me? Teardrops froze in little balls on her cold face. *No other man will want me now.*

Three moons ago, she heard his flute music as it floated past her lodge, soft on the cold night air. Her mother had told her every woman knew the sound of her future man's voice in the music. Not knowing who called, she followed the sound. Quiet footsteps led her to him. She could not see who it was, but went to him even though she should not have until her ceremony had passed. Hypnotized by the beautiful sound, she faced Night Hunter unafraid. The flute stopped, then their eyes met and he lowered her to the ground. It was wrong, very wrong. Even the cold and snow-covered ground did not stop her from lying with him, encased in the warm humpback robe.

Another blast of cold brought her back, reminding her she had yet to find safety, and that she did not have the warmth of another person. She started to drift in her mind, thoughts jumbled. Her body shivered uncontrollably, and her feet ached from the freezing water that had found its way through the sinew used to make her footwear. She rounded another curve in the canyon. Orange-red colors plastered in icy-white greeted her. Her eyes combed for caves, indents in the stone, even a curve that would get her out of the wind.

Nothing! There is no shelter anywhere!

She arched her neck toward the now nearly invisible clouds and cried out. "Creator, help me please. I am young and afraid. I am not brave. I fear loosing my life in such a way. Who would sing my Soul to the campfires in the sky? I would be lost in-between this land and the Spirit's land. Please, Great Mystery, help me to help myself. I know I am weak. I am sorry. I wish I was braver."

She pushed away her snow-covered hair that escaped from the robe, but it whipped around, slapping her face. *Stupid! I smelled snow! Why did I not take my winter footwear?* Her ceremonial footwear soaked up even more of the icy water. She'd hurried, and the air was warm when she'd left. Still, even after her parents had taught her about sudden cold, she had not listened. She had acted as a child, and now must pay for her haste. *Would a woman act this way?*

Cold and exposure started to claim her. Numb feet no longer ached. She could no longer feel the tips of her fingers. *Sleepy.... If I could just rest.*

Thunder rolled and lightning sparked in pink above her. Thunder snow. The old ones said it meant Nature herself was confused, and the cold season was always much worse. At every turn, she found only white ice that clung to jutting edges of stone—no shelter anywhere. She pushed on, head bent against the blasts of cold pelting her face. Ice concealed the uneven ground, and the tip of a hidden stone tripped her. Frozen ground rose up to meet her. She lost her grip on the robes, and gasped when the icy water splashed up her dress. With numb hands, she pushed herself into a sitting position, and laughed.

I finally feel warm. Am I seeing the last place of my life? I should have stayed and accepted Night Hunter's offer. He was not so bad to look at when he did not wrinkle his face in anger. He did smile at me the first time we saw each other. I did not see anger then.

Instead, I lay here freezing. So sleepy.... If I could rest but for a short span.

"No!"

She reached out for the pack her mother had given her, hoping she had missed extra clothing. She clung to the rocky face of the canyon wall, pulled herself up and reached her arm behind herself to pull the pack off her back. The canyon's snow crusted wall gave in and some hand-like thing pulled her through.

Her own hands touched fur, and she screamed.

Chapter 2

Falling Rainbow fell on musty robes and backed away in terror. Tiny eyes scurried past her. The only sound that met her ears did not sound like her own breathing. She held her breath.

It could not belong to her! It had to be a monstrous creature.

She scrambled away until her back hit the cold, hard wall of the cave, and awaited her fate. She would not—*could* not—go back out into the cold, blinding snow. Bright sparks drew her attention as a small fire lit up the cave.

"Who has come to visit me?" An elder man stepped into the light cast by a fire. "Do you know it is the wrong time for visiting? This cold season has brought much snow, and now Nature forgets the time of snow has past. Pull a robe over you, silly child—*after* you get out of your footwear. They soak my robes. Your lips are blue. Get out of all your clothing so you can get warm. Well, do not act like an animal caught in Bear's cave. I do not wish my robes to be soaked. And you, girl, the bad Spirits will find you, make you sick if you do not listen to me."

Her eyes widened at the sight of the elder. Relief mixed with fear made bile climb up into her throat. He appeared harmless, far more concerned for her.

His eyes... they look as one does when they are not connected to this side.

She stared, her mouth agape. She pulled off her footwear, dragged a dry robe up to her chattering chin, and stared at the elder before her. He had his head turned and talked to someone she could not see. She squinted to see a tiny mouse on his shoulder. The mouse took a piece of food from him, and ran off to eat it somewhere in the darker part of the cave.

"We help each other." The man spoke without looking up. "They eat my dried foods and keep me company. Those who are soon to pass to their campfires in the sky—I ease their burden with a fast end."

He smiled warmly at her, most of his teeth gone. "Come closer to the fire, child. Please get out of those clothes. No harm will come your way. I heard you outside, crying out, and I knew you needed help, so I pulled you in."

She finally found some words. "They go to the campfires in the sky? I thought only humans went there."

"Well, where then, did you think all other beings go? Into nothing?" He cackled, leaned back and stretched. The little fire had grown large enough to warm the cave. "The Great Mystery creates all creatures. Why would only humans be chosen to live in the sky and make campfires at night? Do you not have storytellers in your band who teach you the stories?"

Confused, squinted eyes stared back at her from a mass of tangled hair filled with stardust. It fell past old, thin shoulders that showed through the holes in his worn tunic. "Do not be shy. Get out of those wet clothes and toss your own robes before you ruin my robe!"

She glanced around for something dry. A stack of carefully folded clothing lay within her reach. In the dim light she saw fur-lined footwear, a long tunic and leggings, and reached for the tunic — fur-lined both outside and inside. Carefully stitched strips of black, browns and whites created the colorful and warm looking piece of clothing. She glanced up to see if he watched her.

"Oh my, do not look at me so. I will look away." He grinned and turned his head.

She kept her eyes on him while she questioned him. "Who are you? Why are you in this cave? Where did — "

The elder held up his hands while still facing away from her, and chuckled as he spoke. "You ask questions, but do not wait for the answer before you ask another. Slow down, girl. I am called One Who Wanders, or Wanderer, by my friends."

"I am dressed. Please turn around... and thank you for helping me. I know I was about to fall into the sleep that takes away life. I... wait. You have friends? What kind of friends would allow an elder to live alone in a cave?" She fingered the furred leather on the warm, dry boots.

The elder stared at her, sadness reflecting from his eyes and tightened brows. "They are all gone. Went to the stars long ago. I stayed behind." He tossed her a comb carved from bone.

"Stayed behind? You speak as... as." She did not want to be rude and call him addled. "Why did you stay alone in the canyons?" She caught small handfuls of hair and tried to pull the comb through, but gave up and placed it beside her.

One Who Wanders grinned and exposed what few teeth remained. "For you, of course. You came just in time." He handed her a carved, wooden bowl. Firelight reflected on the small animals painted on the sides. Two wolves faced each other and a mustang stood by a small human figure. "Eat, and do not wonder what you eat. We all return to the same source. This keeps the Circle whole."

Her belly protested too much to worry if she ate dried meat, or fish or.... She raised the bowl, smelled the hot food, but stopped and said a silent prayer to the Spirits. She then raised the warm liquid to her cold lips with hands that still shook. "My hands hurt some. I am sorry if I spill the... food on your nice robe.

He nodded her way. "Good, good, I see you are respectful. Someone has taught you something, at least. And I see your lips are no longer blue. Good thing I found this cave a full cycle of seasons ago. It gave me time to fill it with food."

Another mouse climbed up his shoulder, and he stopped talking to feed him. He looked up again and continued to speak with the same kind voice. "I had to bury it so my little friends did not eat it all. I found thin robes in here, too, carefully stitched with sinew around the edges. They worked well for wrapping food. The other robes with the humpback's hair on them were a bit worn, but I mended them. I could tell they had been here for some time, neatly stacked and waiting for me to find them. Whoever put these robes here took great care in tanning them. I am grateful that these huge animals roam the grasslands."

"One Who Wanders—"

"Oh, call me Wanderer like my friends." He leaned over and offered to fill her bowl again. "Good thing I made extra. I see you are very hungry."

She looked up from her bowl and into eyes that stared right through her. They had a soft blue glow. He wore a worn, quilled yellow and white headband that reminded her of the zigzags on the canyon baskets that a trader brought occasionally. Her father had actually traded a good robe for one.

She guessed Wanderer had seen around fifty-five winters, maybe more. "Where are your friends?

"What friends?" He reached for another bowl and dipped it in into the warm food, then leaned back and blew on it. "Good this time! Much better with the dried root plants added in. I saved them for when you would come. My friends would have enjoyed this."

She squeezed her eyebrows together and smacked her head. "*Your* friends who call you Wanderer. Where are they?" She tried to show only respect for the elder, but he made her mind crazy.

He jabbed a finger above his head. "There. Not to worry, little one, I will do you no harm. I had two wonderful women in my lifetime and do not want for another... even if you are a pretty one." He cocked his head her way as a mouse scurried over the robe she sat under. "Do not mind them. They, too, mean you no harm." He pointed to her hair. "My, your hair is long and thick, a bit tangled up. Your round face gives you Doe's eyes. I must admit I find your long nose and wide lips beautiful. And your square jaw, where did you get that from?"

She reached up and felt her jaw. "I... I was born with it. Is it ugly?"

He laughed loud enough to send mice racing for cover. "You are too pretty to have an ugly chin! Even your voice has a soft sound. I know you must sing as beautiful as birds do when they seek a mate. You must be... what... thirteen winters old? I can see many men will want you. Your beauty comes through well. I find you very good to look at."

"I am fourteen winters and a woman! Can you not see that?'

He slapped his robe with his hand and grinned. "Oh, yes, I see that now. Only a woman's voice would speak so loud as yours. And... so sweetly." He cleared his throat.

He jerked upright, stiffened and grabbed for her. She squealed as he reached over and put a hand across her mouth to silence her. "Shhh! Do you hear that? Cover your head and let your air out quietly. I hear crunching on top of the snow."

She spoke through her muffled mouth. "Could they be your friends?"

"Remember, my friends do not live in this world anymore. Shhh... voices!" He let go of her, covered her with a robe and tossed dirt to strangle the fire. Smoke started to rise and he tossed a robe over it.

***

"Night Hunter, why does this... this girl interest you so? I have seen many beautiful women in this band and our own. Why not choose an older one with enough sense not to runaway in a snowstorm!" Mustang hooves stomped in the snow as the men jumped off them.

The sound was loud enough for Falling Rainbow to hear inside the cave.

"Brother, listen well to me. She holds Power that belongs to a man. If I take her as my woman, I will also claim her Power as mine. That old father of hers thinks too highly of her. After all, she has much growing yet to do in mind and body. I will take her back to our band and say her father, as a special gift, gave me her Power. I will then gain the favor of the hairy-faces who came to live with us."

She tried to peek out, but an old hand pulled her back.

"They think we are as dead blades of grass, to be walked on. I will show them it is they who are to be walked on!"

"Are you sure Falling Rainbow came this way? I see no tracks, nothing to show she—"

"Brother, if there were any tracks, the snow that slaps at our backs would have covered them." He huffed and jumped on his mustang. "Stupid girl. I tire of searching for her! We will return and wait for her. She has no place to go but back to her parents' lodge. She might be there already, and here we are, riding in wet, freezing...."

Sounds of mustangs moving made her dig deep in the fur. She found it hard to breathe slowly. Her hands clutched each other and she bit at her knuckles. She was sure they heard her pounding heart.

"We go back and see if she has returned. If not, we wait. If she hides in someone's lodge, her own body's needs will force her out."

"Good, I saw two women whose faces were full of smiles when I mentioned to an elder woman that I had no mate. My night may not be as boring as yours."

***

Wanderer acted as if no one had nearly found the cave they sat in. "Falling Rainbow? Now, I simply do not understand that name." He tossed the robe off the dirt, scooped it away and restarted the small fire. Another mouse ran up and took an offered nibble of food from his hand. "How does a rainbow fall? Please tell me how your name came to be."

Dim light in the room came alive as he added sticks to the waking fire. He snuggled in his robe much like a child awaiting a good story.

She cocked her head toward the cave entrance, which was once again hidden by snow. "I... do you not worry? What if those two decided to come back? And what Power? I have no power. So his smile at me when he called with his flute was not real."

The bowl that she picked back up leaned sideways in her hands, as a mouse dared to put a tiny paw on the bowl's ledge.

"Ahh! What are you doing?" She jerked backward and sent the bowl flying. It thudded in the back of the cave and made a wobbling sound. She shrieked and quickly put her hand over her mouth, and glanced back and forth. "Do you think anyone heard?"

He tossed his head back and laughed. "I would say every mouse in here did!"

"No, humans. Do you think Night Hunter and his brother heard?"

"Night Hunter? Well, if he had, he would be here by now. No, child, he did not hear. You are safe. The night is very dark. The Mother we walk upon must have a tired daughter. She has chosen to sleep this night. Gather your things, Falling Rainbow, and I will gather mine. We must be ready as soon as Father Sun wakes."

Falling Rainbow sat stiffly, open-mouthed. "What... where... I am not going home! Night Hunter waits for me!"

"Of course not, child. It is time for us to move on. I will show you the paintings. When we reach them it will be time to rest for the night."

"How did you know I have been looking for paintings? I did not tell you."

"No, you did not, did you?"

"Then how did you know I looked for the paintings?"

"Curl up and sleep, girl. The fire will soon go out and we will loose its warmth. I wish to be asleep before then." He turned on his side and scooted down into the robes.

Without a word, she slipped into the robe, grateful to be safe and warm. Sleep overtook her exhausted body.

Chapter 3

"Push! The baby is not going to come out with you just squatting, girl. I know the time has been long, but you are nearly there," Bright Sun Flower said.

Animal Speaks Woman tried to be helpful as her man's grandmother wiped her sweaty brow. She no longer wanted to be a mother... but she did—her emotions, befuddled. Two days of pain had weakened her body and mind. From somewhere inside the lodge, a young girl who knew nothing of birthing pain yelled, "Push!" *She can say push all she wants, but* she *does not have to squeeze her own insides out!*

Her mother kept telling her how she would forget all the pain once her new baby rested at her breast. *Ha! That is what every woman who comes to see me says.* Even Running River, with enough children to start her own band, had come earlier, smiling and offering words of comfort. *Comfort! The woman's last child slid out so fast she had no time to reach the birthing lodge.*

She spoke through the sweat streaming across her lips. "Mother, can you not see the head? Your hands are small! Reach inside and guide my baby out. How can such a tiny baby be so hard to get out? I will never do this again. Never!"

Morning Star rubbed her back. "Slow your breath down. You panic. Do you want your baby to be afraid all her life? The calmer you are, the more peaceful your baby's life will be. See how your little sister sleeps? I stayed calm and—"

"Mother, she is not giving birth, I am! Of course she sleeps in peace!" She put the leather back between her teeth, bit down and grunted.

"Daughter, first babies can be this way." She reached down and felt for any signs of the baby's head. "Lie back for a bit and allow me to rub your legs, and Bright Sun Flower will rub your shoulders. You feel tight. Makes Baskets needs to nurse her son, but she will return to help sing to your daughter, to let her know she is welcome."

She listened to songs her mother and Bright Sun Flower sang to the unborn baby, telling her how good life would be, what a happy place she was about to enter. They reminded her of the songs she and Shining Light had sung to their unborn daughter, preparing her for life outside her belly. Some of the songs were to teach the girl things she would need to know about life.

She groaned as her belly tightened again.

***

Shining Light sat sulking while several women came and left—throughout the night and past Father Sun's rising.

Flying Raven Who Dreams tried to comfort him. "Most women do not want us men bothering them while they are in the birthing lodge, Son, which is why we are farther away than you want to be. You cannot change how they feel. This is the women's business, not ours. It has always been this way, which is why your mother waved us away just now. They do not want us here. Birthing has always been a private thing. I was only able to help your mother give us our daughter because we were all alone."

"Father, I no longer care!" He thrust out his arm in agitation. "Look at how tight the lodge is closed. Why must the lodge sides be down? Do they fear bad Spirits or us seeing inside?" He scooted away from his father and stood. "I am going behind it to open a small spot. She needs clean, cool air. The air outside has the blessing of Sister Wind. They barely gave the flap time to close before tying it shut."

Before his father could grab his tunic, he slipped away.

"Shining Light, let the women be. We are not even meant to be this close! Soon Father Sun will rest and the night air will cool."

He ignored his father and, silent as a mouse, crept on his knees behind the lodge. He lifted the bottom and placed a short, fat log under the flap—high enough to allow a cool breeze inside. He met up with White Paws' wet nose. The wolf had hid inside the lodge by the back edge.

Animal Speaks Woman clutched the fur on his back with one hand. She moved her head up to see Shining Light, and smiled. She mouthed the words, "*Soon... soon.*" Another spasm hit her hard enough that she bolted upright.

White Paws tried to lick her arm, but Shining Light pulled him back while her hand still gripped his fur. He whispered to the wolf. "How is it that *you* get to be inside and *I* do not?"

He leaned on his knees toward the wolf's face. "Even though I am a Holy Man, they will only allow me in if they need my help. Grandmother is there as birthing woman and Holy Woman. Should you even be here? What about *your* four pups? I know your mate takes them on small hunts... and... you should be there, with *your* babies, not mine!"

White Paws, his fur a darker grey now than when he was a pup, cocked his head and let his tongue flop out to one side.

"I am happy that human women only give birth to one! I have heard of women having a second one, but hope that never happens to us. I would not allow anyone to think my second child was a bad omen! Women are funny creatures."

A loud grunt from within the lodge sent the young man and wolf scurrying from the back of the lodge. White Paws left behind a handful of his fur. Before they could run to the safety of nearby trees, a shadow towered above them.

"So, Grandson, do you wish to be a birthing woman?" Bright Sun Flower's familiar squished fruit-face glared down at the pair. Her wrinkles no longer raced across her face, but her scowl could still make people stop in place.

"Grandmother, I... um... was pulling White Paws away. Now I too go away. Perhaps a walk will comfort me." He stood up and dusted off his leggings and tunic. He turned to leave, but looked into his grandmother's softening face and stopped.

"You act as my grandson—my little Feather Floating In Water—rather than Shining Light. I see the boy in the way you act, even if your body and face are of a man. I see the muscles on your body but still see Feather in your expressions. And your silliness!"

The years of age had melted away from her when they entered the Sacred place of Tall Trees. Her eyes still held a soft blue glow.

Power. Her power has grown even more here. She no longer has pains in her knees either.

"Shining Light, I know you worry, but this is the nature of things. Your woman is fine. Your baby will come when she is ready." Bright Sun Flower smiled and placed a basket in his hand. "Go gather swamp plant fluff. There is plenty still clinging to the tops of last season's plants. Your new baby will need it to keep her bottom dry."

He gratefully took the basket, and scampered toward the still waters that pooled at the bottom of falling water splashing over boulders. Small white flowers reached out from emerald moss along the edges of the pool. Never would he tell his grandmother no, even if he *was* a man and could say no if he wanted.

He turned to talk to White Paws, but the wolf's tail stuck out from the birthing lodge. "Maybe he has learned to turn invisible. Not one person appears to notice him. Yet *I* try to give Speaks fresh air and *I* am chased off! Perhaps I need to grow fur and—"

Shining Light took one step too many and sunk one of his feet in the soft mud surrounding the swamp plants. He sat down to pull it out, coming up with a naked foot instead.

"I am a soon-to-be-father who still acts as a boy!"

"You are a boy."

"I am not!" He spun around to face the intruder, his cousin. "Gentle Wisdom, you do not act so smart today. I am past fifteen winters now, not a boy!" He flexed his muscles. "How many boys have these?"

Some others his age had yet to go on their first Vision Quest, but he had proven himself long ago. "My mother and my woman both tell me I am good to look at. I am *not* a boy."

"Then why do you argue with me? A man would remain silent when bested." Gentle Wisdom crossed her arms and stared up into the treetops.

"Bested! You learn more strange words from the other Peoples you visit. What is 'bested?' Gentle Wisdom acts like a child, not a girl about to become a woman. You should still carry the name Chases Butterflies. Why Blue Night Sky gave you the name Gentle is something I will never understand. You are—"

"Shining Light!"

He turned to the sound of his father's voice, who motioned to him.

"Come."

He dropped the basket and ran toward his father.

"Shining Light, do you want your footwear?"

He turned to his cousin, who smiled as she waved his footwear in the air, and he limped back, glaring at her grinning face.

"Thank you." He grunted as he snatched his footwear back, and took off again before his cousin could tease him more.

His grandmother roared with laughter as he hop-raced to the birthing lodge.

***

Makes Baskets opened the flap and brought out a squalling baby. She cooed at the bundle she brought toward Shining Light. "Your daughter, son of mine, has made me a very young grandmother. She tells all she has arrived. Her face is round like yours and she wears your square chin, but has the eyes and soft mouth of her mother. And such thick hair!"

She cuddled the baby so close in the folds of her elk skin dress that the new father could not see his daughter.

"Mother!" He held out his hands. "My daughter, please. I would like to see her also."

She stuck her tongue out at him, then grinned. "You must be careful to hold her head up and cradle her bottom."

"You forget that I held Sparrow Hawk when he was welcomed into the band, and did fine."

Her youngest son, Sparrow Hawk, was now two winters old, thirteen winters younger than his big brother, who had grown tall enough to stand face-to-face with her, his squared jaw matching hers.

"I only tease. Here is your sweet daughter." She handed the now quiet newborn, wrapped in rabbit fur, to the new father.

He looked in surprise at Makes Baskets. "She is so small! As long as it took, I thought she would be much bigger! Look at those tiny hands grab my finger. Awww... she is so tiny I could carry her in one hand."

A new mother's voice boomed from the birthing lodge. "Man of mine! You think she is tiny, eh? Next time *you* give birth! Bring me my tiny daughter, Man-With-Big-Hands. I will *show* you tiny."

Makes Baskets motioned with her head to go in, but Shining Light stood there, not moving.

"Mother, is she angry? She sounds like She Bear, not a human! I am not so sure—"

"Go in. She sounds no different from any new mother. You must unwrap your daughter and tell your woman that you were mistaken, that your daughter simply *looked* small in all the rabbit fur. Make big eyes to show that you now see how large she really is. Now go, do as I say and all will be well."

***

Flying Raven couldn't help but smile as Makes Baskets turned, walked over to where he sat, and eagerly took the food he offered his woman. She inspected his full cape of Raven's feathers, which reached his waist just like his hair. With a half-cocked smile on her face, she watched her second son, Sparrow Hawk, sing in his arms.

"I think we have another special child," she said. "Soft Breeze sings in your arms and tells stories as if she lived another life. Now our son sings words I swear I understand sometimes." She reached out to his face. "You are so handsome. Our young son has your bright eyes and slender nose. He did get my square jaw, so some of me will be in his face as he grows."

"Now, woman of mine," Flying Raven said. "You know why we both dreamed of Sparrow Hawk before he came to be with us. He has his own song, even if we do not hear it that way. You told me the night before his birthing that you heard singing. You have changed so much since that flash flood in the canyon. You now dream, see bits of the future. I wonder who this rainbow girl is that you dream of. Shining Light has dreamed of her and a bear that is white. He says he knows the carved White Bear, given to him by Blue Night Sky, the Great Elder, is not from the place of much snow, but of here. Even if we have snow and sometimes cold winters, he says Blue Night Sky thought it was in a land very far from where we now live. I have yet to see this bear — or dream of this girl — and I am Holy Man."

He stared deeply into the trees as if these visions might appear.

*****

Shining Light and Animal Speaks Woman were alone with their new baby daughter in the birthing lodge. He sat next to his mate, unwrapped the newborn, and boasted on what a big daughter he held. "Do we give her the name of Turtle Dove as my father's grandmother said to, or do we wait and see what name the Spirits will offer?"

"Shining Light, I am a bit tired. Please put our daughter beside me and allow me to rest before we decide. I know since you are a Holy Man like your father, your dreams tell you her name, but I think the vision you had long ago has already told you." She yawned and closed her eyes.

He smiled and placed his daughter next to his sleeping woman. As he stood to leave a bear's outline appeared through the lodge's wall. His arms tingled and his heart raced, as if he had been running for a long span. Dizziness forced him to reach out and grab the lodge's flap. He had only seen White Bear from far away, and then but for a flash, and now she appeared to be right outside.

The tingling... it had started again.

*****

Hawk Soaring sat next to Flying Raven, the new grandfather, and laughed as Shining Light tried to swallow words he'd already spoken. Hawk Soaring pulled his hair into one braid down his back. It held the dark luster of a much younger man. Gone were his wrinkles and sunken eyes. His jaw now pushed forward with the help of his teeth.

Not a single person appeared as an elder anymore. Their new home indeed held the magic that he had dreamed of as a child.

"I seem to be in trouble most sunrises, anymore. Bright Sun Flower thinks I spend too much time away from our lodge." He chuckled, stood and stretched his back. "I may not be aging anymore, but stiffness still takes anyone's back who sits straight too long."

He motioned for Flying Raven to walk with him.

They wandered into a meadow bursting with new life. Busy birds dashed past them in their search to fill hungry mouths that peeped from nests above them. The men walked on a rich, green carpet filled with flowers that burst in an arc of spectral colors unknown beyond the Forest of Trees. A doe jumped up and dashed into thick underbrush, white flowers spraying everywhere.

Hawk Soaring raised his head to stare into the clear wildflower-blue sky. "Such beauty here, but I do miss the reds and oranges of the canyons. I would one day like to go back."

He felt himself drifting away and refocused his mind. He picked up a stick poking out of the rich, green grass and twirled it in his hands.

"Heh, I told Bright Sun Flower when our daughter was born, that with the baby being so small, I could not understand why no one reached in and pulled her out. Animal Speaks Woman spoke the same words to her mother this day." He shook his head and stopped to watch a pair of Eagles drift into the misty treetops.

He sucked in air. "Wrong thing to say. For a woman who was supposed to have been so weak, Bright Sun Flower clawed at my arm like Eagle ready to tear his meal apart. I left for that night, and went to the lodge meant for men with no mates."

Flying Raven leaned his head back in laughter. "When Soft Breeze decided to greet us, not soon after that flash flood in the canyon, Makes Baskets woke me and said, 'Wake up, man of mine, our daughter comes.' Before I could get the robe out, which we had brought for that reason, Soft Breeze was nearly all the way out! We had barely enough time to slip the robe under Makes Baskets. Perhaps after the first it is easier."

The soft patter of feet and giggles came from behind the pair. "Here, catch, man of mine who did not feel birthing pain most of the night before his daughter slipped out." Makes Baskets swung Soft Breeze into his arms while their boy Sparrow Hawk tottered over and clung to her dress, bouncing and begging to take his sister's place. "I slept for spans of time, my belly waking me in spasms before that breeze woke me, letting me know my daughter wanted out. You appear to have forgotten that Sparrow Hawk was in no hurry. I remember hearing you pacing and praying... for two sunrises."

Soft Breeze pushed her arms against her father's chest and leaned back. "I remember too, Father. You pull on your hair too!" She jumped from his arms, giggled and danced in a little circle. She had a softer jaw line than her mother, and a round cheerful face with shiny eyes to match. She wore Hawk Soaring's nose, long and slender.

"Father was a worried man!" She put her little hands on tiny hips and danced around the three adults, her little braids bouncing. The shells brought by a trader tinkled against small elk teeth that decorated her dress.

"He ate the ground down around the lodge like this. I know! I watched." Her small feet stomped in a circle and her face wrinkled up with feigned worry. After stomping around three times, she fell over in laughter, legs kicking upward.

Makes Baskets scooped her daughter up in the air and rubbed noses with her. "Silly, silly little one, I would have liked to see your father act so! We will go now and leave these adult men to care for the little boy who will one day worry for his own woman... which is a long, *long* way off." She eyed Flying Raven. "A long way off."

She looked up at the darkening sky. "Our granddaughter has been born on a moonless night. I wonder if that means she will be able to see in the dark better."

Without another word, she turned, took Soft Breeze by her hand, and went back to the birthing lodge. Soft Breeze twirled around with a toothy smile and waved before turning back.

Hawk Soaring put his hands across his mouth and chuckled while staring at Flying Raven's bewildered face. "Even when they are but babies they have power over men."

Chapter 4

Shining Light shuffled beside Bright Sun Flower. "Why is it my woman cannot get our daughter to take food, Grandmother? Dove has lived two days and will not take nourishment."

He spoke in soft tones away from everyone else. Too many people had followed him with worried eyes since his daughter was welcomed into the band.

Bright Sun Flower inhaled and pursed her lips, then stared up at the pair of Eagles playing in the currents. "The birth was hard on them both. Your woman and daughter are strong. I know you do not want to leave them, but I think it is time you go pray, maybe give an offering. I see you pacing too much. You worry your woman, and she is scared enough. I watched her this morning sitting in front of your lodge, staring off. She must eat more, and I will go make sure she does while you are gone."

"Do you think the moonless night caused this?" His tone was serious as he pulled his fingers and popped them.

Her lips turned into a thin slash. "Of course not. Do not give your mind to silly thoughts. The whispers from the women are just that, no more." She turned to see some of the women staring their way, and cleared her throat loudly. "We live in a new land, and only good things have come our way since we have been here—good things!"

The women scattered.

He relaxed and some of the tightness in his shoulders let go. "You still have a strong voice that others listen to! I know Grandfather does not wait long before he comes when you call him."

***

Shining Light took his grandmother's advice, and gathered his Sacred items in a pouch. His woman had spent much time quilling it, in all white with the natural black tips. The entire pouch, except the bottom, started in a small Spiral and expanded to the edges.

White Paws trotted behind him as usual.

The early season awoke, showing off its colors of greens, rusts, and a mix of white and yellow flowers that competed with thin-spiked purple-pink ones for the light beneath the trees. The trees themselves glistened from tiny water droplets on the green moss that grew on one side. Several soft, tan-eared plants, which the people found good to eat once boiled, climbed in a Spiral up the trunks.

He stopped to watch a new butterfly struggle to come out of its cone-shaped home on a branch of a small tree, which had kept him safe as he turned into a yellow and black beauty. "Look, White Paws. See how he readies himself for flying? I wonder why we are not born with wings. Maybe it is a good sign, seeing one only now finding his way out of the wrap he made for himself."

He pointed to two more climbing out and testing their wings before they moved on. "New life is everywhere."

Light filtered through the trees along the animal trail they shared. The pair wound about the path covered in vines, to where the rainbows fell with the waters. Many times, he came to his favorite spot simply to watch the rainbow fall and splash into the water. He laid out his robe away from the stream's edge to avoid its getting damp, and started a small fire within round stones he had placed there the last time he prayed.

He stood with Sacred Sage and waved the smoking, tied stick of leaves to the four directions, as well as above to Creator and below to the Mother they walked upon, and allowed the plant to go out. On his knees with raised arms, he reached out to the Great Mystery. His hair dipped past the bottom of his back and swayed as he prayed.

"Creator, many children have been welcomed since we found our way here. I know you did not let the Spirits guide me, and bring our Peoples here, only to allow my new daughter to go back to the stars."

Loose Sage nestled in a colorful shell that a trader had brought back from the salty waters. He put an ember from the small fire in it, and added a short breath to help it spark. It burned until another breath stopped it, allowing the Sage to smolder. He then took out Eagle's wing and brushed the rising smoke over himself and White Paws. The purifying smoke of the Sage filled his nostrils and covered his body, cleansing away anything bad.

He tried to center himself, to find the path into the Circle. He envisioned a path and started his walk in the middle, up a gentle sloping trail. The trail started to form a Spiral that he followed until it became a Circle.

He breathed deep the misty air. The smells of tangy moss and sweet flowers drew him in. He stood to sing and dance his prayer, his arms raised. White Paws joined with his howling. Above, somewhere in the trees, Eagle called. Chants from the Ancient Ones joined in. All of life created music. The falling rainbow shot sparks of colors as Father Sun danced through each color—first yellow, orange-red, red, purple, purple-blue, blue, green—each with its own song.

"All I have that is truly mine, I offer to you. Please have pity on our new child, your child, and give her strength to live. Take the strength from me. Please."

To him, time did not move. He glanced toward White Paws, who now walked the Circle with him. His howls mixed with the distant song of his pack, seemingly everywhere behind them.

Somewhere a rattle shook to the beat of his heart. It shook deep in his mind as Sister Wind whispered her song in his ears, through his body. He swayed to the music that came from within. It flowed through his body and mind. He took out his obsidian knife and put it to his skin, ready to make small cuts.

'*So my Shining Light is well, and has his daughter.*'

"Blue Night Sky?"

'*You expected someone else? I told you I would be here, watching over you, and now yours.*'

"What can you do to save my daughter?"

'*Young one, I can do nothing but offer guidance. You have already saved her by your willingness to sacrifice the only thing that belonged to you.*'

"My daughter will live?"

'*Go see. Your Power of love and willingness to sacrifice is more than you understand.*'

Soft laughter vibrated all around him, and the colors of the rainbow surrounded everything.

'*There is more for you to do now. I know you remember the Spirits saying that. I know you dream again....*' Blue Night Sky faded into the rainbow colors.

The sound of rustling brought him back. He caught sight of a large white bear rising up on her hind legs for a brief span before she moved among the trees, her cub following.

"White Bear, are you really there?" He stood to get a better look at the movement making its way through the trees. The white She-Bear and her cub stopped, looked his way, and moved on.

Father Sun had started to lower. White Paws jumped up to lick his face and then trotted off into the near darkness.

"Darkness? How long have I been here? Dove, my daughter!" He jumped up, gathered his Sacred items and pack, then raced back toward camp.

***

Animal Speaks Woman sat at the edge of camp and sang to her daughter. She rocked her body back and forth while sitting among a small herd of deer — four does with their six young ones.

Shining Light stood back, not wanting to ruin the scene before him. *Such wonder here in the forest. They have no fear of her.*

The animals stood with ears twitching, then meandered back into the forest.

Animal Speaks Woman twisted around and waved for him to come closer. Their daughter suckled in her arms. "Your daughter has saved all her hunger for this day. Your grandmother told me where you went, and not much time passed before our little Dove expressed her hunger."

She pulled down her robe so he could see as he sat next to her.

He ran a hand through their daughter's hair. "My mother was right. Her hair will be very thick."

He gathered them in his arms, squeezing both. "All is well in our lodge now, my woman." He rocked his family from side to side. "Speaks, you have given me a wonderful gift. You called her Dove. I never told you the story about Turtle Dove, did I? She was my father's grandmother who, in a dream, said she wanted me to name my... err... our first daughter after her, so her grandson could hear her name again. Father took great care of her. I remember how, after the burial ceremony, everyone sang her home. I guess too many words spilled from my mouth, so my mother kept me away, but still close enough that I could watch. After the singing, he left to go into the canyons, and a young woman's Spirit followed behind him. I knew it was his grandmother, only she was happy and young again. It was the first time I saw a true Spirit... besides the Ancient Ones who told me to bring the people here."

She leaned her head against him. "I heard doves calling the morning she came to be with us. One flew into the lodge and stood by the flap. You call her Turtle Dove. I will call our daughter Dove. I know what you did—singing, praying. I saw it in my mind. I also saw Blue Night Sky's Spirit in our lodge. She stood smiling, then was gone just as fast. We, your daughter and I, were alone, so I said nothing to anyone."

She raised her head to stare into his eyes, and sighed. "I know."

He pulled away. "Know... know what?"

"You dream again, and plan to leave soon. You know I can sense other's thoughts, though sometimes I still wonder whose thoughts they are, but mostly only yours. I want to go, too. You might need me, not to call the animals, but I have a deeper feeling. I had a vision of a rainbow falling into the waters, and of another woman with child. I wonder if this is why. Soon I will be on my feet. I am strong."

"Speaks, you just gave birth—"

"No matter, we are a strong people who heal fast, not weak like the hairy-faced ones. You remember one of the hairy-faces cut his arm while skinning a deer?" She held out her arm. "He lay for days refusing our help, until his wound swelled and turned deep purple. It was then that you went to him and healed him in two sunrises. I remember you telling him Father Sun would help him to heal, but he laid there in the dark, moaning. Even our children do not act that way."

She shifted her daughter to her other breast, cooing to her. "We are strong because we believe we are. We put the Power of thought into our minds, push it in deep until it becomes truth." She rubbed his arm.

"I *am* going." She got up and walked back toward the lodge, leaving her man to sit and stare after her.

He watched her until the darkening sky hid her from him.

"Me too." Gentle Wisdom plopped down before he could get up and follow Speaks. "I may not have Power as you and Speaks, but I will go. It is a promise I made myself when I was only a little girl, cousin."

"Go chase butterflies, Gentle Wisdom. I am a father now and I need to go—"

"Yes you do, and I am going too!"

"How is your wisdom gentle? When Blue Night Sky first started to name you Carries Wisdom, I thought that was a better fit. You like to tease so much!"

Someone pushed him from behind. "Hey! Who pushes me? I am not a boy to be pushed—"

A soft nicker answered him.

"Sandstone, why are you not with the other mustangs? And... and you drag your baby out into the darkness. What if he fell? His light grey body would be hard to find." He reached out and rubbed her muzzle, soft as rabbit fur. "Like you will answer me."

Sandstone pushed him again and nickered louder. She stepped in front of him this time.

"Women! How can *you* know what is in my mind?"

"So when do we go, Shining Light who is not a boy?" Gentle Wisdom shoved him and laughed. "Men, they think they know so much!" Her voiced lowered and she glanced around. "Do not speak of this, but... I became a woman last moon."

"Cousin, you what? Why do you keep this a secret? You should have had your New Woman celebration and... and... where did you go to do this? You know women have great Power at this time. You can drain a man!"

She put her hand over his mouth. "Shhh! If my mother hears, she will get all silly and start searching out a man for me! I do not want a man." She crossed her arms and stared ahead.

"Where did you go during your moon time?" Shining Light grabbed her arm and made her look his way.

She jerked her arm back. "I told my mother I was going to see Wandering Wind. She has a baby now and lives with her man with the hairy-faces three sunrises away. I told her I wanted to walk, so I could gather herbs. She handed me a basket, told me to take it with my other things, to be careful and have a good journey. And I went to sit under the falling water." Her lips spread into a smile. "I sang my own new woman song!"

"Tell me you did not—"

She put her head down. "No, I did not go to your place. That would be disrespectful." She looked back up and smiled again. "A woman knows not to do such bad things."

He turned and, without thought, hugged her. "In my heart, you will always be Chases Butterflies, my little burning fire. Now you are a true woman who burns brightly. I would not think of leaving you behind. I see you wander off for sunrises at a time, and know you go to other bands to learn from them and pass on what you learn from others. You soak up knowledge as a thirsty plant soaks up rain, and still you thirst for more."

She reached out and squeezed his shoulder in the darkened forest. "I am a woman and your friend always, not just your cousin who likes to tease you."

Shining Light's voice became serious. "Besides, I will need someone to cook for me. My woman will be busy with our daughter."

"Perhaps you need your hair shortened. It now flows down your back!"

He scrambled to get out of her way, before she cut off a chunk with the knife she had unsheathed from her knee-high footwear. He raced away, laughing at her threats to feed him the sharp, spiked legs of the hopping bug that lived outside the forest.

He needed to tell his father and his mother the time had come for him to leave the forest. *My daughter just born and now I must leave? What danger awaits us? Should I let Speaks leave with our baby? A man would say no!*

Chapter 5

Falling Rainbow watched Wanderer pack and laughed when he placed the mice into little sewn compartments inside of his outerwear. He had made them from several thicknesses of furred hides in colors of different tans, browns and off-whites. She could see that not one strip of hide or fur had gone to waste.

"How long did it take you to make your... your colorful outside wear? Never before have I seen one with so many little inside pouches." She watched him scoop up baby mice and place them with their mothers in pouches packed with swamp plant fluff. "And... why *are* you taking the mice?"

"Hmm? I cannot leave them here. Who would care for them? We have been together for a cycle of seasons. It took some doing, but not one of the adults will make their waste in the pouches. I had to make them understand that, if we were going to live together, they had to go outside the cave. After about two moon's time they understood! At night, I taught them to sleep in pouches so they would be ready when we would have to leave."

She sat stunned, mouth open. "When *we* would be ready to leave? Wait, you taught them? What about their babies? Who taught them?"

"I just told you, I did. I was not about to live in a place where mice made their messes! I had to clean out my home many times a day. I offered them food when they would go outside instead of inside." He shook his head. "Silly girl."

"Again, I ask, what do you mean for when *we* had to leave? You and the mice?"

"I need to pack my things now that you have finally arrived." He chuckled and crawled into the narrow back of the cave. "We as in all of us, of course. I can feel you stare at my back, girl. Do you not understand that everything happens as it is meant to? We may not like what happens, but happen it will."

***

The turquoise sky had cleared but the chill remained. Early season weather could turn as fast as a fish headed for a net. This time, Falling Rainbow smiled at Sister Wind's cold shoves at their backs.

"Our tracks will be covered and Night Hunter and his brother will not be able to find us." She twisted around. "This outerwear you made fits me well. And the footwear... it is all so nice and warm." She cocked her head at Wanderer as he tried to keep the mice in the pouches. "Why did you make the extra clothes? Did you need something to do while waiting out the cold season?"

"For you, of course. I could not let you travel in this cold with what you wore. It took me moons to get enough furs to make the insides so they would be warm. I made them, so when it became warmer you could pull out the fur lining." He paused and glanced around. "I need to go back to your camp and get us two, maybe three mustangs. That way we do not have to carry so much on our backs. You will be safe here." He pointed to a curve away from Sister Wind's grasp. "Just go past that boulder and you will see a small cave. I put a thick hide in some time ago, in case I had to move."

"You are going to my... the... camp and stealing mustangs? I will not let you go alone. Besides, one mustang will come to me if I whistle for him. I have a way with the mustangs." She jumped against the canyon wall as a chattering squirrel scolded above on a narrow ledge. He sent snow flying onto her shoulders and hit her with several acorns. "*I am* going with you." She squeezed her outerwear closer around herself.

"Good idea, this whistle. I need to hear it. Make this whistle for me. We do not want to scare them into running." He opened his mouth. "See? I have few teeth with which to make a whistle. I make a flapping sound instead."

She had to turn away and stare at the ground before she lost her straight face. "He only answers to me. Many of the females have bellies with babies. They are so big they waddle." She spread her arms at her sides and showed him how they walked.

He ran his hand over his mouth, but a laugh escaped. Trying to hide it made him cough.

"We cannot take them. You need to let me go back with you, to get the ones who do not have babies in their bellies or babies to care for. The male I whistle for... the hairy-faces did something to him so he cannot mate. Another like him stays at his side. I *will* go with you." She pulled up her footwear and tied it. "Take the smile off your face! Show me where we are to go." She nodded her head toward the path as she adjusted her pack.

He sighed. "They told me you would be a strong-headed, stubborn female. All right then, *we* will go to your camp. But I know a much shorter way."

"What? Who told you I was strong-headed?" She swirled around, crossed her arms and raised her square chin.

"The Spirits. Who did you think, the mice? They do not speak to me. Here, put on these hand warmers. We have a ways to go. While we walk, tell me how you came by your name." He turned around and waved for her to walk beside him.

She really wanted to give him a shove more than anything, but no one did such a thing, especially to an elder, no matter how crazy he made her. She hiked her pack up and tied it so it would stay in place.

She cleared her throat, brushed back stray hair, and hurried to catch up with him. "My name is from a story my grandmother, Song Bird, told me. Some say it was in her mind, yet others say it is true. She dreamed of rainbows falling down water that came from cliffs, and told me that I must find my way there. She also told me of the paintings, to find them and follow where they say to go."

She put her head down. "Song Bird went to the stars two winters ago. I held her hand while she crossed over. She told me I could say her name, that she wanted her sister to hear it someday. I have no one left who will speak of this place to me now. My father honored her dream by changing my name from Girl Who Rides Mustangs to Falling Rainbow. No falling water exists here except very small ones." She raised her arms and glanced upward. "I have never seen one, anyway, just those trickles that come with the melting.

"This place must be real, not some elder woman's stories of regret for not following her sister and her people to this place. She said her sister's grandson dreamed of this land. I know his name is Shining Light, but little else about him. When I asked more about this place, people laughed at me and called it a child's story."

His white brows squeeze together as he scrunched up his face.

"Do you believe me?"

"Of course, Falling Rainbow, that is why I am here." He stopped and grabbed her arm. "Dangers await us, girl. We will have some time to rest once we get the mustangs, but when we relax the most, things may start to happen." He held her arm as they stepped around the stones that had fallen from the canyon wall

"The hairy-faces? I do not understand. The hairy-faces do not come this way anymore. They did not find the yellow stone here. Some settled about a moon away from our camp, but leave us alone... until they want women." She squirmed under his grip and shuffled her feet. "We have had to move farther away, twice in the last six moons, to stay away from them. My friend —" She choked out the words. "—she disappeared in the darkness along with two others just before the cold came. A bad storm hit, preventing anyone from searching for them. Before the storm, two families sent their men in search of their lost women. They did not come back."

She tightened her jaw and spoke through her teeth. "I would fight until I drew my last breath, before I would become a slave."

"I am sorry you have had to know the bad side of life, but even that teaches us important lessons. Do not keep the hate inside you. Only you can feel it, and it slowly kills anyone who refuses to let it go from them. It weakens and sickens them. They either become bad and do harm to others, which will still get them in the end as bad Spirits consume them, or their Spirits shrivel and die because they are full of bad thoughts."

He stopped and leaned against the canyon wall. "I watched this happen once. When I was a boy, a man lost his prized bow. At first, he searched for it where the men had been hunting. Not finding it, he started asking everyone if they had seen it but maybe did not pick it up. Everyone said no.

"As the warm season started to turn cold, so did he. Even though he created a much nicer bow, he was still consumed with finding his old one. He became bitter and everyone avoided him. It ate at him until one day his belly hurt and, soon after, his head pained him so much he would cry out. It was pain he created himself from so much anger. The Healer offered to help him, but he refused, no longer trusting anyone. Deep in the cold season he refused to leave his home, as the pain in his body made his mind crazy. His woman left him and took their children. He had no one to care for him anymore."

He sighed. "My father allowed the bad Spirits to take over his mind, and in his anger he would lash out at anyone who tried to help him. He was no longer the gentle man I knew. He shouted one day when a horrible blizzard kept us all inside our lodges. He shouted and shouted. Everyone knew it was him, so no one went to his aid. They knew he would push them away. The next sunrise, he was no more. One of the people found him in the snow, next to the tattered branches and covering that was once a warm home. He had ripped it to shreds." He arched his back, pushed off from the wall, turned, and walked on.

"Your father? I am so sorry!"

He did not respond for a short span.

Finally, he turned and said, "If you keep your eyes open as we travel, no harm will come to you. Fox, your Spirit Guide, will help you stay hidden."

"How... how do you know who my Spirit Guide is?"

"Keep walking. We have to move faster." He stared ahead and picked up speed. "Fox is also my Sprit Guide. How do you think I have lived where I have, right along the path animals use, and not been seen? Not one hunter ever looked my way. I am grateful Fox, a master at hiding in front of anyone and not being seen, chose me. It is a special gift. Fox has also taught me to go within, to heal myself from pain when it becomes too much for me. Now we walk and save our wind for breathing, not talking."

Chapter 6

Darkness crept through the canyons, creating looming shadows. Falling Rainbow jumped as Wanderer grabbed her arm again.

"Inside these large boulders is a small cave. We must leave everything we do not need." He took off his outerwear and the mice scattered. "They will be safe," he mumbled.

He took off his pack and pulled out a long tunic. "Pull out the long tunic your mother made for you. It will be warm because she layered it as I did mine, but it is looser and you will be able to climb better with it now that Father Sun lowers. We have little time before we will not be able to see at all."

"How did you know my mother made it? I did not even know. I was about to dig to the bottom of the pack—"

"Shhh! No time for questions. And whisper! Once we catch the mustangs, we need to keep them at a trot if we are to make it back here before Father Sun wakes. Sister Moon hides—just a sliver shows—and this will help. When we get to the top, stay low to the ground, girl. No sense taking chances of someone being awake."

He pushed her forward and pointed up. "We climb here. It will take us right to your camp, just over those boulders. Seek the way with your hands. You will feel it."

"I have never climbed down this way—too slippery for me—and now you ask that I climb up?" She arched her neck up and saw not a path, but a good place from which to fall.

"I lived where your camp is. The hairy-faces came in the night, and only a few of us made it over these boulders to hide in the cave. Long ago, other Peoples made handholds on the boulders, which we will use to climb. Be careful—some are worn and shallow. I will follow behind you in case you fall. Feel for the handholds. They are spaced about an arm's stretch, all in a row."

"I will not fall. I am strong."

"I hope so. I am not. If you fall, I will too."

"Then why did you tell me to go ahead of you?"

"I told you, in case you fall. Whisper."

The first one was easy to find. She stretched way out, and had to feel back and forth, for the second one.

Wanderer pushed one of her feet up. "Pull yourself up, and each time you do, put a foot in the last handhold you had your hand in. Understand?"

"Yes!"

"Whisper."

Each step was a nightmare. Darkness took away any chance to see where to put her hands. Her nails broke, split and hurt. She clenched her teeth as rocks fell and rolled past her feet. Wanderer, sputtering from below, told her that his mouth tasted the dirt she had let loose. One hand found a plant of some kind. She pulled it, but the roots let loose and she squealed when she lost her grip. Hands from behind pushed her against the boulder.

"How did you get up to me so fast?"

"Shhh! Keep moving."

Cold sweat formed on her forehead, down her neck and inside her clothing. Small plants seeking their own grasp on life covered the worn holds. She had no choice but to rip them out. "Wanderer, the plants are letting go... and... and I do not want to kill them."

"Silly girl, you are not killing them. Their roots grow deep within the cracks in the wall. Stop worrying. You need to keep focused on finding the top."

"I feel it!"

More sputtering from below told her he had gotten the worst of it. *Now I understand why you had me go first — not only to help me place my feet, but so my mouth and eyes do not suffer as yours do from falling dirt. Maybe you are not so crazy, but kind, with a good heart.*

He tugged at her one dangling foot and whispered, "Once we are over the boulders, get on your knees. Count twenty sets of ten as you crawl, one time for each knee, and you will be at the edge of camp. Move, so I can get up."

"How do you know where my camp is?"

"Shhh!"

Both stood on the edge of what would have been a very long fall, and crouched, crawling toward the camp.

"You have not camped here long, have you, girl?" They neared the edge of the camp.

"We settled in just as the snows started. No one had done much exploring yet. We grouped close in case the hairy-faces found us again. Now that I think of it, we were silly not to have set up guards right away. Night Hunter walked into camp during my ceremony, and no one had sent any messages to other bands. It was too cold. I have no idea how it came to be that he showed up." She stopped and stood to stretch her back.

"Get down, girl! Whistle, call your mustang—quiet whistles. Mustangs have good ears."

She crouched and let go a long, slow whistle Sister Wind would have envied, and turned to Wanderer. He was gone.

Not long after, two mustangs followed the sound.

When the animals came up to Falling Rainbow, her tears flowed freely. "Father? How?"

Her father walked between two more mustangs, each carrying loads, and held their lead ropes. She patted them both on their light brown necks, then stepped through the middle and squeezed her father.

He squeezed her back with a force that took her air away. "I will miss you, Daughter. Wanderer and I have planned this day for some time. When Night Hunter and his brother showed up, I knew it was time for you to find this Shining Light."

She pulled away from him. "Father, I do not understand. How did you know? When did you meet Wanderer? Why must I meet this Shining Light?"

He held her face in his hands and pulled her closer. "Beautiful child of mine, the Spirits will guide you. Listen to them, to the whispers in Sister Wind. Listen to Wanderer. He is a Holy Man with great Power. Do not ask so many questions. Allow yourself to find the answers. They will come to you. I made your mother stay in camp in case Night Hunter was about. She says to think of her often, and perhaps you will come back this way. I know you will."

He hugged her once more and moved away, glancing back several times.

He was gone before she could ask how he knew she would return. The silence spooked her. "Wanderer, Wanderer? Where are you?" A hand covered her mouth.

"Shhh!" He let his arm drop. "You did not need to call out for me! I went to find good, strong mustangs to ride, but your father already waited for me. He heard your whistle and knew it was not Sister Wind. He has special ways."

"He told me you and him were friends. That he knew you were coming."

"Yes, of course he did," he whispered, then patted Falling Rainbow on her shoulder. "Watch me."

He rubbed the mustang's neck, brought up his muzzle, and breathed into it. "Lets them know you are greeting them. Allow them to do the same. Heh, he gave me Night Hunter's creature and said no other animal is as fast. He said to tell you we have the four fastest animals in the band. Night Hunter will rage for some time before he sets out for you. You have a very clever father. He sent the children out to lead the other mustangs away, so the camp has only old ones and the ones soon to give birth, or those who have babies only a moon old — none he can ride."

He handed her the rope to Night Hunter's animal.

They rode where Sister Wind had blown most of the snow away, creating a quiet path to ride side-by-side.

He leaned her way and whispered. "When we get back down the canyon to pick up my mice, we will change mustangs. The dark grey male of Night Hunter's is full of Power, but your father wanted you to have his best horse, this light brown one with the white hair on her neck and tail that I ride. She has what the hairy-faces call 'vi-bran-te.' She is young and may be hard to handle, but she did not have a young one this season. I mentioned this one's wild ways to your father, and he chuckled. He says you are a master at riding these four-legged ones, and that she is for you. Once we are back down on the path, we will trade. I only wanted to see how it felt to ride her."

He tapped the mustang into a trot and waved for her to follow. "We must get to my mice before others find them and make a meal of them."

"Mice? We really go back for your mice?"

"Whisper. Yes, we go back for my mice."

"But mice are everywhere. Why not get others?"

He let out a slow breath. "Because we are companions, girl. Now hurry before someone sees us besides your parents."

She heard a soft cough and turned just as both her parents waved. "Never before have I been without them." She waved back, unsure if they could see her so far from their tiny campfire. *I will be back!*

"Good thing you are a woman. Women are brave, or at least act brave, when they leave their parents' lodge." He smacked her animal's rump. "We must hurry. When Night Hunter wakes, we had better be far away. His heart is cold, and he will hunt us down. I know he either has made promises to the hairy-faces, or has made them afraid of him. Your father told me that Night Hunter has offered them the yellow stone, even though he cannot give it. They do not know this. For that reason alone, they will follow wherever he leads."

She leaned sideways to speak.

His wave silenced her. "We will have time to speak later. Now hurry! We must ride all the way through the canyon where we left our things and my mice."

She glared at him even though she knew he could not see her, and tapped the dark animal forward. "Go fast, mustang no longer Night Hunter's."

By the time they made it back down to the cave in the boulders, Father Sun lit the canyons well. Wanderer took little time gathering his belongings. "We need to trade animals. Your parents have packed everything you need, and whatever is in this little pouch." He tossed it her way. "Something about paints."

"Can we not rest here? I am so tired that my eyes burn."

"No, little one, it is far too dangerous."

She spotted Fox and turned to point her out, but her Spirit Guide vanished. She jumped off her animal, closed her eyes, and asked Fox for protection. "Guide us true, keep us safe, and warn us of dangers. Give us your cunning, your inner sight."

She raised her hands to Creator as Wanderer came from the cave. He too raised his arms in a prayer to Creator.

"It makes my heart feel good, girl, to see you pray. Your father taught you well. With both of us having Fox as our Guide, we are going to be fine. Fox will warn us, as will these little mice. You see, they may not speak, yet I hear them whisper in my ears when danger approaches."

He chuckled as he scratched one mouse behind tiny grey-brown ears. "And you thought they were only some crazy elder's play things. We must hurry. Night Hunter will soon realize you are not in camp."

He finished placing the mice in their pouches and jumped on the dark grey Mustang. Fox trotted by again.

Falling Rainbow said, "Vi-bran-te, huh? I like the name Heart With Fire. That will be your name, girl."

After she had tried four times to jump on Heart With Fire, Wanderer reached over from atop his mustang and caught the mustang's neck hair to still her. Heart With Fire tried to pull away from his grasp, but Falling Rainbow managed a fast jump up. Human and animal swirled around several times before she got the animal pointed in the right direction.

"How did you get on her?"

He grinned. "Your father had her front legs tied, and waited until I got on her before he untied her legs. That was a good idea."

"You could have mentioned that before I danced all over with her. Ha! I change her name to Fire Dancer!"

Wanderer chuckled and led the way.

Each trotted on a mustang and led another animal toward the path leading out of the canyon.

"Wanderer, do you dream?"

"Of course, silly. How else did I know you were coming?"

"I did not dream of you. You said Fox is your guide also. Why would you tell me this? No one tells another—"

"I felt it. To know we have the same Spirit Guides shows we are both cunning."

"I follow an elder I do not know, yet somehow my parents knew of you. Am I a captive, or did I escape? Perhaps I am both, one who escaped and one who is held captive by a... an elder." She slid from Fire Dancer to readjust and tighten her pack.

Fire Dancer twisted around until Wanderer caught her neck hair again. As Falling Rainbow danced once again in circles with her mustang, she caught a glimpse of something on the newly fallen snow.

"Wanderer, prints... human prints!" She jumped on her mustang and pointed at them.

He leaned over. "Snow still fell when we left, so they cannot be ours. Fox did try to warn us, and we paid no heed. Stupid."

He started to jump off to get a closer look at the prints, when laughter on top of the high boulders spooked the mustangs.

Chapter 7

Shining Light's face dripped with sweat. He fought to free himself from the dream, from the swirling Spiral of the dizzying colors, until he heard the voice. He stopped fighting and allowed himself to be pulled in. He felt calm, warm as he swirled within the Spiral. Words he did not want to hear came into his mind, as clear as if he listened to someone in his family.

'Shining Light. Time... time has come for you to leave, go back toward the canyons.' A blue color joined in the Spiral. *'Spiral — cycles of life. Shining Light, you must help the Spiral, the never-ending dance of life, continue to grow, evolve. It is the path to Creator. The Circle of Life depends on it... on you. Prepare your body, your mind... your Spirit.'*

He woke, his closed eyes still following the Spiral of the swirling colors. Father Sun shocked his eyes as he opened them. The illumination made him groan, roll over, and face the ground. The night before, he had chosen to lie outside the lodge under the trees, where he could be alone to think about White Bear and her cub he had encountered on his walk. She had stood tall, as tall as the black bears, but was more docile and had not approached him with warnings, as a mother bear normally would.

Is she real, or a Spirit Bear?

Her eyes were black and her fur more of an off-white color. Twice now he had caught her and the cub watching him. Only a handful of the Peoples that shared this wondrous place had seen her. Those who had were awestruck and paralyzed at her beauty. One man told him he had seen a black She-Bear with a white cub.

How is this so? There must be a white bear father hidden deep within the trees. The Sacred Bear prefers to live deep within, where much moss grows. It is as if the sky opened up and snowed moss from the sky. I wonder why she leaves her land to seek me out. It is many days' walk away from us. So rich is this forest in beauty and Sacredness. I wish to live nowhere else. I miss the colors of the canyons, but these falling waters, colorful birds, and a little spotted one who I learned not to get so close to, keep me searching for more things I have yet to see.

He thought he was alone, and rolled back over and stretched his arms, surprised that Soft Breeze, his sister, slept curled on one side. She now rolled into one of his outstretched arms. White Paws and Moon Face slept on the other side, curled tail to nose. The rest of the pack began to stir in the circle around them.

Soft Breeze turned in her sleep and faced outward from his shoulder. White Paws stretched, and his Wolf Brother's back leg flopped onto his face.

"Soft Breeze, what are *you* doing here?" He jumped up, spitting out fine hairs and clumps of dirt from the wolf's leg.

She rubbed her eyes and frowned. "You woke me from a good dream! I was riding Sandstone in the clouds, and we were about to jump over a rainbow! You sure are a noisy sleeper. Now I will never get to jump over a rainbow!"

She sat up and giggled at the wolves. "I hear some people say you are more wolf than man. You have people ears and a people nose, too." She stood and pushed his hair away from his ears, then pushed at his chest. "Sit up. I want to see if you have a wolf tail!"

He rose to his knees to brush mud off his tunic. *Muddy wolf paws!* "Silly sister, I do not have a tail. If I had one, you too would have a tail. Do you?"

She put her hands to her mouth. "Do I have a tail, brother?"

"Well, I have not looked. Maybe you do! Better get Grandfather to check." His eyes grew big. "If you do, you will have to come live with the wolves!"

"Mother would have told me, silly brother. Well... I *think* she would have. Maybe you better check." She turned, trying to see for herself.

He patted her behind. "No, I guess you are safe. Why did you sleep next to me, and not with Mother and Father?"

"They got up early." She rubbed her behind and tried to turn around and look once more. "Sparrow Hawk would not sleep, so they took him for a walk. They told me to stay put, but I did not." She leaned over and pressed her face into his.

Her sweet smile and bright, mischievous eyes reminded him of a boy once called Feather. He tousled the hair on top of her head and grinned at the memories. "You are not being very good to run off. What if they came home and saw you were gone?"

"Oh, they already did! I sat up when they came this way and waved. They giggled in their hands and left." She rolled over on her belly and picked at a yellow flower. "I like yellow flowers." She jumped up and ran off with the flower.

"Wait, Breeze! Where are you going?" He jumped up to grab her, but she raced away and yelled, "Grandmother! I go give this to Grandmother. Wake her up with a surprise!"

Shining Light giggled as his grandfather hollered, "Soft Breeze, that is my belly you have just plopped on!"

He remembered when he had found the very old bone, and had to chase White Paws into the lodge to get it back. He had dived on top of his grandfather, who had been sleeping moments before, in the same way.

He stood, stretched, and twisted in a circle, the dream vision momentarily forgotten. "Lazy wolves, why were *you* all sleeping with me and not out hunting, teaching the pups? Can I not find solitude when I seek it?"

Wolves stretched and rolled on the ground. Pups wrestled in the grass while Moon Face looked on.

"Why are you here, Moon Face? Did you drag these pups from your den? What goes on here?"

White Paws pushed his nose into his Human Brother's hand.

Shining Light vibrated from the spiraling colors as he touched the wolf. "No one hunts this day? Why *are* all of you here?"

He closed his eyes and the Spiraling vibration of colors was still there. A heavy sigh came from deep within. It was time to go back.

"So, this is why all of you are here." He twisted to face the mother wolf. "Moon Face, how old are your pups now? Four moons? So you teach them to hunt, and they can now move with the pack some."

He reached down, dug his hands into White Paws' fur, and became serious as he stared into his Wolf Brother's eyes. "Will you leave your family behind as I must? Perhaps we have a few moons before we must leave."

He knew better. The warning tingle increased as he spoke of staying. He lay over White Paws. "Ahhh, old friend, I need to go seek guidance. I hope Speaks will understand. We both knew this day would come, but I had hoped our daughter would be much older. She is only now greeting the people of our band."

He stretched once more and scratched his back on the shedding bark of the log he slept next to. He stared up at the trees and wondered, *Why now?*

He walked softly to their lodge in case Animal Speaks Woman slept. As he drew closer, he could hear her singing to their new daughter. *What words do I use to make her understand she needs to stay? Blue Night Sky's stubborn blood runs in her veins. She will be as her Guide, Fox, who finds a way to do as she pleases.*

He slipped past the front of the lodge, and a roasting duck that his grandfather must have brought. The rich scent made him pause, mouth watering. He would not eat this day, and maybe not for many days. He had to fast, purify his body to show the Spirits his strength and willingness to do what he must for a vision.

He went through the open flap and could hear her singing, but where was she? "Speaks, have you blended in as Fox does?"

She laughed and appeared in front of his eyes. "I am good, am I not?"

"How *do* you do that? You blend into our lodge just as Fox blends in while she waits for a meal to walk by."

She stared up at him from where she lay resting on a raised platform made from grasses and leather. He had watched her double-stitch the seams. "Man of mine, think: how is it that you see things only Mouse would see, or go into your mind as Bear would, or know how to heal others' wounds? You are silent, like Wolf, as he stalks his prey. You have the ability to make people listen to you. How is it that you teach others to listen to their words before they spill from their mouths? You turn before a person approaches. Your gifts are many and they come from your Guides, as does mine. I also know you *think* you will leave me behind."

Her sly grin told him he was not going to win any discussions this day. "I... I need to go. I need to know more of where I am to go and why. For four full cycles of seasons, we have lived here. I wait still to find the Ancients to learn from them. They brought us here, but then vanished after Gentle Wisdom and I met them. I still get a glimpse of them in my dreams, but they say I have much more to learn. Perhaps this is more of the learning I must do. But to leave the forest! I must know why. I—"

"Water and food when you are ready for it." She tossed him a pack she had sitting next to her, and nodded toward his Sacred Bundle. It contained his items, Sacred things only he knew were in there. "Even without my being able to touch your bundle, I hear it sometimes, calling out, whispering, and even singing. Take it and go. Gentle Wisdom waits for you. She will be the one who watches from afar, to make sure no one else comes near."

"Do you know...?"

"That she is now a woman? Of course. We are as close as blood sisters, you know this. Now reach down and hug me. I want to hold you, feel your breath mingle with mine, feel your skin touch mine." She reached out to him.

Her scent drew him in, called to him. He knelt down and Speaks squeezed him against her and their daughter, who slept on her breast in a sling. *Her hair, clean, smells lightly of... of....* "I could lose myself in your smell, your soft hair...." He reached for her face. "Your—"

She pushed him back, laughter so soft and inviting that he tried to reach out to her again. She stilled his hand with her own. "Never forget this, how it feels. You are not meant for lonely nights any more than your father or grandfather."

His eyes wandered over her face, her body, soaking it into memory. "Even though we have been together a cycle of seasons, I still find I need to see you with my eyes, my hands...."

"I love you as I have since my eyes found you, even when you ran away like a scared rabbit with Fox trying to catch her meal." She chuckled. "I will never forget you running into me. You left me with a bleeding nose. I saw the shine you had for me in your eyes when you were but a boy, but you raced off as if I was going to eat you!"

He hugged her once more, holding her tight, feeling her face against his, then stood to reach his Sacred Bundle. "I need to go—"

"I understand."

He cocked his head and gave her his best squished face. "Why is it you can finish my words before I can get them out of my mouth? Never mind, I may be better off not knowing that answer. I will be back when I can." As he stepped out of their lodge, he turned. "Do not pack your things, Speaks. You *will* stay."

He dodged a thrown piece of wood and dashed out as stinging words tried to bite him, grinning as he made his way toward his Sacred place.

Only a full cycle of seasons ago I was without a mate. Now I am a father! The word does not yet roll off my tongue with ease.

A sound made him stop. "Gentle Wisdom, do not follow me so close." He turned to scold her.

His eyes grew large at the sight of White Bear and her cub before him.

Chapter 8

Shining Light froze and dropped his pack with a soft thud. White Bear acted as if she had no cares, no concerns for the human who stood in front of her. Not even when White Paws slipped in beside him did she move. He let go of the breath that tightened his chest as White Bear turned around and disappeared into the smaller trees, her cub chasing after her.

The wolf nudged his shaking hand. "Is she... her young one real? They do not look like Spirits. Why does she not attack us, White Paws? Bears are very protective of their young, why not her?"

The wolf trotted past his Brother a ways, then turned back and sat.

"I know, *I know*, keep going to the falling waters." He picked up the pack and continued his journey.

Once there, he squeezed through the narrow passage and crawled across tiny pebbles, which also made up the walls, and up into a small cave. It led to the back, far enough away from the water that the splashes could not reach him. It was a good place to speak to the Spirits, to ask for advice when answers would not come in his dreams.

He turned to motion White Paws through, but the wolf was not there. He inhaled deeply and shrugged with the exhale. *White Paws never leaves me unless there is a reason.*

He pulled out two hidden robes from within a small dry cave at the back of the falling waters. A spark of light showed the interior well enough that he could light the Sage, inside part of a large shell that glistened in blues and greens.

He used a whittled stick and one wide piece with a hole on its edge, and twisted the longer, round one back and forth in the hole until the small bit of grass under the wider piece smoked. He blew on it, bringing the fire to life in the Sacred Sage, and blew it out, permitting the Sage's smoke to rise toward the glint of light. He moved the shell about, cleansing the small cave, and then brought the smoke over himself, even the bottoms of his feet. He set it aside and allowed it to burn itself out.

He wrapped the robe around his body, sat still with eyes closed, and concentrated on the drumbeat from within his chest. Each beat took him deeper and deeper still. He began his song, a special song that had come in a dream while the Fish People still lived in the canyons.

"I AM HERE. HERE I WAIT FOR ANSWERS TO BETTER UNDERSTAND VISIONS THAT HAVE COME MY WAY.

TO UNDERSTAND BETTER WHAT COMES TO ME IN MY
DREAM VISIONS, MY WAKING LIFE VISIONS.

TO LISTEN AND LEARN WHAT I MUST TO BETTER THE
LIVES OF MY PEOPLE. I COME, I WAIT... I WAIT.

I AM HERE, WHITE BEAR, MOUSE, GRANDFATHER WOLF,
WHO ARE MY GUIDES.

COME TO ME AS I OFFER MYSELF TO YOU, TO CREATOR,
TO YOU MY TRUE MOTHER THAT I WALK UPON.

I WAIT... I WAIT... I WAIT."

Gentle Wisdom showed up at Shining Light's side, took her small obsidian
knife, and cut tiny pieces from his skin. He did not look her way, already
approaching a trance, following the Spiral within. She vanished as quickly as
she'd entered.

Sounds from the powerful falling water entered the young Holy Man's
mind and body. His mind blended into swirling colors of the falling water's
rainbow and he sang louder, knowing the Spirits would choose their own time
to speak.

Within what felt to him to be only a few heartbeats, White Bear and her
cub sat before him, and Mouse sat on the mother bear's leg. His eyes widened.
He reached out and felt for White Bear, but she vanished with the sound of
Wolf echoing inside the waterfall.

He sang on, repeating the song over and over... waiting.

A chuckle bounced off the dirt walls.

"Blue Night Sky? Are you here?" No answer came, only the sound of the
water as it rushed past.

Thirst overcame his weakening body. He refused to give in; after all, he'd
only been there a short span. Eyes still closed, he continued his song.

His voice faltered and became too sore to sing anymore. He reached for
the water bladder, undid the tie that kept the water secured, and hoped to still
his burning throat. Dirt poured into his mouth.

"Water, I need water! Why is there dirt in here?" He spit out the dirt and
used his robe to clean out his mouth. "How can this be? Spirits, why do you
trick me? Have I not shown proper respect?"

'Silly Human, we have waited for you to ask for our help. Why did you not speak
up?'

With his voice barely above a whisper, he croaked, "What? I have sung to
you until my voice could stand no more."

Mouse emerged from the air, jumped onto his shoulder, and sat next to his
ear. 'I heard your song. I wanted to hear you speak. I offer my thanks for the food you
leave out for me every time Father Sun wakes. My knowing, my ability to dig deeper in
search of answers — these are the gifts I have given you. Have you forgotten my gifts?'

"No, I have not. Every day I have found a use for your great gifts. People
come to me when they have a question, when no answer comes to them. I have
used your gifts to help them find the answer they seek. I feel their emotions

and become them so I can help them to see what they seek. I walk in prayer always, thinking of my connection to Great Mystery, to you, to all my Guides, and as I walk upon our Mother, I give thanks for all living."

A feminine voice responded, 'Then, why are you here?'

He jerked his head, popping his neck. Before him, White Bear lay on her side. Her cub played with her tail.

"You... are you real?" He reached out, but felt only air.

'Of course I am real. Have you not seen me and my young one watching you? Have you been able to heal those who are sick? Have you forgotten my gifts? I told you, when your mind is in need of healing, seek the silence so it can filter out the noise that clutters it. I gave you special gifts – the gifts of healing and of patience. I now also give you the gift of forgiveness.'

"Forgiveness? I hold no anger against anyone. Why do I need this gift?"

'Do you toss my gift away, Human? I freely give you this gift.' She rolled over and faced away from him.

"No... no... do not turn away, Great White Bear! Please forgive me... please." Tears raced down his face. "Forgive me, please." He bowed his head in shame.

She rolled back over and her cub landed at his feet. He reached out and, this time, felt the softness of her young one's fur. He leaned over and cried into the cub's fur.

'So, perhaps you need my gift, after all. I forgive you.'

'Shining Light,' Mouse whispered in his ear, *"take this gift, as you will find need of it.'* Mouse touched him with his tiny claws. *'Always remember to treat every gift as the most special thing in your life, and they will be there, part of you forever... forever. Listen well, my Brother, and go out into the grasslands once again. You are needed.'* Mouse vanished.

Tears still fell as he rubbed his face in the cub's fur, until she ambled back to her mother. Voice shaky, he spoke with words that were as quiet as Sister Wind on a still day. "I gratefully take this gift. I understand what it is like to have need of it now, and will treasure this gift as long as I breathe."

'As a young cub, you must learn lessons firsthand. This one gift will see you through so much in your life, young one who still has much learning ahead of him. Just because you are a man and have a family does not mean your learning has stopped. Leave the Land of Trees, and know I follow. And, Shining Light, know you must take your woman with you, and Gentle Wisdom. Fear not their bleeding times, for they will not continue until you all have returned.'

"Why must I leave, and bring risk to my new daughter? This is my home now. All of my people live here safely, away from danger as the Ancient Ones promised me so long ago. Bear? Bear, where have you gone?"

He tried to sit up, but he was too weak and fell back against the rough dirt wall.

Wolf sat within the circle of rocks. *'Bear goes to find food for her young one. The young one grows fast and demands much of her time, as any child does.'*

His smile grew wide. "Grandfather of White Paws, I have watched you walk on the edge of my dreams ever since I first met you, when I became a man. I know you protect me, as you do Grandmother when she goes deep within a dream."

'*So you remember my gift to you, then?*'

"I remember all my gifts. You gave me your courage and a determination to see things through. I am a teacher, and others listen to me, as you said they would."

'*Good, you have learned much, but as Bears says, you have more to understand. Learning is something every creature does, from first breath until last. Know now, you must protect another as I protect you. She comes from the canyons and is your blood relation. With her come more people, some good, others dangerous. I give you two moons, then you must leave. This woman has already left. She has things to learn before meeting you. Prepare for a long journey. You must always be watching with your eyes and your mind. Do not allow yourself to think you and yours are safe, not even for a short span. Now go... I will be at your side.*'

Shining Light rubbed tired eyes, and White Paws licked his face. "Hey, where did you come from? I thought you had left me. I should have known better. You would never leave my side."

He hugged him and reached for the bladder that held water at last, not dirt.

Chapter 9

Wanderer's mustang slid on a slushy patch of icy water and into the canyon's damp red wall. He fought hard to regain control after the laughter that spilled down into the canyon had spooked the animal. Mustangs called out to each other as they, too, slid and hit the bodies of their companions. One of the brown ones carrying packs slipped and crashed into Wanderer's leg. He grunted and reached out in pain, and bent his leg to assure himself that it had not broken.

The sound of slush worried him. Falling Rainbow might lose control of her mustang and slip into the red ice and mud herself. *I know it was Night Hunter's laughter that sent these animals running. This half-frozen ice has made things worse!*

He reached out and grabbed Falling Rainbow's mustang as the animal reared, her hooves curling backward as she pawed the air. The mustang's eyes, wild with fear, showed more white than brown.

"The mustangs smell of sweat after that long run. Combined with the icy water, they risk getting sick if we do not dry them off. Jump down. We must get them all to walk. We are far enough away to be safe. I do not believe he has the men he needs ready. And we know your father had all the mustangs he could ride hidden.

"Hold Fire Dancer's leather leads and walk her. No, do not allow her to run in circles, become her... whisper soft words. I know you can do it. Your father said you have the gift. That is it—reach up, pet the sides of her face, whisper, tug the nose rope gently to get her to lower her head, and breathe into her quivering nostrils."

Mice squeaked their own fear. One climbed into his hair and clung to the strands near his ear.

"As mouse says, *'Your eyes can only deceive you if you use them. See inside your mind and the true sight will come to you.'*" He jumped off his mustang into the freezing slush. "Believe in yourself... believe. Allow all doubt to leave your body. It is a weight that you carry inside and can make you feel heavy. It gets into your Soul and causes harm, makes you think you are not worthy. That is why your gift can hide from you."

He calmed down as he spoke, as did his mustang. He made his way to the brown pair who still shook in fear.

"Not trying so hard will allow you freedom. When we think too hard, we find ourselves lost. Simply let go. Fire Dancer will respond. Remember my words always. You will one day pass them on." He kept an eye on her as he rubbed both packed mustangs' legs and rumps with dried grass he had pulled from the jutting stones along the canyon's wall.

She took off her hand warmers and leaned forward to reach Fire Dancer's thick, coarse neck hair, and gently stroked it. When the mustang's breathing became even, so did hers, and Fire Dancer dropped her head. Falling Rainbow stood still for a short span, breathing slowly, and then made her way back in front of her mustang.

Wanderer felt her become one with the animal, and smiled as Fire Dancer lifted her muzzle and breathed on her human. The air misted as the pair shared their mingled breath. Woman and mustang blended, became one, shifted into each other's realities, and then pulled away. Fire Dancer stood with the calmness of an old animal, waiting for hands to guide her.

"Very good. You see, letting go allowed your own fear to vanish, and she, not feeling it, relaxed. Now pick a bunch of dry grass that grew on the canyon wall last season, and as I am doing, dry her off." He held more dry grass in his hands, already wiping down the packed mustangs' chests.

"Your father told me the truth about your ability. He said to remind you of it if I saw the need." He chuckled and began drying off his own animal.

"If you stay calm, they will also. I have learned that many animals know what we think by watching how we move, not just sensing it. It has taught me to watch people. If you approach them with anger, they back away. I learned if you walk slowly, with your hand out and down low, an animal will either stand still or, if they trust you, will come up to see why you hold out your hand. I was able to pet a wolf once long ago. I tingled from her Energy. She sniffed me, walked around me while I held still, and then disappeared before I knew it."

Falling Rainbow nodded. "I would one day like to touch a wolf, feel their Energy, as you have. I still vibrate from being one with my mustang. I am still... with Fire Dancer, and do not wish to pull away."

"Never pull away completely. You will want to keep that depth so she will respond to you without your asking. I once had a dog like that when I was a boy. Heh, I used to sneak him inside the lodge until I got myself caught. My mother made me sleep outside with him. Her mistake. I never wanted to sleep inside again."

"Ha! Cold season must have been fun for you."

"Oh, we snuck in, or I think we did. There was always food waiting for me... so perhaps not! I see you try too hard. Relax your own muscles, set your mind free. You will know when you can let go of your thoughts. Your body will feel light, and your mind will then follow. It takes time, and you need to do it every chance you get—when you ride, walk, eat, even before you sleep. Each time you approach Fire Dancer, you will be more connected not only to her, but to every living being.

"We need to walk our four-legged companions so they can get the tightness out of their bodies. Tightness leads to muscle cramps, as it does in humans, and it can hurt. We will walk them for a while." He took the lead. "Watch for stones. You must look down as well as keep your eyes forward."

"How do I do that?"

"Stop thinking so hard."

After a good span passed, he heard her take several deep breaths, and turned to face her. "Soon, soon we will be at the paintings. There we will allow the mustangs to graze. I see worry on your face. Do not worry so. Night Hunter must gather men he will lie to about the yellow stone. He cannot act alone. He is not so brave. Father Sun will rise several times before he makes his move. By then, we will be in a warmer place, and our mustangs will graze on grasslands — new grass that right now fights to push its way past old growth, waiting for animals to seek it out."

He turned and breathed into the soft muzzle of his mustang, and stroked the thick neck hair. He moved over to rub the softer hair on the animal's face. He remained silent, unmoving.

"I name him Fast Shadow. He likes the name, and so do I." He jumped on Fast Shadow and twisted to see if she was doing the same with her mustang. "You two will make good companions. Already she stands still for you. Jump on. We need to keep moving while Father Sun still shines on the canyon walls."

The pair made their way through the widening canyon. Father Sun warmed the opening space. Birds, once hidden in budding thickets, now fluttered past, showing red breasts, yellow heads, and soft greys mixed with darker blue-tipped wings. They flew upwards into the turquoise sky.

A young Mouse slid from his shoulder and bounced on the ground. "Oh no, grab that baby mouse, will you? He might jump into danger before his time. We all have our time with destiny, but his is not now. A dream will tell him when."

"Mice dream?" She jumped off Fire Dancer, who stood in place instead of trying to get away.

"Of course they do, silly. All beings dream, even stones." He stared at her as if seeing her for the first time. "Who are you?"

"What? Wanderer, you know me. Why ask such a silly question? Has your mind left you? And what do you mean stones dream?"

"Later. Tell me who you are." His expression turned serious. "Well?"

"I... I am Falling Rainbow of the Beaver People, daughter of — "

"I know that."

"What has this to do with this little mouse?" She held out her cupped hand where the mouse sat.

"You remind me of him, running away without knowing where he goes or why. I am glad to see that you caught him before he found trouble."

"Why not let him go? He can hide in the clumps of yellowed grass. Aww... he is nothing but a tiny little creature with big eyes." She held him by his tail and petted his body. "He is so soft, and look at his whiskers moving about so fast."

"Perhaps you would like to care for him and his brood? His mother has weaned them." Wanderer's expression was serious.

"I... I do not know how to... how to — oh, catch him! Wait, he is crawling into the fur around my neck. How many are in his brood?"

"Six."

"So many! I am, umm, truly honored but... but... I am not so sure a mouse brood would be such a good thing with my being on Fire Dancer. What if she—"

"Here, silly, I only tease. It takes skill and time to know their ways. Besides, you have yet to take care of yourself. When you can tell me who you are, I will let you care for a mouse." He pointed to a place ahead of them. "We fast approach the paintings. We need to go one ahead of the other when we get to that narrow pass. You will miss it if you do not look up."

Wide-eyed, she quickly placed the baby mouse into his open hands, then jumped back on her mustang and urged her forward. "Where? I do not see the passage."

She pushed Fire Dancer harder. The animal jerked back and she fell on the muddy ground.

A laugh escaped as Wanderer tried to act stern. "Slow down, woman who acts as a child. The paintings have been there for cycles and will not vanish before we get there." He leaned to offer his hand.

"I am not acting as a child, I am simply... excited, nothing more. I *am* a woman."

He helped her up and aided in smacking the clotted mud from her clothes as she mounted. "Yes, good thing you are a woman. You might have fallen harder." This time, nothing could contain his laughter. "Ohhhh, my girl, a few moons ago, before you became a woman, you would have made yourself look very silly!"

Her face turned the color of cold unmittened hands. "Heh, good thing the furred clothing that you made me is in my pack. It would have been ruined. I have much to learn. I... I will admit this to you and apologize for being so bold. I still do not understand your question about who I am." The heat on her face still showed.

He turned Fast Shadow sideways, took the woman's chin into his hand, and pulled her eyes level with his. "We never stop learning. We only stop with our last breath. You and I, we will learn from each other no matter the age I have over you. And I still learn from you."

"Me? How so?"

"I never had a daughter—all boys, seven of them. Now you will teach me what it is to have a daughter." He let her chin go.

"So, am I a teacher?"

"We all are."

She cocked her head. "Where are your sons now?"

He stiffened at the question, and his heavy eyes welled with water threatening to spill over. With a jerk of his hand, he slapped them away and whispered, "Someday... perhaps someday I will tell you."

He rode ahead of her.

Chapter 10

Twice seeking guidance, first for his daughter, and then for answers to the dreams that invaded his sleep, Shining Light leaned against a tree, his legs stretched in front of him. He rubbed his bare feet against the softness of thick moss and short grass; it helped him relax. White Paws and Moon Face stretched out on either side of him. Their eldest female pup from their first litter cared for the newest pups and helped teach them to hunt. His grandmother had named the wolf Bright Beauty for all the colors in her fur. She had done so on the day she, his mother, and he nearly lost their lives to the flash flood.

Much Power came to us all that day. Mother saw both sides — this land and the Spirit land. She became more in balance with herself and life. Maybe when we are faced with such closeness of leaving this side, we let go of things that do not matter so much.

He had watched Bright Beauty race by with the four pups mixed among the rest of the pack only a short span ago. Teaching pups did not fall solely to the parents, but to the entire pack. All females made their own milk for some reason. He shook his head in wonder that the young ones had nursed on different females. They kept up with little trouble now.

He chuckled and reached out to both parents. "Just like my own people, your pups have more than one mother and father. The whole pack, like our band, takes responsibility for every young one and watches them as they would their own. Your pack teaches them what they will need to know to live and grow, to become responsible pack members. Our children will carry on traditions to be taught all over again to their own children."

He sighed and relaxed his arms on the two wolves, then leaned back and closed his eyes.

The peace lasted only for a short span before a dream misted into his mind, in which he was as Mouse.

He clung to a bit of what seemed like fur, his ear twitching. Whiskers sprouted from his long grey snout. His ear flicked, eyes wide as a young woman screamed and pushed her four-legged companion hard. Too hard. The mustang began to fall back, stopped and stood still, heaving as white foam flecked the light-colored animal's shoulders and sides.

A desperate cry garbled by Sister Wind rushed past Shining Light's — Mouse's — flickering ears.

The woman twisted her back as men came closer, men of the Peoples, and men of the hairy-faces mixed among them. Laughter echoed from one of the pursuers.

Shining Light dug his tiny claws deep and tried to hold on as an elder man shouted. It was then he realized he rode on the elder's shoulder.

The elder man took an arrow, and blood spattered on Shining Light's grey mouse fur. The elder's screams were not for himself, but for the woman who desperately tried to kick her animal into moving faster. The elder reached behind his shoulder for his bow, causing Shining Light's mouse legs to flay out as he fell to the ground.

Shining Light squealed and clawed his way up the mustang, lost his grip and, once again with legs splayed, fell toward the muddy ground....

Shining Light woke drenched in his own sweat, lurched forward, and gasped at the taste of blood in his mouth. The heart that belonged in his chest choked him as he swallowed. Clutched in his hands, White Paws' fur gave way. He brushed his mouth, and blood from a sliced lip came away on his hand.

"So real. I *felt* what Mouse did. I did not mean to pull your fur so hard that it came out."

Both wolves stood in front of him. White Paws moved forward and licked blood from his face. Moon Face whined, moved over and rubbed her head against Shining Light's side, while wriggling her body, tail tucked.

"You forgive me without question." He pulled both wolves closer and turned his head to one side. "Always, you wolves have comforted me, stayed with me when my dreams scared me awake, never once shying away, but ever comforting this pup who still grows and needs his pack for guidance. Guidance no human could ever give... not even Animal Speaks... sweet woman of mine."

***

Animal Speaks jerked forward while standing in front of Gentle Wisdom. "Did... did I just? Shining Light had a vision, a bad one. I felt his fear!"

She handed her baby to her companion and raced into the trees. The shells on her fringed sleeves clinked against elk teeth that covered the top half of her dress. Panicked birds flew from low shrubs.

"Shining Light, where are you?"

Small animals raced for cover. His mustang, Sandstone, raced beside Speaks, her young one at her side. With no thought to her safety, Speaks grabbed hold of the mustang's neck hair and flew across her back, almost falling off on the other side. Now one, woman and mustang surged forward, Sandstone's little four-legged grey shadow fighting to keep abreast.

Sandstone reached the falling water and stopped abruptly at its edge. Speaks slid sideways off the mustang's back and into the water. The grey baby whinnied as he caught up to his mother. His now darker grey and off-white neck hair and his little flickering tail shook. He leaned into her for comfort, and the mother reached down to nuzzle her young one.

"So, now my woman has learned to fly?" Shining Light leaned up on his knees then stood, a grin on his face.

She stood up, dress hanging low from the water's weight, and spit out water and hair. "You ungrateful...! I was terrified when I heard you yell out in my mind, and you... stand there... smiling?"

Water ran from the seams of her dress and into the river. She flipped her hair over her shoulders, her hands visibly shaking as much as her legs. She splashed out of the water, swinging her arms rapidly as she approached him.

***

Her face held much anger and she tightened her hands into fists.

"Speaks?"

Shining Light swallowed as Sandstone turned to him with an expressive glare of her own, then trotted to him and pushed him down!

Animal Speaks sloshed her way to him, sputtering words he wished he could not hear. They stung him like the small winged ones angered by Bear's swat at the hive.

"At least Sandstone understands my horrible fears!" She tried to kick his leg, and tripped.

He squealed as a cold, wet and frustrated woman fell on top him and pounded on his chest. "Speaks, I only joke! Are those tears in your eyes? I do not remember seeing your eyes spill water before, not even when I peeked in as you brought our daughter to us. Are... are you angry with me? I am sorry you fell into the water!"

"Birthing pain is hard to bear, but I bore it knowing I would bring new life — bring us our daughter. You see pain in my eyes because to lose my heart, my Soul, would not be as bad as losing you. I felt your fear, and it terrified me!" She sobbed as Shining Light held her.

His own eyes spilled over. "My woman, my joy, can you forgive this man of yours?" He held her until their soaked clothing glued them together. "Please say you forgive me. I cannot bear your anger. It hurts deep inside, as a loss I have never felt before."

He pulled them apart and leaned on his side, shivering not from cold, but despair. "Please, Speaks, I love you more than there are trees in this forest, more than there are drops in the falling waters. Not so long ago you gave me a daughter, yet you raced toward where I might be with no thought to your own pain. You are indeed a strong woman! You are my heart."

She smiled through watery eyes. "To you, my man, I give my heart and life to do with whatever you wish." She slapped his chest. "Just do not ever, *ever* leave me behind to wonder if you are safe... or alive! Do you understand? My heart would surely die. My Soul would turn to dust and blow away."

She stared at him with a mix of love and somberness. "I forgive your silliness."

Sandstone nipped at his toes. "Hey! I am a beaten man. Even my mustang has her say." He scooted against her again and smiled.

I am forgiven. Now I understand my new gift that White Bear has given me, and it's great Power. To be forgiven gives me a good feeling in my heart. I cry with tears of joy inside my Soul.

"May our lives always be filled with moments of such joy... only drier." He smiled.

She smacked him on his head, spraying him with water.

Chapter 11

Makes Baskets stood with crossed arms, glaring at Flying Raven. "Many say they wish to help your son. Even the hairy-face, Tall Smiling Warrior, says he will go. *We* have two small children who need their father. I will be terrified enough with Shining Light leaving. I will not be twice terrified!"

Flying Raven tried to look stern at his woman, but she matched his expression. "How can I not follow *our* son? He is still so young, even if he is a father himself. He is my child... and yours." He tried to reach out and touch her face, but she pulled back, her eyes still sparking in defiance.

"I have spoken to a Holy Man whose camp is nearby. He will visit everyday when I am gone, to see to the needs of our people. You, woman of mine, are strong, or I would not leave you. Your mind is as sharp as your tongue."

She let out a slow breath. "If you had not smiled when you spoke your words about my tongue, you would have heard it! If we did not have two babies, I would follow you. I thought to never have my heart filled by a man again, and then you came along. My heart would stop beating if you did not return, man of mine."

"Woman, I *will* return. If I had danger waiting for me, I would know. Do not forget I am Head Holy Man of the Wolf Peoples. I have power to see —"

Shining Light stepped in between his parents, soaking wet, and spread his arms to keep them apart. "Mother, Father, I am not taking an entire band back toward the canyons! I am taking Gentle Wisdom... and," his voice lowered, "and Speaks. I know they will only follow if I dare to sneak out without them. And I am not a child! You *have* two children. You both know the Spirits will watch over us, and only what is meant to happen will happen."

Flying Raven's woman's expression changed, and with eyes squinting, she shook her finger at their son. "You will not dare take your woman who gave you a daughter less than three moons ago! I will not allow it."

Animal Speaks Woman stepped forward, also soaked. "You, my man's mother, have no say. I am going to pack right now." Animal Speaks stomped off with a grinning Gentle Wisdom on her trail.

Shining Light shrugged. "Who can tell a woman with fire in her heart that a man knows best?"

His mother's face bloomed with heat, and Flying Raven could not help but laugh at his son's words. Everyone nearby stood motionless.

"It is women who keep bands together." Her voice rose. "Our 'fire' comes from our worries, our cares for our families! If we did not have a voice, which comes from our hearts, you men would act before a single thought. Women have Power, strong Power."

She mumbled something no one wanted to repeat, and headed toward her mother's lodge.

"Son, I *am* a Holy Man among the people, but not with your mother. To her, I am but her man." He looked her way. "A man should have his say!"

"I heard you, Raven!" she yelled without looking back.

He turned, shrugged, and stomped after her.

***

Shining Light grinned until he saw his own woman with arms crossed staring his way. *No sneaking away for me. I need Fox medicine to disappear, and Speaks has it, so I know she will be right behind me no matter if I leave in darkness.*

He knew from his grandmother's familiar steps behind him that she had heard everything.

She placed her hand on his shoulder. "Grandson, the Spirits will always be with you and yours. As I said a long time ago, things happen as they are meant to."

He turned to face the woman who had molded his young life. "I do not want to put Speaks and our daughter in danger. I have no idea what is out there waiting, or who. I would like Father to follow, but Mother is not happy with that and, as you know, she is *so* stubborn!"

"As is her son." Bright Sun Flower sat on the ground and patted a spot next to her, and Shining Light sat. "Do you want your grandfather to go? I know he wants to. He says he seeks an adventure. Most of our band is content to stay, yet others, who were wanderers before we came here, have a need to do so again." She reached out and grabbed his shoulder. "Grandson, I do not want you to leave without protection. You cannot do it alone."

He twisted away from her grasp. "I do not know what is out there. In my vision, I saw a young woman and an elder fighting to save themselves from men of the hairy-faces... and someone else. I do not know how many there were. It could have been only a handful, not so many that we need to worry. Perhaps I could do it alone."

Bright Sun Flower squinted as her voice changed. "You *are not* so smart if you think you do not need help! We are a band of combined people, many bands of combined Peoples, who would rush to your aid. Listen well to me, my inexperienced warrior grandson — you will *not* leave alone."

He knew she spoke loud words so others could hear them.

"We will call a Counsel and speak of it more there. I leave now to speak to Flying Raven, your father, yes, but also our Head Holy Man."

He had yet to use his bow against another person, and did not wish to do so, but to put others in danger? With his pride hurt, he stood and walked away from camp and into the trees.

White Paws bumped into his backside.

"I would not dream of leaving *you* behind, ever. I could not leave without my Spirit Guide, who lives in a body to be at my side."

Tonight... I leave tonight with Gentle Wisdom. Perhaps Speaks will be sleeping.

Chapter 12

Wanderer led Falling Rainbow to the old Fish People's camp to wait for Night Hunter and his followers to pass. "We allow them to get ahead of us. That way, we know how many follow him. We are warm and safe here. If Night Hunter could get only some of the hairy-faces to follow, he maybe bribed them. If there are more following, that would mean they believed his story about the yellow stone. Either way, we must know."

He rubbed his shoulders. "It is not so cold this day, yet I have chills. I can feel much in the old Fish Peoples' camp, from babies crying to an elder woman who they sung to the stars."

He sat by her on an aged log next to a tree that overlooked the old camp. Lodge polls lay in bunches with chattering animals racing through them. If not for the polls, no one would have known a camp had ever existed here. Plants had taken over most of the land. In the distance resided the only thing that marked this as a camp of the People—a burial place partly given back to nature. Saplings and large shrubs hid what may have been the path to the grounds. Old hides flapped from the thick arms of mature trees. Still a Sacred place, it would never be disturbed by any human.

"It must have been very hard to leave their loved ones behind. I had to—" He cleared his throat and stood to stretch.

"We must prepare for a cold night. No large fire tonight, we must be careful. The air is warm, but soon the cold will come with the darkness." He nodded toward an area where a huge boulder guarded the way into part of the canyon. "We can have a small fire over there, and that will be plenty to keep us warm. Our mustangs can eat, but we must keep them tied as the hairy-faces do, by their front legs, so they can only take small steps. Even with binding as we have done, they like to roam as they graze.

"I feel restless. Maybe the animals do also. I know mustangs can feel what we feel when we are riding them, so why not when we are near them? I will take care of them once we unpack and see what we have to make a shelter." He raised his arm and swatted at the air.

Falling Rainbow gathered her robe about her and turned in a circle twice, each step slow, precise. She listened and looked for their stalker. Even from where he stood, several strides away, he could see her wide eyes and tense face. He needed to get her mind away from her fears.

"Woman, what do you think of the paintings and carvings? Do you think we can find your Shining Light and his band?"

Her frown changed into a smile. "Yes, I *think* so. I saw Father Sun at the end with an arrow pointing to where the land gets cold." She wrapped her robe tighter. "Thank you for showing me what my eyes have sought for so long. I must have walked near it many, many times! I feel silly to know I was but one path away from it. The path was so thick with dried raspberry sticks that I decided not to walk that way, always choosing another. I even went partway into that path to eat the fruit!"

She started gathering deadfall to make a small fire. "I wonder why they chose that canyon. The pictures told of how an elder named Feather Floating In Water led his people here, but he did not live past the first cold season. They had plenty of fish, deer and rabbits. Song Bird told me that Shining Light had visions of the land dying as the people and animals ran away from the grey land. He could feel the hairy-faces when he was only eight winters old."

She held a log and seemed to stare at nothing. "To have such dream visions for one so young must have frightened him. We now know the hairy-faces were real, so why not this place of Tall Trees? Imagine a boy who became a man while still in the body of one so young, and having to get adults to listen to him. He had help from a Great Elder who taught him much, guided him to the center of the Circle. I wonder who she was. The People named themselves Fish People. My aunt's sister, Bright Sun Flower, was one of them. My aunt spoke of these people often, or I would not know what I do."

Wanderer again batted at something invisible above him. "I do not think the raspberry stickers were the reason they chose this place. The canyon they chose has very little light on the wall where the paintings are. It keeps them safe from Father Sun's ability to fade paint. Further into the canyons are paintings far older, ones where red paint shows handprints and people with broad shoulders. They are so old, they flake away in some spots where Father Sun hits them. I saw Circles in Spirals — ongoing life — painted there, so they had the same beliefs we do. With each Spiral there is growth, learning. Never forget the Spiral represents a broadening of consciousness, the opening of the mind."

He stood, leaned over and picked up a basket, which someone had tucked away in a robe and placed within a clay pot. "Woven baskets, like the one here, start with one circle. To make it grow into something, another circle is made and another until the basket is completed."

Several mice crawled out on his shoulders, down his arms, and jumped. Again, he batted at the air. "We need to use Sage if we are to stay this night."

She nodded. "I will do that for you. Mother taught me how important the Circle of Life is, that we are all joined, and how easy it is to harm the Web of Life." She stared at the old circles that were once fire pits. "When I was a child, I remember the storyteller gathering all the children into our Counsel Lodge for a story. Perhaps you would like to hear it?"

"I would. I love to hear stories, but we must make sure we are safe first." Two more mice leapt to the ground, wrestled with each other, then dashed into the lodge polls and raced back out. They then vanished into red-orange stones.

"I nearly forgot your mice. I have not seen them poke out their heads until now. Where do they go?"

He shrugged. "To wherever mice go. Maybe they look for food, mates, or want to stretch their legs, as we do. Of course, they have more legs than us, so they may be gone for some time."

Her eyes followed his hand waving in the air, as if pushing Spider's web away. "Do you not worry about them? How can.... I mean, every creature sees them as food."

"They have their own destiny, as do we. Inside, each mouse understands this, as does every creature we eat. If respected, as I told you when we met, when they go to their campfires they tell their relations, and that respect will lead to them returning if they choose. Maybe I would like to be a mouse and have some old warrior feed me! When they tell me it is their time and ask me to end their lives, I do so for them. Maybe they do not want to feel pain. I do not know. I never asked. Pain is not a curse. It helps us in many ways, but the final pain for some is hard to bear. It is better to allow them peace if possible. When my time comes, and if I am in pain, I would want someone to show me mercy."

She paused, put her sticks down, and sat next to him, her face pinched. "How does pain help anyone? When I was little, I fell from a tree and the bone in my arm cracked—as bone we crack to eat the marrow out of does. I remember screaming and crying. I was but five winters old."

"Little one—"

"I am a woman."

"Yes, yes... but to me you are...." He reached out and ran his fingers through her hair, then put his hand down and played with the creases in them. "Never mind. Pain told you that something was wrong with your arm. Had it not hurt, you would have gone on playing, maybe damaging your arm so much that you could not use it now. It stopped you from harming yourself even more."

He paused as a pair of mice danced around each other, and he smiled. "Soon, more will fill spots in my clothes."

He played with his bent fingers. "These fingers I broke when I first learned to use a bow. The arrow broke and I grabbed it, and the arrow point sliced two of my fingers nearly off. The Healer did his best to sew the skin back on, but they healed crooked. That pain taught me to be much more careful! Sometimes it can guide us, help us to focus on something besides ourselves, take our mind beyond the pain. Like my fingers. They hurt when rain is coming, and they tell me about rain before my nose does. I can stop what I am doing and seek shelter if I am not near any."

His eyes followed the broken path toward the burial ground, and he let go a long sigh. "Pain is a teacher. Those who have not felt real pain cannot reach out and comfort another. My first woman's head would hurt her so bad, she would beg for herbs to kill the bad Spirits in her head. Other times I would see her leave our camp, go off on her own."

He paused and looked toward the entrance to the canyon. "She would just roam and allow her mind to do the same. She would come back and paint the pictures her mind remembered, some so beautiful the whole band would gather to see them. Many would ask her to paint them something." He wiped a tear that tried to follow a line down his face. "I still carry one of her pictures with me. It faded long ago, but I can see it in my mind."

He turned and smiled at her. "I am leaving my mind's path, going backward instead of where we need to go. When I went on my Vision Quest to receive my adult name, my uncle took pieces of flesh from my arms so I could feel it, acknowledge it, and then move beyond it to seek the Spirit Land. Yes, pain is a great teacher. Listen to it, and it will guide you places you would not otherwise have found."

He stood, stretched, and shuffled toward the canyon entrance. "I need air."

***

Falling Rainbow watched him go into the canyon. She wanted to follow, but knew his mind needed to seek peace. Much pain came with him speaking of those his heart yearned for. She wanted to ask him of his past, what had happened to his family, but each time he spoke of them, she could see she asked too much of him — far too much. She would let him be.

Meanwhile, the camp needed tending. She was, after all, a woman, and should not allow fear make her cower and wait for his return. She unpacked the mustangs and tied their legs as she remembered her father doing, while trying to avoid mice as they leaped on and over her.

Maybe these mice will teach me things, as they have Wanderer.

One landed on her shoulder, and this time she did not jump but scooped him up in her hands. "So, Mouse, tell me about this mysterious elder named One Who Wanders."

The mouse sniffed her hands and jumped down to chase after another, intent on catching his target. She shrugged her shoulders, and made her way through the overgrowth toward the large boulder Wanderer had pointed out as a good place to conceal a small fire.

The pouch her mother had prepared for her would have a clay bowl and Sacred Sage along with Cedar, both cleansers for bad Energy.

I wonder if Wanderer will notice I cleansed the old camp.

After finding her clay bowl, she set it down and busied herself making a small fire from twigs and grass. She transferred a bit of burning grass to the clay bowl where the Sacred plants nestled in the bottom, and blew on it. After it caught, the fingers of fire reached up. She blew it out and allowed the smoke to rise. She cupped her hand and brought the smoke to and over her body, down her knee-length hair, and even the bottoms of her feet.

She meandered about the camp, and let Sister Wind guide the smoke over the log where they sat, allowing the smoke to rise up in the branches where Wanderer swatted the air. She made her way, step by step, toward the tied mustangs. She ran the smoke over them too, saying a prayer for the good Spirits to welcome all of them to the camp. Her lungs took in the deep cleansing scent and she sat on the log, clay bowl at her side.

The chatter of Fox caught her attention, and she backed away, forgetting the Sage and bowl.

Chapter 13

Wanderer ambled along the canyon path through melting snow and muddy puddles until he came to a clearing. He stood by the meandering river along the edge of an orange-red canyon wall, and followed the off-white splashes that wove in and out of the wall.

I wonder where the colors come from. But this off-white, what is it?

He raised his head and let Father Sun warm his face. The time of baby animals had arrived. Beside the path, new Sage plants wakened, and taller light-green plants with fern-like leaves and stems swayed in the gentleness of Sister Wind. Ahead, dark evergreen trees bowed to the weather and Sister Wind's will. Many were ancient, and some offered a small nut the Peoples would put in pemmican in the late season of falling leaves.

"Such great beauty. So many colors that my mind cannot name them all. The strange shapes of these rocks have me wondering if maybe, a long time ago, another kind of Peoples, much taller than ours, lived here and piled these stones on top of one another." He scratched his head at the six stones piled on top of one another. "They look as if Sister Wind could knock them over any time she pleased! The dark green shrubs hang off the sides, yet seem to be very happy to be there. Everywhere I look, I see wonders that, to me, appear impossible—great many-colored stone hills that look like they once had water race past them."

He heard the laughter of a small boy and turned, but there was no child. *My mind teases me.* Still he put his hand up to his eyes and searched the banks of the river. The movement of the waters was the only sound in the canyon.

Why do I see a boy tossing stones in the river? A man as old as me walks beside him. What is this vision?

He took a few steps toward the river and saw a grey wolf. He paused, dropped his hand from his eyes, and stepped even closer. "Wolf, what have you to tell me? Are you a Spirit or does my mind still tease me?"

His old legs shook and his chest barely moved. He could not help staring as deeply into Wolf's eyes as Wolf did into his. His legs gave way and he collapsed to his knees. He fell sideways, and reached out to hold himself up.

"Wolf, why do you come to me?"

'Follow the river....'

"The river? This is how we find the people Falling Rainbow seeks?"

'Follow the river as it spills out into the land of grass, where the humpbacked ones live.'

Wanderer thought he heard the boy's laughter again, and jerked his head toward the sound. "Why do I hear this, Wolf?" He turned back to hear the answer, but saw only the river. "Wolf?"

Legs still shaky, he stood, slapped off the mud, and raised his arms to the turquoise sky. "Great One, I thank you for Wolf's visit, but to follow the river? That will put us out, exposed in the grasslands. I worry this may not be wise." Only the rush of the river and chattering birds greeted his ears. "How will I do this and keep the girl safe?"

'Trust in yourself and the Spirits, Great Holy Man. You have waited long to find this girl, and you know nothing will happen that is not meant to. Trust... trust.'

Again, words whispered in his mind, *'Follow the river... follow....'*

He had received the only answer he would get. Fox barked from somewhere, and he picked up speed back to the old camp. "Fox barks not only to warn of danger, but to keep me paying attention to others who may be watching."

He trotted back to the hideaway and, out of breath, leaned against the entrance. He smelled the campfire but did not see Falling Rainbow.

"Girl... err, woman, where are you?" He stepped cautiously and searched for movement, finding none except his mice and the mustangs. He approached the log they had sat on and peered about the camp.

He tiptoed about the old camp, his voice barely above a whisper. "Sweet Mother, why did I leave her? The Spirits told me I was to guide and protect her. Me, a crazy old man whose mind wanders more than his body."

The red stone he had told her to ready a fire behind moved. Fox ran out and scampered into the canyon.

"Falling Rainbow, where are you?" He stepped closer, pulled out the knife in his footwear and readied for a fight. "I am not so old that I cannot fight good enough to win! Who is there?"

"I, Falling Rainbow, am here, where you told me to be. I was about to cleanse the camp when Fox barked. I watched her fade into the red stone, and it was then I heard voices, so I ran to hide where Fox also hid. I waited to see who might be there. I thought it was Night Hunter, but I saw no one."

She stood up, revealing herself. She too held a knife, but slid it back in her footwear. "I heard Spirit voices! They said something about following the river. Frightened, I did as Fox had taught me, to become my surroundings, and then I waited for you."

She rushed over to him and wrapped her arms around his waist. "When you came in the camp, I was still hearing voices and was not sure you were you." She hugged him tighter.

"Silly, who did you think I was, a Spirit? You know me and the way I look. Maybe you are going crazy, too. Perhaps Fox is only telling us to be aware and ready."

"What? I never said you were crazy."

"Not in words, no. Maybe living half in the Spirit Land does make me crazy, but if this is so, I am a happy crazy. I still get to see my... never mind." He shook his head. "You are not the only one who heard voices. I also saw, though I have no idea what I really saw."

He scratched his chin before batting at the air again. "Spirits, but *not* Spirits. Wolf came to me and said we are to follow the river. I saw... saw... a vision. That is what I saw: a vision—a boy and an elder walking along the river, and the boy laughed several times as he tossed stones into the river." He shook his head again and pulled her away. "You had me terrified! Next time you do Fox medicine, remember I am real and you do not need to hide from me. It is my destiny to guide you."

She squinted and cocked her head. "Guide me? Who says this?"

"Spirits, of course. When Father Sun rises, we will follow the river. Wolf told me Night Hunter would not think to go that way. We will not stay as I had said."

"I would like to go see the paintings again before we leave. They... they felt so alive to me. I could touch them and see in my mind. I think I even saw people carving and painting them."

He chuckled. "That is the gift of Energy. To feel as deeply as you do is a Sacred Happening. I too would like to see the paintings once more before we leave. For now, we must take turns watching for Night Hunter and his brother."

He glanced up and spotted a place where they could watch for any danger. It felt familiar, even though he had never sat there before. "Look up there, by the tree, where the ground is bare. I will sit there when Father Sun sleeps, and we will leave when Father Sun wakes again and spreads across the land. The snow melts fast now, and Night Hunter will soon see that our tracks were not hidden, and will turn around. Maybe he will go back to see if you returned to the Beaver People. If so, we will allow him to pass back this way, and we must be ready to leave. We will have several sunrises to lose him if we follow the river, should he decide to keep looking for you... and for me."

Chapter 14

Shining Light rode Sandstone while White Paws trotted at his side. He still fumed that his grandmother had gotten her way in the Counsel Lodge. She had reminded the people that no one should venture out of the forest alone, no matter how tempted. Everyone had nodded in agreement.

Even if he knew she was right, he felt bested once again. To pack, prepare food, and choose the strongest mustangs to drag enough poles for one lodge took two sunrises. Even though he agreed to wait, between his grandmother and Animal Speaks Woman, he had enjoyed no time to himself. He could feel eyes on him even as he had slept.

Women! How is it they get their way?

Head raised, he ignored Gentle Wisdom and Animal Speaks Woman, who spoke in not so low whispers and muffled laughter about babies and men behind him.

He twisted around on Sandstone's back to look at his father, grandfather, and the hairy-face who also followed, but at a further distance. He had told them they needed to be farther back to keep their eyes open for any dangers. To his surprise, both his father and grandfather had agreed. The truth was he wanted some time alone this day, if being within listening distance could be called alone.

He grinned and felt lighter at the sight of wolves fanning out around all of them, in the growing grasses. The wolves could always pull him from a bad mood. Moon Face's pups kept up well—when she did not have to call them back with a stern howl. Blue Waters, his woman's dog, danced around her mustang with a wolf pup on his heels.

Wolves and dogs living together, yet separate. And the mustangs! Enemies when they are wild, but they relax and have no fear of these wolves who would make them a meal... if they chose to.

It did not take long for them to lose sight of the great Forest of Tall Trees and spill out onto the grasslands. They were a half moon away. The land, he had to admit, was nice to look at. Grass of several lengths and colors hid the spiked oval-shaped plants. He remembered to keep an eye out for them. Every time they stopped, everyone checked their mustang's hooves for any stickers.

He leaned over and glanced at the circles in which the plants grew, and remembered his grandmother teaching him about the Circle of Life. They would soon bloom in the same circular pattern, in whites, yellows, and different shades of oranges. He chuckled at the memories, now understanding that he had worn out his grandmother with his racing through the canyons. She never complained, and always would sit him on her lap and tell him stories, some that she had already told him many times. Now he understood their meanings, and would soon tell his own daughter the same stories.

A bump against his footwear brought his attention back. Sandstone's young one nickered at his mother and tried to nurse.

"I know, little one, you must eat, as must Moon Face's pups. Once again, I thought only of my own feelings." He smiled down at the mustang's young one. His neck and tail hair, frosted in yellow-white, contrasted with his grey body.

On his other side trotted Thunder, Sandstone's first-born daughter in their new lands. Stubborn. Too stubborn for anyone but Shining Light to ride. As red-brown as the rich ground in the Forest of Trees, she stood a hand taller than her mother, had a more boxy face and darker stripes on her legs. Thunder never allowed any male near her, even when her breeding time had come.

Four winters old, she should have had her own baby, not still pester Sandstone for attention. She did not try to nurse, but did not like it when the new baby did. Others laughed, but Shining Light had to take her aside every time and "talk" to her. He often jumped on her back and raced with her across the land, until she stopped on her own. The only problem was that Thunder would then refuse to turn around unless Shining Light got off and walked beside her.

Another woman who gets her way.

He glanced at his woman, and she wrinkled her face in response and pulled her mustang even with his. She understood his thoughts. Animal Speaks Woman learned of his thoughts by watching his body movements, a skill he had tried to learn from her.

He trotted on ahead of her.

His grandmother would have come, also, if his grandfather had not made her understand that if she came, so would his mother, Gentle Wisdom's mother and father, and all the children with them.

He threw up his hands at his thoughts. "Why not bring the entire band back out into the open?"

He jumped off Sandstone, swung up on Thunder, and sped off before anyone could react to his outburst. The mustang's speed gave him joy. He leaned forward, and she took the hint and raced faster. Without glancing back, he knew no one would even try to keep up. Thunder always won every race the men challenged her to run. The prize offered was their mustang if they lost. Shining Light was rich with mustangs. Many came offering hides, arrows, and handcrafted necklaces to get their animals back. He would laugh and tell them to take back their four-leggeds, and to stop tempting him with so many goods. He had no use for more than his little family needed. Things only dragged him down.

Why take more than one needs? Where would I put it all? Build another lodge for things I would have to go look at, puff out my chest as the hairy-faces do when they acquire more than their fellow companions? How silly to think items make you rich, better than others. Sharing makes you rich, and... equal to others. I have too many mustangs and must do a giveaway when we get back — a giveaway to others who have less. Yes, this is the right way to live — to make sure everyone has enough.

Thunder slowed down, stopped, and tossed her head in the air—her way of saying, 'I will run no more. Now, we walk.'

"Thunder, why must you run so far?" He put his hand to his brow and shielded his eyes from Father Sun. "I can see no one!"

She reached up to nibble on the new tender leaves in the grove where they stopped.

"I cannot even see my people, and... and look at White Paws! A good thing this human is wise enough to carry water. Wolf, why do always insist on chasing after this mustang? You know she is crazy. I wonder where she got this crazy blood. Not from her mother!"

White Paws lay on his side, panting hard enough that his belly bounced up and down in unison with each breath. He glanced up once at the sound of his name, then plopped his head back on the newly grown light-green grass.

"I know, old friend, you are never far behind me." He jumped off Thunder and sat beside the wolf. "You must calm yourself before I give you any water, so get your nose away from the water bladder, silly. You will only waste it on the ground. I need to go gather the long grass along the side of the hill, to rub down Thunder before she chills."

As he approached the mustang, she came to meet him, her muzzle dripping water.

"Water? While White Paws and I thirst, you found water behind the hill and helped yourself? I hope you do not get a bellyache. The last time you drank too much, I was up all night walking you." He reached out, hugged her around her thick neck, and inhaled deeply. "You have a sweet smell like the others, but you have a sharp smell like the pines. Why have you chosen me, Thunder? Was it because I was there when you were born? Your mother acted like she had no idea what was happening. How can this be so? Do not all females know what to do? Okay, so Speaks needed help. But I bet if she had been alone, she could have had our daughter."

He looked in Thunder's chocolate eyes. "Maybe not. What do I know about birthing? I understood enough to help pull you out only because I had watched others help their mustangs. You were big, maybe too big for Sandstone." He rubbed her chest with the dry grass. "I thought my father's mustang, Flies Like Wind, was your father, but you do not have even a hint of his color. Maybe your father is among the hairy-faces' mustangs?"

She shoved her face into his when he stopped to ponder his own question.

"How is it your wild brothers and sisters do not need rub downs? In the past two days, I have counted three small groups of mustangs who ran at the sight of us, racing up hillsides so thick with shrubs that we could not follow. They stood up on those hills and... I swear they laughed at us! I saw no one running after them with grass, offering them rubdowns. I think this is a trick that one of you thought up to get rubbed all over! A trick we poor humans fell for once, and now it is accepted as truth."

He worked on her neck and down her legs first, then her back, as she grunted with pleasure.

"Sneaky trick. Perhaps I will try this with Speaks the next time I come home from hunting. I could say, 'Sweet woman of mine, I have come far with meat. I had to carry it, having too much for Sandstone's back. Oh, I am so tired, and in great need of a rub down.' She would chase me off with a willow switch!"

He tossed the grass and she followed after it.

"Thunder, you have stopped in a place that would be good to camp in, if the others can find us! This valley with a hill protects us if Sister Wind gets too strong, and there are plenty of fallen branches, a few long logs, much grass, and... we have water."

He eyed his laughing mustang as she raised her lips and twisted her head at his response. "You must have smelled the water. Crazy mustang!"

White Paws stopped panting so hard and nosed the water bladder.

"Here, my faithful companion. I do wonder why you do not just go over to the stream. Have you also decided I am good for being a slave?"

He knelt and placed the water bladder between his legs to steady it, and poured it into his cupped hand so White Paws could get his fill. Then he too sat and drank. Before long, he stretched out next to the wolf in the shade of the large boulders that sparkled in the light. He watched as Thunder grazed, and his eyes drooped in response to his cooling, relaxed body. His breathing became even, slow, and his mind drifted.

The old camp came into view. He was above it, sitting on a low cloud – so low he could see the mice playing. The elder tried to gather them up, calling to them. The young woman laughed as he bent to scoop a pair into a pouch in his outerwear. The mice jumped on his head and squeaked, and the elder tried to scoop them up before they bounded off. Instead, he slapped his head.

Shining Light laughed as the elder raced after each one. He called to the elder. "They only play with you, tease you. Continue packing to leave, and they will run to you if they think you leave them."

The elder jerked his head up in bewilderment. "Are you the wolf who told me to follow the river?"

"Um, river? Ahhh, yes, follow the river... as... Wolf said. I will find you." He nearly woke when he realized he looked at the camp the Fish People had come from.

'Who are you? I am crazy, talking to air!' The elder grabbed some smoldering Sage and waved it in the air.

A gentle kick surprised Shining Light. He sat up while still laughing, and rubbed his eyes.

"So, man of mine, you now laugh while you sleep?"

"Speaks!" He turned his head to discover that everyone had set up camp while he slept. "How did you find us? And how is it that I slept through you setting up camp?"

He sat up and scratched his head. "I... was going to come back, but White Paws was tired and thirsty, and I just lay down next to him to wait until he was ready to go back, and... fell asleep. Really, I was about to get up. My dream was funny, not like most of my others, and I talked to the elder! I really talked to him, Speaks, and saw our old camp, too, by the river where Blue Night Sky came to us. I saw where our lodge once stood and...."

Animal Speaks Woman rolled her eyes. "You still talk like that boy I once knew. Of course, as I remember, you had to stop running away from me first. You acted as if I was going to eat you! You are still just as silly, only now your mouth—"

"Hush, you two." Gentle Wisdom strode over with her hands waving in the air. "You sound like my mother and father, who are now old, but still—"

"Gentle Wisdom, your parents are not so old! They are wiser, that is all." Hawk Soaring shook his finger at the misinformed girl.

Shining Light yelled, "Grandfather! Is everyone here, then? How did you know where to come? Heh. Silly question. You followed Thunder and White Paws' tracks. I had no idea I had fallen asleep!" He pointed to Thunder. "It was her fault. She ran White Paws so hard he fell over gasping for air when she stopped. I have no idea why—"

"Hush, Grandson. As when you were a boy, too many words spill from your mouth. Try breathing now." He shook his head, chuckled and mumbled as he went back to the camp. "Maybe still is a boy."

Gentle Wisdom stood with her arms crossed, laughing. "Bested. You are bested by a mustang!" She stood over him, waiting for a response.

Shining Light tried to scoot closer to Thunder in hopes of jumping on her back, but she trotted over to Sandstone, turned around and gave him her lip-rise-over-her-teeth grin.

She teases me!

The smell of roasting meat made him decide that maybe food was a better idea than running off on a crazy mustang, anyway. He slipped past Gentle Wisdom and reached for the meat, now roasted to a crisp dark brown. He pulled his knife and sliced off a piece that was so hot, he had to chase it with his hands. As it cooled, a wolf face jumped up, grabbed the meat and raced off.

Flying Raven, who sat on the log in front of the pair, wore a wide grin. "Well, Son, now that you are done eating, perhaps you would like to share your dream with us?" He licked his fingers. "Your woman sure knows how to make meat—the right amount of wild plants to taste, how to wrap it so the juices are captured, and.... Why, Son, you sit as a deprived child might. Did you not get enough to eat?"

Shining Light glared at his father's pretend concern, until Flying Raven reached behind his back and pulled out a chunk of meat wrapped in swamp plant leaves.

"Father, you saved my belly!" He grabbed it and tore away the leaves. From the corner of his eye, he watched a sneaky grey figure slink toward him. He was about to shout at White Paws, when one of the new pups put her head on his knee. "You have a mother to feed you."

He raised the treasure above his head. A hand grabbed it and a giggling Gentle Wisdom tore through the camp, waving *his* meat in the air.

"Hey!" He tore off after her and yelled, "Give me back my food or I will make you eat caterpillars!"

Chapter 15

Speaks tried to reach out and pet Thunder, but she hid behind Sandstone. "Those two!" She nodded and laughed as her man and his cousin shouted at each other like children. "They are good for each other. She reminds him to let go of his worries in a way I never could."

The pair raced up grey boulders, using shrubs for handholds.

"Flying Raven, how is it Thunder will only allow Shining Light to touch her? I am Animal Caller, yet she hides from me too." She sat on the log next to him and rocked back and forth with her baby snuggled in her sling. She stopped and reached down to pet her dog, Blue Waters, who pushed her hand with his nose. The bluish-grey dog scooted over for more attention, and she scratched his neck.

Flying Raven turned his head toward a flock of birds darting in and out of the trees in the grove where they camped. Leaves had started to fill in the tree branches, creating a green drape through which the cornflower-blue sky flickered. He stiffened at the birdcalls, put his meat down, and moved his hair behind his ears.

Speaks tightened her hold on Turtle Dove, and her eyes darted about as she spoke in a low voice. "What do you see?" Her dog tensed with her, and stood growling. "Do I need to grab my bow? You know I am good with it. I practiced much in the forest, and I brought food into our lodge as well as yours." She bit her lower lip.

He turned and patted her shoulder. "Do not worry so, Speaks. Ravens call and I became alert, nothing more." His voice sounded reassuring to her, but his head jerked away as if searching for hidden warnings only he knew about.

"Tell me we are safe, Holy Man. Tell me I have not brought my daughter into danger." She clutched the sky beads Shining Light had given her as a binding gift.

He did not respond, turning instead to Tall Smiling Warrior, who walked through long, spindly sapling branches that slapped his leggings. "Are those tracks you found, while we followed Thunder to find my son, old? Fresh?" He raised an eyebrow at the hairy-face's silence.

Tall Smiling Warrior made his way to the remainder of the cooling meat, tore part of it off the wooden spike, and ripped into it. He stood and ate without looking up. "There are many tracks to sort through—mustangs with no riders, human prints from those who most likely tried to catch them, and all a few days old."

He dropped his carryall from his shoulder and drank deep from the water bladder Animal Speaks offered him. "We are a long ways into the grasslands, the kind the humpbacks like. Tracks are easy to see, but mixed with many animals. Some were fresh from mustangs heavy with riders. They could belong to hunters from bands looking for food. What I did find was... um... well, let me show you."

He whistled, and a young woman heavy with child rode in on a patchy yellow and brown mustang, her head held high. Sad, sunken eyes showed even more with dark circles beneath them. Her oval face was slashed with an angry, noticeable scar across the length of her round jaw. She wore a man's tunic, old and worn, that did little to cover more than her thighs. Her feet, red and swollen, were bare. She held tight to the mustang's ropes, the tenseness in her body showing that she would race away if anyone came near. Wild, tangled brown-red hair hung below her waist.

"When she first saw me, she tried to get her old mustang to run. I caught up to her and, right away, she put her head down. I am at a loss for some of what she says. All I can tell you is she is terrified, with child, and has no man. When I asked her about why she was alone, she shrugged, said something about being a slave since she was a child, and that she comes from the land of sunrises. She flinched when I tried to touch her hair, acted as if I was going to hit her. I told her I would not do such a thing, but she would not look at me. I asked her if she was hungry and she glanced my way, but quickly looked away again. I told her to follow me. She acted as if I had captured her and held out her hands to me. She has old and new scars on her wrists. This poor girl has not had a good life. She is maybe sixteen winters."

Animal Speaks Woman cautiously walked over to the frightened woman, arms extended to show she meant no harm, and smiled. She motioned to the pack on her back, and the thin woman took it off and tossed it to her. "Now you. Do you need help?"

The woman jumped down, but stepped back several paces. She reached for her tangled hair and pulled on it. Her willowy body made her belly stand out more than the eight moons along that Animal Speaks Woman guessed her to be.

The woman wrapped her thin arms protectively around her belly, and stared everywhere but into another person's eyes. "I am slave, nothing more. Last man who owned me beat me as a warning that if I had a girl child, he would kill us both. I took an old mustang and, in the darkness, ran for my baby's sake." She looked into the only other woman's eyes she saw. "You are not a slave?"

"I am called Animal Speaks Woman. And how are you called?" She tried to take the stranger's hand but she pulled away. "I am not a slave. At one time, I ran with my mother and her grandmother to avoid the... the...." She stared at Tall Smiling Warrior, who motioned her to continue. "...the hairy-faces who tried to kill us." She pointed at the hairy-face before her and smiled. "Not him, he is a good man. You have nothing to fear from us. My man is a... um... Spirit Man? You understand?"

She nodded. "My name changes with every man who owns me. My mother called me Sparkling Star. Why are you not with a band?" She jumped when Thunder came up beside her.

Speaks laughed and slapped her thigh as she held onto Dove. "Well, you have a friend I have not been able to make! Her name is Thunder, and only my man can touch her... and now you."

Thunder rubbed her head against Sparkling Star's shoulder.

"Come, you must be hungry. Do not mind my dog or the wolves you see running through the grass. They are all... companions, protectors. Sit, and I will speak to you about why we are out here."

She stretched her hand out. "You are no longer a slave. Never will you be one, among us. Perhaps you can tell us more about where you have come from, and why I see something I have never seen before — red in your hair. Sparkling Star, what a beautiful name."

***

Shining Light licked his fingers. "Told you I could outrun you! You have shorter legs than I do. I am a man, not a boy, and it is *you* who is bested! I am a father and do not have time for silly games."

Gentle Wisdom sat close to him and leaned her head on his shoulder. "You will always have time for silly games. It is in your heart that you are still a boy. Perhaps when you have many children and are too fat to chase them — "

"I will never be fat. I have you to steal my food!" He grinned and pushed her head off his shoulder. "Oh, look, my silly Cousin, Spider has chosen to nest in your hair."

Before he could run his fingers through her hair, she screamed, stood and shook her hair. "Where? Where! Tell me now or I will shake my hair over you, cousin who is worse than silly."

He rolled backward, kicked out with his legs, jumped up, and darted back toward camp. He turned to see if she followed, and tripped over a small shrub. "Do not stand over me and chuckle as I sit here with maybe a broken leg. You are going to have to carry me back." He frowned, looked down at his twisted leg and made moaning noises.

She gasped. "Light, I did not mean to make you fall! I am so sorry. I acted as a child and forced you to chase after me for your meal." She started to kneel when... he jumped up and raced off. "You are a boy, and a mean one!"

He slid to a fast stop and nearly skidded down the hill. Gentle Wisdom did not stop, and found herself tasting dust as she landed on her backside next to him. Without looking at her, Shining Light offered a hand while pointing with his other. "That woman does not feel right. I feel sickness around her."

"Woman? What woman?" She spit dust from her mouth, let go of his hand, and brushed her arms free of more dust. "A woman! We have a new woman in our camp. Look Shin — "

"It was I who told you, cousin. Where has your bested mind gone?" He slowly made his way down the hillside, not taking his eyes off the woman.

Gentle Wisdom followed behind him, trying to push him out of the way. "What do you mean she does not feel right? I wonder where she came from. We go racing up the hillside, come back and have a strange woman in camp. I can see something in her hair — red something." She put a hand over her brow. "She hides behind Speaks. She is scared for some reason. Now I can see her belly! Light, she is with child."

He did not respond, but continued his way into camp. He felt a light shove on his side and reached down, knowing it was White Paws. "So, did you enjoy my meal?" White Paws trotted past him and headed toward the young woman.

As Shining Light approached, the woman sat on the ground and stared at her lap. A soft breeze moved her hair, and the red-brown hair wrapped itself around her shoulders and face. She did not try to brush it away.

Her face is oval, not round as ours, and her hair... dark but more like the color of a humpback.

"Shining Light, my man, will not harm you, Sparkling Star. It is fine to stand and look at him. Do not be afraid. Please stand." Speaks offered her hand to the unresponsive woman, who only rubbed her arms with her hands. When she dropped them in her lap, palms up, calloused scars marred her small hands.

White Paws settled down next to her and put his head in her lap. Her voice but a whisper, she rubbed the fur on his back. "Wolf, you still find me. If you had not been catching me food, I would have not made it as far as I did." She hugged White Paws as if he were an old friend.

Shining Light knelt beside her and tried to lift her chin. "I see you have made the best of friends already. Now allow us to be your friends, your family. You have nothing to fear from any of us." His voice was soft and soothing. "Now I understand why each day he vanished with his pack for long spans. I thought he searched for danger. You have been following us. Or maybe White Paws led you to us."

She averted her eyes. "I will be called Sparkling Star, the name my mother gave to me."

"What is Sparkling Star?"

She pointed up with her finger. "That is what the hairy-faces call the campfires in the sky."

"Please look at me. It is not against our ways. You can look at me, any of us, and not worry you look into the eyes of someone better than you."

He smiled as she raised her head and stared at him with soft brown eyes. "You are good to look at, beautiful one. Where do you come from?"

She turned her head away from him and would not speak, but trembled as he tried to touch her face again. Her neck had a red line that had come from a rope. "Sparkling Star. How is it your mother called you that?"

She turned her head back toward him, but did not glance up again. "My mother heard the name and said it sounded soft. I come from the land where

Father Sun wakes. A long time ago, my mother was a slave to a hairy-faced one." She shot Tall Smiling Warrior a quick glance before turning away to stare at her lap once more. "We were taken from men who fought with the hairy-faces and lost. They took us back on the big salty waters in a floating thing made of wood — where my people came from, but... another direction."

She shook her head and tears splashed onto her dress. "I was around seven winters old when something happened to my mother, and the hairy-faces gave me to a people who thought I had gifts after seeing red in my dark hair. When I was about ten winters old, they decided I had no gifts and traded me to another people, and those new people traded me again. This is all I know." Her eyes dulled and she wrapped her hands around her belly.

Shining Light could feel that she suffered from "split-apart," a pulling apart of the body and mind. It caused sickness, made a person forget who they were and forget their purpose in life. If the two parts did not pull back together, the sickness would get worse.

He looked up at his father, who nodded that he already understood why White Paws had led her to them. The wolf knew she was very ill.

"Tonight, Sparkling Star, we will gather to hear a story my grandmother told me when I was a child. For now, my woman and cousin will help you with cleansing, new clothing, and will feed you." He reached out, showing empty hands. "You are safe."

He stood, allowing Animal Speaks Woman and Gentle Wisdom to take her to the small pool. As she went with them, a grey fog floated around her. White Paws and Blue Waters both followed. Moon Face came up and sniffed the woman, and then she and her pups also followed.

The wolves, and even Blue Waters, also know. This I can feel. Sickness... it is deep within her.

Chapter 16

Wanderer felt a chill and rubbed the fur sleeves that hid his arms. He paced back and forth, searched the sky, and listened for any sounds.

"Falling Rainbow, wake up. We must not stay another day. Spirits are whispering, but I cannot understand them. This is not normal for me. I feel uneasy and cannot stop the chill bumps from growing on my arms." He made a chatter call and mice appeared around them. "Time to leave, little ones."

Falling Rainbow rubbed her tired, dry eyes and sat up from her sleeping robe. Father Sun had only started to rise, and a chill still gripped the red-orange hideaway where they had slept. She crawled out from her robe and rubbed her arms, reached for a few small sticks to add to the smoldering ashes, and looked up with brows pinched.

"I cleansed the whole camp last night. What is it? What do you feel? You call to your mice so soon?" She watched them appear from every place her eyes searched. "You had said we would stay for a bit longer, at least for part of this sunrise."

"After talking to Spirit Wolf, and then to a man I could not see, I sat up on that little perch all night and listened to sounds in the darkness, and the Spirit Wolf stayed in my mind." He continued to pace. "I want to leave before we have to worry about Night Hunter finding us too soon."

"Too soon?" She stood with her mouth open. "What do you mean too soon?"

He continued to pace. "One night here is enough. Do not panic. We are safe, little one, this I can promise. I just need to move on from this camp, nothing more. Before we leave, I want you to go climb up to the perch and look out over the land. I have never seen such beauty anywhere before. These people must have been sad to leave such a place. Come, we go together while my mice eat. We will eat as we ride." He took out several strips of dried meat, shredded it, and tossed it on the ground.

His mice tried to drag the shreds, one on each end pulling away from each other.

Falling Rainbow laughed. "How many are there?"

He tilted his head and gave her a quizzical look. "I have no idea. Why would I count them?"

"So you would know how many you have and be sure none get left behind."

"If they want to come, they will. I do not own them. They do not belong to me — they belong to themselves. As we belong to ourselves. We may share our lives with others, but no one can truly own another animal or person. That would mean they would own everything about them. How can we own another's body, and mind, and even their thoughts? No one can ever do that." He cocked his head at her. "I have heard of other Peoples having slaves, but surely it is not true."

She stood, facing him, and reached out to touch his face, but pulled back. "I am so glad you waited in that cave for me. You are a true teacher and a good friend."

"What makes you think I waited for you?"

"You... you said you did." Confused, she scrunched up her face.

"Did I?" He grinned and motioned for her to follow him. "You will never forget what you see. The Spirits told me you would find yourself up there."

"Wha... Why?"

"Just follow me, girl."

As they reached the top, Father Sun continued his rise over the land. What first appeared below as light purple turned off-white, and blended into the burnt sienna canyons. The rich turquoise sky appeared over the colorful canyons in a mystical beauty.

She sighed. "I feel the pull of the magic, of all the beauty before me. As many times as I have wandered these canyons, never once did I think to climb up and look down into them. Look down below." She pointed at new growth.

Even as high as they were, she could see greens, both light and dark, showing through spears of light that flashed across the patches of melting snow, making it sparkle. The azure river twisted and swirled around the canyons, and spilled out into small lakes surrounded by rich green plants.

"It is as if the cold season left down there long before it left up here. I am sure it must be warmer down below." She turned, excited, and bounced up and down. "I just know flowers bloom in the valleys!"

"Good thing you are a woman. You might have bounced off the ledge!"

Her laughter brought a peace-filled Energy to the air. "My eyes will never forget what I see, not even if they grow dim with age."

She pointed to small herds of deer and elk that milled around. "So much beauty! And we are going to ride through it. As soon as I can, I want to pull out my dried paints and put this all on a hide for children and ones still in their mother's bellies. My mother was wise to pack them for me."

"So now you know who you are." He crossed his arms and continued to stare out over the land. "Remember when I asked who you were?"

"Um, yes... yes I do. But—"

He nodded at the scene below them. "You are a creator of beauty, a storyteller through your painting—the same way as those who painted on the walls so long ago. We would have never known they lived had they not left their paintings behind for us to see."

"Yes, I... I understand." A smile played at the corners of her mouth. "She Who Paints: perhaps that should be my name."

"Oh, no, I love your name. Promise me you will keep it." It was not a question.

"I promise. I only joke. My name has much that comes with it that I wish to remember. Perhaps someday a dream might add to my name." She rolled her shoulders forward. "I miss my family. Know this: I, Falling Rainbow, will one day return and bring them with me."

"I believe you, sweet one... I believe you. I will go get everything ready to leave. I want you to stay up here and put everything you can into your mind."

***

She turned and reached out. "Wait. I want to tell you about a dream I had before we knew each other. It is a simple one, but I now understand it. I saw many faces in my dream—some good to look at, others twisted and not good. My dream showed me babies, children, young people, and then elders. Their faces changed as they aged—some became more gentle, while others grew angry."

She took in the brightness of his eyes and watched them sparkle. "I can see a person's Soul by looking at their faces. As I stare into yours, I see all the things in your life that made you who you are, how life changed you, hurt you, and brought you joy. I know your Soul, Wanderer." As she gazed across the land coming alive with Father Sun's light, Night Hunter's face came to her.

"Of course you do. You are a painter." He smiled and went back down the path, leaving her to memorize the view.

Night Hunter's face is smooth, with a line between his eyes—a worry line. Now that I think about him, he does not seem so bad. I wonder if his father put the idea in his head that I had Power. I can paint and heal with herbs, but nothing more. I have dreams sometimes, which show me things in my own life, like everyone else. I hold no Power—or do I? Painting is my Power.

She scanned the land before her. "I see Power everywhere, not only in a person's Soul. All I want to do is find Shining Light's band, see the place they now live. If it is a good place, I want to lead my people there. My wants are simple. My life is simple. I like who I am." She raised her head and smiled. "No more will I question who I am. I know."

She turned away and headed down the path.

"You have everything packed, including the mustangs. You are fast for one so ol—" She caught her words before they spilled from her mouth, then jumped on Fire Dancer.

For the first time, she felt life could be lived simply, without worry of gaining material things, or needing to be known for something to gain respect, as she had seen in others. Respect would come naturally if one deserved it— unlike Night Hunter, who tried to take it from others, which she now understood he could not.

No one can take another's Power.

She glanced up at the perch and wondered if it held magic. So much flowed into her mind while she stood there overlooking the land. *So pure, untouched. May it always be so.*

She smiled and tapped Fire Dancer into a trot, and they made their way toward the paintings one more time before following the river.

Wanderer chuckled. "I think you are ready to care for a mouse."

Chapter 17

Shining Light made sure Sparkling Star had plenty of food and a soft robe. He placed his own pack under her robe so she could sit up and enjoy the fire. "I promised you a story, one that will teach and remind us all of something important."

Animal Speaks Woman and Gentle Wisdom sat next to the woman whose arms rested across her belly. Sparkling Star smiled for the first time since he had seen her. Her face held color, but he could still feel the split-apart. She rubbed her belly, content. Her hair, combed smooth, shined red in the fire's light. She wore a light brown elk dress belonging to Speaks. Sky beads alternated with elk teeth to her waist, and her footwear was quilled in Spirals of white and black-tipped quills. Her bright eyes held beauty, and her relaxed face did not look like the terrified young woman from earlier.

"The story I want to share is one my grandmother, Bright Sun Flower, told me." Shining Light settled next to his grandfather, Hawk Soaring, and nodded his way. Flying Raven sat on his other side. The three formed a small half circle, placing the storyteller in the center where everyone could see him. The only sounds came from the crackling fire.

He made sure everyone sat in comfort and nodded to each person. "We have come a long way in a short span, and a good story will remind us of home." He reached out for Dove as his woman passed their daughter to him. "This story will prove how truly blessed I am, as we all are.

"A long, long time ago, the Animal People and the two-leggeds shared the same campfire and spoke the same language. For many, many seasons, this was so. Everyone was happy and shared everything. No one had more than the other. But a few two-leggeds began to mumble to each other, 'Why should we share?'"

Shining Light changed his voice for each being in his story.

"One night, a Human brought it up while everyone rested around the fire after a long day. 'I do not need the Animal People to help me. My woman finds the best roots,' he said, and puffed out his chest. 'I can create a fine, warm shelter because I have hands.'

"Another Human boasted that he, too, could keep his family fed better, and also bragged not only about how he could make a warm shelter, but hunted better than even Eagle. He said that his family did not suffer the cold as the Animal People because he, too, could make fire with his hands. This Human's eyes roamed around the fire, staring at the Animal People. 'Who among you can build a shelter as we can?' He waited for an answer, but not one of the Animal People spoke up.

"It was not long before all the other Humans spoke up about what they could do, about how special they must be because Creator gave them hands. They all stood to leave.

"Only dog decided to follow them. Dog knew someone had to keep an eye on the beings who thought themselves better than all of Creator's other creatures. The rest of the Animals were too offended to follow and watch over the Humans. After all, they had taught the Humans everything they needed to survive. Sadly, the first Human Man to speak up left as Father Sun woke. 'I will go and take my family where we can find more food.' He and his woman packed up their belongings. The Humans, now losing their place around the great campfire, mimicked him."

"Dog sighed and stood, saying, 'Someone must help these foolish two-leggeds. I will take my family and go.'"

No one in the semi-circle took their eyes off the storyteller. Custom dictated that they sit still and listen to every word. Even Flying Raven, Head Holy Man, gave his son this respect.

"After the now lower-cast humans and Dog left, the rest of the Animal People decided they would not abandon their Human Brothers and Sisters, but would no longer talk to them face-to-face. Instead, they decided, if humans needed to seek their advice, it would only be through dreams and through Vision Quests, which required the humans to prove themselves worthy through sacrifice.

"It did not take long for Dog to decide that he, too, would no longer speak to the humans. They expected Dog and his family to pull their drags, and only tossed them scraps. Still, Dog and his family stayed. Someone had to, after all, now that the Humans had no one to help them. Dog took pity.

"Seasons passed, and Humans grew less sure of their abilities. Food became scarce. Unable to find animals willing to give their lives to better the lives of the Humans, they had no hides to keep warm and no meat to keep their children's bellies full. They made shelters from Tree's branches, but did not ask Tree first. They just took. The branches became brittle. Soon, Sister Wind tore them apart.

"Humans fell ill. They became lost and did not understand why. It was not long before their illness affected every part of their bodies, including their minds. No one paid much attention to other Humans in their band anymore. Many simply wandered away, and no one saw them again. People fought and told each other bad things. 'You are the reason this has happened. You are not worthy to be Human. Even the dirt has more worth than you.'

"Dog felt great sorrow for them, and spent many days in search of the campfire that once held many four-leggeds, winged ones, and ones who crawled on the ground. He howled his sorrow, but none appeared, not even Spider. None. Dog howled his woeful mourn once more, turned and went back to watch over the Humans.

"When he made it back to the camp, he saw Humans wandering without purpose, without reason, their eyes blank and empty. No one helped anyone.

Even parents paid no heed to their children. Dog knew what had happened. He howled in camp and was able to utter the word: '*Split-apart.*'

"One elder, whose hair held much stardust, remembered the word. He stopped his pacing and turned to face Dog. He knelt down and hugged the four-legged before he stood and spoke. 'My people, hear me,' he shouted. 'I, once part of the Great Circle of All Living, have this to say.' He raised his arms wide. 'We have lost our way, and in doing so, we have lost ourselves. It is time to reconnect with the rest of all living. We must sing, dance, and seek guidance. We need to call to the Spirits, to the Animal People, who we abandoned at the Circle of Fire. We must ask that we be put back together, both body and mind.'

"'This pulling apart of the body and mind is a sickness, and has made us forget who we are. We have forgotten our purpose in life, our reason for being. A dis-ease has formed, and we all suffer greatly for it.'"

"'But how do we find our way back?' asked a woman with hollow, empty eyes.

"The elder turned to her and said, 'Ask for dreams this night. Ask for help to understand, to find our way back.'

"Each person had a dream. In their dreams, they were all told the same thing the elder man had told them. After leaving the Circle of Fire, they lost a great connection to all living. No longer connected, their minds had no guidance, and their bodies were dying.

"Everyone gathered in a circle, held hands and sang a song many thought they had forgotten."

'WE ARE CHILDREN OF THE CIRCLE OF LIFE,
OF ALL LIVING... WE BELONG. WE ARE CONNECTED.
WE ARE CONNECTED, AND EVERY LIVING BEING IS CONNECTED TO US.
OUR MINDS AND BODIES ARE ONE WITH EACH OTHER AND THE CIRCLE OF LIFE.
HEAR US, GREAT MYSTERY, AND ANIMAL SPIRITS. HEAR OUR PLEA AND BRING US BACK TO THE CIRCLE OF LIFE.
THE CIRCLE OF LIFE... THE SPIRAL OF LIFE....
HELP US REMAKE THE SPIRAL OF LIFE, THE BEGINNING OF ALL THERE IS — WILL EVER BE — THE SPIRAL OF LIFE.'

"The people wept, danced, and sang until no one could stand anymore. They each took turns going on Vision Quests, offering themselves as sacrifices, danced, fasted, and sang until each found their way into the land of visions.

"They were happy for Dog, and through his message, he saved many Human lives. To this day, Dog is welcome and guides us still... if we listen. My story is finished."

He stared directly into Sparkling Star's eyes, at her tears, but she did not look away this time.

"How... how do I save my baby?" Her voice shook with grief.

He spoke in the same soft words as before. "All I can do is offer advice. You must decide if you are willing to do it." He stood, made his way over to her, knelt down and, without shame, wrapped her in his arms and rocked her. "Only you can heal yourself. You have been told for far too long you are not worthy, that you did not belong to yourself, but to others. Your mind believed this terrible wrong.

"Your Soul hovers above you, waiting to rejoin. There is no whole self until the Soul returns. Sparkling Star, be the woman you really are. You have worth. You are beautiful in the eyes of Creator, and in our eyes, too. Your baby will not live without you. You must tell your baby that it does not matter if a boy or girl comes from your belly. All are Sacred and have value, worth—all belong."

He squeezed her tighter as great sobs came from the slight woman. "Say it. Say you have worth, are needed, and have purpose."

She spoke through gasps for air, her mouth quivering. "I... I... have worth. I have worth." She clenched her fists. "I have a purpose in life." She rubbed her belly and moved Shining Light's arms away. With one hand on her belly, she looked down and spoke. "You, my son or daughter, are dearly loved and wanted. I want you... love you... *need* you to make me feel whole again."

Speaks and Gentle Wisdom came to her side.

Speaks turned to Shining Light and smiled through her tears. "We will care for her now, man of mine."

He nodded and left the group. White Paws stayed next to Sparkling Star.

White Paws is needed here. I need to go clear my mind.

***

Hawk Soaring watched his grandson until he was no long visible. "His grandmother and I are very proud of who he has become." He turned his attention to Flying Raven as he added more sticks to the fire, and nodded toward Sparkling Star. "Our newest member has found peaceful sleep next to Gentle Wisdom. I do worry that we may not be able to travel fast enough with her. She is weak, and too much more bouncing around on her old mustang will not be good for her. Perhaps I should turn back and take her home with me."

He watched her belly rise and fall, the only movement she made. "Raven, did you hear me?"

Flying Raven stared into the spitting sparks as the fire danced, following the sparks up as they rose into the sky. Hawk Soaring could see his mind was elsewhere. He touched his arm, and Flying Raven jumped.

"Hawk Soaring, I am sorry. I did hear much of what you said. I know the girl will slow us down, but came to us for a reason only the Spirits know about. As you know, nothing happens without reason. We must listen with our hearts for the answer. Too many times, I have seen people toss something out, only to retrieve it later. Perhaps they do not find it because another saw usefulness in it and took it. So it is with Sparkling Star—we see her worth that another did not. I hope no one comes looking for her."

Hawk Soaring shook his head. "I have much age on you, Holy Man, yet it is you who teaches me... like my grandson did tonight. He added to the story he told, and it all made sense in the end. I will remember how he told it so I can tell his grandmother. That will make her more proud of him, and yes, she will gloat once again and tell me his strong mind comes from her side." He looked again at the woman sleeping next to Gentle Wisdom. "If anyone comes for this woman, we will defend her as we would any other band member."

Both men settled into their sleeping robes for the night. "I am honored, Hawk Soaring, to be part of your family."

The elder watched Flying Raven still himself and allow his mind to become part of the campfires in the sky.

***

"Speaks, we have little food, and now we have another to feed." Shining Light reached for her hand.

She pulled away, twisting her hair and tying it into knots. "We packed much meat so I would not have to do this until much later. You do not fully understand what this does to me—why I eat more plants than meat, or why I ask you to bless the hides as I scrape them. I know each animal is prayed over, and we ask Creator to take them to their families, but to me it is not enough. Even the scrapings to me feel Sacred. I always give the wolves every tiny piece so it will not go to waste. When I call the animals, I feel everything they do. I become them. I hear myself calling them to sacrifice themselves."

Her hands shook when she let her hair go. "I become their ears, hearing my own call. I see through their eyes as they glance about their herd. Young ones nod to the older ones as if they are asking them if they will go. The old ones paw the ground, snort, and shake their heads in resignation. Old females go up to the ones they last brought into their herd, they say their own parting words through nuzzling them, and turn to walk away. Males, who know the next cold season might take them, also follow."

Her eyes became distant and she made no move. "I am them coming to us. I feel each hesitating step they take, and know just before they show themselves." She looked deep into her man's eyes. "They pray as we do, did you know this? They tell their relatives to expect them soon, and then they come close enough and turn so your arrows will drop them quickly. They do not want to feel pain any more than we do, but the pain is there. I feel it. I am with them as each one of their Spirits try to cling to their body, one last attempt to stay connected. Then their Spirits let go."

She grabbed his arms and squeezed them, and her eyes brightened. "Eagle Woman comes for them! At first, she is all Eagle, but as she extends her claw, her claw becomes a hand. Her face becomes Human, with long white-yellow hair. For each animal, she becomes them, be they Deer, Elk, Humpback, Rabbit, Bird, even Snake, and all reach for her. She takes their hoof, paw, claw, or Snake's head, and pulls them up."

She paused and looked up. "Light, man of mine, I have followed their Spirits up into the campfires. I see something, maybe a rope that holds them to the Mother. It snaps and drops, and I have never been allowed to follow beyond. Always Eagle Woman comes to me and tells me to go back. Before I can speak to her, she says my time is not yet come. If I followed, I would not be able to return."

She lowered her head and whispered, "I will call the animals, but know, as always, I walk away and will not return until it is over." She raised her hands and whispered her song.

"You are not meant to hear my song. No one is." She lowered her hands. "Go get your bow. They will soon come, and I now leave and take Dove."

She gathered a robe and left. Sullenness followed her walk.

Chapter 18

Two moons passed without incident. Falling Rainbow had stopped many times to add paintings on the hide Wanderer had given her. Father Sun's warmth gave beauty to flowers, shrubs and trees. Birds darted through the leaves that Sister Wind's gentle song moved, going to and from nests filled with hungry, peeping babies. The turquoise sky changed to a cornflower-blue, and alabaster clouds floated by in shapes she had never paid attention to until now. She put a hand over her eyes to watch three Eagles as they disappeared and reappeared, floating on warm air currents.

Falling Rainbow marveled at the amazing scenery.

Snow no longer dominated the land. The familiar red ground changed into a mix of browns, and the river had become wider, no longer held captive by the canyon walls. Different kinds of grasses blended into the brilliant burst of flowers, showing off oranges, yellows and purples. Shrubs' dark green leaves showed white tube flowers, over which buzzing winged ones danced in search of the rich nectar. Life awakened everywhere.

She tried to focus on what plants would make good paints, but noise from Wanderer, who followed behind, made her twist around on Fire Dancer. His fidgeting on his mustang and twisting around to stare behind them distracted her, and caused her to fidget too. His neck was as busy as the birds flying past. His mice jumped from their hiding places to the ground, chasing each other.

At first, she thought he was watching the mice. He had told her a few days ago that soon they would go their own way; that it was in their minds to search out new places and food.

"Why do you keep looking everywhere? This whole day you have been restless."

He stopped Fast Shadow. His brows connected together and his eyes squinted. "All this time, we have had no trouble. I started to feel safe and was wrong to do so. I can feel something is not right—feel it deep from within. I sense eyes are watching us—human eyes. Wolf said Night Hunter would not come this way, but that does not mean he might not have come from a different way. I do not so much feel danger as I just sense being followed. I do not like it, not knowing for sure."

Cold fingers walked up her spine. She twisted back to stare at the sloping ground on the other side of them, and slowed her mustang to be even with Fast Shadow. "You have me scared. Why do we not move away from the waters and go farther out onto the grasslands?"

"We only have three water bladders, and I am not sure how long they will last. We also have our mustangs to worry about." He spoke to his mustang. "Fast Shadow, we need to move into the shelter of those trees."

He pointed and tapped the mustang's sides a little too hard. The sharp turn made his pack mustang slide sideways, and the biggest pack broke loose and fell. Fire Dancer panicked and reared, throwing Falling Rainbow to the ground still grasping her mustang's ropes.

Before she could get up, an arrow whizzed past. She gasped as Wanderer cried out.

Wanderer's eyes squeezed tight as he gripped his bloody shoulder.

Falling Rainbow pulled him to the ground and dragged him behind a boulder that barely hid them both. He clenched his teeth and gasped, as she broke the shaft of the arrow and tossed the arrowhead to one side, then broke the end of the shaft that held the feathers, and pushed the stick through the back of his shoulder. He fell unconscious.

***

The smell of meat roasting roused Wanderer, and he tried to sit up, his eyes still closed.

"No, do not do it by yourself. Let us help you."

He squeaked out raspy words. "Us? Who *is* us?" He opened his eyes, but his vision was too blurry to focus.

"Umm, well... It is Night Hunter." Falling Rainbow leaned over to brush hair from his face.

His eyes shot open. "Night Hunter! Are we now captive?" Again, he tried to sit up.

This time, she pulled a pack to brace him upright. Blood covered his tunic.

"I will need to take your tunic and wash it. I have fresh broth for you to drink, and healing plants also." She reached for the clay bowl with the broth. "Your wound is stitched closed, and moss packed in mud now draws the bad Spirits out. You must not move much, or the fine stitching Night Hunter did will pull out. He helped me to gather the fresh medicine plants that I might not have found on my own. He remembered passing them at sunrise. Drink the plant medicine first."

She held it up to his protesting lips.

"How has this come to be that the man we run from now tends the wound he caused?" He reached for the knife hidden in his knee-high footwear.

A mouse sat close to his ear and he nodded. "I did not mean to sound ungrateful, but what has changed? Why are you here, Man Who Seeks To Steal Power?" He glared deep into Night Hunter's eyes.

Night Hunter dropped his gaze and squatted next to the elder. "Some people say you are crazy, that you live with mice. I see mice and a look in your eyes that has me thinking they are right. Since Falling Rainbow is with you still, perhaps she too is now crazy."

"Yes, we are all crazy. Answer my question, pup. Why are you here? Where is your brother?"

Night Hunter's lips curled. "My brother now has two women and no desire to do anything but be lazy. Being lazy does not gain favor from the Spirits. Soon he will be fat and no longer fast on his feet. His mustang will groan from his weight."

"Why are *you* here? To shoot an old man?" Wanderer's voice rose and his face turned hot, but soon he grew cold as he tried to sit up further.

Night Hunter avoided staring Wanderer's way. "I have had much time to think. When we did not find you, Falling Rainbow, we turned back to the camp." He turned to face her. "I talked long with your parents. I also went on a Vision Quest, fasted for four sunrises, and on the fifth, had a vision—one that has changed me to my very Soul. I promised your father I would watch over you and help you on your journey, which I now know was meant to be."

He reached out, turned the meat, and continued to look at her. "You have much beauty and are very good to look at. You... the Power you have over me is for another reason I have yet to understand. I thought you had to have Power, as your father, the Holy Man. Greed... it made me blind. I learned to see again in my Vision Quest. I did not know greed could wrap itself so tight around one's Soul, drag them into darkness and make their heart turn black. I gave away all my possessions before I left your father, so I had nothing to make me greedy. He gave me the flawless, nearly white mustang and her matching young one, who will one day be a strong male. I call him Flying Cloud.

"I felt honored and shamed both to take such a wonderful gift. When I told him I had nothing in turn to offer him, he said that I did, and he wanted to be sure I gave him that gift—to protect you."

"You do understand I—" She looked away.

"I know you have no desire for me. I follow you to my own destiny. The Spirits told me you would lead me there." He smiled at her wide eyes. "We are friends, yes?"

"Yes, but no more."

"Stop, you two!" Wanderer glared at them both. "I still want to know why this arrow of yours found my shoulder. I am in pain and you two make silly eyes at each other."

Falling Rainbow said, "Night Hunter was aiming at an injured deer. He thought to have a good meal for days, and also to end the deer's pain, like what you told me about mice when they were injured and sought release."

"Night Hunter has no mouth of his own with which to speak? I am old and may not live long enough to learn why I looked like a deer!"

"Elder, Grandfather of the people." Night Hunter raised his hands, palms outward. "I am sorry my aim was not so good. I did get the deer we are about to enjoy." He smiled at Wanderer, but jumped up and moved away when he saw the movement of the elder's knife.

"Come back, boy, I only want to open your shirt for you!"

Falling Rainbow burst out in laughter. "Wanderer, you will live, and... well, he *is* a better hunter than you. I am tired of so much rabbit and birds not smart enough to run away, and I welcome a change to eat... um.... I did not mean it that way! Please do not look at me with that face. I have never seen so many wrinkles squish together on one face like that! I have grown to love you and... and...."

She turned to catch up with Night Hunter.

Wanderer glanced their way, grinned, and reached for the roasted meat.

Chapter 19

"What would you have us do? Leave while you go off?" Animal Speaks Woman waved her free arm in the air, with Dove cradled in the other inside her sling. "Leave you and go forward, you say. You will be safe, you claim." She shifted Turtle Dove from one hip to the other, and waved her arm toward the camped people who listened but looked away. "You leave the safety of others behind!"

"Speaks, understand me! I am a Dreamer, and when dreams call me, I need to be alone." Shining Light sighed and hugged his woman and daughter close. "Watch over Sparkling Star. Move forward. Go toward where Father Sun rises and find the river. My father already knows where to go. I need not to worry that you women are not protected."

She pushed him away. "We *women* know how to use a bow! You forget, man of mine, I was running with my band from the hairy-faces before we met. Even as a girl, I carried a bow when we hunted, and were hunted." Her face reddened as her voice rose. "My young life was filled with fear. Must I feel it again?"

There was no convincing her. He reached out and pulled them both to him again. "You knew long ago that this was to be my life. I must do this, sweet one. White Paws, Moon Face and the new pups will stay with me, and the rest of the pack will move on with all of you."

He stepped back and twirled the sky beads draped across her neck between his hands. He let them drop and shouldered his pack, turned, and started to move away.

She took a few steps with him, then stopped and let him go on alone. "My heart follows you. Bring it back to me."

He turned back and saw tears stream down and catch the corners of her quivering mouth. "Speaks... if I take your heart, I will leave mine here with you."

Too many nights had passed since he held her against his bare body, felt her caresses, and now it had become unbearable. *Spirits, forgive me if I do wrong. I know I go against what I have been taught.* He turned and took her hand.

She smiled, and together they made their way toward the stream behind the hill.

Speaks sighed softly. "I heard a whisper as White Paws looked up at me — or was it only in my mind? He said your love and mine binds us together at the Soul, that our connection will never be broken. It goes beyond this life. Who knows what great knowledge animals might pass on to us?"

She knelt beside the wise wolf that followed them. "You truly are wiser than we humans. We ask questions without first looking within for what we already know."

Shining Light knelt next to her. "If our daughter is as smart as you, she will travel far in this life. Her path will not be as rocky as some." He took his daughter gently from her sling and laid her in the soft grass. He then drew his woman to him. "I long to feel your body under the robes. I weaken at your touch, your...."

He held her close and breathed deep her scent. Father Sun warmed them as they lay next to a sleeping Dove. His woman's fingers explored his face, and he responded with his own. They caressed each other's bodies, exploring as they had their first night together. Intertwined tightly together, they shut out the rest of their surroundings.

***

Shining Light sat staring through a dream haze into the familiar small cave. The ancient bear skull sat undisturbed after all this time. He turned around, expecting to see Speaks, but she was not there. White Paws stepped from behind and pushed with his muzzle. *'Go forward, Brother.'*

He glanced around. *Only me and White Paws.* The other wolves, and even Sandstone, were gone. *How is it that they know? Only White Paws ever dares follow.*

Sister Wind teased his hair with chilled fingers, sending shivers throughout his body. He swung his pack off and took out his robe to chase away the chill.

As he prepared to unpack his belongings, Sister Wind's breath spoke in his ear. *'No, not here. Go around to the other side of the hill.'*

He picked up his pack and followed a tiny trail that began at the mouth of the cave and zigzagged around the steep hillside. "So small, looks as if Mouse made this trail." He stood on his toes to avoid several mice that darted back and forth. "Ha! Mice did make this trail, but why am I following it?"

As he rounded the side of the hill, his hair crackled and rose above his head. The mice vanished, and a cold settled into his bones. He stopped, unsure of what to do. His Wolf Brother leaned into his back, urging him to keep going. Sister Wind sang in his ears, and above him Eagle called. He looked up, but saw only Father Sun ducking behind the clouds, then slipping back out into the empty sky. A voice sounding like the Great Elder, Blue Night Sky, floated in the air. He followed her voice.

A small mound of stones sat piled in the middle of a flat area a few steps before him. From around the stacked stones, lines of other stones spread outward, forming rays around the pile. The tips of the rays connected to a Circle surrounding the deposit of stones. A few of the stone rays shot past the Circle as if they were meant to go on forever. In each of the four directions, a small Circle interrupted the line of the large Circle. Each of the small Circles enclosed just enough space for a person to sit.

The Circle's Energy felt as if Father Sun heated it. Slowly, he paced around the edge. Down the slope that ended in a pile of stone sat several white mice-like creatures staring back up at him. He blinked several times, and the creatures turned into one small, white bear. He squeezed his eyes tight and opened them again... and saw nothing. He shook his head and moved on.

Born at sunrise, Shining Light felt himself drawn to the small Circle that would be greeted by Father Sun first. He stepped into the Circle and sat. White Paws sat outside the Circle, his tail swishing back and forth. Each swipe pushed away pebbles and exposed tiny plants with deep purple flowers.

"Will you stay, old friend? I do not understand this strange circle of stones, and do not want to offend any Spirits. I am sure I heard Blue Night Sky, but my mind maybe teases."

He undid his pack and took out his oval shell, which contained Sacred herbs and the pipe passed onto him by his grandfather the day of his Vision Quest. He lit the Sage, and stood to pray and sing as he offered the lit pipe to the four directions, and to above and below.

***

The night air chilled Shining Light. He called to White Paws, and the wolf snuggled next to him. He covered them both with his robe.

How long have we been here? I thirst.

He uncurled from his robe and reached for his water bladder. He drank the cool water, and poured some in his hand for White Paws, but the wolf sat up and stared into the darkness.

Why does a circle of stones float above me? Colors, so many colors... and it is dark! They dip and twist like birds playing in the breeze. They must be clouds the way they float. How could stones do this?

He patted the ground and felt the sinews of someone's hand, and jumped. "Who is here with me?"

'I am here, boy.'

"Blue Night Sky? Why can I not see you?"

'I am here, in front of you. I sit on a stone next to White Bear. She is pleased with the story you told the one soon to give birth.' The Spirit of the Great Elder wavered in front of him.

Intense, metallic indigo surrounded Blue Night Sky, and blue sparkled at the ends of her hair that floated around her. Her voice vibrated. *'Soon you will meet a man who is not only a Holy Man, but much more. Some say he is crazy. He is not so crazy. He sees the futures of others, and lives between this land and the Spirits' Land. What he tells you, you must not tell another, not even your woman. I know this Elder well, better than others ever have or will. He also leads a Peoples to the Land of Tall Trees. Age has less to do with the body than the mind. Remember this well, young one.'*

Before him, within the blue glow, White Bear and her cub appeared. He reached out for his wolf, but he was not there. "White Paws!" He twisted his head, searching. "Do not leave me... please."

'Look here, boy, I pet your wolf. Have you forgotten your way inside the Circle? Look around you. The center is the womb of all living. As a Spiral, life is born, grows, becomes, and continues outward, ever outward.'

He looked to where she nodded. Beyond the second stone that stood between Bear and Blue Night Sky, a new vision appeared.

Children played as Father Sun shone golden rays upon them. Rich emerald grass grew above their knees, and dogs of many colors—whites, browns, reds, and yellows—jumped to grab leather balls. People of many colors—red, white, pale yellow, brown, and black—stood talking to each other. Lodges in a center circle had wooden squares made of logs behind them. He jumped when the front of one of the wooden boxes opened and a woman came out carrying much food.

'This could be the future... or not. One day, Peoples will have a chance to join one another and be as one. Greed, the inability to forgive, and selfishness can destroy the Spiral, so the Circle of Life will die.'

He pulled away from the vision before him. "Where do so many Peoples live now? And the wood lodges they live in, did Tree give them permission to take so much? They look happy together. Their children all run and play together. How can this be so, that greed lives among them? They have everything they could ever want! One supports another, and so it continues on and on. What could ever change such a wondrous place of great joy? This I do not understand. This place is as one big giveaway where everyone benefits from one another, shares everything they have. And I see great respect, even in the children's eyes."

He turned to a silent Blue Night Sky. "I have missed you, Great Elder... and your wisdom. I carry you in my heart always. You helped me face my fears, and speak about the dangers in front of adults who were not so sure a boy knew of what he spoke. I hope my daughter carries your gifts, and then I will see you every day of my life."

'That wisdom is within you. You are in my heart, boy. Feel me as I feel you. Listen well. As seasons move forward, as people are born, life continues, but much will be forgotten.

'Each person born must hear the stories of our Peoples. Many will not listen, but some will. Those who listen will make a difference. Those who do not listen will have hearts as black as a moonless night, and as frozen as the coldest of cold seasons.

'It starts with one person passing on this story. You must be one of the people who will pass on what you learn here, what you have been taught since before you were born, when your parents sang to you. Find a way every day of your life to pass on this knowledge. The future depends on it. If you and others do not do this, the only thing ahead is a great darkness for not only our people, but the ones I have showed you. All will suffer. As the story you told about the split-apart... it will become very real, and most will not have anyone to tell the story you told. Tell it to everyone you meet, and around campfires, even if you must teach it in sign words.

'Another people of fair skin come this way, and will take away all they can by means you cannot yet understand. Until this time of great greed passes, if it does, our

people must remember who they are, and never forget, if they are to break out of this darkness. They will have to bring their children away from anger that they will feel, and show them the old ways. If not, all will be lost and the Peoples will be no more. Never forget the songs, the dances, the very reason we exist – to make life better for the next to be born. Be they Human or Animal, all beings will pay for the greed of a few.'

"I will pass on this knowledge, Great One, but I am only one man."

'This place is a Sacred place no one has seen for many, many generations. When it was built, the Peoples joined here in hopes of returning every early season to watch the land turn green, to renew their hearts, and to keep the memories alive. Somewhere the Peoples forgot, so those children could not tell their children about a place they had never seen.

'Teach each child wherever you may find yourself. Sing songs and create a new dance to remember this early season of Nature's birth. Scatter seeds of knowledge you will now save for when the warm season goes to sleep.... Never forget, Light Who Shines So Bright.'

"I hear chanting and see the Ancients swaying. I have not seen them since we left the canyons."

'They are wherever you are. They are your ancestors.'

White Bear stood on her hind legs, towering over Shining Light. Her voice rumbled for attention. *'I, White Bear, say this, young Human Cub. The story you will tell is one that needs repeating for many, many seasons to come. My kind stay hidden within the Land of Tall Trees, knowing the hand of the future can be a harsh one. It depends on whether Humans listen to your words and pass them on. As I taught you, forgiveness instead of anger, teaching instead of walking away, guidance instead of silence – these will be the way. The only way. Your Four-Legged relatives will watch from their lands. What comes to pass between our Peoples will depend on you Two-Leggeds. Remember my words. If your kind will heed these words, then perhaps our kind and yours will one day speak again.'* White Bear and her cub faded into the indigo mist.

Shining Light heard a small noise, as if a tiny creature had cleared his throat.

Mouse sat on the Great Elder's knee. *'I only need to remind you to look at what appears to be too simple. If it seems that way, then beware and rethink your decisions. See with your mind. I have said my words.'*

White Paws stretched, yawned and faced his Human Brother. *'These visions are to show you how you can help the Peoples of now and beyond. I hope that the teachings will be passed on for many generations. The Circle would suffer, and so would the Peoples and Animals yet to be born. If these words are not heeded, one day the Circle will shatter, the Spiral will come undone, and life will become unbalanced.'*

Shining Light again marveled as colors swirled above him and slowly faded. On the ground, the Circle of stones, each lightly glowing, also faded. The last thing he saw were the Ancients chanting as they danced around the Circle. They started to fade....

He woke with his arms curled around his Woman. "Speaks, my sweet one." He sat up and looked around. Father Sun hid behind grey clouds and a mist hung low. *How long have we been here?* "Speaks, wake up."

She sat up, looked into her baby's calm eyes, and touched the beginning of rain on her daughter's face. "How... how long did we sleep?"

"I have no idea, but I had a dream vision while wrapped in your arms. You must have magic I do not know about." He reached to pull her closer.

The loud crack and jagged yellow streaks across the sky startled them. Dove cried out, and Speaks scooped her up, wrapping her daughter inside her own dress. "We must hurry back. Soon darkness will take the land."

Water broke open from a darkening sky. Shining Light grabbed onto his woman as their feet slipped and slid on wet grass.

"Shining Light!" Animal Speaks Woman yelled. "I fear I may lose my footing. Get in front of me and take Dove, please!"

As he reached for his daughter, a whinny caught his attention. Thunder galloped toward them, slid to a stop, and pressed her muzzle into his side. "Hand me the baby and jump on Thunder. She somehow knew to come to us."

Speaks jumped on the mustang's wet back and held onto her neck hair. "It would be safer for the baby if you carried her back."

Shining Light could only nod, grab Thunder's tail and hold on. The mustang kept her pace slow.

Just ahead, White Paws howled and human voices responded.

"Father, we are here! Follow White Paws!"

Another sharp slice of jagged yellow dashed across the sky and split into crooked fingers. Shining Light's father waved a fire torch ahead, and the mustang, without prodding, headed his way, to the place where they had erected a small lodge earlier in the day.

Shining Light handed Dove to his father and helped Speaks down. Thunder trotted off toward the other mustangs.

He crouched and entered the crowded lodge to escape the rain, and settled in next to Speaks.

Sparkling Star had her head in Gentle Wisdom's lap, and both women spoke softly. Sparkling Star's expression showed worry.

Chest heaving, he tried to slow his words. "I see that while this lazy man and his woman slept, others readied a nice lodge and a warm fire. Even a pit has been dug around the lodge to guide the waters away. I am glad to see others with sense that I did not have."

After he gave everyone praise, he added wood to the fire. "A dream took me to a strange place I wish to tell you all about."

Some things he would not speak of, but much of it he would. He asked for permission to sit next to Sparkling Star, and took Dove with him.

"Your child and ours will be the first ones to hear of the message the Spirits told me needed to be passed on. If someday you move on, you must remember this story. Tell your child the story many, many times, until he can tell it to you." He turned to stare at everyone, one at a time. "This is our responsibility—to pass on this story to every person we meet. We are the beginning of something very old. We will bring it back to life."

He was about to ask where White Paws was, when several wolves raced in and gave everyone a good splashing with their shaking. Instead of shouting in anger, everyone covered themselves with robes and laughed.

Once they all settled back in, he spoke of the story. Energy filled the lodge. Everyone remained silent, but grasped the hand nearest to them, something most never did.

***

Father Sun greeted Shining Light as he slipped out thinking he was first to awaken. He raised his hands in greeting the day, and thanked Creator for being alive and having a good family. He sang his song of thanks.

The smiling face of Sparkling Star greeted him. Thunder moaned under her massaging hands as she moved from the mustang's neck and shoulder down under her legs. "She is a sweet mustang. She leaned my way when I worked on her rump and back. I had to push her up and off me, and she understood I could not bear her weight, and stood straight. By working my fingers into her body, I too felt calm and relaxed, in spite of some belly pain. She even turned sideways and rubbed my head with her face! As in your story about the Animal People, they still find a way to help us."

She rubbed the mustang with the edges of her hands, digging into Thunder's muscled thighs. The mustang shifted so she could reach a different spot. "I have never had such pleasure go through me as I do now."

"Yes, they do find ways to help us. Some do not see it as well as you. Many may not understand it, but our lives would be much harder without their guidance." He lifted his face to Father Sun's warmth and inhaled. "The land smells good this day, and nowhere are there grey clouds to worry us."

He dropped his gaze back to the mustang, who remained calm and steady. "She has never taken to another before as she does you. Always Thunder has moved away from humans." He nodded his head toward Sandstone and her nursing young one. "Sandstone is her mother and has had two babies since Thunder, yet she has tried to push her mother's new babies away... until now. You calm her and she calms you. No more do I see you cower when a man approaches you. I would say you are good for each other. You and Thunder belong together. I do not think the old one you rode in on will mind."

She put her head down. "He lies not far from here. I think he left with the rising of Father Sun. He took me many, many sunrises away from the hairy-faces, and the warrior who kept me as he did his dogs. I will not forget that mustang and his gentleness. I wish I had given him a name."

"Creator will not care that he has no name. He will lead him to his herd no matter what."

Her face clenched into a pinched expression. "Shining Light, I must slow you and your people down one more day. I am afraid, and do not understand birthing pains. I have never had a baby before, and never have I seen one born. This day I ask for your women's help."

Chapter 20

Falling Rainbow waded in the shallow part of the stream and dug her toes into the soft sand, carrying her knee-high footwear in one hand. The cool water felt good as it swirled around her ankles and calves. Father Sun had blessed the land with warmth, and the fragrance of newly bloomed flowers filled her nose.

"I do not remember so many colors all bursting forth in the canyons. I have seven hides painted with my memories that I one day soon wish to share. You need to see them. Painting is my Power, Night Hunter." She made sure he understood her words. "I have no other Power. I have also learned no one can take another's gifts away and make them their own."

"You no longer need to follow that... that strange man. I will not bother you anymore, and I am sure your parents would sing their joy to have you back." He walked on the bank, his hands behind him.

She stopped and turned his way. For the first time, she really saw him. Muscles rippled as far down as she dared look. He wore only a breechclout. His long, obsidian hair shone blue in the bright sun. It hung loose and danced down his strong back, with the tips of it playing at his waist. Eyes so bright, alive. A light breeze tickled his rounded jaw with a few loose strands. His long straight nose, his lips....

She jerked her eyes away and forced herself to look forward and continue wading. "I know they would like me to return home, but I must go on. This Land of Trees that I have always heard as a child's story, it is real. I must be able to prove it to my people." She lifted her dark, tanned dress as the water became deeper. "Maybe at first you were the reason I fled, but now I see you were but the hand of the Spirits. You forced me to find my courage to go forward. When Wanderer first came into my life, I was not sure how to act, what to do. I thought he was crazy, had left his mind somewhere. I know better now. He too has guided me."

She continued wading but stole looks his way. "He is deep within the Circle's Spiral and lives both inside and outside of it, all at once."

Night Hunter turned to her. "Maybe you are now crazy. I do not understand how a person can be two places at once." He nodded back Wanderer's way. "He heals fast, very fast for an old... err... elder. My Vision Quest told me to follow the Mouse Man—whom you followed. I thought maybe I had fasted for too long." He shrugged his shoulders. "Who am I to question the Spirits? I tried to get my brother to come, but he was busy exploring his new — " His face reddened.

"He was not meant to follow your path, but his own. We cannot guide someone where they are not meant to go. Perhaps your brother will find his own meaning to life that no one, not even you, can show him. We all walk the same path, but many trails lead to this path. Trails lead us, not others."

She climbed out of the stream and sat on the bank to allow her feet to dry, tossing her footwear to one side. She ran her hands over the soft grass and tiny purple flowers that the first days of warmth brought, and above her Eagles swayed and called to each other. Fox slipped by partly hidden in the new growth of shrubs on the other side of the waters. She stiffened.

Night Hunter's words drew her mind his way. "How is it a new woman can know so much?"

"I was not a new woman when my parents made the ceremony for me." Her face grew warmer as she fought to keep her head up, facing him. "You used some trick to call to me. I fell for it. For a brief span I thought you cared for me!" She snapped and turned away from him. "How could you, a man of the People, do such a thing? Were you not taught... your father... never mind! He must have had a hard heart."

He knelt by her side. "I am so sorry for what I did. My heart was not right. My mind was dark from thoughts my father put there, that I had allowed him to put there. He hungered for Power. Perhaps he thought that if I had Power, he too would have it. I will not go back to tell him he was wrong. I will never go back."

He started to reach out to her, but she pulled back. "I am sorry for the fear and grief I caused you. I want nothing from you but to allow me to follow you and, and that cra... Elder who walks in both worlds." His face softened. "I will not harm you. Ever."

"Night Hunter.... I call you by your old name. How are you called now?"

"My name did not change. None of that matters right now." He sat next to her and cleared his throat. "I must tell you something. It has been nearly five sunrises, and the Elder has healed enough to ride. We must move on."

She caught the stern stare and the feel of fear that shot from his eyes. She put her hands up to her mouth. "The hairy-faces follow you."

"Yes. They think I know where the yellow stone is. I told them that I did when I wanted you—your Power." His hand shook as he reached out and touched her shoulder, and he quickly put it down. "I am so sorry for my wrong thoughts, for believing I could take away another's Power. I have learned every person is special, that each of us has our own medicine, and everyone's Power is needed to keep the Spiral growing so others may learn from it. My Vision Quest told me no one has the right to another's medicine. I learned much. My mother's Spirit spoke to me. She gave her life so I could live. I was only two sunrises old when I lost her. Until my Vision Quest, I never knew anything about her. My father gave me to another woman to raise, and took her as his woman. My brother is not of my blood. I am of my mother's blood. She told me to follow you. In my vision, she also told me—"

"You speak of your Vision Quest to me. This is personal and shared with only your Holy Man, perhaps your mate... or the Peoples as a whole if Spirits tell you to do so. Tell me now why the hairy-faces still think you know of this yellow stone, why you came to us knowing they would follow."

She squeezed her fingernails into his bare arm. "You bring danger to Wanderer, to me. You must go." She reached for her footwear and shoved them on.

He stood before she could. "Falling Rainbow, I came because my Vision told me to. I am not the same man who... who.... Forgive me, please." He hung his head.

She could see his lips quiver. He really did mean it.

My emotions are so mixed up! He is not the bad heart I thought he was. How is it that he can do this to me? Is he to be part of my life? No! I am free to be who I wish to be. "Perhaps, in time, I will learn forgiveness. I ask again, why do they think you know where the yellow stone is... and why, oh why, did you lead them to us? Could you not have followed from afar?"

"Woman, I thought I was. I took another path, yet somehow it led to you."

Wanderer's voice intruded, sounding rushed. "Destiny. Destiny led Night Hunter here. Now we must pack and leave."

Falling Rainbow twirled around and faced Wanderer. "You should not be up. You are—"

"Fine. We have little chance if we do not leave now." He nodded toward Night Hunter. "You will pack my mustang and ready your own as Falling Rainbow packs her things. Once we are ready, you will remain and make our camp look as if only animals have been here. We will ride in the waters for some time, and you will follow before Father Sun rests."

He adjusted his sling. "Woman, I need you to make my wound clean with fresh medicine." He turned, scooted through the grass with his footwear, and made clicking noises as he headed back.

Night Hunter slapped his thighs and chuckled. "What is the crazy man doing? Calling mice?"

"Yes, you foolish man. Do as he says if you wish to follow us. Better yet, perhaps you should go another way."

She hurried to catch up to the Elder. *How did he know we were talking about the hairy-faces?*

***

Wanderer clicked his tongue and tried to clap his hands. "Rainbow, please gently clap your hands to call the mice who are coming with us. I cannot do so."

She did as he asked while Night Hunter ran ahead of them both to the camp. "How did you know we spoke of needing to leave? Are you ready to do so? I need to make sure you do not bleed. I—"

"Hush. Use your wind to hurry, not talk."

"But how *did* you know?"

"Dream. Now go get Fire Dancer ready. We have about three sunrises before they find us."

Mice followed, running behind and beside them, and others already milled around the camp. As they approached the camp, Wanderer chuckled as Night Hunter stomped his feet while packing the mustangs, muttering about mice and crazy people. "Fine young warrior to allow tiny creatures to bother him so."

Night Hunter's voice deepened as he pulled his hair back and tied it with a jerk. "Mice! There really are mice... everywhere! What good are mice? They get into food, chew clothes, and make their nests in footwear as you sleep!"

Wanderer turned to Falling Rainbow. "Since I have but one useful hand —" He glared at Night Hunter. "—I ask for help with gathering them and putting them in their pouches."

"Of course. I know how important they are to you." She went to his pack that leaned against a young sapling, and pulled out his coat with the pouches.

"I made it so the outer part would untie, knowing there would not be so many mice in time. Pull off a layer since only some of my companions will come with us now. Also, it is too warm to wear it. I will need to make it into a bundle that I can tie on Fast Shadow —"

"You *are* crazy! "Night Hunter stomped his feet as two tried to crawl up his boot. "We run for our lives, and you stop everything to gather mice?"

"I have stopped nothing. It is you who stands there instead of packing my mustang."

He whispered in Falling Rainbow's ear. "Heh, only seven Mice still follow me. To him, it must appear as so many more. Some warrior."

A mouse leapt off the pack Night Hunter had put on his own mustang. "I heard you! I do not fear them. That mouse probably ate half my pemmican or chewed a hole in my leggings!"

Wanderer shook his head, motioned for her to follow, and walked away mumbling. "To think he is to be your mate...."

The words stopped her. "My mate? You *are* crazy!"

She flew onto Fire Dancer and kicked her into a run.

Chapter 21

"Stay here, you will be all right. This is only your baby wanting to come out." Shining Light trotted toward camp calling for his woman, leaving Sparkling Star even more scared and unsure.

Fear lanced through her heart. Never before had she felt such pain! She said to the child inside her belly, "It feels like my belly will come apart and you will shoot out! I knew when I felt more than a few kicks I was in trouble. The wide eyes on him makes me wonder why a Holy Man, a Dreamer, would act calm, yet I saw his body tense in worry. Does he know?"

She cradled her belly protectively as the pain she had felt all night intensified.

At sunrise, she woke to a sharp pain, which had forced her to get up and move around. She had left the lodge, and the pain went away for a good span, so she and Thunder walked side-by-side. It was then she had found the old mustang. After saying a prayer over him, she went back to camp. Shining Light woke and found her, and her pain came back as they talked. When she told him she needed help, a warm gush had run from her body and down her legs.

Now, she waddled into the stream to wash away this strange occurrence, leaned over, awkward as a child first learning to stand on her own, and splashed water on her thighs. Blood stained the water.

No one had ever allowed her near the birthing lodge in any of the bands to which she had been traded. No one had spoken to her about babies. No one had allowed her to even hold a baby.

Oh, why did I slip out of the lodge even before Father Sun woke? I should have stayed near Speaks! Now I cannot walk.

She raised her arms to ask for protection from Creator, but quickly dropped them back around her belly. Her cramps came alive, as if a big cat had attacked and ripped through her.

By the time Speaks and Gentle Wisdom found her, she had sunk to her knees, still in the stream, her body quivering. Both women splashed their way to her, helped carry her to the edge of the waters, and sat her down.

"Please do not allow any harm to come to my baby." She grimaced and held her breath.

"No, no... breathe." Gentle Wisdom's lips stretched into a smile.

Sparkling Star noticed how stiff Animal Speaks Woman's body looked, as if she held herself tight against something sorrowful. More frightened than before, Sparkling Star spoke to hold off the worry that poisoned her mind.

"I know I am about eight moons along, so I did not worry about the cramps I have had for several sunrises. The cramps were few and the pain small. I have felt movement. I... I thought everything was fine." She studied Animal Speaks Woman's face, seeking reassurance as she helped her back to camp. "I bleed too much, I know. I saw it in the waters and feel so tired, dizzy."

No one spoke to her. They rushed her inside the lodge.

Sparkling Star stiffened at the sight of the Head Holy Man. "Flying Raven, why are you still here?"

He had already cleared a place over the fire pit and lined it with a robe. "I know women always feel the birth is easier if they squat. I helped my woman bring our daughter from her belly, and we had no time to worry about a pit. I held Makes Baskets up."

Sparkling Star grunted as Speaks sat her down against a rolled-up hide. She looked up into the Holy Man's eyes. "I hope I get to meet your woman. You speak of the pit you dug. This is all new to me. I will need guidance." A sharp pain made her cry out. She slapped her hand across her mouth.

Speaks took her hand and held it tightly. "No matter what you have been told about a baby being born weak if the mother cries out—know there is no shame, no truth to this. Put your hand down. When the time comes, we will give you a piece of leather to bite on to protect your teeth, not to silence you."

Sweat already formed on her face as she glanced up at Speaks and Gentle Wisdom. "I will need the Holy Man. Flying Raven will know what to do."

"A shadow baby? Is this why you ask his help?" Speaks knelt at her side. "My man told me he felt them while he told the story about the split-apart. We will not leave you. They are just babies, not bad omens. No harm will come to the second child, but how did you know?"

"I did not—not until I heard Flying Raven whisper it to Hawk Soaring when they thought I slept, the night that Tall Smiling Warrior brought me here. I worried they would cast me out, so I stayed very still to hear more of their words. Flying Raven only said that he would pray for help. I cried that night, to know I was not going to be treated as a cast off robe. My eyes water much more often than anyone here. It is because of my blood, not all of the people. I am weak. I am sorry."

Speaks held her hand tight. "You are not weak because your eyes water more. Look what you have been through to get to us! Any woman who carried babies in her belly would not have been any stronger, and... and you took beatings, they starved you, used you as a pack animal!" Speaks' tears flowed free. "You are strong! Look, White Paws has come to be with you. You will be fine!" She squeezed her hand again. "We all care about you, sister."

"Sister, you call me sister. I am honored. Other bands, they say only bad things can come from a shadow baby." She lurched forward and clenched her teeth.

Flying Raven wiped the sweat from her face. "We are not other bands. Two such births have happened to women who took hairy-faces as mates, and nothing bad has happened to any of their Peoples."

Gentle Wisdom stared at her, tears now rolling down her cheeks. "And because you are half hairy-face woman does not mean you are not strong. Do you remember our talk last night? Power comes from within, not from who you are or are not." She reached down and hugged her. "For that... that creature who put these babies inside you to call you only half human makes him the bad one, not you. You have all of us women crying because we care."

Shining Light poked his head in. "I cannot help but feel the fear inside. Speaks, allow me room — "

"I will do no such thing! She is terrified and needs women to be with her. You leave, and take our daughter with you... please."

"Speaks, I am a Holy Man. I can be of use."

"I handed you our daughter when I went to help Sparkling Star because I knew your cousin would follow, and there is no other women in camp to care for her. You need to tend to Dove. We have enough hands in here already."

Flying Raven raised his hands. "Silence, you two women. Shining Light, get your bundle and place Sage around the lodge to keep bad Spirits away. While you are out there, tell Tall Smiling Warrior to keep watch with your grandfather for anyone who might come near. I have this feeling we are not alone. And no, Sparkling Star, no one bad approaches. If they did, my son and I both would know. I prayed for help after Father Sun slept. I knew of your pain just as you did, and I think help comes. Wisdom, I know you care for her. Hold her other hand."

Gentle Wisdom held her hand and reached out to hold her.

Through the pain and sweat on her face, Sparkling Star smiled. "Wisdom, I am brave as long as you are here."

She turned and stared at everyone, smiling through her wet eyes. "I never knew anyone could care so much for one person. My old mustang knew what he was doing. Every time I turned him one direction, he would turn again after a few steps, toward your camp. I was so tired, I gave up trying to make him go... go... I had no idea where I was going, just away from danger."

She cried out and squatted over the pit.

Chapter 22

"Stop arguing or I will stop my mustang and bind your hands together and declare you mates right now!" Wanderer smiled to himself as the pair behind him became silent. Without looking back, he continued. "We have a very important matter to take care of... at least I do." He took off his wrap. "It is too warm now, anyway. I ask that you both be aware of the mice. Make sure they are safe for me. They have taught me much.

"Even as a boy, I would sneak food out for them, and one day I had found an injured mouse, with one of his legs curled-up and stiff. He was so thin. I picked him up, kept him in my pocket and fed him. Soon, another joined him. Ha! It was not long before I had so many mice that my mother found them in our food. Once again, I was banished from our lodge. Heh... my dog, my mice and I started to live in a cave near the camp. That is how it started for me, being without other people. An old Healer came to live with me and taught me much. There will be another sunrise for the rest of my story. This is not it."

Two mustangs trotted up beside him, and Falling Rainbow and Night Hunter asked the same question, and not about his story. A stern glare from him stopped the questions. "We are there. Look ahead instead of at me."

Several people scurried about carrying water and robes in and out of a lodge.

He tapped Fast Shadow into a trot. "We must hurry."

Even with his arm in a splint, he jumped off his mustang and sent mice scattering. He ran for the lodge over the rise, leaving his companions to deal with what came their way.

Wanderer shoved past the people and knelt in front of a terrified woman whose face was as deep purple as a canyon sunset. Sweat soaked her face. The thin muscles on her arms tensed as she gripped another woman's hands, but they had begun to lose their grip. Her eyes rolled back in her head and she fell backward against the rolled hide.

"Remove the roll and lay her flat." He eyed the large wolf who sat to the side. "I find it warm in here. Roll up the back for good air. Perhaps we would have more room if the wolf went outside?" He still wondered about the Spirit Wolf and felt uncomfortable. "Just make sure he is not so hungry that my mice fill his belly."

No one had time to wonder at the new arrival. They simply obeyed.

"Falling Rainbow, in here, now!"

"I come." She lifted the flap, and stared after the wolf as he passed only long enough to blink twice, then bent and climbed in. "What can I do?"

"It depends." The Spirits had shown him only parts of this in a Vision. "If the first child is where he belongs, the second who is not will have a better chance. No matter what, I will need your small hands to guide the second one out."

"Second? A shadow child?" She put her hand to her mouth.

"Stop that and wash your hands, then mine." He turned away to keep water off the mother. "That is right. Now that your hands are clean, wash mine." He held his hands over a greased pouch that held a water bladder.

"I am sorry, Sparkling Star—"

The woman leaned up. "How do you know my name?" She cried out before he could answer, and twisted into a ball.

"I must ask you to allow me to touch you where your babies will come out. Will you allow me to do so?"

She nodded rapidly.

"All the men, leave." He waved his hands over his shoulders.

"Gentle Wisdom, your hands are small also. I may need you to help guide the second baby out if Falling Rainbow is busy with the first one. Animal Speaks Woman, go above her and place yourself behind her, with your own legs on either side. She might need help leaning forward for the first child."

He looked at Sparkling Star. "When I say push, you do not stop."

She arched forward, and Speaks leaned into her. "How do you know who we are? Who are you?"

He ignored her. "Good, this is good. The first one is going to come out as he should. This will help his brother because he will leave the passage wider."

Sparkling Star gasped. "Brothers? I will have... boys?"

"Push!"

She sounded like Mountain Lion about to attack an intruder.

"Baby! I see a head." Gentle Wisdom tried to push Wanderer out of the way.

"Girl, get back! It is I that must help this little one. You will ready yourself to take him, instead of Falling Rainbow. The rest of you women who are not giving birth, sing! Sing to the Spirits, sing to Creator, and sing to the new boy who is to become a new band member. Welcome him."

Sparkling Star pushed with all that she had in her.

"Breathe while you push, woman—short, fast breaths. It will help you. He comes, and the right way: face down. That means his arms are at his side. Good, good."

The baby needed no help and soon lay in his arms. He handed him to Gentle Wisdom. "Take out my boot knife and run it across the fire to purify it, then cut his rope where I show you."

An unmoving Gentle Wisdom just stared.

"Now!"

She jerked from her trance and did as she was told.

He helped Gentle Wisdom cut the rope on the first baby. "Also, clean out his mouth and nose, then tap the bottoms of his feet so he will take his first breath. Wash and dry him so he will not get a chill. Now you will know what to do when his brother comes."

The baby cried for a short span. "Awww, he is all wiggles!" Gentle Wisdom moved over to show the new mother, who dripped with sweat.

She nodded and smiled. "Great Holy Man, I thank you for answering my prayers. I prayed for many sunrises for help." Only a short span passed before she yelled and clutched her belly again. "I feel so helpless. A woman should know what to expect. Not even when the other women saw my belly swell did they offer guidance." A tear escaped her eye.

He nodded. "They are lucky to be inside a lodge. My first woman, while we traveled in the cold season, gave me my son on a robe under a pine tree!" He laughed softly at the memory. "Women are amazing. They are the true Power of the band."

He leaned over into her face. "Now, daughter, granddaughter of the People, catch your air and relax. Your second son comes, and he will need help."

He turned to Gentle Wisdom. "Cover that baby. You must have a small furred robe ready... right?"

Silence.

"Right?"

Animal Speaks Woman nodded her head toward a pack. "Wisdom, in my pack is one of Dove's wraps. Take it, sit back and hold him. Sing softly to him and welcome him."

Wanderer nodded. "If I need you, I will let you know. Sing him a good song, one that lets him know he has come into a good place."

He rubbed Sparkling Star's belly, massaging it. "Relax, new mother, the circle that held your child must now come out also. There will be some pain with it, but not like giving birth."

As it came out, another spasm hit, and she bit hard on the leather that Speaks had placed in her mouth so she would not break her teeth.

The lodge filled with song as the second baby tried to come out to greet his older brother. Wanderer felt his bottom and moved to the side. "Rainbow, take my place and do as I say. Place your fingers inside, very slowly now. Do you feel his head?"

She shook her head. "No."

"Sparkling Star, as hard as this is for you to do, relax yourself and breathe as you would while walking slow. Rainbow, watch to see how he works his way out. When you see his legs, reach in and gently bend them so they are out and not in the way. Then we wait to see where his arms are."

She moved his legs as gently as she could.

"His arms look to be straight up. Is this bad?"

"It is not good, but we can make it good and save the baby. Hold onto the sides of his hips and *very, very* slowly, turn him. Good, that is good. Now reach up inside by his arm and gently pull it down. Good. Now you must turn him back, and do what you did, only with the other arm."

"Yes! You did it. Now his head should come out as you put your hand up under his chin--and make sure his head is up a bit. Do not pull. He will come out on his own."

Wanderer sat back and rubbed his shoulder. "Heh, *you* did all the work and *my* shoulder hurts. Now help me get out the circle that baby had around him, and everything will be fine, just a little blood to worry over." He inhaled deeply and let his air go.

He glanced toward Animal Speaks Woman, who talked quietly to the new mother while wiping sweat from her smiling face.

Thank you, Mouse, for your help. My eyes might have missed their camp.

***

Shining Light scratched loudly on the flap. "Hey in there, I hear babies and laughter, but no one comes out. And there are mice out here! Is Sparkling Star okay?" He paused and waited for an answer.

"Also, I am wondering who has joined our little band besides this man out here that will not get off his mustang. He glares at Tall Smiling Warrior as he would a dangerous animal."

Speaks yelled back. "Everything is fine. Two, healthy, baby boys now greet us, and a man called Wanderer, a Great Holy Man, sits with us. There is also a young woman who sits here smiling. She wishes to meet you."

"Why must women tease so! Who is this Great Holy Man? This woman?" He still spoke through the flap. "These mice! The wolves will eat them when they get back."

A gruff voice responded. "I, the Great Holy Man, will have Wolf for my next meal if my mice are harmed!"

A young woman crawled out, hair stuck to her face. She stood and brushed it away, her square chin exposed.

He glanced into her familiar eyes. "How is it that I think I should know you?" He received a hug in response and started to pull away. "My woman—"

"Silly, I am Falling Rainbow, your cousin. I have traveled far to find you. It was your woman who spoke your name to me." Her face widened into a smile and she hugged him again. "I knew I would find you! The trees? The Place of Tall Trees, is it real? I am sure it must be. Why else would I find you... or you have maybe found me? I am so happy, I could burst with joy. I am—"

Wanderer crawled out of the lodge and squeezed his way between the pair. "Girl, I knew you had a fast mouth, but I had no idea that one human had so many words inside her! We need to gather the mice together before... before your wolves return. A Spirit Wolf told me to follow the river, and I saw a boy who looks a bit like you—" He turned as Hawk Soaring came up to him. "—and you, but older. How is it that you look the same, but so much younger? Are you the son of the man I saw? But then the boy—"

"Now who has a fast mouth?" Falling Rainbow glared at him, put her hands on her hips, and tapped her toe on the ground.

Shining Light's eyebrows rose as his mouth flew open. "You talk to the Holy Man as if he is your mate, and without respect? And Great Holy Man, why does a black Dog Spirit follow you?"

"Heh, so you see him. He was my companion when I was a boy. I named him Dark Sky With No Stars. He always answered better to Dog. He still watches over me. Sometimes we share secrets."

He met the blue glow in Shining Light's eyes, and the two stood staring at each other. He nodded. *Power.* He knew this young one in front of him. *The Boy!*

"Will someone tell me why this hairy-face is here?" Night Hunter's mustang pranced in circles, her young one mimicking his mother's movements.

Shining Light reached out to grab the mustang's rope. "All is well here. Come, jump down. You are welcome here, as is the hairy-face man. We are all a bit surprised by so much happening so fast. We must tend to the new mother and her babies."

"And my mice!" Wanderer spoke loudly. "I do not want them to be food for your... your wolves."

"Please, Great Elder, gather your, um, mice. I will go find White Paws and his pack. Everything will be fine once we all sit and speak over a meal."

Falling Rainbow tapped his shoulder. "Wanderer, what dog?"

***

Shining Light headed toward the lodge and scratched the flap. "Speaks, is all well inside?"

"Yes, man of mine, all is well. I will stay here with Gentle Wisdom, who appears to have heard nothing. Her arms are full of babies and her mouth is full of smiles. Sparkling Star is well. Now go, and let the new mother rest."

He turned back and walked toward his father and grandfather, who were doing their best to explain Tall Smiling Warrior to Night Hunter.

"Crazy things happened here this day. I am going to find White Paws, maybe take my time." He jumped on Sandstone and pushed her into a trot. Her young one, now large enough to keep up, raced after his mother.

Chapter 23

After several sunrises, the newcomers and the band flowed together like two small streams enlarging into one another. Everyone, that is, except Night Hunter and Tall Smiling Warrior. They continued to eye each other with wariness.

It did not ease when, every morning, Night Hunter reminded them all that danger from the hairy-faces closed in with every sunrise.

Sparkling Star spoke of her desire to leave, and insisted she was well enough to move on, but Wanderer shook his head in response. She still walked too slow and acted uncomfortable.

***

Falling Rainbow strolled beside Wanderer along the narrow stream below a small mesa, several days after the twins had been welcomed into the band. "How is it you knew the people of this band? Did one of the mice tell you?"

"I told you, mice do not speak to me."

"I saw one on your shoulder before you raced into this camp."

"That one likes to sit there and see where he is going. He remains silent and does not bother me with silly questions."

"My questions are now silly? You have guided me, taught me—" She stopped and looked into bright, laughing eyes. "You tease. Was it the... um, was it Dog who told you?"

"What dog?"

She smacked the top of her head.

"I would be careful. You never know what might come out of your ears that you might need." He picked up a stone, turned it over, righted it again, and then put it back.

"Why did you pick up that stone?"

"The stone had an answer for me." He gazed ahead.

"Had an answer for you? How can a stone speak?" She walked in front of him, her eyes squeezed together in puzzlement.

"Not in words as you and I know. I have gotten answers from trees. Sometimes they tell me about the weather, animals." He shook a finger at her. "Pay attention to animals. They know when things are about to change. You see a clear sky but they see danger. You go to higher ground and wonder why, until you hear roaring water behind you. Squirrels busy putting food away means you better do the same. If birds become silent in the trees, there is a reason, and you had better look around, maybe even hunch. Could be another human coming your way you do not want to see, maybe even a dangerous animal. Always watch animals, even mice. They listen and see in a way we cannot. They do not just run to play with each other. Sometimes they run so another creature will not eat them. Maybe a big animal that would eat you, too."

"Fast mouth! Never before have you spoken so many words so fast! Better be careful. You might use up all your words for this day, and have to wait until Father Sun wakes again to fill your mind back up."

"Silly one." He grinned and went past her. "Come, Dog."

"Smart mouth!" She stopped, her eyes going distant as he continued walking ahead of her. A smile spread across her lips as she trotted after him. "You feel the answers—see them also. All of Nature guides us if we watch, listen, and smell. I finally understand."

"Do you?"

"Yes. One has to listen and feel with their heart. A mouth can speak, but only the heart can hear the answer."

"Ha! Yes, every day you learn more. Not all answers can be heard." He took a deep breath. "Such a nice place, full of smells I never knew. Even the Mother we walk upon has a different smell from the canyons." He turned to her. "Go get your paints, lay out your hide, and paint the smells, Rainbow."

"What? You just told me not everything can be seen by the eyes, or heard by our ears, and now you tell me I can smell and paint what is before me. Show me how this is so."

"Do not stand there looking silly. Sit with your paints, and you will be able to paint what you smell. Think of Sage. Close your eyes and smell it. You will see it better."

She shook her head and cocked it at him. "Rainbow... for several days you have called me Rainbow!"

He chuckled. "You mind changes so fast, you will one day forget what someone has just told you. What else would you have me call you?" He strolled on, not looking her way.

"You know of what I speak. Only family, and the ones you care about, do you call by their heart name."

She twirled around. The light-colored, smoke-tanned dress that Wanderer had given her fell past her knees, but split up the sides for ease of riding. An arc of yellow, orange, red, and green quills shaped a rainbow on the front. Wanderer had painted purple and blue quills, instead of searching for the rare colored quills to complete the rainbow. Elk teeth graced the top of the dress from the neck to her breasts.

"When you gave me this beautiful quilled and beaded dress, I never dreamed...." Her voice stuttered to a halt. "How long it must have taken you. And my footwear! They fit so well, even around my ankles. You must have worked while I slept. I am without words."

"Never will you be without words."

Water threatened to spill from her eyes. She blinked hard. "Only family would give such a gift. When you handed it to me, after the darkness took the land, and walked away... I had no idea. I thought it was a robe to cover myself with until I unrolled it."

He stopped, shuffled his feet and looked down. "I was not blessed with a daughter. You treat me as if I am a normal human, not a *Great Elder* or a crazy man. I chose to live alone after... after I lost my family. As a Holy Man, I am not allowed some of the same emotions as others. I am expected to be there for others, to be there when I am needed no matter how I feel."

He raised his head, and a worn and tired face stared back at her. In his dark eyes, she saw his Soul. "I love you, Wanderer."

She stepped closer to him and threw her arms around his thin neck. She buried her face against his elk hide tunic and cried so hard she shook.

He wrapped his arms around her and cried with her. "I smell Father Sun in your hair. I love you too, daughter of my heart. You have given me life. I guess the Spirits sent me more than a girl to save. They also saved me."

He leaned back. "Now paint me a picture I can smell." He put a flower in her hair behind her ear. "Beauty for beauty."

***

Shining Light sat on the hillside with legs crossed, his hands on either side rubbing White Paws and Moon Face. White Paws yawned and stretched across his Human Brother to shove himself against his mate.

"White Paws, you have such a large family!"

The pups chased their older brothers and sisters in a blur of colors across the top of the bluff.

Twenty-one wolves! He laughed, remembering the huge eyes on Wanderer when Shining Light rode back to camp with more wolves than the Great Elder had ever seen at one time.

"*You are the crazy ones, not me!*" Wanderer waved his hands above his head. "*Why have these wolves not eaten all of you before now? A band who runs with wolves, or are you wolves only pretending to be humans? I understand why I heard that Spirit Wolf in the canyons. He led us to a band of wolf humans so... so. No, that cannot be right. My dreams told me... Sparkling Star... a small band of humans sought us to save us. Or were we to save them?*"

He sucked in both lips and rubbed White Paws. "Much time has passed since I have seen someone outside the forest with the glow of such Power. I cannot help but miss my grandmother now."

He had watched Wanderer scoop mice from his shoulder into Falling Rainbow's hand. Afterward, the pair had headed for the stream, the woman leading him with her free hand.

From the hillside, Shining Light could now see over the flat grasslands until the ground and sky met. Sparse trees dotted the land along the small stream that disappeared past his eyesight. Was it so smart to camp in the little valley?

When Father chose this place, it was because Thunder and I had fallen asleep on the grassy hillside. Sleep! How could I do that away from the others? A warrior would not have done so.

As soon as Wanderer told the new mother she could travel, they would return home. He glanced down at the pair who had found them, and felt a pang of emotion watching them. He missed his mother and grandmother even more, and let out a sigh.

He ran his hand down his tunic, and the beautiful new shirt Speaks and his grandmother had made him. His woman had painted White Paws and Moon Face in the center, and his grandmother quilled the sides in yellow. His first one, which Speaks had made him long ago hung in their lodge, outgrown. Beads and teeth from the outgrown tunic decorated the darker tanned deer hide he now wore. Long fringe swayed from the bottom and reached a hand's length below his waist. His loose hair waved in front of his face, tickling him like Turtle Doves' small fingers did whenever she touched his face.

I must change before something happens to this beautiful tunic. I should not have brought it out here.

"Grandmother, I wish you sat here with me as you did when I was a child in the canyons. Why does my inner voice still say danger? If it is not the hairy-faces that follow Night Hunter, what else is out there? Or are they still coming?

"Everyone had made their peace by the third sunset, for the most part, and slept around the lodge. Night Hunter and Tall Smiling Warrior now talk some. Speaks and Wisdom sleep with the new mother. And I sleep on the ridge with the wolves, Sandstone, and her baby. Thunder has an unusual attachment to Sparkling Star and stays near the lodge. At least now Sandstone's baby can nurse in peace. Me, I still need to be alone for sunrises. Perhaps that is the way of a Holy Man."

Gentle Wisdom plopped beside him. "You have climbed up here for three sunrises and sat until your belly calls for food. What do you look for?" She nodded her head at the wolves. "I think you are a wolf human as Wanderer says. You go off as they do, and I have even seen you howling with them. I never told others it was you. I know it is deep in your being and I... know how you feel, Cousin."

She cleared her throat and played with the fringe on the bottom of her tunic. She had quilled above the edge in small yellow and green Spirals. "I prefer dressing as a man, wearing leggings. It makes travel better and I am... am better fit to wear these than a dress."

She wore footwear that came just above her ankles. She looked down and followed the design of quills with her fingers, the pattern woven into a Spiral in green and yellow quills that followed on the outside and completed a circle.

"Sparkling Star and I are going to live together. It is not that I do not like men, but I feel more comfortable with her. We... we connected with each other." She threw a stone down the hillside.

"I know. You may think I do not see or sense things about you, Cousin, but I do. The older I get, the more is revealed to me through dreams, visions and life. You are a Warrior Woman.

"Wisdom, look up at me. Your lives have mingled and I know you care for her. There is no shame in being who you are, who your heart tells you to be. We all must make our own choices and not allow others to do this for us.

"Our parents choose our mates. They want for us what they feel will be best. Women are the ones who are given to a man by their fathers. I hear women talk about this. I also hear them say that they might not have found the right mate on their own. I also know of bands who think nothing of allowing their older children to explore early in their lives things our band frowns upon. None of it is wrong, only different."

Wisdom watched Wanderer and Falling Rainbow walk, arms wrapped around each other. "There should never be shame in being who you are." She rested her chin on her knees, arms clasped around her legs.

Shining Light nodded. "No, there should not. You forget your little brother, Knows Both Sides. Your mother and father were proud to welcome him into the band. Before she decided to walk her own path, Blue Night Sky told your mother she carried a baby who would be a Twin Spirit, one who will be both man and woman in his heart. He would be one that people would seek out for advice on many things, like their mates, children, someone who would just listen to their problems. Knows Both Sides will have a life that will know both loneliness and joy."

He reached for her trembling hand. "Walk tall. Be proud, Warrior Woman. Your mother and father will be proud to know they have two special children. It is deep in your being." He grinned widely at his now smiling cousin.

"Your heart will not be sad if I have no children?"

"You have two. Sparkling Star and you have two children."

"My heart overflows with love for you, Cousin. You always know what to say... even if you are only a boy." She punched his arm and laughed.

Chapter 24

Shining Light stood with hands shading his eyes. "Wisdom, look out across the grassland. I see wild mustangs, maybe. I hope that is all I see. They are too far away to know if they might be the hairy-faces from my dream, or if they are running as wild mustangs do. Run and get Tall Smiling Warrior!"

He had hoped with Wanderer and Falling Rainbow in the camp the dream would not happen. *How can it happen? We are ahead of them.* He looked toward where the pair had been walking. "Wanderer! Falling Rainbow! Come back and go into the camp. A group of mustangs come our way."

Wanderer dropped his arms from around Falling Rainbow. As she ran toward the camp, he strode toward the top of the hill. Tall Smiling Warrior raced to the top, ahead of Hawk Soaring and Flying Raven.

Within a few paces, Night Hunter was at Shining Light's side. Fear rode like a wild storm in his eyes. "Where is Falling Rainbow?"

Shining Light glared at him. "You worry about only one woman? We have four women and three babies to worry for as well." He spoke in a stern voice. "What are you not telling us, Night Hunter?"

"I... just worry for Rainbow because—"

Tall Smiling Warrior interrupted him. "If it is the hairy-faces, it is better that I go alone. Even dressed as my new people they will talk to me. Maybe they will think I know where the yellow stone is. The first night everyone ate together, Night Hunter told us that they followed, and asked if we wanted him to leave. We said no, so we stand together."

He lifted a hand to his brow. "See how the mustangs follow one another? It is the way of my old people."

Night Hunter's voice shook. "We must get Falling Rainbow away from here. If it is the hairy-faces, they seek her. Before I... I learned... before the Spirits in my Vision Quest taught me what they did, I told the hairy-faces if they took her from the old... from Wanderer, I would lead them to the yellow stone. My eyes only saw greed, a way to Power. I will stand and fight. Go. Leave from here. This is my shame to bear. It is shame that feels as heavy as a wet humpback robe." He raised his hands to his eyes. "You have maybe until sunrise before they reach where we stand."

He looked straight ahead, head held high. "My mustang... take her and the young one, and give me one of the older ones. I will give you as much space ahead of them as I can."

Falling Rainbow stepped from where she hid, listening behind him. "You do this for me? Why?"

He turned her way. "You know I am the reason they still follow. I have brought this sorrow upon you, all of you." His eyes stared over her head, out across the grasslands.

He took a breath and raised his head. Fire spit from his words. "They do not understand our ways and said my Vision Quest was unholy. They told me only they had a true Holy Man. They even mocked your father. My anger came back, and I told them I had more yellow stones than anyone had ever seen. For my lies and greed, I will take my stand here. I will fight until my last breath is torn from my mouth, will fight to protect Rainbow and to protect this band."

He touched Tall Smiling Warrior's shoulder. "I claim this man as my brother." He stared into his eyes. "You are not all the same. Some, like you, only seek peace. You have only honored me since we met."

Tall Smiling Warrior put a hand on his shoulder in return. "Others of my kind are filled with greed and we cannot know who is who, so I will go speak to them. They have not yet seen us and will think I am alone. Perhaps they, too, seek peace and leave the others. We will not know until we meet them."

Shining Light spoke up. "He will not be alone. We will follow in the grass as we did before the mustangs came. Gentle Wisdom will —"

"Be at your side, Cousin, as always." Gentle Wisdom crossed her arms and stood between the men, whose faces all showed the same confusion. "I am a Warrior Woman." She stood, head held high, and looked past the men at the advancing mustangs.

"Wisdom, you have the right, but who will care for the other women and babies? Speaks must stay behind and care for Turtle Dove. Even if Sparkling Star could care for three babies, I would not allow it. No child should be left without a parent."

He saw Speaks below. From the stiffness of her pacing, he sensed her fear.

Wanderer spoke. "Night Hunter will stay." No one would say no to the Great Elder, not even another Holy Man, unless he matched him in age. "We will give them time to come closer as we prepare the camp for battle."

He turned and walked away. Falling Rainbow dashed after him.

***

Shining Light and White Paws roamed down the dry gulch, away from the others. This day they would make their way toward the hairy-faces.

"White Paws." Shining Light dropped to his knees and hugged the wolf. "You have a large family and pups. Moon Face must stay with the pups, as my mate must stay with our daughter." Amber eyes bore into his. "I sense no fear from you. I know you and your older children will follow us, yet I am scared. Never before have I faced this kind of fight. If five hairy-faces can be said to be a fight. I fight for not just my woman and daughter, but for others. All this time I have called myself a man... have I really been one?"

Sister Wind whirled and whipped, pelting him with dust and sand. Dark grey clouds filled the sky, hiding Father Sun. Lightning slammed into a dead tree across the gulch. He threw his body over White Paws as a hail of splintered wood exploded around them.

'*Boy, stop feeling pity! You are a Holy Man. Young, yes, and you have much to learn. Look up at me.*'

Shining Light raised his head. Sister Wind calmed and the sky cleared. "Blue Night Sky, what am I to do?" He pushed to his feet. White Paws rose with him, tail moving excitedly. "I feel shame. I have a family, yet do not feel like a man. I have yet to truly prove myself as a warrior."

'*Have you no memory of standing before all of the Peoples to speak of your dream visions, of danger if they did not follow you out of the canyons? Have you forgotten that, when you were only eleven winters, you raced down the hill on Sandstone to save your people? Have not your visions showed you things only a true man of Vision can see? Do you see me now, Shining Light?*' Blue Night Sky stood before him, surrounded by the purest blue, the color of the Spirit. Her hair, once bright stardust, was now darker than Raven's wings and swirled around her. Obsidian eyes sparked with deep blue specks, and her body shone with the Power of youth.

A surge went through him, to his very core of being, and Power filled him.

Behind her, the faint white of a bear appeared. '*I, White Bear, have only this to say — forgiveness.*'

White Paws jumped into Blue Night Sky's Spirit World. She leaned down and rubbed his head as he spoke. '*Human Brother, do not question who you are, what you are, or your own uncertainty will cause you to doubt, and make you weak. A man does not make a warrior. It is the warrior facing the enemy who creates the man.*'

He stood tall and raised his head. "I am a warrior." He clenched his fist, raised his hand, looked up to the sky, and shouted, "I am a warrior!"

Skies calmed and clouds vanished, as if there had never been a storm. The tree struck by lightning stood tall, untouched. Eagles called to one another as they drifted on air currents.

Chapter 25

Night Hunter bolted toward Wanderer and shook him awake. "Rainbow is gone."

"My shoulder is still sore, you crazy man! Every sunrise, she goes to greet Father Sun, to pray and sing alone." He rubbed his eyes and looked around. "It is still dark." He sat up and listened to the night sounds. Mice jumped from his robe as he tossed it aside and stood. "Wolves are still out hunting, and I do not see any lightness rising. What are you doing up?"

"I sleep very light, unlike old men."

"I still heal from a man who calls himself hunter and shoots old men! Perhaps you should feel the sting that I do. The fire still burns. I will hold your hand over it." Babies cried. "Now you have the women awake. Get more sticks for the fire. We must see what has really happened."

Robes flew open at the voices of the two men. Sparkling Star's babies started to cry louder. She put them to her breasts, as did Animal Speaks Woman with Dove to quiet them. Blue Waters whined and rubbed against Speaks. The air, still cool, brought everyone to the fire seeking warmth. Mustangs nickered and moved about.

***

"Shining Light?" Speaks pulled Dove from her breast and stood. "Where are you? Light!" Her eyes darted about. "Gentle Wisdom?"

No answer.

"Gone! They are both gone." She thrust Dove into Flying Raven's arms and ran to where the mustangs huddled together.

Sandstone's front legs were tied and her young one nursed.

Speaks' stomach felt empty and knotted. Nowhere could she spot Thunder. She closed her eyes and spread her arms out at her sides, trying to calm her mind, and to ignore the words of the men next to her.

"Old man, Great Elder, what does she do?" Night Hunter squatted next to Wanderer.

"Be still," he whispered. "She calls for the wolves. White Paws would not leave her man's side."

"How do you know this?"

"Shhh.... Be still, pup."

Rustling sounded from the underbrush, and Speaks opened her eyes. "Only Moon Face and her pups. What has my man done?"

She cried out and dashed up the hill, and barely noticed the rest of the camp following. At the top of the hill, she swung around and directed her anger at Night Hunter. "Where is my man?"

Night Hunter ducked his head. "Animal Speaks Woman, I do not know! I only just woke myself. I sat up and did not see Rainbow. I ran looking for her and found her mustang gone. I paid no heed to anything else. No one else." He put his hands to his face. "I am so sorry."

Her heart dropped to the ground. She moved past him and stumbled back down the hill. She knelt by the fire, her mind spinning like waters beneath a frozen river, and fed it small sticks until its flames rose and licked at the sticks she held above it. Her mind was in deep thought. The pain from the fingers of the fire forced her back and she dropped the sticks.

When Wanderer knelt beside her, she did not turn, but spoke quietly. "He said he could not sleep and left my side. Many nights he walks. I did not worry."

Wanderer spoke softly. "Holy Men must seek the Spirits' guidance alone."

She turned to face the Holy Man. "He rides Thunder. He seeks no Spirit's guidance, but speed. What does he seek, Wanderer?" Blue Waters whined. "I am not angry with you, old friend." She dug deep into his fur, clinging for comfort.

The Great Holy Man met her eyes and spoke in a gentle voice. "You must trust him to follow the right path. He will do so."

She leaned into her dog's solid body and wrapped her arms around him. "Moon Face knows where her mate is, I sense it. White Paws keeps his secret." She buried her face in the dog's rough fur. Voice muffled, she said, "Oh, Blue Waters, if only you knew where they travel. But you are not of the wolf pack, and they do not share their mind with you."

She jerked her face up, understanding. "Shining Light heard Falling Rainbow leave camp. He followed her. And Gentle Wisdom followed him." She spun on her knees to tell Wanderer, but he had vanished, silent as a mouse into the darkness. She put her head in her shaky hands.

Hawk Soaring stood. "We also must leave. I will not allow my grandson—"

"No." Flying Raven came from the darkness. "You and the others must stay. We may need to make a stand." He swayed his granddaughter back and forth in his arms.

"You are right, more so now that we are but two men. Night Hunter no longer squats next to where Wanderer was, and I never saw Tall Smiling Warrior at all." Hawk Soaring pressed Flying Raven's shoulder down.

"I know you want to follow your son, but who will guard the mothers and babies? Are we so sure there is only five of the enemy? I know it to be true that where we think only one group is near, another is often close by. Remember when we rescued Tall Smiling Warrior's woman? We learned they only waited for another group to come. Had we been but a few sunrises later it may have gone very wrong. For what we know of them, they could be surrounding our camp right now."

Animal Speaks Woman ran to Sparkling Star, who warmed herself by the fire. "The fire must be small, only enough light to see by. We have no way of knowing anything right now."

***

Flying Raven, still holding onto Dove, stared across the fire at Speaks. "I will not leave, but I will follow my son."

He laid the sleeping child on a robe next to the tiny fire, went to the lodge, and came out fully dressed with Raven's cape wrapped around his shoulders. He prepared to walk into the darkness, looking up at the near-full moon. His son would count on this being enough light. He also had a good idea what Shining Light planned to do.

Shuffling sounds brought Hawk Soaring next to him. "You cannot go into the Spirit land as your son can. I have come to help you find your way to the Center." He held out his obsidian blade.

Flying Raven stared up at the twinkling campfires in the dark sky, their brilliance dulled by the fullness of the moon. "Not much light to cut by. Do not slice me in half." He chuckled, knowing Hawk Soaring's great skill would aid him.

"You are smart, like your son. I know you have not eaten in at least two sunrises. You prepared yourself for something you knew might happen. I may be good, but I will not chance cutting you in half." He brought out a shell smoldering with old grass. "We will have a small fire. It will help you to focus and aid me as well. Sing, Holy Man. Prepare your mind as I prepare this fire."

Flying Raven Who Dreams dropped his robe, exposing his arms, and started to chant his song. He felt the blade slice into thin skin many times before his mind followed a mist as it swirled. Before him, the Ancient People swayed and sang, dancing in a Circle. His mind followed their dance, and he found himself within the Circle, dancing with them, arms intertwined. He sang louder to honor them.

He danced with them until his legs could hold him no more. He fell in a dizzying Spiral of colors and songs, and heard the cawing of Raven. He tried to stand, but had no arms to prop himself up, only wings. He spread them and took flight.

'*My Brother, I welcome you. Are we here just to fly?*' Raven flew beside him, around him, and in front of him.

"Brother Raven, I am honored that you welcome me and allow me to fly with you. You have kept my senses keen since we left the forest. Without your constant presence in my life, I would not be the man I am. I must ask for your help. I am here to do more than fly. I seek my son and five others who follow him. He goes into danger. I wish to know where he is." Power surged through his wings and moved them faster.

'*Slow down. You will not get there faster. We are not in the same place as he. A long span for him is but a flash of lightning for us. He is where he needs to be, as are those who follow. Destiny guides them though they may not know it. Even the Great Holy Man, One Who Wanders, has this knowledge. He is a man of Great Power, but follows his heart without his mind's help. You need to remind him. Do not think he will be angry. He knows we all learn from each other no matter our age. No matter how great other people think Holy People are, you learn something new every sunrise. Even your granddaughter will teach you.'*

Flying Raven slowed his wings but not his need to know where his son was. "Brother Raven, I am honored with the words you offer me to learn from. I will not forget them. I ask again, please show my son to me, to ease my own worry."

'Man of Raven, you cannot change what is to happen. This is the destiny of others, not yours.'

"Please! Please show him to me. I, a mere man, beg you." He felt himself losing contact. "No, please, I need to know where he is. Show me this and I will ask for no more."

Below, a lone rider was out ahead, too far ahead for the others to catch up. Behind that one, two riders trotted at a fast pace, and farther behind, still two more riders raced full out.

Despair pierced Flying Raven's heart. "Darkness could make the mustangs fall, Brother Raven."

Silence.

Ahead of the lone rider were seven mustangs. Two carried packs and five carried riders. As Father Sun climbed above the horizon, one rider drew even closer to the oncoming riders.

"No! No! Brother Raven, allow me my wings again." Flying Raven stood alone in the grass.

Chapter 26

The hairy-faces surrounded Falling Rainbow's Mustang and forced her into a rocky canyon.

"They caught her! What was she thinking?" Shining Light slowed Thunder. "We cannot go in after her without knowing what is there, and we are alone." He watched as her mustang disappeared.

Thunder reared and twirled around as Gentle Wisdom's mustang slid in closer. "Now I see riders behind us!"

He squinted. "By the riding style, they must be of the People."

Gentle Wisdom raised a hand above her eyes. "Light, I think it is Wanderer and Night Hunter. One mustang has a young one who tries to keep up."

He clucked to Thunder and the mustang shot toward the riders. Gentle Wisdom's shorter mustang soon fell behind.

He tried to speak low, worried that voices would carry in the open land. "Thunder! Stop, calm down. You nearly threw me off, you silly, crazy mustang!"

Thunder stopped as two mustangs rode up, though she still stomped her feet and swished her tail in protest.

"Wanderer? Night Hunter! Who is with the women?" Shining Light strained to see who else might have followed.

Wanderer glared at him. "What are you doing out here?" His voice was stern. "I thought we had this decided."

"We did, but when Falling Rainbow left, Thunder woke me calling after one of the other mustangs." He scratched his head. "I thought I had this all understood in my mind. She was safe. Tall Smiling Warrior was to.... Where is he? Did he stay in camp? My mind is dizzy with thoughts. I need to stop—"

"And think." Wanderer leaned forward on his mustang and pointed to where the hairy-faces had raced off with Falling Rainbow. "Women think with different minds than men. I saw the changes her face made, kept making, while we sat around the fire making plans. I allowed my emotions to get in my way. Rainbow was the first person to touch my heart with the fire of love."

Night Hunter stiffened. "Love? Crazy Mouse man. Even now I see mice on your shoulders." His mustang pranced and twisted. "I love her, I... *love her!*" He wiped his eyes. "She is stubborn, fights with me when we talk. She is not a woman to have for a mate. She—"

"She belongs to herself." Wanderer spoke softly. "We must stop arguing and use our minds as warriors. We let our hearts get in the way, and could die for our mistakes. Of all of us, I should have known better. She has filled my heart with the joy of knowing a daughter. For the first time, I allowed someone into my Soul. Not even my women ever got that far, and I loved them much."

Gentle Wisdom cleared her throat. "May I speak? Falling Rainbow is our cousin. That is why we two rode after her. I know you men see me as only a woman—" She nodded toward Shining Light. "—except you. You see me for who I am."

Wanderer eyed her. "I know who you are and who you will become, Warrior Woman. Your words have worth. Speak them."

She pointed toward a mound of large boulders. "We know where they went. They will hide and maybe wait for us. Father Sun has made us easy to see. I say we ride the other way until we can find a place they cannot see us. Not back to camp. They will then know where to attack if they choose."

She shifted on her mustang, gathered her loose hair and retied it. "Only five of them? How do we know? Darkness may be our only chance in this mix of tall brown and short green grass." She reached for Brown Dog's ropes. "I say the dark is our best chance. Creator will find us even in the dark if something happens to us, and take our Spirits. I believe this with my heart. I will wait until Father Sun nears sleeping, then come back." She tapped Brown Dog and headed in the direction she suggested, her back straight and head held high.

"Fine Holy Men you two make!" Night Hunter spun his mustang around and followed Gentle Wisdom.

Wanderer raced after them.

Shining Light held Thunder in place though she reared, kicked, and called to the other mustangs. "Thunder! Thunder... calm down." He reached out to rub her neck and scratch her ears. "I am trying to understand what Mouse said to me in my vision. How can you know what I say, eh? You are not White Paws." He let out a low whistle.

Wolves rose from the grass.

He jumped down to reach out for White Paws, but Thunder nearly pulled the ropes banded around her nose from his hand. He was unable to bond with her as he had Sandstone. He had tried since she was only a sunrise old, but her mind was hers. He stood and faced the mustang, rubbing the sides of her face, and she bobbed her head and nickered.

"Why you chose Sparkling Star is a question I may never know the answer to, but you must help me this day." He put his face up close to her, breathed gently into her flared nostrils, and took her breath in return. "Thunder, I must save my new cousin. I need your help. Please allow me to do so."

He closed his eyes and tried to slow his breathing and reach into Thunder's mind. She snorted but stood still. There was a dim connection, but enough for him to put his thoughts in hers. He used pictures in his mind to show himself hugging Sparkling Star, who came into his mind from hers, and he reflected the image back. Thunder relaxed and let him in.

"Thunder, we need help to protect all our females. Sparkling Star is one. So much danger awaits us. I need your help."

The mustang breathed in his breath and gave hers back. She shuddered, stepped back and stood.

He had reached her! "Thank you, girl. I know Sparkling Star belongs to you, and you to her. That will never change."

He stood still, one hand tangled in Thunder's neck hair, and eyed the wolf. He let go of her hair and, with a tug on her rope, walked the mustang toward where Gentle Wisdom had gone. "White Paws, what am I to understand? Do the hairy-faces want us to follow?"

He needed to leave from where they might be watching him. "Perhaps, White Paws, they will think we have all given up if I go the other way, as everyone else has done." He watched the ground and allowed Thunder to do as she pleased.

He paced across the dry grass. It crackled with each step beneath his footwear. "Why does it appear to be too simple? Do I miss something?" He ambled on, thoughts spinning in circles. "I know they expected us to follow. We did not. To get into the rocks, I would have to let Thunder go."

Sister Wind raced past him, and the cold air curled around his body. He did not think anymore than the rest of them about the cold, wearing only his breechclout. The cold season had passed and green decorated the land. In the distance, small herds of the big humpback beasts rumbled with their young beside them. The need to hurry whispered through his mind.

"White Paws, please stay with me. I need your help." He knelt down on the cool grass. "The clouds gather. Perhaps they will come this way. We will all be wet, but this may be what we need. Perhaps the Spirits are watching over us, giving us a chance."

He stood, raised his arms and shouted, "Why am I here? Why is my family here?"

Sister Wind responded with more strength than before. His voice set Thunder in motion and she reared, turned and ran. "Thunder!" He raced after her, wolves speeding past him.

White Paws turned her, and she came back as if nothing had happened. She slowed to a trot and stopped in front of him, tossing her head.

"Girl, *why* do you act so... so... I cannot find the word I seek. No mustang I know acts the way you do. You are like a sharp raspberry thorn I cannot pull from my skin!"

Her lips curled back and she nickered at him. He reached for her ropes, but she stepped back out of reach and pawed the ground.

"You act silly." He turned away from her and crossed his arms.

She shoved him with her head and nickered again. He turned to scold her, and she trotted back toward the boulder where Falling Rainbow had vanished. He ran after her, wolves in tow.

She slowed when she reached the rocky canyon, and stood submissively.

"Thunder...." He bent low and held his legs, breathing hard. "What... why...?"

The mustang nodded her head toward the boulders that led toward a narrow entrance.

"What are you trying to show me? Go in there, up the big stones? Is this your way of helping me?" He headed toward the side where he could climb without worry of anyone seeing him.

White Paws followed to the bottom, but had to wait with his pack.

Shining Light searched for handholds as he climbed the rough grey boulders. He turned to see where the wolves were, but they were not there. He hesitated. No noise came from within the boulders. Courage pushed him on, and climbing higher he found a place where a grown man could slip through. He used this spot to get a better look.

Deer... I see only deer! No one is inside this hidden spot. Not one human. Not Falling Rainbow. What goes on here?

He jumped down, motioned to the wolf pack, and flew onto Thunder's back, tapping her into a full gallop.

Thunder ran faster than he had ever known her to do. She left the wolves far behind. Her muscles tightened beneath him.

Somehow, she knows more than I ever understood. I thought she was just a Mustang who would never grow up.

***

"Where is he?" Gentle Wisdom glanced back as she paced back and forth, twisting her hands.

She turned to Wanderer. "Now what? You must have a way to find him!" She stomped up to him but stopped short. "I am sorry, Great Holy Man. Shining Light is more than a cousin. He is my true heart friend. He is the only one who understands me."

Wanderer tilted his head to one side and watched her with kind eyes. "I know more about you than you understand, Warrior Woman. Do you think I see you as a girl who will one day take a mate and bear children? I am not so blind. I see you guiding people, protecting them as you risk your own life. Power follows you, not as a Holy Person, but as protector."

He patted the log he sat on, and when she sat, he leaned over and whispered, "I know your Spirit Guide."

She tried to jump up, but his hand held her down. "Tell me!"

"No." He shook his head and looked deep into her eyes. "It is not time. You will learn soon."

"How?" She searched his eyes for answers.

Wanderer pushed to his feet. "You must earn the right to know."

She gazed up at him, pointed at him, and leaped to her feet. "I will earn my right to know my Spirit Guide this night." She blinked and called after him as he moved off into the darkness. "Wanderer? Holy Men! Who can understand them?"

Thunder shoved her from behind. She turned as the mustang trotted away. "Maybe I will make jerked meat out of you, Thunder! Thunder? Where is Shining Light?"

She twirled around and into her cousin's arms. She shook with excitement and then shoved him away.

"Why did you not follow us? Where have you been... I have been crazy with worry!" She beat on his chest. "Cold, you must be so cold. I was smart enough to grab a robe." She dashed over to where the robe lay, grabbed it, and tossed it his way.

"I am grateful, Cousin." He wrapped himself and crouched, hands over the fire.

Thunder nickered and trotted up to the mustangs. She circled them and led them off at a trot. Gentle Wisdom's hobbled mustang whinnied after them.

"Jerked meat!" Wisdom yelled at the wayward mustangs.

Wanderer and Night Hunter sprinted after them, leaving Shinning Light to warm himself.

She saw him staring into the fire, not paying heed to his surroundings. "Rest, Cousin. We will talk once I get your wild mustang back. Men," she mumbled to herself. "Why did they not tie their mustang's legs? Ha!"

She untied the ropes hobbling her animal and jumped astride.

"Women would have known to tie their mustangs, but we have different minds than men. That is why they need us."

With a light heel against her mustang's side, she broke into a gallop to catch up to the runaways.

Chapter 27

Night Hunter sat at the small fire next to Shining Light. "I am very happy to see you, but I am not so sure about your mustang. It is good Flying Cloud is tired and called to his mother, or we may have never seen any of them again."

Thunder grazed on the far side of camp, away from the rest of the mustangs. She eyed him while she grazed. No one had thought to grab ropes, and that left Gentle Wisdom to herd them back toward camp.

He stood, walked back and forth, and stopped in front of the young Holy Man. "Why did Falling Rainbow run away? What was she thinking?"

Fear burned in his heart for the woman he loved. He stomped away from Shining Light and the fire, but he spun around, raised his arms, and slapped them to his sides.

"I see pity in your eyes for me. Pity Rainbow, not me." Anger heated his words. "We have two Holy Men right here! Right in front of me. Why do you not use your Power to make her return? Where is she? Holy Men have Power. Use it!"

***

Shining Light's lips tightened. "Brother, Power does not work that way. I have no magic to offer you. If we had special Powers as you wish we did, then I could raise my arms in the air and command her to appear. I could make food already cooked show up in your hands, and you would never have to hunt again." He bowed his head. "What I can do — what I *will* do — is ask the Spirits for guidance, and pray to the Great Mystery to give me visions."

He stood, allowed the robe to drop and put his hands on the troubled man's shoulders. "My guides offer their help, but it is up to me to understand what they tell and show me. I am only a man, not Creator."

He saw such fear in the man's eyes that he wanted to find a way to calm him, but could not even calm his own fears.

"Brother, trust in the Spirits. Never in my life have they led me down the wrong path. Do *not* lose faith in yourself. That is most important. You lose that, and you will wander the rest of your life unsure of who you are, why you even live. Remember... split-apart.... No one can live like that for long. It eats at your Spirit, destroys you, and you will not even know it. Others will, but you will fade in your mind and become a walking shadow. Do not take other's choices for your own. We all choose what we do, then must live with those choices. If you take on another's, your own will be mixed in — another way to have a split-apart."

Night Hunter nodded. "I am sorry. My worry consumes me, Holy Man. You are right about the split-apart. I would not do Rainbow any good then. I need a walk. Darkness has always comforted me. Even if some say darkness is where a Spirit wanders forever, I say darkness is calming." He grabbed his bow, shoved shrubs out of his way, and vanished beyond the flickering fire that cast is own shadows about the camp.

***

"Let him go, young Holy Man." Wanderer tossed broken sticks into the fire that reached up as if grabbing them from hunger. "He blames himself and needs to be alone. Let him think on your words, they were good for him to hear... and good for me also."

The fire crackled, giving light to the surrounding darkness. Shining Light pointed to Thunder. "Great Elder, can you tell me why she led the mustangs away from us as she did? If not for her, I would have never went back and saw the boulders were empty of humans. And now she has stopped us from going back together. She is a smart one, the smartest mustang I have seen."

Wanderer turned toward Shining Light and Gentle Wisdom, who sat next to her cousin. "She keeps us away for a reason I do not understand. Things unfold this night that will change the way we see things."

Gentle Wisdom lifted her eyes and turned his way. "Is this why Tall Smiling Warrior has left us?"

He continued to toss sticks into the fire. "He, too, takes the blame for Falling Rainbow leaving. It weighs his heart down. He knows the hairy-faces are brutal, thoughtless. This is why he is no longer with them. For whatever reason he left, I am sure it is to help her."

He leaned over to see her better. "Little one, trust me. I am not so crazy that I would risk another's life. I see worry on your face. Trust the Spirits as your cousin says." He dropped his eyes to stare into the fire.

Three mice hopped from his pocket and crawled across his shoulder. "Hmm? Oh yes, you are hungry." He tore dried meat and gave them some. "Why do you not go eat seeds?"

She jumped up from her spot and stood before him. "I have seen what the hairy-faces do to captives. Have you?" She placed her hands on her hips. "I do not mean to be disrespectful, Great Elder, but I am going after my new cousin!"

He stopped feeding the mice. "I know full well what they can do, girl." He squeezed his eyes shut, his grief clear as he put his hands up to his face and his shoulder curled in.

She stepped closer and scooted in between him and Shining Light. Her lips quivered. "I am sorry. I only think of myself, my own worry. Like Night Hunter, I fill with anger too fast, and my words come out before my mind has a chance to stop them."

He opened his eyes, moved his wet hands away from his face, and looked up. He patted her knee, stood, and went into the darkness.

As soon as he was away from the firelight, he fell to his knees, raised his arms skyward, and allowed emotions to find their way from his heart.

***

Shining Light moved next to his cousin. "Wanderer is more than a Great Holy Man. Some things I cannot tell you, but this I can. He carries the burdens of many, along with his own grief. That is the way of a Holy Man. Many choose to live alone. Some even move away from their band. We... we feel much from others and take it within ourselves. Sometimes, no matter how hard we try, we cannot let it go, even though we may not show it."

Night Hunter returned and sat on the ground before him. "I saw Wanderer and knew to leave him alone." He glanced away, then back again. "Shin— Holy Man, I did not understand any of this. I thought Holy People prayed, offered guidance and healed others from their pains, but also had Power to do other things. I feel great shame at my anger." He pushed himself up to leave.

"You choose to be angry by the way you see, by the way you feel what has happened. Listen well to these words and they will heal you. They are from the Spirits. They say to look beyond appearances to find the center of the problem, like Tree's root—if there is an infection, it can take over the whole tree and kill it. The mind creates emotions. Emotions, if painful, can cause illness. Only if we know the 'root' of the problem can we heal ourselves. Wanderer has found no reason to seek forgiveness for himself. You and he are much alike. Like him, you hold everything in your heart, but unlike him, you bring it out, but still do not let it go."

The warrior stared into his eyes, then looked away. "I did not mean to—"

"You do not disrespect me, Night Hunter."

The man looked back into Shining Light's eyes. "How is it that one so young as you can know what you do?"

"Age creates wisdom, yes. Youth urges us to seek out Power. Somewhere the two combine. Age is but a place in time."

This time, Shining Light stood and sought the darkness.

Chapter 28

Shining Light walked away from the camp. Sister Moon's brightness did not allow him the total darkness he sought, but it would be her light that also guided him. Hunger snapped at his belly.

How long since I have put food in my mouth? Two days? Three? None of us have eaten well, and we have food! I tire, feel weak, yet Power pulls at every part of me. In slow motion, he turned his face upward. *The campfires in the sky should be dull, not so bright with Sister Moon at her strongest. So much Power this night. Rumbling from the distance moves closer, yet holds back, waiting... waiting... for what?*

He raised his arms and sang softly to the beat of his heart, his Soul. He stopped to pray. "Creator, Great Mystery, I, your child, seek guidance. Forgive my begging for help. It is not for me, but my people."

Fur brushed his bare legs. "White Paws, Wolf Brother, what do I do to protect everyone?"

'Brother of mine, Power fills this night for you. Use it.'

Shining Light drifted toward the campfires in the sky... or was it the campfires that came down to him? He held his breath as one campfire landed next to him. A man sat before it playing with a twig. The flame neither grew nor lost its brightness.

'Did you know we never have to add wood to the campfires in the sky? They are Spirit fires that never go out. We feel neither warm nor cold. We just are. Some wait alone by a fire, while others are very crowded. We wait for our relations to join us. We do much visiting and never sit alone for long.

'Feather Floating In Water, I asked that you carry my name when you were born. I am your relative from long ago. I carried that name until I came to this place of wonder, where names are as unimportant as time. I have watched you grow from a boy and become Shining Light.'

White Paws passed Shining Light to go lay next to the campfire, as if it was where he belonged.

'Sit, young one.' He motioned to him. *'You know me in your heart. I led the Peoples to the canyons where they split and became different bands. I was old and knew to lead the Peoples as far as I could. My "Spiral," my cycle of life, had come to an end.'*

Shining Light scooted closer to the fire, then reached out and ran his hand across it. "It has no warmth, yet I feel warm. Great One, why are you here?"

The air filled with vibrating laughter.

'I am no greater than you, so do not call me that. We are the same, only in different places. Since life does not end, but shifts to a different place, never fear death, even if it comes to the ones you love. It is but a word, as Blue Night Sky told you a long

time ago. Stop worrying. I know you fear for your people, your family. I am your family. Every being is part of your family.

"*Do you know that trees talk? They talk to each other, and to you, if you will listen. Stones are the true Great Elders, not Humans. Sometimes all you need to do is pick one up, hold it, feel the Energy. Also, little one, trees pray. Did you know that? Sister Wind helps carry their prayers. All living beings pray. Plants, animals — it does not matter.*'

"What does all of this have to do with Falling Rainbow? The hairy-faces who took her, or she gave herself to... I am unsure. I asked for guidance, to be sure I do the right thing this night."

'*It has nothing to do with it, yet it has everything to do with it. I take this time to speak to you. Listen well, young one. Pay heed to signs in Nature. Mouse told you to close your eyes and you will see better. Do you understand?*'

He sat for what felt like a long span before he answered the Great One. "I must listen to Nature, to follow not just my heart, but to see simple things that others do not — things I have not seen myself, such as the time Grandmother did not pay heed to the signs when I was a boy. I had begged her to go with me to see White Paws' first pups. The signs that day warned of changes in Nature, but I had distracted her so much that we almost drowned in a fast-moving flood."

He sat in silence once more, filling his mind with his relation's wise words before he spoke again. "Father of my Grandfather, I am confused still. How will I know what I see?"

He stared into the campfire, hypnotized by the movement of the flames. A vision shot up from the flames and became mustangs with riders. The riders forced the animals around boulders and across the land toward the camp where his family and Sparkling Star were. The riders circled around the back of the camp and took everyone by surprise.

"No, they took the camp! They did not hide in the grasslands." He looked up to speak to the Spirit, but found only darkness.

The grass crunched next to him, and Wanderer appeared. "What are you doing out here, boy? I thought I heard voices." He stared at the robe next to Shining Light. "Ah, you sought guidance. Sister Moon is almost past her strength. We must act now. I hope you are ready."

"Wanderer, I saw —"

"I know, boy." The Great Elder slipped past him and headed toward camp.

He and the wolves hung back. White Paws responded with a jump onto his chest, his amber eyes boring into his own.

"Just as always, I feel so... so connected to you, as if we are, and always will be, as one. I think you know it is time. If I am right, and I believe I am because of the visions from the fire, and because of Wanderer's urgent words, we all must go now." He looked up at the encroaching clouds. "Sister Wind begins to whisper through the leaves, and brings clouds. I smell rain. The Spirits are with us this night!"

The wolves raced ahead, leaving him to catch up.

When he entered the camp, every mustang was ready, even Thunder. He called to her, and she trotted his way. "So, now you come to me as your mother would have. You really *do* understand much more than I thought. You showed me the big rocks were empty, and kept us from leaving this camp by chasing off the other mustangs. And you would not let anyone near you until now. Who put your nose rope on?"

He rubbed the sides of her face, came around, and swung onto her back. She remained calm.

Gentle Wisdom trotted over to him on her own mustang, her smile visible as she neared. Even in the dim light, she could not hide her pride. "She came to me! For days I have been having visions, just out of my eyesight, of mustangs. I can feel Power from them. I slept a little while waiting for you men to come back, and I dreamed of riding on a pure white mustang, but we were flying! I felt... joy, and my heart beat faster than ten crickets! I had a Vision of teaching children and sharing my gifts. I have always thought I needed to be bold to be the Warrior Woman that I am, but it is not the only truth for me. I can, and will, defend our people with my life, but I am also Gentle Wisdom, one who passes on knowledge as a teacher. The story you told Sparkling Star will be one I pass on.

"Shining Light, everything will be okay this night. I know it is so. I felt it, not saw it. I am also a Dreamer Warrior Woman, if such a thing is real. I feel pure Power this night! And yes, I feel bold, strong!"

With one fist raised, she tapped Brown Dog into a trot and followed Wanderer and Night Hunter.

Shining Light shook with the Power that escaped from his cousin. He passed them all on Thunder, with wolves spanning out across the grasslands. Spears of lightning stabbed the ground in yellow and pink, as it exploded into Eagle-like claws clutching the grasslands before him.

Chapter 29

Sister Wind whipped the clouds closer, and noise growled deep within the clouds. With the last strike of speared yellow through the sky, Shining Light could see the hill in front of their camp. As they neared, muffled voices carried over the hill's rise. In the lead, he motioned everyone to jump off their mustangs.

Before he turned Thunder loose, he whispered, "For once, this small span, listen to me. I know you are smart. You proved this." He curled his lips inward and raised a brow at Thunder. "The woman you have bonded with is down there, on the other side of the hill, with her babies... and so is Speaks, so you must be still and wait. Will you do this for everyone down there? I am counting on Falling Rainbow being there also. You need to stay put. We cannot risk lives. I know if I tried, you would not allow me to tie your legs. Do you listen to me, Thunder?"

She made no move, not even with her expressive face. Her muscles tightened as he rubbed her shoulder.

"Thank you."

He turned to find everyone standing half a mustang's length away. Night Hunter opened his mouth as if to speak, but Wanderer tapped his elbow into the man's belly to silence him.

Sister Wind howled louder. So many clouds gathered that they hid the moon, and the air vibrated with Energy, but no rain fell on the four people who crouch-walked toward the top of the hill. As they reached the crest, they lay flat and peered into the camp lit up by a small fire. It struggled to stay alive as Wind punished it, keeping the flames low as it sparked upward, begging for life.

The hairy-faces looked above at the coming storm, and raced about the camp gathering their weapons. They tried to catch mustangs that reared and backed away from the trees that held their ropes. Not one had legs tied. As hard as they tried to calm the animals enough to grab for their legs, something kept spooking them. They doubled their ropes around the trees until the mustang's heads were nearly against the trunks.

One hairy-face shoved Falling Rainbow in behind two other women who climbed into the wind-whipped lodge.

Night Hunter tried to surge forward, but Wanderer pushed him back to the ground.

Across the camp, Flying Raven and Hawk Soaring sat restrained to saplings that whipped sideways in the wind.

Shining Light motioned to Gentle Wisdom. "Warrior Woman, call out in Owl's voice so my father and grandfather will know we are here."

She turned with a questioning look. "I can see Tall Smiling Warrior standing behind them. At least I think it is him. I see the way he dresses. Now we know where he went. I worried for him. He has been good to us."

"When he hears you call out, I am sure he will know it is you and cut them loose. Remember, he has heard your call before, when we rescued his woman from the enemy hairy-faces before we came to live in the forest." He pointed toward the anxious mustangs below. "I am sure it is him who keeps spooking their mustangs, and he will also cut them loose."

Night Hunter tapped his shoulder. "The hairy-faces are not stupid. They, too, will hear an owl in such a storm when owls would not fly."

He shook his head. "This is a chance we must take. With a storm upon them, they will worry about other things and their ears will be deaf to an owl calling."

He tapped his cousin with his wrist and rose to his knees. Before Gentle Wisdom's Owl cry died in the wind, he let out a long, loud howl. In response, wolf howls cried out and encircled the camp. Yellow spears forked across the turbulent sky and lit the camp below in brilliant light.

He continued his howls along with the wolf pack, and watched the hairy-faces stumble after their crazed mustangs while holding onto their weapons.

One slowed and turned to look back, and several wolves dashed out of the shadows. He raised a knife and a wolf cried out. The rest of the pack surged forward, and the hairy-face's screams filled the air. The storm's fury chased the rest of the enemy as they ran. Swollen clouds ripped open, and rain pelted them as they tried to escape the torment. Darkness absorbed the enemy and their mustangs.

Shining Light and his companions slid down the muddy hillside. Clouds moved away from the camp as if the Spirits allowed Sister Moon's light to shine through.

Tall Smiling Warrior stood between Flying Raven and Hawk Soaring, who both rubbed their wrists.

"Thunder!" Shining Light turned to go back for her. "Tell Speaks I go for Thunder. I will — "

Tall Smiling Warrior grabbed his arm. "No, the mustangs will be fine. We must get inside and guard the women in case they try to come back. I will remain outside to watch." His forehead rose in lines. "Just give me a dry robe. We must watch out for them and keep everyone away as I find out if the enemy your wolves attacked still moves. I will do what they did not... if they did not already."

The men ran into the lodge and every woman, except Falling Rainbow, spoke at once.

Speaks squeezed Shining Light until he begged her to let go. "You squeeze our daughter!"

"You are soaked, man of mine! You men go outside and get those things off. We will pass out our robes, *dry* robes, so get back in as fast as you can and leave your clothes inside by the flap. Hurry, I am not done squeezing you!" She called after him. "You only have on your breechclout! You could get sick from bad Spirits finding you. I will make a fire in here. Oh no, give Smiling Warrior a robe! I know he must be miserable."

"I am fine. I will be back soon. No one needs to come my way!"

Shining Light called into the lodge as he stripped off his breechclout. "Why does Gentle Wisdom get to undress inside? The rain stops anyway. Pass us robes, please!" He wrapped himself inside the warm robe and raced back to Speaks' side. He wrapped her and Dove in the robe with him while Speaks squealed at his wet hair. "Is Smiling Warrior all right?"

He stared at the flap. "He does what he needs to do. You now call him Smiling Warrior. He is our friend, so I too will call him Smiling Warrior."

***

Gentle Wisdom told the story of how everything unfolded, with expressions that made everyone laugh and relax, especially when she spoke about a certain crazy mustang. Sparkling Star sat close to her, nursing her babies with an expression of contentment.

Against the back wall of the lodge, Falling Rainbow huddled alone and silent in her robe.

Wanderer moved closer and sat with legs crossed next to her. He leaned his shoulder against hers as if he knew how alone she felt.

Shining Light saw her rigid response, even with Wanderer next to her. He cleared his throat to gain attention, and the others fell silent. "Rainbow, I have something of great importance I want to share with you."

She kept her head down. "I caused this. I wanted to keep everyone safe. I sought to make them think that you had left me behind. They laughed at my hand signs. I tried to speak what words I knew, but they grabbed Fire Dancer's ropes and pulled her into the hollow stones. She fought out of fear, and I had to beg them not to kill her."

"I told them the words, 'yellow stone,' and they let her go. They pulled my mustang through a small opening so those who came after me would not see us. When Shining Light crawled up the boulders and searched inside, they waited on the outside, where he could not see, until he left, and then followed tracks to our camp."

Her eyes welled and her lips quivered as she fought to gain composure. "The only reason they did not harm you was because I told them you had found much yellow stone and had many of your people with you, not far away, that waited for your return."

She clenched her dress at the knees. "I told them you always had someone guarding you, even if they could not see them. I then raised my head up to the tops of the boulders, and told them I was only a woman and you would find a way to silence me if I spoke. It was then they tied a strip across my mouth. I have no idea why they did not kill me. I think they wondered why you even tried to rescue me. Perhaps that is why they kept me."

She scooted back even more. The only noises in the lodge were babies gurgling, the occasional pelting of rain, the crackling fire... and her shuddered words. "Please forgive me. I deserve to be cast out."

Shining Light scooted closer and squatted in front of her. He spread his hands wide as if encircling the people in the lodge. "Rainbow... we are as the wolves, loyal to our own. Our strength comes from one another. This is how all can survive. What you did was very brave. You were willing to give your life so others could live. You have honored all of us with such a great, great gift. Not one person in here believes you are a bad person to be cast out."

He brought his hands across his heart. "Each one of us has a purpose." He pointed toward Animal Speaks Woman. "Caring for the young, calling the animals." He turned toward where the men sat. "Some provide food for us all."

He turned, pointed out everyone and spoke their name. "Sparkling Star has brought us knowledge of what a woman slave must bear. We will never forget it. She has brought joy into Wisdom's heart and helped her to understand more about who she is. Each person is important, respected and loved. The strength of the wolf is the pack. This is what White Paws has taught me. My grandfather has a Spirit Guide who has helped us with his eyes above us. My father has Raven in his name for a reason. He is also a powerful Holy Man. Both Grandfather and Father teach me more every day of how I, too, can become more and one day pass on my knowledge, just as Wanderer has guided you and taught you much.

"Night Hunter... he has learned the most, I think. He knows who he is, but had to be willing to sacrifice for the Vision Quest to learn. Not everyone is so brave. He brings us together by what he has to offer. Did you know he can see well in darkness? More so than anyone I have ever met. Rainbow, he risked his life to find you. Do you understand this?

"Smiling Warrior has much courage, and left to find you while the rest of us were still trying to decide what to do. He will go on a Vision Quest when we get home, and maybe his name will change to show who he has become. He followed me out here with my family, not knowing what he would find. I am glad he did follow. We could not have done what he did."

He lowered his head. "I have become so much more than I ever thought I could be because of each and every thing that has happened to me. I wondered why the Spirits told me to come rescue a woman and an elder. We have come Full Circle. Each of us has helped make part of the beginning of a Spiral that represents the womb, and the path outward that we all make from birth to death. We could not have done so without every one of us helping each other learn all these lessons."

He leaned closer to her. "When one member is in need of help, the band unites and comes to that person's aid. I could never imagine living in a place where others barely knew my name. We need each other. One day, White Paws and Moon Face will sit back as one of their children becomes the leader, and they will teach their grandchildren, as our respected elders teach us. Only an elder can pass on knowledge and wisdom because they have lived long. One day, Rainbow, you too will pass on what you have learned.

"You are part of our band, and when we go back to the forest, you, Wanderer, Night Hunter, and Sparkling Star will be adopted into the Wolf Peoples."

She dropped her robe and sat taller.

Wanderer cocked his head and grinned. "Never have I heard one with so many words that spill out all at once before! Do you breathe much?"

Falling Rainbow smacked his leg. "You have a fast mouth, Wise One. I thank you, Shining Light, for all your words of comfort. You honor us all."

Wanderer cleared his throat and she smacked his leg again.

Sparkling Star spoke up. "I do not have enough food for my babies, so your woman has had to help feed them. They are as your children, brothers and sister. What will your... *our* people say when they see I have two babies? Will they worry which one was born last?" She squeezed her sons tightly.

"Which one was born last?" Shining Light cocked his head and grinned. "I did not see which one came out last. No one will ask. As Wisdom said, she has seen the women who are with the hairy-faces have two children, and not one is called a shadow child."

He turned to Smiling Warrior. "Do you know of such a word used in your camp?"

"Never. And I am sure it will not ever be a word used in my camp. So if Sparkling Star is not wanted—"

Gentle Wisdom lifted one of Sparkling Star's babies. "My mother will cry when I say that I am a Warrior Woman, but will cry more when she sees these babies. She will call them grandchildren."

Chapter 30

Falling Rainbow glanced up as Father Sun pushed through the last of the clouds, painting an orange-peach color in the sky. *So beautiful. Last night was for hugs and sharing stories — stories I will never forget.* She picked through wet wood to start a fire and dry out footwear and clothing. With an armload, she turned and stared at the sagging lodge.

Its flap opened, and Night Hunter stepped out. "Shining Light and the others still search for the hairy-faces and their mustangs?"

She turned away. "They found three of their mustangs, but no hairy-faces. Shining Light rode a different way with Smiling Warrior after they came back with the animals. Flying Raven and Hawk Soaring continue the search, following tracks they said went back toward the big boulders. Wanderer and Gentle Wisdom hunt."

He plodded his way to her and squatted to help pick out wood that would burn. "You understand I am not lazy by staying here. A man needed to stay behind." He dropped the wood, stood, and reached out and turned her to face him.

She tried to turn away, but he held her fast. "Speaks and Sparkling Star search for greens to eat. They will be back soon."

"Woman, I care for you. You have taken my heart."

She put her head down. "I do not know what I feel. You make my mind crazy with thoughts that were never there before. Leave me be."

He pulled her chin up and held it so she could not look away. "I do not believe you."

She pulled away and busied herself with the wood again, not looking his way. Sticks and pieces of wood flew everywhere, some hitting him. She mumbled to herself about her parents and their asking him to look after her, then bolted upright and shook her finger at him.

Before she could speak, he reached out and touched her hand, holding onto it.

"Stop! What if others see you grab my hand? They will think you take your freedom with me. I am a woman of the Beaver People, and we do not act this way. We have customs." She yanked her hand back and tried to turn away, but he twirled her around to face him.

"You do not act like a woman, sometimes. You are too independent, like Gentle Wisdom."

She reached out to punch him in the chest, but tumbled over the strewn wood and landed in his open arms. "Why do I find myself in your arms?"

He held her tight and stared into her eyes. "Had I not caught you, silly one, your face would be in the mud."

"Let me go! I am not your woman." She twisted from his grasp and fell backwards, landing in the mud he had tried to prevent her from falling in. She took his offered hand.

He pulled her into an embrace. "I know what I did, taking you even before you were a woman. This has dishonored you, and I will do anything— *anything*—to make you understand I am no longer that man. Please give me a chance. You are my heart, and I feel you have walked in my Soul."

Her eyes met his. She reached out, ran her hand across his muscled chest, and shivered.

Footsteps approached behind her. "So, you wish me to do the ceremony now, or wait until everyone else is here?"

She squealed and jumped away. "Wanderer! Where did you come from? I was digging through the wood. I need dry wood to get a good fire going to dry what we can...."

She bent back to the task, hands shaking, and dropped much wood. She hurried toward where she knew Speaks and Sparkling Star picked greens.

***

Animal Speaks Woman elbowed Sparkling Star. "I could hear Falling Rainbow long before I saw her heading our way. Her heart feels much, but she refuses to admit it. My man ran from me for some time before love caught him as a fish in the net. He struggled and fought, and when I almost had him, he wriggled away to run once again." She stood and chuckled. "Now, we are as a dream I never thought possible. Love can be such a silly thing and a wondrous thing, both at once. I was terrified when I woke and found Shining Light gone away from us, and trembled with much fear. Caring for one so deep can cause great joy... and great sadness."

Sparkling Star stood to stretch her back. "I have never known a man's true love, but I now know love in a different way." She turned and hugged Speaks. "I will never want for love again. To know everyone in camp also fought to keep me and my babies safe lifts my heavy heart and raises it with a joy I have never known. As Father Sun rises, so does my heart. I am so happy to know Wisdom. It is as if the Spirits brought us together. Had I not ran away when I did, I would have never met her, or any of you.

"The man who owned me went to go to a gathering and left me to care for his two fat women. They bore him no sons, and he went to find another woman. They sent me to gather wood. It was all gone near camp, so I took the old mustang to carry it back, and they never watched to see which way I went. I never looked back."

She knelt on the robe and rubbed both of her thick-haired sons' heads. They held the same red color as her own, only a darker brown. "That man will never know. I want to give my sons names soon, good names that will not speak of where they came from.

"He is only now finding out that I am gone. A moon has passed. I ran away the very sunrise he left to trade at a gathering, and traveled for many sunrises. I do not think he will look for me. He would not even allow me to sleep in the lodge unless he wanted something from me. No more! I am free, forever free. No more will I feel the sting of his hand... or anything else. I did not think that man's heart ever ached for a woman as Night Hunter's does for Rainbow. I wonder when she will melt her own heart toward him."

Speaks stopped nursing Dove and held her up. "I never knew how blessed I was until I met you. This is also the first time you have spoken so many words about your life. I am honored you have felt comfortable enough to tell me.

"Gentle Wisdom needs you, Star, as the night calls to Sister Moon. She will be there for you."

Both women sat on a robe next to their sleeping babies.

"Soon, Dove will try to crawl away, and I will need to make her a basket so I can hang her in a tree and keep her safe. Already she tries." She touched Star's arm. "We will make our baskets together. I will show you, and we will learn how to make yours big enough for two. On our way home we will pick thick grasses to weave."

Sparkling Star sighed. "Home. I have never had a home, not one I could call a *real* home, where people cared for me. And... and you hugged me in return, without worry that you touched someone beneath you." She put her head down.

"Never again put your head down, Star. You are equal to everyone, not a slave — not ever again, my sister."

Falling Rainbow finally arrived and plopped down before Sparkling Star had a chance to respond. "Men! Why do they think they are so... so... man like!"

Speaks and Star giggled so hard they woke their babies. "Here — " Speaks handed her Dove. " — hold her while I help Star care for her babies."

She scooped up a gurgling Dove. The baby's hand twisted her hair and brought it to her mouth. "Silly Dove, not hair." She untangled her hair and offered her finger instead.

"So you know babies? Dove is starting to learn there is more to life than food. Would you like to help us care for them? They are such a joy. We help each other so we can scrape hides, gather foods, and cook. I can see you will make a wonderful mother, Rainbow."

"Mother? I must have a good man first!" She nodded her head backwards. "He says he loves me. Ha! I know love, and it does not make one feel so strange as — "

"Yes, it does. The first time I saw Shining Light I felt my heart grow wings and flutter in my throat. I was stiff with wonder, stiff with fear. All I could do was stare at him, mouth open. No words would come out. When I did speak... he ran away!" She laughed so hard she wiped away the wet from her eyes.

"Speaks, we just went through a horrible thing, yet you let it go. Do you not fear the hairy-faces' return?" Rainbow's lips tightened and her fists clenched.

"No, I do not. We have strong men—" She nodded toward Sparkling Star, who cooed at the baby she held. "—and a warrior woman to protect us. If they return, which Smiling Warrior says is very possible, I know our men will have a plan."

Speaks took her hand. "Remember, we are a band. Bands do nothing without speaking to others first. A band is only strong if we know what each other plans. I understand you did what you did for the good of us all, but always seek Counsel first. Allow each of us to have our say. Then we decide. When we do not, it will break us apart as it did that night. Everyone was ready to fight for you, but no one had time to make plans. Everyone acted out of fear and concern, especially Night Hunter. Rainbow, his love for you is greater than any falling waters in the forest. Those falling waters are full of Power, so much power you can hear it roar as the waters fall into large ponds.

"There are things you do not know yet, such as why we are out here away from our band. Shining Light's Guides told him to leave our home and come out here. Well, told *him* to come out here. I refused to stay behind, as did his father and grandfather. Gentle Wisdom will not leave her cousin if he is in need. Smiling Warrior knew he would be needed. If they find the hairy-faces, we will need him to make their words. We came as a band—small, yes, but still a band of combined peoples to help one another."

She smiled at the babies she helped nurse. "My man sought to come alone. His grandmother, Bright Sun Flower, called a Counsel meeting to make sure he did not."

Falling Rainbow put her hands to her mouth. "Bright Sun Flower! The sister of my grandmother, Song Bird. I love her already. She is my aunt, and I will soon look upon her face!"

"Love is why I am here, Rainbow. Love pulls us across the deepest waters, the hardest of times, and binds Souls together tighter than the woven basket we put the greens in. His mother and grandmother would be here also if the people did not need them. So many wanted to follow. That is love also. Not like between a man and woman, but love just the same."

This time she turned to Sparkling Star. "Keep love in your heart, for even when you think there is none, there is."

She turned back to Falling Rainbow. "You, young woman, must stop fighting it. Night Hunter is a good man. I know what happened. It happened in the time we cannot go back and change. We can only move forward. Go to him. Walk with him and talk. Allow him to spill his painful thoughts onto the ground, and leave them there as you walk forward, away from what was. If you do not, you will lose the best part of your life, the part that only comes around once."

She looked above Rainbow's head and smiled. "Shining Light, you have returned!"

She ran to him through the mud and puddles and leaped into his arms.

Chapter 31

They knew caution had to be first in all of their minds as they pulled out of the camp. The men fanned out, and Gentle Wisdom stayed with the women. Wolves slipped through the grass around them, with the pups following their example.

Shining Light stayed closer to the women, rode Sandstone, and watched while Thunder kept a careful pace as Sparkling Star swayed on her back.

Father Sun and the clouds teased each other throughout most of the day, creating comfortable riding weather. Mid-season flowers and Sacred silver Sage, mixed with the greens of the grass and darker green shrubs, created a beautiful palate beneath the azure sky. He learned that the cry of a wolf, when the hairy-faces ran, had been that of one of the pups. Still, he had to grin.

Smiling Warrior carried the young wolf on his mustang, the pup's front leg wrapped in leather containing medicine plants and mud. The two had bonded.

It was too easy to relax and find distractions. Sandstone's young one trotted alongside his mother, the muscles on his body more apparent than most mustangs his age.

"You must have a name. You have proven your worth, little one. I worried about having to carry you on a drag when we first left. I was wrong."

He admired his coloring—darker grey took the place of the lighter shade, and his neck hair and tail had thickened in a more off-white hue. There was something about his eye color. He had dark eyes, but blue ringed them.

"When we get home, I will start putting some weight on your back. You are going to be big like Thunder. Thunder's little brother... who are you?"

He glanced forward, then turned his head side-to-side. *No time to think about names. We must reach home safely.*

He looked again at the long-legged mustang as it now moved ahead. He had the coloring of a dark storm full of rolling clouds.

"Storm!" *Heh, Thunder, the sister, and Grey Storm, the brother.*

"Perhaps I needed a distraction from our travels this day." He leaned over and patted Sandstone's neck. "Every one of you mustangs has become full of muscle, strong. I see long rides do us all good. I may find it hard to stay in one place now."

If not for the many hairy-faced enemies that search for this yellow stone, I would feel safe to explore with my family in the lands Sparkling Star came from. I would like to see more, and feel the urge to do so. All I have ever known is the canyons and the forest. The Mother is much larger. I need to speak to Smiling Warrior. Perhaps he also feels the need to travel.

"One day... one day I will know more, maybe have a small band to travel with."

Out ahead, Flying Raven turned his mustang around in a circle and rode to his son. "Clouds now change to a deep orange-red. We need to set up camp. Somewhere we have turned wrong." He turned to Hawk Soaring, who looked equally confused. "None of this looks as it should." He jumped down and waved the others toward a stand of trees. "No hills this night. We are in the open but for that small group of trees. Soon the campfires in the sky will show. They will tell us where we are."

***

Hawk Soaring slapped his thigh. "We watched for the hairy faces and lost our own way. Foolish. How did we do such a thing? We grown men were careless."

He raised a hand to shade his eyes, and scanned the land for anything familiar. "Will you help set up camp, Raven? I will help gather firewood. I see the humpbacks have left their waste. It will burn hot and long. Night Hunter was good to get us the grassland birds that would rather walk than fly, so we do not need to eat jerked meat this night." He leaned forward and put a hand up to shade his eyes again. "We men must share watching over the camp."

Gentle Wisdom cleared her throat, but he shook his head before she could speak. "We need you to be with the women and babies. I know you will watch over them."

She sat taller, turned, jumped off Brown Dog, and started unloading the packs from the mustangs.

Hawk Soaring called to her. "No lodge this night for the women. An enemy might sneak up on it."

He searched for his grandson and found him still riding as if searching for something. "Shining Light, tie the mustangs' legs tonight. We must be ready if we need to be."

As soon as he said to tie their legs, Thunder trotted off.

Wanderer chuckled from behind. "Leave her be. That mustang knows more than we do." The Great Elder turned to him. "No mice came up to take offered food. They are also smart. All seven hide. We must be watchful this night. I know an old trick we need to use."

He grinned at the Great Holy Man. "I know this trick you speak of. We will make two camps — one here, with bundles under some robes. We keep the fire going, but move far enough away with the mustangs to see, but not be seen." He nodded his approval. "We will need two watching, so we trade all the way through the night. Flying Raven and I will watch first, then Night Hunter and Shining Light second. Smiling Warrior and Wisdom will go last. I feel Falling Rainbow will panic if you do not stay with her, Great Elder."

***

Wanderer relaxed as low whispers, grazing mustangs, and crickets chirping were the only noises in the open space where they all rested. Half their robes were used for the fake camp. They had shared the remaining five to stay hidden.

Flying Raven and Hawk Soaring shared a robe. Wanderer picked up one of the last two robes, leaving Night Hunter, Smiling Warrior and Falling Rainbow with one between them.

Rainbow Stomped over to Wanderer, and Night Hunter let out a low moan.

He grinned as she settled next to him. "So you wish to share my robe, eh? Does this mean you wish to be my woman?"

She poked him in the ribs and pulled until she had more than her share of the robe.

"Ouch! My body is thin. You forget I am but an old man. Perhaps I will take my robe and go sleep alone, further away from the others. You could share Gentle Wisdom and Sparkling Star's robe, but I doubt you would find much comfort with the babies taking the middle. That would leave you with as much robe as you have left me."

She reached for his hand and whispered. "I am sorry, I was not thinking — and you are not a helpless old man. I know better, so do not tease. I am scared. No fire, and no one is even sure if the enemy will show, but if they do...." She evened out the robe. "If my parents saw me in a man's robe, they would drag me out, even if it was to keep safe."

He laid his head on her shoulder. "I love you as a daughter, and I know your parents would approve."

She whispered lower. "I know you see things. Why have you had no warning about all of this?"

"Oh, I have. I even watched as we moved away from our path. I have never been here, but I knew when Fox crossed in front of me, going the opposite way we rode, that we headed the wrong way."

"What? You knew, yet you said nothing?" Her voice, a higher pitch than she meant, drew attention.

Shining Light left his warm place next to Speaks and crawled toward the sounds of their whispering. "I have had no vision of this. Why did you not say something?"

"You were not meant to have a vision. We do not always get warnings. If we did, we may back away, try to avoid what is meant to happen. Our future would maybe change if we could see it. We are no more meant to change the path the Spirits place before us than the waters are meant to switch the way they flow. Do not worry for your family. They will not come to any harm."

"Great Elder, you make bumps raise on my body. Now no sleep will come to me this night. I need a walk. I will return in time for my watch. I wear the tunic and leggings my woman was smart to pack for me. I will be hidden in the dark colors."

Shining Light spoke to his woman through her protesting, then his father and grandfather through their warnings, and finally picked his way past the others with White Paws at his heels.

May Creator watch over you, young Holy Man.

***

Shining Light still had most of Sister Moon to see by, and he kept his ears keen for any sounds. Owl called in the distance. Fingers of chills climbed up his back, and the hairs on his arms and neck stood.

I do not need to hear Owl's warning! Enough has happened already. I need to go back.

He turned to go back, but dizziness overtook him. He dropped to his knees and put his arms out on either side for balance.

White Paws hunched, then moved backward.

Blue sparks flashed before Shining Light's eyes. Closing them made no difference; the color stayed as intense. "Why is this so? Who calls to me? Blue Night Sky? Only you would have such brightness. Your Spirit color blinds me to all else. Are you here? You must be! Blue Night Sky, do not make me fear so. Owl—"

'I know, boy. Owl is here with me, not in your space.' Blue Night Sky reached out to White Paws, and he slipped past the fallen Shining Light to her. She sat, but not on the same ground as he. She hovered above, inside a Circle of rainbow colors. White Paws sat with her, his fur reflecting a deep blue.

"Why—"

'Listen well and you will know why. Still so many words spill from your mouth. Perhaps one day you will sit as Holy Man and listen as others speak, especially those from the Spirit Land.'

She moved so close that he reached out to her, and he gasped when she pulled him in. "I... I feel so warm, loved. Never before have I had such Power move all the way through me. I am one with all there is. I have no fears, no worries, and do not even feel the burden of a body! What is this place? Not even the center of the Circle has done this to me."

'Silly boy, you still ask questions. Feel where you are. You are deep within the Circle of Life, deeper than you will ever feel as long as you have a body. I see you have walked the Spiral. You have opened your mind, expanded your knowledge. There is yet another lesson for you, one of many that will come your way as you live to become a Great Elder yourself. You cannot teach what you have not experienced personally.'

Colors faded and Blue Night Sky vanished.

White Paws lay beside his Human Brother as if neither had ever moved.

"Such peace! Were we really there with her?" He turned and extended his arms around his Wolf Brother. "Are you real, White Paws? I mean, in my space and my people's lives? I feel you, see you, yet somehow you know things before I do, react with a knowing I do not have. You truly are a living Spirit Guide. Not that Spirits are not alive... or... are they?"

He put his face in the wolf's fur and breathed in as one would after a clean rain.

White Paws jumped up and ran a circle around him, then grabbed his tunic and pulled until he rose to his feet.

"What are you doing? Sweet Mother... something has happened in camp."

Chapter 32

Shining Light stumbled over stones in the semi-darkness and raced to the hidden camp with White Paws beside him. In the distance, people shouted and wolves snarled.

The fake campfire is larger than it was!

He gasped when he reached where the women should be. "Speaks! Father! Grandfather!"

"Slow down, Shining Light. We are here—the babies, Rainbow, Sparkling Star and me. We are here, man of mine."

He twirled around as Speaks reached for him and held on. She murmured with relief, "Father Sun soon rises. You have been gone most of the night."

"Where is Grandfather, Father, and the others?" He tried to pull away from his woman.

"The hairy-faces came and attacked our fake camp. Even here, we heard their laughter as they beat on the robes filled with only our packs. Your father crawled to us, told us to be very quiet, and then rushed to join the other men. Gentle Wisdom, torn about what to do, stood until we urged her to go, to be the Warrior Woman she is. I told her we were not helpless." She held up her bow. "Moon Face pushed her wounded pup down when he tried to follow, then she left. He stayed until he heard his pack's fighting, and before I could reach him, he was gone. I thought wolves obeyed their parents as our children do theirs."

"They do, or are supposed to.... I must catch my air." He held onto her shoulder.

He let go his woman and turned toward Falling Rainbow's voice behind him.

"My fault. It is all my fault."

"Listen well, Rainbow. You cannot take blame where there is none. The Spirits brought us out here for their own reasons." His voice shook and he grabbed for Speaks again. "I go now."

He leaned down and squeezed his Brother Wolf's fur. "You stay here and watch over them."

White Paws moaned. "I know your family is there Brother, your little wounded one. I will find Moon Face and send her and the pups back here to you."

"Where do you go, man of mine?" She held him as tight as Fox held his meal, her nails digging into his arms.

He peeled his arms free. "To my Father, Grandfather... the others. I cannot hide and cower as a rabbit fearing a wolf. I am a man. I claim my right to be called warrior. Stay put."

He trotted into the dark, loose stones rolling under his feet. "Spirits, protect my people. Show me and guide me."

Fear rained down on him, but fear would not be what led him. Energy coursed through his blood, and courage grew in place of fear.

He raced into the fake camp with no thoughts for himself, howling as Wolf and racing forward with boot knife in hand.

In the center of the camp, both his grandfather and father fought hand-to-hand with hairy-faces. Night Hunter stood over two unmoving men, while Wanderer stood watching something in the dark, blood trickling down his arm.

Shining Light stood but for a blink of an eye before racing to help his grandfather.

The Elder stood, and blood not his own spattered his tunic. "It is done, Grandson. We must find Smiling Warrior."

He glanced back at his father, who made his way to Wanderer. The fire blazed tall.

Gentle Wisdom stood in the middle, dazed.

"The women!" Shining Light shouted. "Wisdom, go to them and keep them from harm. Hairy-faces may be out there that we have not found. They are without a warrior to guard them and the little ones!"

Wisdom stood, staring at the fallen man before her, with blood on her hands. She gave him a nod and called back, "Go help find Smiling Warrior! I will care for the women. They are not without weapons, and I know your woman knows what she does. You must not worry for them." She ran toward the hidden camp.

"Wisdom, wait! Take Moon Face and her pups back with you. The one pup who limps." He scooped up the pup, even though he was nearly the size of his mother, and ran to her. "Now go. Moon Face will follow you with the rest."

***

Wisdom trotted with the heavy pup and found nowhere to lay the pup on the ground. She frantically searched in the dark for the women and babies. Nothing. "Star! Speaks! Rainbow! Where are you? Come out."

A small fire came to life. Still, she could see nothing.

"Please do not frighten me so!"

On the far side of the clearing, shapes wavered into sight—movement, yet nothing visible.

Her eyes strained to see past the small fire. "Stop this!"

Speaks and Rainbow came out first.

Fox Medicine. Rainbow also? "Talk to me, Fox Medicine people!" She readied her bow, uncertain if the shapes were truly her people or the trick of a bad Spirit.

Sparkling Star's voice floated from the dark shapes. "I am here."

"Ha!" Wisdom dropped her bow. "Star, where are you?"

Sparkling Star emerged from the darkness. "I am safe. I do not yet understand this... Animal Guide protection, but I am sure I will learn. I have had no dreams to show me who guides me."

Wisdom stepped forward, put the pup down, and hugged her. The babies protested and she stepped back. "Your babies, they must have names. It is not good for them to not have them. Spirit, the Great Mystery, needs to know how to call them if something were to happen. Not that anything will happen."

She knew she should not have said what she did.

Sparkling Star's voice shook. "In... in one band I was... was captive in, they did not name their young ones until they had reached a full cycle of seasons. No one told me why this was so! What will become of my babies if they have no names? No one would even *speak* to me unless it was when *they* had something for me to do."

Wisdom, my name is Wisdom, yet I spoke with foolishness! "Your babies are safe." She hugged the shaking Sparkling Star. "No more are you part of any band but our own. When we get back, perhaps even before, I am sure they will have names. I did not mean to speak as I did."

Animal Speaks Woman's worry showed on her face through the glowing firelight. She held a bow. "I found his bow, only too late. Wisdom, my man... did you see him? Is he... safe?"

"When I ran to find all of you, he ran to find Smiling Warrior, who chases after the enemy who got away. We must put this fire out and go back toward the place where we hid. Wanderer is injured."

She heard Falling Rainbow's deep intake of air, and twirled around. "But not so bad, Rainbow, only a small injury on his arm. Stay behind me and take each other's hand." She stomped out the fire and moved forward. "I must go be sure my cousin is safe, so I will leave you there. I have no worry now. Fox Medicine is everywhere this night. As I walk in front, I do not even hear movement behind me."

I must learn to hear my own words before they spill from my mouth! I must earn my name before my Spirit Guide will honor me.

***

Shining Light heard scuffling ahead. He did his best to stay silent, but stepped on a stick. He stopped. The noise ahead continued.

Father Sun, now waking, exposed the two fighting men, and two more lying in the grass.

I must defend my people!

He rushed ahead screaming, knife in hand. Before he could reach the fighting men, the enemy fell... and so did Smiling Warrior. Shining Light scrambled to his friend's side and fell to his knees. Enough light shined across the land that he could see no movement from him. Around the skirmish area, the three enemies made no move either.

Do I scream for help, or are other enemies about? He put his finger on Smiling Warrior's neck, felt for jumping in his neck to show he still lived. *Sweet Mother....*

At first, he whispered, "Creator, Great Mystery, I beg for your help. This man has shown great bravery and has risked his life to save his adopted... his people! His wounds are bad and he bleeds much."

A scream roared from within his heart. "Do not let this man leave us! He has women and many children who need him." He stood and faced Father Sun. "Hear me, Spirits! This man is good. Creator, show me what I can do to heal him."

'You have the Power, Shining Light.'

Fur brushed across his face, and a faded image of White Bear floated in front of him and went through him. Her cub followed.

He reached out but felt nothing. "What is this Power I have? To bring a man back from the Spirit Land that he clings to? More of him is there than here!" He dropped down and put his hands across Smiling Warrior's heart. "Come back, please."

Behind him, Flying Raven stood with Night Hunter beside him. A high-pitched chant sounded behind them, as Wanderer sang and came forward.

Shining Light looked up as Speaks and the other women headed his way. "We must clean his wounds, add fresh moss and mud to draw out the bad Spirits. Speaks, Rainbow, go and find healing plants. I will stay here."

In a Circle, the entire wolf pack sat with noses raised, howling. One pup held up a leg and joined in the howling.

Much Power comes. I... I feel so much Energy. "Wanderer, help me, guide me."

The Great Elder knelt by his side. "We will all help, but you, young Holy Man, will be the one who speaks to his Soul. We will all guide you by song and prayer, but this is a path you alone must follow."

Everyone left to gather needed items, except Night Hunter, who dragged the fallen enemies away, and Wanderer, who had his hands on Shining Light's shoulders as the young Holy Man leaned over the wounded warrior.

"You know what to do. Blue Night Sky taught you much."

"How, Wanderer, do you know of Blue Night Sky?"

"Blue Night Sky was my oldest sister. I was but five winters old when she took a mate and became part of the Red Bear People. We were a moon's walk away when she followed her mate, a trader, to his band. One day, her mate did not return, and my sister decided to become a trader in hopes of finding him. She traveled with her son for several cycles before learning old age had claimed him. She loved him so much that she never took another mate.

"I only saw her once every few cycles of seasons. She settled down when her son found a mate back among the Red Bear People. By then, our band had moved even farther away. I do not mention my band's name because I am the last.

"Yes, boy, I am related to your woman. I will tell her later. It was my sister, from the Spirit Land, who led Falling Rainbow, Night Hunter and me to you."

Night Hunter pushed aside shrubs and stood over the Holy Men. "Mouse Man, you still make me crazy. Now you say your *sister* is related to Animal Speaks Woman, and that Rainbow *and* me—"

Wanderer waved him away. "Go gather firewood. We will speak later. There are things we Holy People have to do this night. Night Hunter, you have proven yourself well. Keep guard for us."

"Maybe I need a mouse. Maybe crazy is not so bad. When I yelled out my cry of battle, I swear I heard mice with their own battle cry." Night Hunter's voice held respect, not his usual banter. "You saved my life. I owe you much. I had no understanding that an elder held so much strength. You ripped the enemy from my back before he could do any harm. I, Night Hunter, call you brother." He nodded to Rainbow, and the pair left together.

Wanderer turned to Shining Light. "Crazy has its ways. Now you see a couple, where only one had held love for the other, together, following and staring with crazy eyes at one another. Had she known her future, Rainbow might never have come with me, and gone back to her Peoples instead. Night Hunter maybe would have had a hairy-face's spear in his back."

Shining Light pinched his brows and tightened his lips.

"Oh, do not look at me so, young Holy Man. Life begins at the start of a Spiral and grows to become part of the Great Circle of Life. This night, you must find the beginning of the Spiral and walk to the center of the Circle. Go deep as my sister took you. Your friend is there, confused. You must help him decide where he will go. His Spirit is only partway in his body, which also means he is partway into the Spirit World."

Chapter 33

Shining Light knew he must find Smiling Warrior, but how?

Wanderer and Flying Raven chanted and sang. Wolves sang. Other voices he recognized sang somewhere. Gentle Wisdom made small cuts in his scarred arms as she, too, sang.

His belly grumbled from the meal they had eaten the night before. *Not the best way to find the center. My belly still has food. Stop thinking. Do as Mouse says to do. See without my eyes. Keep them closed!*

His cluttered mind would not let go. *Grandfather Wolf, I need you! White Bear... Mouse... where are you?*

'*Who dares enter to take a Soul from me?*'

"From you? Who are you?"

'*I am Guardian, Protector of Lost Souls. I will guide this one. You may leave.*'

"I... I cannot. He has a mate and children who need him."

'*So do many who enter here.*'

"Who are you?"

Fawn approached. Blue swirling colors mixed with browns and surrounded her. '*I am me.*'

"Fawn? I do not understand. I thought to meet—"

'*Who, Eagle? Bear? No, Little One, you will talk to me. There are things you must decide.*'

"Decide? I do not understand."

'*Do you have love for your people, Shining Light?*'

"Of course I do."

'*All of your people, even those who are not of your blood? No matter what they did before they came to be part of your band?*'

"Why do you ask this? Of course I love all of my people."

'*Then go get the one you seek, and we shall see.*'

"Wait, how do I find him?"

Wolf howled and Ancient Peoples chanted. The swirls of blue and brown vanished, and before him lay a meadow filled with many flowers. Sister Wind's soft voice moved through them as she sang. Lodges stood in a distant grove of trees. He walked toward them, but they vanished. Only the meadow remained.

Shining Light shook his head, trying to clear the image from his mind. "Tall Smiling Warrior, I have come to take you back. Where are you?"

'*Here, I am here, but where is back? Back.... Oh, yes... now I remember. We sure showed those little red-brown people who were stronger! They feared our hairy-faces, thought we were Spirits in flesh! Heeha! We took their gold, burned down their huts and made them slaves. We took their gold back to the ship and set out to get more. We kept finding more and more, but then we crossed a dry place with sand and very few plants. We lost some of our women and children there. I do not remember how long ago that was. I never had a woman, so I did not have anything to lose.'*

"What is gold? And who are the little red-brown people you speak of?"

'The yellow stone. Hehe, we had to make up a name so they would understand what it was. Learning their words was like trying to understand a dog. You know, the little red-brown people who ran before our mustangs in fear. They called them big elk, big dogs! Can you believe it? They — '

"You killed my Peoples? You burned down their homes? You are evil! Why Deer would take you anywhere...." He lunged out and found nothing but air.

'Who speaks to me?'

"I, Shining Light, speak to you!"

'Shining Light? Oh no... I know you. I feel dizzy, not myself. I am Tall Smiling Warrior! I have three women of the Peoples, and many children! My body... what has happened to it? It feels... as air. Shining Light, I have great fear! What is this place? Where are my women, my family? My Wolf People.... So afraid.'

Both men now faced each other, standing in the same meadow.

Shining Light stood with fists clenched and faced his enemy. "You do not deserve those women or children! You are evil!"

Tall Smiling Warrior reached out both hands as streams of tears raced down his cheeks. *'Sweet Mother! I remember... I am not that... that hairy-faced man anymore. I ran with my women right after I joined the band of the Likes To Fight People.'* He stepped closer. *'Remember? You helped me get my other woman from the enemy hairy-faces. You were so young. You came charging down that hill all smeared in ash! Ha! You saved us all from a battle. You... you saved us. I owe you much, little friend. Your bravery stopped much killing that night.'*

Shining Light stepped back, away from his reaching arms. "Your people killed many of the Red Bear People!"

'Not I. Surely, not I. The hairy faces are many, and we were everywhere.'

"How do you know? You say we are the little red-brown people, as if we have no worth! Get away from me. Perhaps Deer will take you to the campfires in the sky and... and drop you!"

Tall Smiling Warrior put his head down. *'I cannot say I was not there. All your people became as a fog in my mind. I obeyed my leader and did as I was told, as any warrior might. But I am not that man anymore! That man no longer lives. I am of the Wolf People. Please forgive me, Shining Light, for the wrongs I have done to all the Peoples....'* His voice faded and he fell to his knees sobbing. *'Forgive me. Please find a place in your heart that still has kindness, forgiveness. I could not live without your forgiveness.'*

Fawn stepped forward, her round eyes deep pools filled with compassion. *'Forgiveness has great Power — the Power to heal, the Power to help others move on, the Power to help others forgive themselves for the wrongs they did. You can heal another through forgiveness, and help them to find healing that is beyond their reach.'*

"Forgive? You want me to forgive him for all the men, women and children he killed?" He turned around and started to walk away. "To where do I go?"

He twirled around and confronted the warrior whose face had begun to fade. "To tell my people what you have done?"

'*They know, yet they adopted me, accepted me. Why can you not? Your grandmother welcomed me with her arms wide. I am not who I was. People change! Not all of us are bad.*'

"Not all are bad... I remember Blue Night Sky said that. She said those words, and I felt them come from her heart." He looked down at the man on his knees and shaking with sobs.

Fawn whispered, '*He came on this journey to protect you. Are you now willing to accept what is no longer, who he was and is no more... and protect him? Give your life for him as he may have done for you?*'

"Fawn, can you forgive?"

Fawn turned her back to him. '*It is not me who must forgive. I neither judge nor condemn as Humans do.*' She walked through the meadow to nibble on flowers and looked back. Once again, her deep, round eyes drew him in.

He felt the same feeling he had when Blue Night Sky had pulled him into the Spirit land. The same peace-filled Energy entered him and absorbed his heart.

'*I remember Blue Night Sky. She was a kind, gentle woman whose bright smile lit up day brighter than Father Sun. Where am I, Shining Light?*' The warrior stood. '*Where am I? I feel as if I am fading, losing myself. I can no longer see you! Where are you, my friend? I am afraid!*'

Somewhere wolves called to one another, and Sandstone and her two young ones whinnied. The Ancients chanted and Sister Wind carried their voices. All waited.

His throat tightened as he reached for the warrior's fading hand. "Friend, fear no more. We humans have much to learn from the animals. You called me friend, and you are my friend. What was done is over, no more. Take my hand, Smiling Warrior. We go home."

***

Smiling Warrior gasped for air, jumped up and screamed, "Pain, so bad! No, what has happened?" He fell back and his hand smacked his chest. "A stickiness between my fingers? What is this—" He raised it up to his face. "Blood. Am I to never see my family again?"

Night Hunter knelt at his side and held his bloodied hand. "Welcome back, brave Warrior Man."

Shining Light took in air. Speaks held him in her arms, and he cried hard tears.

Smiling Warrior heard him gasp for air. "Is he wounded badly?

Speaks turned to him. "He will be fine, Smiling Warrior. He brought you back from the Spirit Land." She held her man while Dove gurgled next to them on a soft robe.

She leaned next to her man's ear. "Dove... she has the blue glow in her eyes. I am glad you will be here to help her grow."

Smiling Warrior tried to sit up again. "I may be wounded, but my mind is still with me. Speaks, what is this Spirit Land, and how can Dove's eyes be blue?"

Wanderer helped Night Hunter hold him down. "We must care for your wounds."

"But what about Shining Light's wounds? I do not remember what happened to me. I was not here, but in a meadow of flowers. And a sweet little fawn was there. Where is the fawn? Where is this place? Are we home?" He tried to push his way up. "Shining Light!"

Wanderer pushed back and placed a pack under his head. "Shining Light's wounds are not as yours. He does not bleed from wounds of the body. Do not try to understand. We will take care of you. You will heal if you want to. You are safe, and so are your women and children. Drink this plant water. It will help you to sleep and take away the pain."

He took the drink, made faces and tried to push it away. "This tastes worse than swamp water!"

"Bitter as it is, you must drink it." Wanderer held up his head and forced the liquid down his throat.

***

"Are we out of danger? Have we journeyed home? I had a strange dream I wichh tah tell mah fammmily." His words slurred and sleep found him.

Shining Light, too weak to sit, lay down. His breathing returned to normal.

Speaks motioned to Wanderer. "I do not understand what has happened, only that he brought our Smiling Warrior back to us. Where was he, Great Holy Man?" She clenched her man's tunic and tried to not allow tears. "His whole body feels hot!"

Shining Light opened his eyes. "I am fine, woman of mine. Just tired. The journey was long. I had to find my way within the Circle to where the Spirits live. It was a place filled with many emotions. I have learned that some lose their way and the Guardian of Souls must show them the way in. Some fight and refuse, will not accept that their Souls now walk with the Guardian. They find themselves tied to the Mother where they do not belong.

"Some remain on the Mother, forever searching, and not knowing what for. Smiling Warrior was one of these Spirits. He and I talked about things I do not wish to—"

"Sleep." Wanderer ran a gentle hand across the young Holy Man's brow. "There will be much time for you to tell of your journey... if you wish to. Your woman and I will sit beside you. Rest... rest."

***

After Shining Light dropped into a fitful sleep, Animal Speaks Woman turned to Wanderer. "Please tell me what happened." Her eyes were rimmed with tears threatening to spill over.

Wanderer sat back on his heels. "Deep in the center of the Spiral, the Guardian of Souls lives. Smiling Warrior was trapped, unable to let go of the Mother, and so found himself caught in between the land of the Spirits and our land. Your man was able to reach him and guide his Soul back to his body."

He sighed and gazed toward the stand of trees. "Your man has great gifts, special gifts. He will never be the warrior he thinks, but a greater one — the warrior who seeks to heal, guide, and save people from themselves."

He stood and raised his arms. "Great Mystery, Guardian of Spirits, I thank you for bringing this young one back from his journey to save a Spirit who had lost his way. Thank you for showing this young one to the deepest part of the Spiral, where the Circle begins, and to the deepest part of his own Soul. I thank you for bringing this young one back to his people."

He put his arms down and, without another word, Wanderer left.

***

Sleep... sleep. Am so tired. My body feels as if I have run for days.

Shining Light pretended to sleep, so that he could hear Wanderer's words. If not for the Great Elder's help, he too might have been lost. He swore Wanderer's hand had been on the back of his tunic while he sought to go deeper.

Too tired to listen anymore, he drifted into disjointed dreams: huge boats on large expanses of waters, wood lodges, strange-looking mustangs, people with skin and eyes so light they appeared as Spirits.

'Some not so bad, some with hearts hard and black as sharp obsidian.' Grandfather Wolf's eyes became his. *'See the many people who will come this way. Most flee, seek a better life, but a few see only greed. The few lead the many, force their ways onto their own kind. You, Shining Light, must always seek out the Peoples who would follow you into the Land of Trees. One day, your Peoples will return to your lands. Until then, you must keep as many safe as you can.*

'A darkness comes, and with it, emptiness — not just of the land, but of the heart and Soul. Animal Speaks Woman must call the animals to safety. One day they, too, will have no home. Greed for their skins and meat will cause some of them to be no more.'

He shook as Hawk flew down and settled beside him, preening his red tail feathers. *'I, Hawk, am here to give you new Power. Your grandfather will aid in teaching you my ways. He has waited long for this. Listen for my cries and be aware. When you hear me call, open yourself to receive messages that you thought were beyond your abilities. They are not. Honor me, and I will honor you.'*

He sat up fast, felt dizzy and fell back. A fire burned nearby and people sat around it speaking, but his mind had not yet come back. Their words sounded slurred. One came his way and knelt beside him. Blue lit up this person's eyes.

"Rest, Grandson, and allow a true sleep to find you. Hawk flew above me this day and I sought him out. You are full of a Power unknown to our people.

You have much responsibility yet to come into your life. You are as Blue Night Sky and Wanderer together... perhaps more. Rest. We start back soon. Smiling Warrior heals."

"Grandfather, how long have I been here?" He turned his head back and forth, seeking his family and Smiling Warrior.

"A few sunrises. Now sleep, boy." His grandfather went back to the fire.

His woman turned. For the first time in a long while, he saw her eyes glow blue. There was something soft in his hands, and he pulled it to his face—a red tail hawk feather.

From above, Hawk's cries pierced his mind as sleep once again found him.

Chapter 34

For seven sunrises, everyone took turns staying with Smiling Warrior. His face reddened from the heat within. He spent much time mumbling about both lands — lands of the People, and of the hairy-faces.

Shining Light stayed with him more than the others did, with White Paws at his side. The man was his responsibility; he had brought Smiling Warrior back from the Spirit Land.

He sang healing songs and spent time with his arms outstretched toward the sky, asking the Great Mystery to spare his friend's life. Shining Light would sit by his side and speak to him, telling him of the beauty in life he would miss out on. He spoke of his women, his children, and how much love they held for him.

The whole time, he held the feather Hawk had gifted him. It comforted him. How Hawk's feather came from the Spirit Land to be in his hand remained a mystery, one he hoped to know soon.

Do I have more Power, as grandfather said? Why can I not take away what tortures Smiling Warrior? I must be careful not to think I am more worthy than I am. When someone thinks this way, his heart carries beliefs that are not true. He becomes a believer of his own wants and makes others believe in them also. Soon he realizes his wants are lies he made up, but refuses to admit it, and becomes as harmful as bad Spirits. I will never do this! I must be careful. Seek guidance always. My own fight to gain my strength back lasted three sunrises, but Smiling Warrior has fought seven more than me. What can I do?

He held Smiling Warrior's hand and spoke to him as he would anyone awake. "I remember your women well. Mourning Dove was the one we rescued. She is good to look at and has given you three fine sons. And her sisters, your other women, have also given you fine children: two daughters and two sons. You have much to be grateful for in your life. One day, your grandchildren will sit at your feet as you tell them stories of your adventures. Many children will seek you out!" He wiped the sweat from Smiling Warrior's forehead. "You are not so hot today, and you wake long enough to drink the healing plants. Soon the bad Spirits will leave your body."

He reached out and took his other hand. "My grandmother told me that even when there is sickness inside a person, his Spirit listens to what others say. My woman spoke of your bravery, of how you ran into the pretend camp screaming like Bear protecting his territory. Gentle Wisdom also spoke of you, saying that it was a great honor to fight next to one who showed such bravery. I know you have never been on a Vision Quest. I would be honored to be the one who guides you into the other land. I know your Spirit Guide waits for you."

He leaned over to check Smiling Warrior's wounds, one in his leg and one—a deeper one—in his side.

"They look fine. You lost much blood and scared all of us. The moss holds nothing but mud, no more bleeding. You are healing."

"You sure talk a lot for a Holy Man." Smiling Warrior grimaced as he tried to live up to his name, offering a big smile. "I thought they were always silent when they sat next to someone." His voice was raspy, and he groaned. "Water please, my friend."

"You are back! You fought the bad Spirits and won." At the sound of Shining Light's loud words, White Paws jumped up and ran to the wounded man's side. He licked Smiling Warrior's face and wriggled with excitement.

Shining Light stood and tried to pull the wolf back. "I had no idea that White Paws.... Of course! He thinks of you as a member of his pack."

He held up the water bladder for Smiling Warrior to drink, and continued to jabber. "You have slept long. Your body had much healing to do. Still does. I, too, had to rest after going into the Spirit Land. You were much taller there. I am fine now. I—"

Smiling Warrior stopped drinking and pushed the bladder away. "You did what? I was where? You speak crazy words."

He scrunched up his eyebrows. "You do not know, do you?"

"Know what? All I remember is the fighting and being wounded. I fell, and now I wake with you talking my ear off."

"Ear? It is gone? I did this to you?" He pushed aside Smiling Warrior's hair.

The man bellowed and grabbed his side. "Oh, Shining Light, it is... an expression only, meant to say that you have spilled more words than I have ever heard you do before. I have heard that as a boy, you were seldom silent." He settled back down, but his laughter still rang across and beyond the small stand of trees before them.

"Funny! I understand now. You spent too much time with my father these past seasons. Now I know what you two laughed about while sitting at my parent's fire. Many times I came to visit, and there *you* sat!"

He crossed his arms and sat silent for a short span. "I am happy you are awake and have humor with which to tease. Perhaps you need more children to keep you busy. That way you have less time to visit my parents. Perhaps Gentle Wisdom needs a talking to about what stories she, too, has told. She is younger than me, and her mouth holds so many words that she cannot keep them all in. I must take her for a walk and see what she has—"

"What goes on here?" Wanderer stumbled through the shrubs and knelt beside Smiling Warrior, competing for space between a wriggling wolf that he could not move, and a Young Holy Man. "You two go." He pushed the wolf away. "We do not need him opening any wounds! You two pups go and run together. Shining Light, you have too much energy saved up from being here for so long. The Spirits heard you, and now you need to allow me to tend to him."

The Great Elder reached out before he could leave. "You have done well for one so young. You have proven your worth in so many ways. I am proud to call you a Healer, a Holy Man, and a friend. Now, go care for your empty belly. It grumbles as loud as stones bouncing down a larger boulder. Heh, you make enough noise with your belly to scare away my mice!"

"So now you tease! I will have many, *many* stories to tell my children about ears coming off and bellies scaring mice." He started to stomp off, but turned. "Perhaps you, Great Holy Man, need more mice to keep you busy."

He turned and continued to stomp away while laughter followed behind him.

***

Wanderer brought fresh moss and mud to add to the healing plants the women had gathered. "You heal well. By the time Sister Moon is at her brightest again, you will be well enough to travel by mustang."

Smiling Warrior leaned up to protest. "I will heal sooner if I can move around. Have Flying Raven and Night Hunter carry me to the camp. You do not need to keep coming here now that I am able to keep my eyes open. This is not safe, being away from camp." He grimaced at the pull of the old moss from his side wound. "I know my old people well enough to know that if we did not get them all, they will come again. I do not have as much time to heal as you would like me to have, and you know this, too."

"You needed some time before we moved you. Your wounds would have opened up. We moved the camp farther away two sunrises ago. We knew we needed to keep moving. Flying Raven comes with a drag that Shining Light's mustang and mine will pull. We will be in the new camp by the time Father Sun goes to sleep. The ride will be hard on you, but I know you will not complain. You are strong."

"Shining Light? He has stayed with me all this time?"

"We traded caring for you, but yes, he stayed at your side even when another came to take his place."

"I feel bad for teasing him about my ear. Heh... I did not think he would really think my ear fell off."

Wanderer laughed and started to pick up around the place Smiling Warrior had been. "I must admit, I had never heard that either. Now I will have to say it, maybe to Night Hunter!"

"Here, Smiling Warrior, you must drink all of this. I hear the mustangs, which means your drag comes. This will help much with the pain, but you must drink all of it. It tastes bad, maybe worse than swamp water. Do not look at me so! I know you will be happy I gave it to you."

Raven and Shining Light rode around the stand of trees. The younger Holy Man had a hand up to each ear as he rode in. His father tried not to laugh, but his bouncing belly told of his thoughts.

"Drink all of this. Now." Wanderer held up a water bladder and refused to take it from the hairy-faced warrior's mouth until he drained it.

Smiling Warrior's voice began to slur before they had the drag stacked with small branches thick with leaves, and the robe tied over them.

"Whasss the brannnches for?" His eyes drifted closed.

"Softness."

***

Smiling Warrior did not stir but once the whole distance, and that was only to ask Wanderer for more of the ill-tasting liquid.

In their new camp, he woke to Wanderer forcing more drink down his throat.

The camp had a small stream teeming with fish, and many trees that offered shade. Food would not be a problem, and no one would have to leave to hunt. Smiling Warrior could heal in the cool shade of trees in full leaf.

Shining Light sat next to Flying Raven on a robe as Father Sun slipped down, leaving yellow rays shooting back toward clouds.

"Father, how lost are we? I tried to find out by looking up at the campfire in the sky, but clouds keep me from seeing."

Raven looked up in the darkening sky. "For seven nights I have tried to find out. I think we may not have followed the right way for some time. I know we are farther than a half-moon away from camp. We never moved that far into the grasslands before we found Sparkling Star, but we have moved several sunrises since then. This worries me, Son. The hairy-faces may be close to our home."

"Father, I know the Ancients did not lead us to the Land of Tall Trees to have us in danger. I truly believe they cannot follow us into our home. It will be as an invisible web to them. In one of my first dream visions, I saw a web across the land. I forgot about it until you spoke. The web was darker than Spider would have been able to do herself. I remember going up to it, and my hand went through it, and not a single piece stuck. Yet another hand pushed and pushed without being able to get through — I did not see the person, only the hand. Spider came down from her web and chased the hand away when it pushed a third time. I do not think we need to worry."

He hesitated and cleared his throat before picking up a stone and playing with it. "It is not over yet."

Flying Raven flinched and wrinkled his brow. "What is this you say? What do you mean, it is not over yet?"

He turned away from his father and tossed the stone, watching as it disappeared in the grass. He lowered his head and played with the lines in his palm. "Some people, not the hairy-faces this time, follow. I must wonder about the band Smiling Warrior escaped from with his women — the Likes To Fight People. Sparkling Star never spoke of the people her... the person who claimed her as a slave... came from. I think it is his band. Only an important man would have come in search of her, to see if she has a son. She never said she belonged to someone important."

Raven's deep intake of air and tightened jaw showed more than worry. "Why did you wait so long to speak of this?"

"I was with Smiling Warrior when a vision came to me. This was not a dream. I heard Grandmother's voice and thought it was because I wished to be home. Out of the edge of my eye, I saw her standing with arms reaching towards me, but I turned and saw nothing. Soon Sister Wind whispered in my ear." He leaned close and spoke low. "It was Grandmother's voice. She said, 'Never think a campfire's sparkle is by itself. Always another is nearby.' Mustangs walked in my vision, with a rider leaning down and looking at something on the ground. He pointed to another man, then toward our old camp. He dressed as the Likes To Fight People, but had much decoration on himself and his mustang. His mustang had circles painted around the eyes, and several red handprints on the rump. He led another, but without any rider, only a small pack."

He stared off toward the old camp. "We must stay close to each other. Smiling Warrior cannot yet travel, and Sparkling Star is in danger. Her babies are in danger. If this man who hunts her sees she has a shadow child, he may do great harm to all three. He maybe hunts us as well."

He picked up another stone to toss, but stopped and turned it in his hand. "We must decide what direction to follow, and who will take Smiling Warrior. Perhaps we can move him a little each day, have someone lead a false trail, and have another cover up the real trail. I ask much for so few people. We are but five healthy men... and one warrior woman."

Raven sat staring off in silence, his eyebrows curled high in thought. "I am not so sure of allowing one man to make a false trail alone. If he found himself captured, it could mean his life. Call to everyone to join so we may speak of this. We must decide who will take Smiling Warrior, and which direction to follow. That person, and Smiling Warrior, will be the ones who face the most danger."

Chapter 35

"We will not separate!" Animal Speaks Woman stood with clenched fists on her hips. "It is only two, maybe three men we speak of, not a whole band! You silly men think you have answers to everything. We have three babies to think of!" She waved her arms in a wide circle. "We have a large pack of wolves who follow us, and my dog, who does have more sense than you think he has. He has been around wolves since he was only half-grown. We are stronger together than alone. I have spoken *my* words." She walked away rather than sit back in the circle of people.

Shining Light ran after her. "Speaks! Look around you!" He waved his own arms in a circle. "We are in open grasslands. The only trees follow the river, and we needed to move away from it. For the first time in many sunsets, the campfires in the sky do not hide behind thick clouds. Father pointed out that we go the wrong way and are at least five sunrises from where we need to be." He stood in front of her with arms crossed, his face tightened in frustration as he ground his teeth.

"Light, man of mine, listen to the women! We will not separate. And do not think you will go off by yourself!" She handed him their daughter, and the backboard she had made from wood and woven swamp plant root. "Maybe you will wear this for a while. Maybe several sunrises, and only give her to me when she is hungry. I am not so blind that I cannot see you thinking of sneaking off. Put it on."

"I am a man! The *man* is the one who... who—"

"Should make the choices for all of us? Ha! Not in *our* band!" She started to walk off, but turned with her finger wagging. "And as for that wolf of yours, you and he will not go hunting by yourselves. As Wisdom would say, you have been bested!" She stomped off.

Chuckling behind the bested man made him twirl around, ready to argue with anyone courageous enough to come at him again. Wisdom grinned and skipped away before his mouth could spill any words.

***

Shining Light sat tall as he bounced on Sandstone, and stayed ahead of everyone. He refused to give anyone a chance to tease him, and tried to ignore the laughter behind him. It had been two sunrises since they had argued about the board, yet the chuckling still lingered.

I am grateful the board did not fit! He glanced down at White Paws, who stared back up with his own wolf grin.

"I am going to hear about this even when we have more children! My mother and grandmother will tell stories of how a man was bested. They will brag so much that my ears will fall off from the pain of everyone's laughs!"

He tapped Sandstone into a trot. Her young one, Dark Storm, passed his mother and trotted toward Night Hunter's mustang's young one, and the pair raced away.

***

Over the next few sunrises, the journey remained uneventful and everyone relaxed. The wide open, beautiful green land lay under expanses of wondrous white, yellow, and red-orange flowers. An occasional pink and purple bloom made an appearance, catching Falling Rainbow's interest. Many shrubs hung heavy with ripening berries. Trees followed the snaking river, as did the band. The soft blue sky shared its spaciousness with clouds and occasional short rains. The humpback herds were thick, and the beasts did little to run away from the traveling people.

They took time to let Smiling Warrior walk about the camp and build up strength while they hunted.

With a successful hunt, the women took time to scrape hides and relax under the shade, while the men boasted of the hunt.

"It was *my* arrow that took the biggest one down. One arrow!"

Hawk Soaring's voice carried to Falling Rainbow, who chuckled at his boasting. She had spent the last few sunrises painting the beauty before her. Night Hunter had found a log for her to sit on, and she discovered that the mustangs' tails made for good brushes — better than chewed twigs.

Night Hunter poked holes every few finger widths through a new hide, and tied it between two trees with sinews. He pulled the sinew tight around the small trunks to stretch the hide for ease of painting.

She had grown used to him being there for her. "Not so tight. The paint will wrinkle and chip off. I learned this once before, and had to scrape off the paint and try to remember what was there. It was of the canyons. My mind held the memory, and I did paint it again, but I can only hope it shows what I wanted it to."

He leaned on one of the trees, holding the hide in place. "You paint with skill. I see a plant dropping flowers to make fruit. You see different colors of leaves and paint flowers in bloom. You even show the difference in greens between the leaves and forming fruit. You show the fruit as it turns colors. I only now see these things. If not for your paintings, I would have paid no heed." He leaned closer to the hide. "A little red-orange winged one?" He stepped closer to the shrub. "Ah, I see now. There are black spots on them also."

Her soft laughter brought him back to her side, and he brushed his arm against her shoulder where her dress hung down. "Even with my arm, I feel the softness of your skin. It is as your voice. I can feel it teasing my ears like soft nibbles from my mustang's rabbit soft mouth."

"Silly words come from your mouth." She stilled the brush mid-stroke. "My mind is confused with you in it. You make me unsure of my emotions. I do not like that. I need to be in control of my — "

Gentle hands turned her. Her heart raced like a herd of wild mustangs tearing across the land. She looked away, but he turned her chin back. For the first time, she stared into his eyes and explored them. Her breasts heaved with each breath. "Oh my, but you are good to look at. Never before have I seen your eyes so bright. When you smile, your cheek bones rise up, and I see such strength and pride in your face." She bit her bottom lip and allowed her eyes to follow his muscular chest.

He knelt beside her. "You are better to look at than your paintings, and they are done with great skill — a skill I have never seen before now." He ran a hand through her hair. "No matter what part of you I touch, I quiver with a joy I have never known."

He held both her shoulders and brought his face to her hair. "Such a sweet smell. No flower could ever compete with your smell and beauty." His intake of air sounded strong with much emotion.

She responded with her own deep breath.

"Woman, I feel a need for you as great as Eagle feels for the sky. In you I feel free to be who I am." He bowed his head. "I, Night Hunter, wish to take you as my mate. If your father stood before me, I would offer all I had as a gift." He looked up again.

She closed her eyes, leaned her head back, and drew in an even deeper breath. "I... I... my heart is so confused." She dropped her brush. "When I am near you, my throat tightens, I become unsure of my emotions, and my knees weaken. I want to run. Is this love?"

"Each must decide for themselves what love is. To me, *you* are love. Rainbow, my mind overflows with thoughts of you. I cannot use my mind to think of anything else but having you, holding you in my arms, to touch you in gentle ways I only dream of doing. Say you will be my mate, that you want only me as your true heart love... as I do you.

"Tears? Do you have sorrow instead of love, pity for me instead of a need to have me? Do not look away. You will tear my Soul apart with such pain if you say no. I would rather cut off my arms if they were not to know yours around me. My heart is as fragile as Butterfly's wings right now. You could rip it apart with just a word."

She wiped her face dry with the back of her hand.

He reached out, took her wet hand, and dried it across his chest. "Let those be the last tears that fall from your face in confusion. I will walk away and not look your way again." He stood to leave.

"Night Hunter, do not go, please. My heart feels you inside it. You have walked in my Soul. I can no more pretend that you do not exist than I can hide from the feelings within myself." She stood and took his hands. "I, Falling Rainbow, wish to have you as my mate for always. May we sit together at a campfire in the sky when our lives are done here."

They giggled like children and pushed at each other's shoulders, as they sought out Wanderer so he could tie their hands together and do the binding ceremony.

***

Wanderer stood before the couple with a smile so wide his cheekbones hurt. "I knew this was going to happen long ago, before you two even met. My heart spills over with joy. This is a simple ceremony, as we are only a few people, but know this does not mean your lives will be any different than if you stood in the middle of a huge camp of our people."

He drew in the pair before him. They both wore robes Rainbow had painted. The colors of the canyons on Night Hunter's made him sigh. He knew he might never again see those canyons. Rainbow's came alive with the grassland's beauty, with grass and flowers that actually looked as if Sister Wind danced through them.

"The life before you will hold many times of joy. Remember that days not so filled with joy will be there also. It is these days I wish to speak of to you. Many couples do not always agree on what their mate wants. This is the way of life. If you weather the storms in life, you will always find that the clouds of anger, disappointment and sadness pass and show brighter times. It would be easy to walk away from your mate and find another, but I am here to tell you that things have a way of repeating themselves, even if you choose a new mate and think it will not be the same.

"Love that is strong will bind you, as does the rope that ties you together for this ceremony. Think of the rope. It will come apart. Nothing is ever as good as it is when new. Let me tell you that once the new is gone, things will change. It is up to the two of you to remember this as it changes: love will grow only if you are willing to face the bad as well as the good. The longer you are together, the more you will learn about each other. Things will be different as the seasons pass. This has always been so. You both must be willing to talk. Always talk over what has brought you to these changes in your lives, as if you are the most favored of friends. Work out your differences, and the days ahead will look brighter, be brighter.

"Never storm off in anger, or there will be a time you may not be able to mend your words. Your heart will fall and break on the sharpness of spoken words that you really did not mean to say. If you must walk away, do it in silence, so when you come back, you will not have stinging words that you must find a way to soothe. Love is the strongest of emotions. May it always be so for you."

The couple moved their bodies closer, and Wanderer felt a bit of sadness. Rainbow would move away from him, as any child would, but he had such a special bond with her that he hoped he would somehow always be part of her life.

"As I cut the rope that binds you together, never forget this day. Keep this rope with you always. If one day you find yourselves wondering what bound you together, pull it out and talk while holding it, and you will once again remember." He reached out and cut the rope.

Night Hunter caught it before it touched the ground and smiled at his woman.

"Go now, become one with each other—for always and forever. I have finished the binding ceremony." He turned and stood before the small gathering. "They are now mates."

His thoughts reflected both joy and sadness, but the sadness was for his loss of Rainbow, not the newly mated pair. For them, he felt great joy. He had finally completed the binding he dreamed of so many seasons ago.

Smiling Warrior sat on his drag, clapped his hands and shouted, "Joy always to the new couple!" His new companion, who he named Dark Moon, raised his muzzle and howled. "I think it is time I stand like a man, ride my mustang."

Chapter 36

Smiling Warrior would not listen to anyone about his side wound. The skin had mended but for one small place. Wanderer had to redress his wound twice before Father Sun had reached the top of the sky, but he insisted he was fine.

Shining Light and Wanderer rode beside him.

"I am grateful for your help. Without it my life would have ended. A man must be ready for things that might come his way. I may not know what happened, but I was somewhere—not here, not on this land. I feel a special... I do not know the words. My mind is quicker, and senses danger that it never could before—as if my Spirit somehow changed. There is a little fawn beside me, yet as I turn my head... no fawn. When we get home, I ask that you both teach me about this Vision Quest. I am changed and wish to know why. Power I have never known before is now part of me."

Wanderer raised a brow and licked his lips. "When one enters the Spirit Land, they are forever changed. Some are quiet, maybe afraid. Others feel as you do, and need to know why. I know you dream stronger. I see you moving more in your sleep. I did not know you were aware you had slipped into the Spirit Land."

"I was not either. I keep having dreams of Shining Light reaching for me." He turned to the young Holy Man. "I am grateful you brought me back, and will always be at your side, wherever you go, as a friend and brother."

Shining Light half smiled and rubbed his nose with his fingers. "Thank you, my Spirit Brother."

Smiling Warrior tried to twist around to make sure that Dark Moon was still on the drag. "Can you see my pup?"

"He must care for you to stay on that drag instead of trying to follow his pack." Wanderer grinned at the sleeping pup.

"Heh, I took the plant medicine you gave to me, soaked some jerked meat in a small amount, and he ate it. I only sip on the rest if I need it."

Shining Light frowned. "You should be on that drag. I know you plan something. I can sense it."

Wanderer cleared his throat to gain attention. "I, too, know you are trying to be sneaky. You are between two Holy Men, and Flying Raven watches you. You are not so smart if you think you can hide something from such Power that surrounds you." He shook his finger at him. "Shame goes to you for giving that pup medicine you should have drunk. I do not want you to torture yourself like this."

Smiling Warrior stared out across the grasslands at the humpbacks grazing. "These lands are rich with animals, which many people hunt. We do not need to appear weak. One man on a drag might be enough to attract attention we do not need. With all of us riding, hunters or others will approach with more respect, even the Likes To Fight People."

He stopped his mustang. "A good idea, since we are not sure who follows, would be to have Sparkling Star give a baby to each Wisdom and Rainbow. If the man who seeks her is following us, he will see only Sparkling Star and no babies."

He watched her try to nurse both her sons while riding. "She grows stronger with every sunrise, and no longer has to give one of her babies to your woman to feed. If the man who hunts her sees her without any baby, he will ask where the child is. I will come forward and demand to know who asks after my woman. He may laugh, say she is a slave and not worth the fight, then leave once he thinks the baby did not live."

"And if he does not?" Shining Light twisted around on his mustang and glanced behind.

Smiling Warrior stopped his mustang. "If he comes, let me make words with him. I am going up to speak to her about the babies. We need to start now. When they cry, all the women will sit together as they would to feed their own. It will make it look like we only stop to let the mustangs rest, and they use that time to sit and care for their babies. I know it is custom to allow everyone their say. This would be a good time to stop, talk this over, and let the mustangs graze."

***

"Star, do you understand much about this man who owned you?" Hawk Soaring sat with everyone as they rested under trees and allowed the mustangs to eat. The two young ones ran circles around the adult mustangs. "Sparkling Star, look at me. Do not fear. We will not let anyone take them from you. I, Hawk Soaring, will protect them with my life."

Everyone, including the women, told her the same words. She clung to her babies as if Eagle might snatch them from her arms. "I have never before known such a band, but I cannot allow you do such a thing. I... I will leave my sons and go with him before I see anyone's blood shed."

Hawk Soaring sat closer to her in their Counsel Circle. "I am a father and grandfather. My grandson has given me the chance to be a twice grandfather. I know how much they mean to me, young mother. I would go to the campfires in the sky to keep them safe." He reached out to her. "Hand me one of your sons."

She let go of the one closest to him. "He is the one I call Quiet One. Until they have names, I wanted to be sure Creator knew them in case... in case."

"He is a fine boy! Fat, and I can see he is content. I hold a child of the soon-to-be Wolf People." He held him high and everyone nodded. "He and his brother are now part of our traveling band. I say this is so! Aho!" He ran smoke from Sacred Sage over the boy and handed Quiet One back. "Now, hand me your other son."

She smiled this time. "He is called Listens To Night. He lies awake at night, and I see his eyes brighten as he hears night noises."

"Listens To Night, I claim you as part of our band here, and will stand and announce you and your brother's names as soon as we are home, or the new names I feel are possible. You will soon be part of the Wolf People! I say this is so! Aho!" Again, he ran Sacred Sage over the boy, and handed her second son back.

"Woman soon to be of the Wolf People, I cannot claim you as my niece. That would mean Gentle Wisdom would be your cousin. But I bet another here will claim you as a relation." He stared at Smiling Warrior.

The man cleared his throat and stood. "I, Smiling Warrior, man of the Wolf People, claim you as my daughter." He chuckled and stared at Wisdom. "What do you offer me for my daughter?"

The tension broke and Sparkling Star passed her two sons, Quiet One and Listens To Night, around the Circle so everyone could hug them and call them Wolf People babies.

Hawk Soaring raised his hands for silence. "In a Counsel, we would normally have a talking stick. Whoever holds the stick is the only one allowed to speak. We are not at a real Counsel, but this is just as important, as it includes everyone here. I ask, Star, that you tell us what kind of man he is, because he may be following us. We must be prepared if he does find us."

***

She squeezed her sons and looked into the eyes of everyone. "I hope it is so that Smiling Warrior claims me as Daughter, but I will tell you of this man first."

Smiling Warrior nodded her way. "I belonged to a man who calls himself Stalking Moon. He is leader of the Warrior Clan. He has tried for a son for many seasons and has had only daughters, nine in all. He trades for slaves who have never had a child to make certain they are pure. His two mates are to watch over his slaves to be sure no other man goes near them."

Her eyes welled and tears threatened to push their way down her face. She squeezed her eyes shut to stop them. "He gives away his slaves who have girl babies, and all have. He... he gives them to his men. When he saw my belly grow, he made sure his wives watched me very close. I am sure he was not pleased that I had run away, and his mates may have suffered for this. Their Healer told him he had a dream I was maybe carrying a son. He told him he could not be sure because he had two dreams of two babies. One had his back to him. It was then Stalking Moon told me if I carried a shadow baby and harmed his son, he would kill me.

"I told all of you it was because he wanted to kill me if I had a girl baby. I was terrified for you to know I might carry two. He said I was bad medicine, and even if I had only one son, he would give him to one of his mates, maybe kill me anyway."

For the first time since Smiling Warrior had found her, Sparkling Star felt great fear. "Do you still want me as your daughter?"

Smiling Warrior was not one to show emotions, but his chin quivered. "I claimed you as my daughter. Because a son or daughter has problems, does not mean you throw them away. They are yours forever, through bad and through good. You do not toss a child away when they do something bad. You love them more, be there for them, die for them, if need be. You did nothing bad, Daughter. Bad was done to you. None of this is your fault. I, your father, will stand up to this bad man. He will never do this to another woman."

He cleared his throat. "I think I know this man, maybe too well. I once lived among the Likes To Fight people. One of my women belonged to him. She took herbs to prevent giving birth while he had her, so he traded her away. She was too strong for him. We rescued her from the hairy-faces. He had no idea she was the daughter of a Holy Woman. You will get to meet her and all of my other children. I will have more reasons to visit! I am sure Wisdom wishes to stay near Shining Light."

***

"Ha! I am smart. Sometimes too smart. This day, for the first time in my life, I cut away my face hair. Stalking Moon will not remember me now."

Smiling Warrior's wolf pup growled and backed away. His bellowing laughter brought the pup closer to inspect the strange man with no face hair. Tiny steps—one after the other—and the tempting smell of fresh cooked fish the man held, had Dark Moon following his nose one paw at a time. Everyone behind the pair tried to be quiet so the pup would not run, but laughter escaped from hands covering faces, and the pup ran to Shining Light.

"Pup, Dark Moon, you now have a new pack member and must greet him." He chuckled, then roared with laughter. "You maybe could go make water on the same tree! I know he looks... Oh Sweet Mother! Smiling Warrior, I never knew you had so much face!"

The confused pup darted for the man who appeared to be a stranger. White Paws beat him to the fish, lunged for it, and raced off. The pup chased after him. White Paws did not take it to eat, but rather to tease his young pup. Within a flash, he stood in front of Smiling Warrior.

Dark Moon no longer focused on the strange man, but begged White Paws for the fish. A hand reached out for him and the pup sniffed it. Dark Moon became excited and jumped up on Smiling Warrior, who kneeled so his pup could sniff him all over.

"I still think making water on the same tree would be a good idea!" Shining Light ducked his woman's hand as it brushed the top of his head.

Chapter 37

Falling Rainbow came from behind the laughing pair. "I have thought of something no one else has. The babies have red in their hair as their mother." She held out her wrap where she kept her paints, rolled it open, and begun mixing water to the dried powder in a small red clay bowl. "Star, hand Wisdom one of your babies."

She positioned herself so she could spread the paint through the baby's hair, working it in to the roots, then leaned back, motioning to Wisdom to turn the baby around for everyone to see.

"See? No more red hair!" Rainbow grinned at the now blue-haired baby. "The paint will dry black, and no one will see any red hints in their hair."

Wisdom exchanged babies with Star, and Rainbow painted the second one's hair with the same care.

Sparkling Star's expression made Rainbow laugh. She was not so sure about her babies' new hair color. She stared at their paint-speckled shoulders. "This will come off?"

"Well, um, I have never painted anyone's hair before. But they will look good in the baskets. Only their faces and part of their hair will show." She glanced around at all the smiling faces that nodded in agreement.

She reached toward Sparkling Star's hair, and the mother jumped out of the way. "Stalking Moon will know my face and... and if my hair is black, he will know I hide something. Better to allow yourself and Wisdom to carry my babies, you think? Perhaps I should gather wood so we can eat our late night meal. The Likes To Fight People always make a camp when Father Sun is low."

Shining Light trotted to catch up to her. "Not a good idea for you to walk alone." He leaned closer. "She meant well, Star, and they no longer have the red color. Besides, he will not get close enough to see them."

She turned to him and laughed. "It is all right! I am grateful for everyone so willing to help." She cleared her throat. "I only hope the paint comes off!" She bit her lower lip and raised her brows.

Wisdom ran up to them, her bow in hand. "Cousin, I will hunt, maybe get a few ground birds."

"Good idea. This way Star and I can talk while you hunt. I know you are eager to run ahead and do this." He nodded his head toward the thicker grass. "I promise I will stay close to her."

Wisdom dropped her bow. "Your dreams, Light—I can see that faraway look you get that you do not think I can see. I will go ahead." She nodded to Star. "Tell him what you have told me."

Sparkling Star slowed. "Perhaps the others should hear what I tell you, Shining Light?"

She stopped and sat on a log, where a small hill hid them from the camp, and tossed stones in a small pool. A low-running stream trickled toward it, and tiny fish darted close to the water's edge and hid in the taller grass. Her attention was on the shapes of orange and yellow clouds Father Sky painted.

"This land is so beautiful. Green grasses, and blooming yellow and white flowers are as in a race to where the sky ends." She picked up a small yellow stone and handed it to him. "Once in a while I see these. They are so small no one else sees them."

"The yellow stone! The ones the hairy-faces seek. How many have you seen since our travels together?" He tossed the tiny stone in his hand. "I have a larger one that I wear on my neck. A Great Elder gave it to me when I was a boy and warned me to pass it around to others, and to always beware for more. She told me to pick them up, hide them, but I never saw any."

"The stones gather in the corners of streams, as do the fish. I watched the hairy-faces dig up and destroy a small river after they found a handful. The water was so muddied no one could drink it, and I watched as fish floated by. I think it was because fish need water to breath as we need air. I have only found a few of these stones." She took out a pouch she hid around her neck and opened it. "Hold out your hand."

She poured six pieces no bigger than her small fingernail out of the pouch. "I have held these since we left the land of sunrises. This one is the only one I have found in a cycle of seasons."

He reached along the curve in the water when she pointed to it, and pulled out sand. The tiny fish scattered from the disturbance. He held up the sand and allowed it to fall back in the water. "All I see are the tiny sparkles I have always seen in the waters. No yellow stone."

"They are few here. I do know heavy rains push them down the fast moving rivers." She grabbed his hand. "Never speak of this to anyone, not even to your own people."

She stood and led him toward thick grass at the edge of curve in the stream. "This stream is small now, but if you look at the dry sand we stand upon, and how far it reaches past this little stream, you know the waters are larger after snow melts."

She squatted, scooped up a handful of sand, poured water over it and let it run into her other hand. Tiny bright sparks of yellow settled in the creases of her fingers. "Not much, but enough to attract the hairy-faces."

"Star, the pieces are so small they fell through your fingers. To me, they look like the rest of the sparkles. I did not know where to find it until you showed me, but why? Why do they kill for it? There are much more sky beads than this. You must know the story of how Water gave Sky some of its color? Sky felt so heavy that pieces fell and landed in the stones, but the stone was hot and sunk into the bigger stones?"

"No, I did not know that. Slaves were never allowed to hear the stories, never allowed to hear anything that we might tell other bands. So that is where those beautiful beads you wear come from."

He took them off and put the necklace over her head. He hesitated when he saw the red scar around her throat, but looked up in her face. "Now you have something as beautiful as you are."

Her cheeks colored pink. "These are so much nicer to look at than the yellow stone." She took the small yellow stones, placed them in the pouch, and handed it back to him. "For you. I know it is not much to give after such a wonderful gift as you have given me, but perhaps they will be enough."

"They are more than enough. I will keep them hidden and only show my family. All of my people know the story of the yellow stone. They have only seen the one piece the Great Holy Woman had given me when I was young. I am happy they did not find much. You were with them as they hunted the stone?"

She ran her hand across the quilled yellow Spiral that chased around in a circle on her short tunic dress. "Your woman is very skilled. I see she paints well also." She nodded toward his tunic where she had painted White Paws and Moon face. "Perhaps when we get... get home... what a good word... home. I have never been able to call a place home. Perhaps I, too, will learn these skills."

She raised her head and a tear threatened to spill down her cheek. "Yes, I was with them as they dug and tore into our Mother. If trees could scream, they did when they fell from the sides of hills. I saw no respect for anything from these monsters. They fought among themselves and even killed one another over the yellow stone they called gold. Even if only one man found some, he had to be on guard, or they would do whatever they could to steal it. I have never seen anything but this kind of life. Then I saw you, your people caring for one another, giving things like the sky beads you offered to me, and always making sure everyone has the same amount of food. And not one person is treated better than anyone else. No one takes anything from another before asking. Even among your people, warriors get first choice on meat because they are the ones who hunt, but I also watch each man share that favored piece willingly with his mate."

She tossed her head back and laughed. "You always give White Paws and his mate a big piece of the heart and liver."

He chuckled. "They help with the hunt. All the wolves do, so we share equally with them. Many times I have watched ravens help by leading the wolves to where animals graze. We also leave them food and thank them for their help.

"Gold. I now know this word." He scanned the land around them. "I wish to ask you about the land of sunrises you come from, about the people you saw. Tell me what color their eyes were, their skin and hair. How did they get there?"

"I only remember the big boats on the salty waters as a child. I do not know why my mother and I were even on one. I was so young. All I can tell you is I have seen men with hair the color of dry grass, their eyes the same color as mine. I saw a man with eyes the color of sky, and skin so pale that Father Sun made it burn and blister. I once saw a woman who stayed hidden under a... cover on her head and—" She drew it in the sand by the stream. "Like that, with her face hidden. I never did see her eyes or even her skin, only her dry, grass-colored hair."

She shook her head and shrugged. "That is all I can tell you. This was a long time ago. None of those people even looked my way. I am sorry I cannot tell you more."

"I will know more, Star. I trust the Spirits to show me more when I need it. I am deeply honored to have you as part of our Peoples. Your Soul is a gentle one, full of good. What you have learned as a slave you can teach others. They will listen to your words and pass them on so many people will learn how *not* to treat others. You must tell these stories, even if people do not believe you. I was once a boy standing in front of many people. Some believed and followed my band. Others laughed and waved their hands at me, as if to say, 'go away.' Falling Rainbow's people did not believe her. Now she comes to prove the land of Tall Trees is real. She may be going back with her painting as proof.

"We may not understand why things happen to us, and may want to shout at the Spirits, or be angry with others, but as we grow, we learn everything that comes our way is meant to happen. We cannot teach what we do not know. Someone told me this long ago. It makes me wonder what lessons await me—await us all. From the beginning of the Spiral, with our first breath, we start to learn and we never stop, not even as we draw our last breath. We enter the Spirit Land and learn more. Learning is a never-ending Circle, and when we leave our bodies behind, it is only a thin hide that remains."

He looked at her attentive, bright eyes. "I guess I do maybe talk more than others ask of me."

"To me, your words are as raindrops upon the thirsty ground. I have much to learn and I will, because of people like you, Light." She smiled and looked deep into his eyes. "Blue? Why do I see a blue color coming from your dark eyes? I saw it in your family's eyes as well. I think the only one I did not see it in was Night Hunter's."

He reached out and she did not pull away, so he rubbed her shoulder. "You see blue because *you are* special, and soon you will learn why. I am glad the other people could not see how special you are. I saw blue in your eyes, but said nothing. I feared frightening you. Not everyone has the blue, but they are not any less special. Everyone has reason for being. Everyone. We may not see it, or understand, but it is true. Good will come with the bad. I have been told this and have seen it. When we are born and grow, we do what we see. As we age, we see what is truly right and not. Our choices will affect everyone, even those we never meet."

Animal Speaks came and sat before them on the grass, lifting Dove from her cradleboard and letting her wiggle and roll over. "Soon, man of mine, she will roll over and make her way to her father. She has a wise man to learn from. I did not want to interrupt, but your daughter is heavy in my arms. Star, I saw your blue eyes, but like my man, worried too much would make you want to run from us."

Shining Light leaned down from the log to pick up his daughter, and waved her in the air with his hands, watching her big smile. "My daughter is as beautiful as her mother. Perhaps one day, Sparkling Star will have a son who will come to speak for her."

Star stared at Speaks first, then Light. "You would not worry about her choosing a mate who carries the blood of a hairy-face?"

Twigs crunched behind Sparkling Star. "Hey, daughter of mine, I, Smiling Warrior, feel no shame. You do not need to either. We are good people, you and I."

Speaks scooped up Dove and stood to leave. "You and I, father of Sparkling Star, need to leave and allow these two to talk. My man has more words than anyone I know." She chuckled and ran her hand over the top of his hair. "He will spill as many words as there are drops in the waters he sits next to."

She handed Dove to Smiling Warrior, and he swung her above his head and made gurgling noises. The child giggled as she reached for his nose.

Speaks' waved a hand. "I was on my way to look for greens before they get too old to taste good. Perhaps you would like to follow, keep me company? My man talks to Star, while Wisdom and Rainbow talk of babies and mates." She shook her head and grinned. "After seeing Rainbow's face change colors, I thought to take a good walk. Come, carry Dove and walk with me. She loves to ride on your shoulders. We will not go far, as I know you and my man were left to watch over the camp."

Smiling Warrior cooed at Dove and grinned. His wolf pup pawed his leg to see what he held. He lowered the child for the wolf to see. Satisfied, the pup trotted in between them.

"I see your pup no longer limps and stays near you as White Paws does Shining Light. You have healed much faster than I expected, and I think it is because of your wolf." She leaned to scratch the pup's head. "Have you ever heard about a Spirit who comes to be at your side who lives in a body? I think your wolf is one of these." She stopped, spoke soft words to the wolf, and he licked her hand and offered his paw, and wriggled his body when she took it. "He is much like his father! His Energy is strong. I feel tingly. I have pet each one, played with them also, but Dark Moon has... feels so different." She looked up at Smiling Warrior. "Much Strength and Power comes from this one."

Sparkling Star's gaze followed the two as they left hearing distance. "Your woman is so good to me, and shows no anger that I sit with you... and Smiling Warrior walks beside her, not her following him!"

He leaned his head back and laughed. "She is a woman others follow without question. We love each other deep in our hearts. She knows I do not wish for another. Ha! And to think I ran from my woman when we first met. Now my life would have no meaning without her."

She appeared more relaxed and at peace.

He smiled. "You have love in your heart. I not only feel it, but also see it. I am happy you have found such a wonderful thing as love."

"I have seen no anger, no jealously here. Nothing but trust. I am truly honored to be here with you and your band."

He leaned towards her slightly, not wanting to frighten her. "I have something to pass onto you. It is about the Mother we live on. She is more than dirt, stones and a place for water to flow. She is a Healer—Healer of the body, mind and Soul. The elders like to walk barefoot to feel her Energy, her love. In her is the strength to cleanse your mind. Many times, when I go off by myself, I do so with my feet bare, especially after a dream, or when I need to speak to another, as I do now."

He looked down at his bare feet and wiggled his toes, and White Paws scooted closer to lick them. "Silly wolf." He dug into his fur and massaged him. "Much wisdom comes to me this way. It helps me to become one with everything living, to be... grounded. Yes, a good word for this.

"When my mind will not slow down and I find my thoughts all mixed, I walk in silence. I focus on the bottoms of my feet and think as a tree. I push roots from the bottom of my feet, and I can actually feel as the roots go deep into our Mother. My feet, they tickle! When I feel emotions that I do not like, as anger or resentment, and yes, I do feel these things, I ask our Mother to take them away from me and fill my roots with understanding, acceptance, and she does."

Star took off her footwear and pressed her feet into the sandy ground.

"Close your eyes, and drift." He waited as she did so. "Allow your roots to grow, and feel as the Mother embraces them. Let all the emotions that cause you harm flow out away from you. Keep doing this until you feel your feet tingle. Then breathe in and take in the nourishment from our Mother. Allow her to feed you."

She sunk deeper into her mind.

He stood and softly walked away while White Paws remained by her side. He looked back and watched as a blue glow circled the pair.

White Paws helps her to find her roots.

***

'*Do not fear what you see, Human Woman. You are safe. Feel your feet's roots going deep... deep within our Mother.*'

"Who speaks to me?"

'*Worry not. I am Wolf, the one who led you to safety.*'

"White Paws? Where are we? Where are my babies? The other people?"

'*Close by, but not with us. Your babies are safe. No harm will ever come to them... or you. No one comes for you. He is nowhere near here, nor will he ever be.*'

"How do you know this?"

'*No matter. He is no more. Destiny led him to the campfires in the sky. Listen to me. What was is no more. All that matters is what is. Do you feel your feet's roots going deep? Push your roots past the sand, past the dirt, past the layers of rock. Push. Push until your roots feel warm.'*

"I feel it! They are warm, as if in a mother's womb. I remember that warmth. My mother would rub me through her belly and I would feel safe. So safe."

'Let go everything that causes you grief. Breathe deep and let it go. Feel it go down your body, down your legs. Allow your feet to take it from you, and use their roots to push it deep. Deep. Feel the warmth take away all the worry, all pain caused by others. Let it all go. Let the past go. It no longer matters.

'What was the past cannot be undone, so let it go, Sister Human. Go on and cry. It is a cleansing cry, purifying your body, your mind, your Soul. You are free to do as you please, and always will be. Relax now, Sister. Allow yourself time just to feel. To be.'

White Paws pricked his ears. His pack called and he responded.

Chapter 38

Flying Raven rode next to Wanderer and Hawk Soaring. He kept twisting back to check on his son and Smiling Warrior. Even the wolves hung back as if waiting. White Paws and the pup, Dark Moon, trotted next to their Human Brothers.

"Two days and no one follows, but the two of them still stay behind us. My son told me since the dream that brought him out here did not happen the way he saw it, he wonders what to think. I do know he takes on too much worry. He even rides Thunder knowing that she has speed, and gave Sandstone to Sparkling Star to ride. I do not think his dream was wrong. I still feel as he does. Someone is near and maybe needs our help. Sometimes dreams do not show us everything."

Wanderer slowed his mustang. "I understand this well. Once, I had the same dream four times that kept telling me to go fishing at this little pond where there were no fish. Rain had made the puddle the same night as my first dream. I was young and ignored this dream, until it made me crazy. I decided to go grab a net and fish there. I was right: no fish. I walked around the puddle and found an injured baby fox. I had no idea how long he had been there. I did not worry about being bit by the baby. He barely moved. Heh, my mother was used to me bringing home wounded animals. She made him a little bed and made him drink water."

He laughed and sighed. "At first I did not know why the baby lived. He had no mother to nurse him. I woke early as my mother was getting up, and decided to follow her. She took the baby fox to a woman who had a baby. I hid to see what was going to happen. The mother took the baby fox to her own breast! I am sure his teeth must have hurt some, but she kept caring for the fox, and he never left her after he grew up. One day, she went to gather wood, and her fox followed as White Paws does Shining Light. She stepped in a hole that twisted her leg too bad for her to make her way back to camp. That fox raced back toward camp, and then to where the woman lay, and barked until several people followed. Animals are a true wonder. Life without them would be so empty."

Flying Raven and Hawk Soaring both had a good laugh when the Great Elder's mice came out and sat on his shoulders.

"Mouse Man." Raven smiled and held out his hand for one of the mice to sniff. "Why do they follow you?"

Wanderer chuckled. "Hungry, I guess."

Raven's laughter spilled out and his belly jiggled. He trotted off to speak to Light, whose jabbering told him his son was at ease.

Smiling Warrior, seeing Raven ride up, put his hands to his ears and grinned.

"So my son talks your ears off, eh? I have so many stories you have yet to hear—"

"Father!" His son's face twisted up and turned red. "I am sure he does not need to hear stories about children. He has so many children that I am sure he has many he can tell you, especially since his first woman is going to bring another—"

"Another?" Smiling Warrior's face went blank as unpainted leather. He stopped his mustang and stared off. "Tell me why you know this and I do not? How is it you know so much?" He turned toward Shining Light with a face that looked as if he had eaten too much bitter fruit.

"Uh-oh... maybe I need to take Thunder for a run. She is restless. I see it in her head movements."

Before he could take off, Smiling Warrior grabbed Thunder's ropes. "If *you* wish to grow old, you will tell *me* how you know one of my women has a baby in her belly!"

"Gentle Wisdom has a big mouth! I would never.... Oh, I guess I told you a secret you are not to know!" He held up his hands, palms out. "Friend. We are friends, and I know friends do not get crazy at each other, so I will go now and leave you to ponder this happy news!"

Shining Light raced off. Thunder, in her greatest joy, left a cloud of dust for White Paws to follow.

Raven chuckled. "My son does spill words... sometimes too fast. I am sorry. I know the woman is the one who likes to tell everyone. I guess your woman was excited, as she has not given you a child in some time."

"I do not remember telling you Mourning Dove—"

"I think I will follow my son." Flying Raven raced off.

"How is it everyone knows about my woman?" Smiling Warrior yelled after him.

***

That evening, they enjoyed a meal of fresh fish, sweet-tasting roasted tubers, and the last of the early season greens. Everyone waited on Smiling Warrior to speak first.

He burped and rubbed his belly. "Good meal that I am thankful for." He raised his head. "So many beautiful campfires up there. Such beautiful open land. The crickets sound like heartbeats all over the land, and I hear the humpbacks calling to each other far away. Where I come from, the land is not so beautiful, and is crowded with many, many people. I would never go back. The people think they are so smart, but if they are so smart, why do they not have stories as the Peoples here? If they had heard the one about the split-apart, then maybe they would not be so empty and unhappy in their lives."

He stared at everyone, one at a time, and smiled. "I am happy to be here. My people will never know the joy I do, never know true friendship, or the caring loving people I am part of. I care deeply for all of you, even if you know things about my women that I do not."

He kept looking up and grinning. "Maybe I will keep my face without hair. I saw my reflection in still waters. I am good to look at now!"

His wolf pup licked his face as he scooted down to lay flat.

"Heh, my mind must play with me. I hear people singing."

Chapter 39

Sparkling Star washed her babies' hair after she told the little band what she had experienced, and that the man who she feared would never harm her again. "Never in life was I able to let go of so much. Many burdens have followed me, and they are gone... gone! I feel joy deep inside."

She snuggled her babies to her. "White Paws somehow took me somewhere, and I did not really see anything—I felt it! For two days, we have seen no tracks other than our own. My babies are safe, and so am I."

The men watched the mustangs graze while they gave the mothers time to feed their hungry babies. Clouds had moved in and cooled the air. Now that it was warming, the men wore breechclouts and the women wore shorter tunic dresses.

"My tunic you made me, Wisdom, is so soft and easy to pull down to feed my sons."

"I am glad it fits so well. When we get home, I will teach you how to do quill work."

Rainbow leaned forward to admire her sky beads. "It has been a long time since I have seen such beautiful beads. Star, once you learn quilling, I will teach you painting. If you have the picture in your mind, it will follow your hand to the robe."

"I would like to share my beads for all of you helping me with my sons." She turned and smiled at everyone. "So much kindness. Thank you for painting my boy's hair. No one—"

The mustangs called to the new ones approaching. The front rider's hand rose in greeting. Night Hunter reached for his bow.

Shining Light stood. "No. We do not yet know who they are or why they greet us." He raised his hand in greeting, but made no move to go forward, counting nine riders. Three were women, and two rode with small children in front of them.

"We come find Shining Light. We from land of red clay. We made homes of red clay. Our clan once part of large band. Too large. We leave find better hunting. Hairy-faces find us." The lead man sat tall. "Our Holy Woman told me... be safe with him, so also bring our family. I am called Black Bear." He looked toward the wolves, who now stood from the grass with tails up. "Wolves... Holy Woman said not fear them." He clenched the ropes on his mustang and tightened his legs around the animal's middle.

Shining Light lowered his hands while watching White Paws. The wolf lowered his tail, as did the rest of the large pack. He trotted over and sat beside his Human Brother.

Smiling Warrior knelt and wrapped his arms around his wolf pup. "What band are you? And why did your Holy Woman say to find Shining Light?"

"You Shining Light?" His voice cracked when he saw his face. "You, a hairy-face? Where you hair?"

Shining Light stepped up. "I am the one you seek. Why did you come?"

Black Bear dropped his mustang's ropes. "We come much far from home." He slipped into sign language and signed of his band having to separate to avoid the hairy-faces. The Holy Woman was old and refused to leave. Her last words were to find Shining Light.

"She pointed up at campfires in sky, and say follow way they show. You help Black Bear and his family?"

Wanderer stepped forward in excitement. "Black Bear of the Red Clay Clan?"

"Wanderer, so long ago we see each other! We were but young men!" Black Bear swung off his mustang and walked toward his old friend.

The two men reached out and slapped each other's backs. Wanderer smiled. "Black Bear, I was worried you would not make it. We are but ten or so sunrises from the forest."

The Great Elder turned to Shining Light. "These are some of the people I have been waiting for. Food! Make much meat. We will sit, and I will tell you all what they say."

Falling Rainbow jumped off her mustang and stood with crossed arms. "And how did you know they were coming? You will tell us this also?"

"I know much, soon-to-be Mother."

"Mother!" She looked at her flat belly and ran her hands across it. "I carry no baby."

"Not in your arms."

Black Bear looked at the ground near Wanderer. "I see you still have Dog."

Rainbow's mouth dropped open. "What dog! You see a dog? He says a dog follows him and *you* see him? Wait...." She turned back to Wanderer. "*Some* of the people? You wait for more people?"

He smiled and raised his shoulders. "I am always waiting for people." He went back to talking to Black Bear.

"More crazy people who see a dog!" She stomped off, dragging a reluctant Night Hunter off his animal.

"Mates... heh." The new man turned and waved to the others to jump down.

Shining Light extended a hand to the closest woman and her boy, helping them down. "Come, sit. We will make meat for you and your mother."

The boy jumped into his arms as he would someone he had known all his life, and hugged him.

He put him down and offered a hand to the woman, who smiled. "You be my son's friend, you be mine." She took his hand, squeezed it, and then slid off the mustang. "My son, he know things. You are good man." She cocked her head and raised her eyebrows. "I have all my teeth and cook good!"

He stumbled over his tongue until his woman came to aid him. Animal Speaks Woman laughed, waved for the other women to follow, and took the first woman and her son to where the other women sat.

Speaks glanced back at him with a very wide grin.

***

Wanderer sat close to his old friend and spoke half in sign, half in words. "I sent you a dream to follow the stream once you came upon the grasslands. Did you get lost?" He passed him a piece of humpback heart. "For my old friend, I give you a piece of the best meat. Where is the rest of the Red Clay Clan?"

Black Bear stopped eating and swallowed hard. He held the meat and nodded toward Smiling Warrior. He leaned in and whispered, "His kind, but with full face of hair. Three moons ago, they raced through our camp, burned our huts." He shook his head. "They not harm anyone. They just burned homes and go. One dropped something with red, smelly water. I made mistake of drinking, to see what it was." He gripped Wanderer's shoulder. "I saw Spirits! I danced with them. They floated in the air and I felt Power from them.

"I woke with much pain in head, thought bad Spirits had taken mind from me. Those people silly to drink red water. For pain I felt afterward, I never do it again, but I wonder about what I saw... forever."

Smiling Warrior approached him. "Tell Black Bear I had to learn to speak with my hands to survive." He stood before him and signed. "The red drink will steal a man or woman's mind. It will trick them with bad Spirits, telling them lies. Black Bear is wise not to drink anymore of the poison. I was once a hairy-face, but no more. Many are bad people who are tricky, like the red drink."

He explained why he had cut off his beard.

The newcomer, wary as he was, grinned. "We here and will help. We good people. Maybe no one come."

Wanderer put his hand in his friend's tattered tunic. "People always will come. You need better clothes. We can help you with that."

***

Once again, the wandering band had grown.

"Reminds me of our first trip, Father. So many came that we could not count them all." Shining Light shook his head.

His father sat with him next to the dying fire. The only two left awake, they had time to talk to each other as they had in the forest.

Flying Raven rubbed his hands to warm them. "Son, I think this is your destiny, to attract people. When Holy People from faraway bands dream of you, it is the Spirits trying to guide the Peoples to safety. Those who listen will be safe. Those who do not will face a future they never thought possible. This much the Spirits have told me. I am sure there must be others out there like you. We just have not met them. Perhaps they are yet to be born. You could be one of the first to guide people to a place where no harm will befall them. I do not understand what is coming our way, but I sensed the urgency by the way the Spirits spoke to me. They say many, many cycles of seasons have yet to pass before this danger comes our way.

"When you were but a boy, before you lost your first father, I would watch you stare off, and I knew then you had Power. I did not understand what kind of Power, only that it was strong. When White Paws came to you that cold morning when you were but nine winters old, I knew you had to be guided by more than your grandmother. I was attracted to your mother for a very long time, and then had the courage.... As you know, women have a Power over us men and it makes us... crazy. I had the courage to speak up about my desire for her."

He laughed to himself, and a broad smile reached across his face. "She was stubborn, proud, and had Energy around her hard as ice. If that trader had not come seeking her, I might have lost her to my own silliness about not speaking up."

His father leaned his way and whispered, "At least your woman was a Power storm! She went after you as a whirling wind through dead trees, knocking them down. Heh, I did worry she would take you as her mate when she was only twelve winters, and give you no choice when you were only ten winters! She wanted you that bad. Ha! You ran from her like your breechclout had caught fire!" Flying Raven's laughter woke babies and adults both.

"Father, you do not need to allow everyone in camp to hear your silly words!"

Thunder trotted over and snorted her response.

His father jumped up. "I am thinking that maybe this is a good time to give Thunder a try, and see how she takes to me."

Thunder raced off, his father on her back, leaving Shining Light to explain the noise that woke the camp.

"Father, Thunder will make you walk back!"

Darkness had never stopped the mustang before, and he was not sure his father had heard him.

He turned to face the camp. "I have no words to say."

He headed for the calm of the darkness as Animal Speaks Woman told everyone what she had heard, and laughter followed him.

***

Shining Light stayed away from the awakening campfire to avoid any questions, and to see if Thunder was going to bring his father back.

He paced as he talked to himself. "I doubt it. She will run until she cannot, and only then will she stop. Ha! My father will walk home with a sore bottom when she kicks him off. He is somewhere near forty winters and acts as a... a... well, not a respected Holy Man!"

"How does one act?"

He twirled around and fell. "Wanderer, you scared me! Heh."

"So, a respected Holy Man would twirl around and fall on the ground? Good thing you did not fall on a spiked plant, or your woman would be pulling stickers out of your respected bottom!" Wanderer leaned over and offered him a hand while holding smoldering grass in the other. "Now that you stand, gather some small twigs with me. I want to make a little fire for us to sit by. Just use what light comes from the main fire to see. In your mood, you do not want to end up stumbling in a hole."

"I walk nights all the time. I have yet to fall in a hole."

"Or twirl around and fall, boy?"

"Why have you come out here? To tease me?"

"Sometimes it happens that way, but mostly, it is a good way to start." He set the smoldering grass on top of the small twigs and added dry grass. "There, now we can sit away from the others while we wait for your father to return."

"He will return on foot! Thunder will make sure." He twirled his finger by the side of his head.

"Boy, we are all crazy. Some do not know they are crazy, and they are quiet crazy. They spend much time talking to themselves."

"I do not talk to myself."

"Then who were you talking to before I came out here?" Wanderer tossed the sticks he gathered into a pile.

"Oh, but I am not crazy!" The growing fire cast flickering shadows across them. "I just need to work some things out, and talking to myself helps. Especially after a dream or a vision I cannot understand... or maybe do not want to believe."

The Great Elder looked to the sky. "The Spirits do not tease as we humans do. They may do something to make us stop and think, maybe only show part of what we wish, because we already know the answer and need to discover it ourselves." He took out his knife and worked on a small stick, shaving it into a point. "If we always received the answers we sought, we would have much for our minds, but would no longer do many things for ourselves. We would grow old without wisdom, and the young ones would never learn from us."

"I want to have a normal family, be a member of the band who spends his time hunting, playing with his children, sitting with men who tell jokes."

Wanderer nodded. "Light, you already have all that... and more—so much more. You are blessed in ways most of us only wish. You will learn much on your travels outside the forest. You will be able to learn many things, and teach them to others who would not have known of them had you not seen, experienced, and been part of it all. You are a Healer of the body and *mind*.

"You went in and brought Smiling Warrior back to us! I cannot do that, and I live in both this land and the Spirit land. I talk to Spirits as you do to White Paws. I know what will happen before anyone else does, yet *you* went before Fawn. I have never been able to do so, and I have tried. I lost two women and all my sons. I could not find a way in. But I do talk to them because of my gift. They are safe and happy. I only wait to be with them.

"All you have to do is ask for guidance, and it is offered to you. Yes, I know this. Remember what I said about being in both worlds?" Wanderer laughed. "Close your mouth! Sparks may fly in and burn your tongue. Heh, you would not be able to talk. Everyone would miss that!" He stabbed his sharpened stick into the ground and pulled it out. "See the hole my stick left?"

"Yes, and I can speak. No sparks went into my mouth." He waved his hand, to let the Great Elder know of his silliness.

Wanderer pushed the hole closed and tossed his stick in the fire. "No hole, no stick. No one will ever know they existed. Many things are that way. A leaf falls, dirt tumbles down a hill, flowers stop blooming, a human or animal leaves a print—in time, they are gone, nothing to show they were ever there. Some things are meant to be this way, but they did exist for a reason."

He scooped up some of the small sticks to add to the fire. One by one, the fire ate them. "With you, your name may fade, just as mine will, but the things we do will remain. What we teach to a child will remain with him, and he will tell another, and those children will tell others. Important words will always pass through generations, even though no one may remember who first spoke them. That part does not matter. The words do. Your words will influence many people. Yes, I know the magic of the forest. I have been there. Time reverses us once we leave. And leave many times, you will. Your destiny lies far into the future, young Holy Man. You will hear the stories that *you* told being passed on. Be proud of what you do. Many lives will be saved because of you leaving the forest when the Spirits call upon you. Many will follow you back, and many will not, but those who do not will still pass on your words, and those words will stop some bad things."

Several mice jumped out of a pouch and sat on Wanderer's shoulders.

One cast a larger shadow than the others. '*Shining Light, always see with your inside eyes. I know my Brothers and Sisters have already told you this, but you will keep hearing it so you do not forget. The inside eyes do more than see. They feel. Emotions guide you Human creatures, which sometimes gets you into trouble, but they also take you where you need to go. Always think once, twice, perhaps many times before you act upon what you see with your outside eyes.*'

The mouse and his companions climbed back into the pouch.

"Did you hear... did you see that mouse talking to me?"

"What mouse? Mice do not talk." The Great Elder chuckled and stood to stretch. "Put out the fire once you are ready to capture some sleep." He turned and left.

Shining Light stared at where the Great Elder had sat. The flattened grass rose and looked as if Wanderer had never sat there at all.

Chapter 40

Shining Light jerked awake from a tap on his foot, and sat up.

Before him stood his very tired father, with shoulders drooping and his face, arms and legs covered in small scrapes. His breechclout was retied with plant fibers. Next to him stomped Thunder, her lips pulled back, showing off her 'I got you' smile, exposing a few gaps between her front teeth.

He tried hard to not laugh at the pair before him, but how could he not at least say something clever? "Father, did you enjoy your ride? I did not expect you back so soon. Did you stop to give Thunder a rest? Father Sun only now rises."

"If you ever expect to live long enough to have any more children, or even be able to make babies again, I would run very far, as fast as you can!"

He took the hint that his father was not pleased with his words. "Um, Father, I only now have fully wakened. I... I had this strange dream about something I can no long remember. Perhaps a fast walk, or a long ride on Sandstone, will help me to remember!"

White Paws raced to the mustang and ran circles around her, and she pawed the ground as if waiting for Shining Light to jump on and ride her.

He walked part of the way backward to keep an eye on his father. He had never seen him so red-faced. As he trotted away on Sandstone, Gentle Wisdom yelled something about jerked meat.

With a grin on his face, he tapped the mustang into a faster trot. Grey Storm raced past with Flying Cloud. He slowed her down and twisted around to shouts from Night Hunter.

"Brother, I wish to speak to you!" He came even with Sandstone. "I wish to ask you questions about women."

"Women? Ha! I have been bested by Speaks, by Wisdom, by a crazy female mustang, and *you* wish to ask *me* about women?

"What is bested?" He stopped his animal and whistled for Flying Cloud, who spun about and raced back. "I need to name the mother, maybe Soft Cloud, so Rainbow can hear a gentle name. They know my whistle, taught to me by a high-spirited mate who also whistles for me."

"Bested means that a woman has gotten the best of you. I must be the most bested man alive! Women. Never will I understand them." He jumped down as Night Hunter did, and they wandered beside their mustangs. "Animals? I can understand them... except one crazy one who everyone wants to turn into jerked meat. Now Sandstone is sweet. She follows me and has since she came to be part of our band."

He stopped and faced Night Hunter with a crooked grin and put his hands on his shoulders. "I am guessing you ask because you have been bested."

The man squirmed before answering. "I love Rainbow. I would do anything I could for her. In my band, men have the say. At least I think so. Maybe not." He grabbed a handful of hair and twisted it around his hand. "Perhaps they allow the men only to think so. We hunt for them, protect them. Except the two Warrior Women, who always joined in on hunts and helped with any disagreements that arose from another band, it was the men who decided when we moved to the cold camp, and back when it warms."

"What is it you wish to ask of me? Speaks is very strong minded. She is my heart and, yes, I do many things for her. In return, she does much for me also. We have a balance in our lives that took several moons to happen. I can tell you to allow much time to pass between you. You are only now learning about each other. Remember, words spilled too quickly cannot be swallowed."

He bent, picked up a stick and twirled it. Eagles called to one another and he smiled. "My grandmother once told a story to our band in the cold season, which I will never forget. She said, 'Your family is forever. Be willing to always talk, but not in heated words. Never walk away in anger. If you must walk away to think, clear your head and simply say that you need to be alone for a short span. Before you leave, always smile, not glare. One day you may not have your mate. You do not want to have regrets that will stay with you until you yourself go to the campfires in the sky. It would be a miserable life to have these feelings until your last breath.' Remember these words. You both are meant to be together, or it would not have happened."

"I never asked you what I wanted to, yet you gave me the answer. Heh, you are around three winters younger than I am, yet you speak like a Great Elder. Thank you."

Night Hunter reached for his mustang's ropes when another rider came over a small rise. The man stopped when he saw them, and raised his hand in greeting.

They motioned him down. Shining Light held Sandstone's ropes, and Night Hunter's hand rested on his knife's antler handle. The stranger's hair was braided down both his shoulders, which bounced on a nicely made dark brown tunic with wide flaring arms and leggings to match.

"Here we are only wearing breechclouts, and he dresses as if he is making ready for a Counsel." Night Hunter shouted and waved for him to come forward. "Elk Dreaming? How is this so?"

Shining Light's head turned from man to man. "I am Shining Light. Where do you come from?"

Elk Dreaming slid off his mustang with such a wide smile, Shining Light stood back, unsure of what to expect. The man stopped short of touching him.

"Night Hunter, is my daughter well?"

He stared down at his shuffling feet. "We are mates."

"You took my daughter as mate? My little girl?"

"Your little girl has become a woman in all ways, and will honor you with a grandchild in about eight moons."

"Who says this? No woman knows this soon." He shook Night Hunter's shoulders.

"Wanderer! He told her just a sunrise ago. Your hands squeeze my shoulders flat!"

Shining Light listened to the two men banter for a span, unsure when to speak up. He heard Sandstone call to other mustangs and glanced up as they responded.

Many people rode and walked over the small rise.

"People. Many people come!"

He pointed at riders, people walking, and mustangs carrying drags. Dogs followed screaming, playful children. He grabbed White Paws thick neck hair, worried about the new dogs.

"I must warn White Paws' pack before the dogs reach our camp." He flew onto his mustang's back, called to the wolf and raced away.

He stopped in such a hurry he nearly fell off. Sandstone's young one had beaten them back to camp, and now trotted over to their animals and snorted, reared, and raced around them in a circle. Thunder picked up the excitement.

People yelled to each other and tried to get to the mustangs before they lost them.

Shining Light smacked his forehead. He knew for sure they would be thinking about jerked meat once more.

I am happy not to know who their father is! I know he would not be able to make any more babies.

Both Thunder and her little brother, Grey Storm, rumbled ahead of the rest of the mustangs at full speed. Only a few had been caught before they could follow.

"We were all bested by your children, Sandstone." He could not help but laugh. What else could he do? "I will need to watch when you tease the males and see who you go to. Make *him* into jerk meat! Or maybe he is a good male to have. I must trade for him. The wolves! White Paws, your pack... go to them. I must speak of the band that comes our way!"

Chapter 41

Shining Light slid from Sandstone and called to the others in the camp. "Let them work off their Energy. New people come."

The people gathered around him, some not so happy with Thunder and Grey Storm.

He could see anger in their faces. "They will be back. They always return because after Thunder tires, she turns them around. These new people are many. Night Hunter and a man called Elk Dreaming were speaking about Falling Rainbow, so they are not to be feared."

"I am his daughter! The Beaver People come!" Falling Rainbow put her hands on the sides of her face. "Where are they? Why are they here? What happened that they left our camp? Are the hairy-faces after them? Shining Light, speak to me!" She flung her hands in the air, dropped them, and ran past him, but turned back. "Are you not going to show me where my father is?"

Wanderer grinned and made his way past the gathered people. "Finally, we are all here. I hope they brought food. We will need it." He calmly turned to the bewildered pair. "When the mustangs return, they will be very tired, too tired to ride. We may need to hunt on foot. Speaks will need to call the animals." He brushed past Shining Light and Rainbow and muttered, "I do not need the new dogs who come to think the mice are food."

"Wanderer! My father comes and you act as if you knew all the time! How? Why?" She stomped and walked past him. "Crazy Mouse Man!"

She stopped, glanced back, and waited for someone to lead the way. "Will someone please take me to my father?"

Light pointed. "No need. Your man has brought them."

He jumped on Sandstone and rode to Sparkling Star, who sat close to the trees, clutching her sons. "Star, do not worry. Your sons are safe. I will guard them with my life. This is a promise I make to you, one I will never go back on. Also, I give Thunder over to you, now and forever. She has always been yours, even before you came to us."

He tapped his mustang and trotted after several men he spotted ahead on mustangs. *I must find those who chase the mustangs before they decide Thunder would make good jerked meat!*

Some distance away, he spotted his father and grandfather among the people who had given up the chase. "Grandfather, Father, I do not know why or how Wanderer knew of them coming, but Rainbow's whole band is in camp! Her father is not very pleased to know Night Hunter took her as mate without him being part of the ceremony. I heard him say something about wanting many mustangs for Rainbow. Will both of you please greet them? I need to try to catch up to the mustangs before anything happens.... If Thunder and Grey Storm are harmed...."

He called the wolves with a loud long howl and urged Sandstone forward.

***

Hawk Soaring scratched his head. "Sweet Mother, what is going on in camp?"

Flying Raven stared off after his son. "I really, really want to go home. Home!" He turned around and waved to Hawk Soaring to follow. "That boy comes from your blood. I think I might never leave the forest again! This has been even more crazy than the first trip to find the forest! I wish to hold Makes Baskets in my arms and never let her go again, to play with my little children, to sit in front of my lodge and listen to the crackling fire my woman has made, and to hear Cricket's heartbeat when we dance. Maybe we need to do that here this sunset! It will maybe help Falling Rainbow's father stop his growling at Night Hunter. He must give her father gifts. I did see mustangs running with ours that I know to be wild. He needs to catch some as his gift to her father."

Hawk Soaring chuckled and tapped his mustang to go forward. "Heh, I have been in communication with Bright Sun Flower for part of this trip. I may not be a Holy Man, but we both know everyone has their own abilities if they seek to find them. I still hear her loud voice ringing in my ears. I hope my woman has missed me as much as yours must. Mine knows our grandson now howls as White Paws, and worries he will run off with his wolves! Some things that people worry about. They make up things in their minds to worry over. Life is not meant to be lived this way."

He turned back and waved the men of the Red Clay Clan to follow them. "I, too, only wish to go home. But maybe it would be a good idea to wait a bit longer, until my woman misses me more." He chuckled and shook his head. "Shining Light may be my grandson, but you became his father. Good idea, this dance. We will celebrate the new couple, the people, and going home!"

***

"Father, how is it that you are here? And with *all* the Beaver People?" Falling Rainbow held tight to both her parents' hands. "I thought to not see you until I came back with paintings of the forest to show everyone."

"Daughter, we have much to speak on." Her father's eyes roamed to Night Hunter.

"Hunter is a good man, Father. I know he will offer you gifts. We talked long on this and thought to bring them when we came back for you. Come into our camp so we may all sit and speak of our journeys. And, Shining Light is here! Father, Mother, come!" She walked backwards and pulled them toward the camp.

Everyone she knew from the Beaver People followed. Several drags had been made into large baskets with willow branches woven together, so smaller children could ride inside. Other drags held elders and supplies. Mustangs pulled drags with lodge polls while people walked beside them.

A band she did not recognize followed behind her People. "Who comes with you?"

Elk Dreaming's expression changed. "These people who follow we found living in huts made from branches. They were all elders, and had little food. They sent their young ones away to find a better place for them all, but the young ones did not return after a cycle of seasons. No one of their band knows why they did not return. Only nine of them remained after the cold season. We asked how they were called, and one man said they had no name anymore. We adopted them, so they are Beaver People. We will talk more once we rest and eat. We had a good hunt and have food to offer. Come, Daughter who now has a mate, help us get settled. We have been long coming, and we are all tired."

***

Shining Light caught up to the other riders and told them to return to camp and let him bring back the mustangs. The firmness in his voice turned all but his cousin back.

"I see dust ahead, Light. I think they still run."

"Thunder and her little brother have their own reasons, Wisdom. We will take our time. Rainbow's whole band showed up! I am not so sure I want to go back right now." He slowed Sandstone down to an easy trot. "I could not count them all. I did not wait to welcome them after I saw all their dogs. I sent White Paws to gather his family. Only Smiling Warrior's pup remained at his side. I called to the wolves before I left so White Paws will know to follow after me."

He stopped Sandstone and stared ahead. "All I wish for right now is to go home and sit in front of my own lodge. I really have enjoyed all this traveling, seeing the beauty of our Mother again. So much open, free and wild lands filled with humpbacks, deer, and herds of wild mustangs."

He held out his arms and raised them. "Big sky! The winding rivers with many colors of greens, silvers, and red-brown shrubs. The flowers all calling out in bright colors. It has allowed my Soul to grow, and I have felt such freedom. I know my path will lead me out of the forest again, but for now, I need to see friends and family, and to be at rest for a while. Sit around a campfire and tell stories of what we have done and seen. Perhaps a trader's life would be a good one."

Wisdom leaned forward on Brown Dog. "I will have much to explain to Mother and Father." She cocked her head his way. "Will you stand with me, Cousin?"

He stared into her tired, red eyes. Her usual smile was gone and she slumped. "Of course, Cousin! You and me, we are forever friends, not just cousins. I care for you deeper and stronger than I can explain. You and White Paws have been at my side always. My heart would drop to the ground if you ever stopped following me. I know you have new responsibilities, some you never thought would come your way, but it is the same for me. This adventure has brought us closer, taught both of us more about ourselves, made us stronger, filled us with more Power. Ha! Here come the wolves. Yahaa!"

They tapped their mustangs into a faster trot across the lush grasslands and laughed as children, their long hair flowing behind them.

Chapter 42

Shining Light and his cousin approached the camp at a slow pace. "I hope Father or Grandfather warned the new people. We ride in with wolves out front and on both sides of us, with Thunder and Grey Storm leading a tired bunch of mustangs behind."

He stopped Sandstone far enough away that the wolves would not startle the new people. "Wisdom, I need to remain here. I worry harm will come to White Paws' family. I see Smiling Warrior and his pup with children around him, but many wolves mixing with dogs? I am not so sure."

Wisdom sat as tall as possible on her mustang and stared toward the new people. "I count eleven dogs. Remember the first time we were out here? We encountered bands with dogs. The people kept them roped and we had no trouble."

"I remember. There were only nine wolves then. Twenty-one wolves may frighten these people. Perhaps Father and Elk Dreaming will—"

"Night Hunter comes, and Star waves to me." She tapped her mustang. "I go to Star. I worry about the babies."

The mustangs trotted off to greet the new animals, leaving him and an excited Sandstone with the wolves. White Paws stood in front of the mustang, tail down. Shining Light knew the signal. The wolf expressed no threat to the dogs.

Night Hunter trotted up on his mustang and stopped before him. "Falling Rainbow and her father speak of our mating. She defends me and tells him of the hairy-faces attacking the camp, how I helped to save her. I go for a ride, maybe catch mustangs to make her father smile."

Before he could pass, Shining Light reached out and touched his shoulder. "You should stay and wait until we speak to him. Find out why he is here first. It is important to hear his words. This offers him respect." He slid down to face his Wolf Brother. "White Paws, you and your pack stay here. Moon Face, you must keep your pups calm. I know you understand. I will not allow any harm to come your way."

Moon Face cocked her head and went to her pups, which lay in the grass. White Paws and the rest of the pack followed Moon Face.

Shining Light jumped back on his mustang and headed for camp. With his hand up in greeting, he rode over to Elk Dreaming and jumped off Sandstone. "Father of Falling Rainbow, who is mate to the great warrior Night Hunter, I greet you and welcome you to our camp. I am Shining Light, Holy Man. I see doubt in your eyes. Yes, I am young. Please understand I have had dreams since I was a small child, and had great teachers. Still do. As you know, we never stop learning.

"Now I ask this: please keep ropes on your dogs so there is no worry. My pack members, the wolves, remain where they are as a sign of peace. Let us do the same."

Elk Dreaming grew stiff with a tight jaw. The man worried being among strangers.

Flying Raven walked forward, dropped his boot knife to the ground, and looked down out of respect. "You keep your lance at your side. We show empty hands, and ask you to do the same so we may sit and speak."

Elk Dreaming nodded and laid his lance on the ground. "We have hunted and have much meat. I will have our women gather wood, and we will share our food."

Shining Light gave a slight nod. "We will ask our women to do the same."

While the women moved off to gather wood, the men gathered around a small fire on one end of the camp. Flying Raven lit Sacred Sage, smudged himself, and passed it to the next man so he, too, could cleanse himself. Hawk Soaring brought out his pipe for everyone to smoke. No words would be said falsely once the pipe had been passed to every man. To do so would anger the Spirits, and cause harm to the one who spoke with a dirty tongue. Everyone knew the Spirits chose their own time to give out punishment for doing so.

Shining Light waited until Elk Dreaming had settled in, then sat next to him, with Gentle Wisdom next to him, and waited for his father to pass the talking stick to Elk Dreaming. The Elder's tight shoulders unwound and his face relaxed. No one would speak without holding the talking stick. This gave each person their chance to say their words and not be interrupted.

Elk Dreaming held the stick that Shining Light's people had brought with them, decorated in white and black quills. He glanced around the camp first.

Food roasted, and the women sat in a circle to the side of the men's. Falling Rainbow, clearly torn, sat next to her mother. Animal Speaks Woman sat off to the side with Sparkling Star. All fell silent. Even children knew not to make noise.

Elk Dreaming cleared his throat. "I, Elk Dreaming, wish to say this first. My heart was ripped from my body when my daughter could not return to us, and my woman, Paints Visions, could no longer bear the loss." He turned and stared at his daughter and woman, then at Night Hunter. He pointed a finger his way. "He was to protect her, keep her safe. My daughter says he did this. My eyes see a peaceful daughter who is now as confused as I am. This is not good." He waved for her to come.

With eyes downcast, she walked around the men's Counsel Circle and sat behind him.

He motioned for her to sit next to him. "Daughter, I have thought much on this. Night Hunter's Vision Quest was a good one. I hold anger and jealousy that I now let go, and I feel shame for judging a man without hearing his words, feeling what is in his heart. Go, sit by your man." He nodded.

She smiled, jumped up, and squeezed in next to Night Hunter.

"We never thought to leave our lands. Yes, we moved to avoid the raids by the hairy-faces." He stopped and stared Smiling Warrior's way, whose face hair now showed some again. "I hear you, too, helped to save my daughter. I call you friend, not enemy. The enemy I speak of will follow us no more. Our warriors made certain of that. The enemy came in the night and burned our homes. We were not there, but at a gathering. I am happy to say no one lost their lives in our band."

Everyone within the Counsel Circle spoke quick words of gratitude, nodded, then grew silent again.

"Riders came to the gathering where we had only visited for one sunrise. We raced back to our homes, and held Counsel on the ground where the Lodge should have been. This was about ten sunrises after I sent Night Hunter to watch over my daughter. Wanderer tells me your band found themselves lost for five sunrises, and then had to come back. This allowed us the ten sunrises we needed. I know our Peoples do not get lost."

He chuckled at Wanderer. "Thank you, old friend, for helping us to get here. I see your dog still is with you, and your mice! I am happy to be here and know my people are safe. I see this now. We wait to see this land where rainbows fall down water."

He turned to Shining Light. "I see you are more than a legend. Yes, you are very young to be a Holy Man. My daughter has spoken of you since she was a little girl."

He held out his arm above his crossed legs, and the young Holy Man crossed his hand over his arm in greeting.

"She told us you were real and one day she would find you. I know we are related. My sister, Song Bird, told everyone to say her name so her sister, Bright Sun Flower, could hear it again. She told me when my daughter became a woman she would like her first daughter to carry her name. Perhaps my daughter might think on this."

He sighed and relaxed his shoulders. "I am an old and tired man who wishes to eat and rest. I have said my words. Ha! Many, many words." He handed the talking stick to Shining Light.

Shining Light held the stick and tossed it from hand to hand before speaking. "I welcome the Beaver People. Soon, if all of you choose to follow us, you will see much beauty. It is very different from the canyons, but just as mystical. Power lives there as it did in the canyons."

He stood and walked in the Counsel Circle. "I believe in my very being that Power follows whoever calls to it. It is up to each of us to use it wisely for the good of everyone, not only a few."

He lowered his head and found White Paws at his side. "Some get Power and think too much of themselves. Abuse it, and Power goes away, leaving the person as an empty shell. Sometimes it takes a while before they understand they have no more Power, but then they pretend they do and convince themselves they still have it. They become hollow, then dry up as grey dust dead of all its Energy. They find life no longer holds meaning, and it is too late once they understand this. The damage is done, and their punishment is to find themselves in darkness with no campfires to sit by in the sky. They will be alone forever, with only their thoughts of regret.

"These are people who hunt us, take away our land. They will one day know of what I speak. Not only will they abuse themselves, but our Mother as well. She is a kind Mother and will give them a chance to make things right. But even chances run out. This is why it is good that you come. We will all journey together to the forest."

He turned his face to Elk Dreaming. "Before we make this journey, we must allow your dogs and our wolves to make peace. My woman has a dog, and they hunt together now, but when they first met, it was not so. After everyone has settled in and eaten, I wish to bring the pack's father and mother forward with their last-born pups."

He held out his hand toward Smiling Warrior. "My friend and brother, once a hairy-face, holds one of the wolf pups in his arms. I have seen many of your children pet him. Hold no fear in your minds for them, or the man Smiling Warrior. I am part of the wolf pack. Wolves protect us and warn us of danger, even help us hunt. They are Sacred, as is every living being."

He walked around the Counsel Circle again and took a breath as he firmed his voice. "In our band are people some would maybe worry over. I will not put those people before you. That is their choice. But I will tell you we have a woman who bore two babies almost two moons ago. They are healthy and each of us has held them. No one will tell you which was born first. It does not matter."

His voice defied any to argue. "I have said my words, and now need to be alone."

He handed the talking stick to his father, who was next to speak, and walked with White Paws toward Moon Face and his pack. Grey Storm followed, and Sandstone trotted after her young one. Thunder, instead of following him as she had many times before, stayed near Sparkling Star.

Chapter 43

Shining Light withdrew from the new people. Their Energy made his mind dizzy. He had always felt the people around him, but they were of his own band. Even with Wanderer, Falling Rainbow, Sparkling Star and Night Hunter, he was able to stay separate.

Too many come all at once with worries and fears. I cannot push so much away as I did the first time.

"You were younger and had not opened yourself up as you do now." Wanderer shed his tunic and tossed it over his shoulder, wearing only his breechclout. "Many Holy People, as they grow, find being alone is the only way to shake it off."

"I felt you leave the people and follow me. I knew you were there before I heard you speak." He stopped and watched the wolves move on. They needed to hunt.

Grey Storm pushed his arm and nickered while Sandstone moved off to graze. "Grey Storm, you can feel me. You and I will bond." He turned and patted his companion's neck. "Your mother and I bonded when I was young. She spoke words in my mind, and we have been with each other all this time. White Paws and you will be... companions, unlike any humans can be. The wild mustangs see wolves and run away with fear-crazed eyes. I have seen this. Never has a mustang among our band showed any fear."

He took Wanderer's tunic, and placed it on Grey Storm's back to see what the mustang would do.

Storm turned his neck and sniffed it, then grabbed it with his teeth and tossed it to the ground.

"Okay, little one, you are not ready to feel the strangeness on your back yet." Shining Light handed Wanderer back his tunic. "I hope it has no teeth marks."

"Heh, it holds mice inside a few sewed pouches." Seven little mice crawled out. He reached for them, placed them on his arms, and laughed. "They bounce good!" They jumped down and chased each other through the grass. "I have five baby mice in one pouch and six in another... or maybe they have me."

"I am sorry I tossed your tunic without asking! That was disrespectful of me."

"Do not worry about disrespecting me. You could never do so. We are friends and do much for each other."

"You honor me, Great Elder. I am sorry. I forget about your mice. You say they do not speak to you, but they have told me much."

"Oh, they speak, but not in words. They reach me through my inner being, as does White Paws with you. As my Spirit dog does with me. When Grey

Storm is ready, he will reach you. He is very young and may not feel he has words to share with you just yet. You must not try to bond with him until he approaches you. You will know." He checked the baby mice. "I have had these mice with me since I went into the canyon and lived in the cave. I left with about thirty, but most chose to go a different way. I am not so sure they will want to come into the forest. I will miss them if they do not, but we all have choices to make that no one can make for us. We belong to ourselves."

The Great Elder pulled off his necklace, which had sky beads that alternated with other stones, and placed it over Shining Light's head. "I made each bead as I traveled with my old band and on my own. The ones that are not sky beads, I found one at a time. Small stones would catch my eyes, and after asking permission to take them—some did say no, and I put them back—I worked them by chipping them into circles, then spent much time putting holes in each one. They come from many places. The first one I found the sunrise your band welcomed you into this life. They are for you. In time, each stone will show you something. They speak in their own way. You will understand only when you are meant to.

"Sky Beads are very special, much more than the yellow stone—that one never spoke to me. The sky bead is known for good healing Energy. It helps with the mind, and some say they work as a protector. Each stone holds great knowledge that they themselves learned as the Mother was born. Some fell from the campfires in the sky and hardened before landing. They carried the knowledge of our ancestors. Stones *are* our ancestors, the oldest beings on our Mother. Listen to them, respect them, and they will tell you secrets. What you see as a simple stone on the ground is much more."

Shining Light turned the necklace and felt each bead. "The stones are so round." He glanced up and smiled at the Great Holy Man. "How did you know when I came to be part of my band? How do you know all the the things you do?"

He clicked for his mice and they returned. "Age, young one. For many lonely moons, I found my way walking along the Spiral, searching for myself. The person we see in the reflection of still waters is only a skin. We never truly find ourselves through others, either. They reflect who they think we are back to us. Only when we spend time within the Circle, letting go of our skin, of who we think we are, will we find ourselves."

He picked up a handful of dirt and let it run through his fingers. "Each tiny bit of dust tells us something, but only when we are willing to sift through all of it will we ever be able to understand. Some people only hold dirt. Others feel the Energy in each speck. Even what we cannot see lives, and if you try, you can feel the Energy. You do not see the air we breathe, yet without it, we would be no more. When you take in air, you take in life."

Shining Light nodded. "Why did you follow me out here? You have given me much wisdom to think about. I only wanted to get away from all the craziness in camp for a while. I needed to—"

"You needed to hear my words. Swallow them as you would food. Let them move through your body and give you strength. As seasons pass, you

There are only a few you will not recognize.

Shining Light – Young Holy Man, family man with much yet to learn

Animal Speaks Woman - "Speaks" (heart name), Shining Light's woman

Turtle Dove – Daughter of Shining Light and Animal Speaks Woman

Gentle Wisdom – Shining Light's cousin

Tall Smiling Warrior – A hairy-face man (white man)

Flying Raven Who Dreams and **Makes Baskets** – Shining Light's parents

Soft Breeze – Shining Light's sister

Sparrow Hawk – Shining Light's brother

Hawk Soaring and Bright Sun Flower – Shining Light's grandparents

Wanderer – Unusual Holy Man

Falling Rainbow – Young woman whom Wanderer rescues

Night Hunter – Man who pursues Falling Rainbow

Sparkling Star – Pregnant runaway slave

Thunder – Mustang with her own mind

And of course - **White Paws and Moon Face** – The wolves

will find yourself needing to be alone. It is hard on a family. Good thing you have Speaks as your woman. My sister knew what she did, making sure the two of you became mates."

The Elder smiled and walked a different way.

I know Wanderer is right about the need to be alone, but it is from humans, not animals. I feel connected to the wolves, the mustangs. They understand and help me by sharing their Energy. Power comes from them that humans do not have.

Grey Storm trotted over to him. He could feel the innocence of the young one, like a child yet to experience life. The mustang's bright eyes gleamed. Never before had he seen such blue in a mustang's eyes. Grey Storm's eyes were dark brown but circled in blue.

He rubbed the mustang's face and scratched his shoulder. "I can see a blue color in your dark grey hair. Perhaps it is Father Sun's light. By the next time the leaves bud, you and I will explore this idea of riding. Being next to you, I feel the same Power as I do with White Paws. Ha! Perhaps some day, you and I will reach inside each other and—"

'Perhaps human... perhaps.' Grey Storm raced away, kicking his heels up as he did.

He stood, hand still positioned over the mustang's shoulder that was no longer there. He nodded and grinned. "Perhaps mustang... perhaps."

He spent the next two sunrises away from camp. White Paws, ever by his side, rested his head on his leg. The wolf shared his Energy, allowing Shining Light to relax and set his mind free. He sought to find his way into The Circle of Life, seeking his way in for short spans to watch the colors make music. He needed to stay nearby, or Speaks, who came out and left him food, water and a robe at the edge of their camp, would leave the safety herself to find him. He took the robe and water, but left the food. It only interfered in him finding his way inside himself.

She must have understood he wanted no food. She removed it the next sunrise.

The stones around his neck felt different, warmer than the sky beads he had given to Sparkling Star. Each stone bead had different colors. Even the sky beads had black indents his other ones did not have. No whispers came from the stones as he had hoped. *'Only when you are meant to,'* Wanderer had said.

He walked until he tired, then rested on the robe. A stone poked the back of his head as he tried to sleep that first night. Irritated, he pulled it from where it had rested for a long time and started to throw it. The stone felt jagged and warm, but darkness had stolen any chance of looking at it.

"Stone, it was wrong of me to pull you out of our Mother. I should have moved over." Before he turned around to put it back, Sister Wind caressed him with her warm breath. He was alone with the two mustangs, who moved about grazing.

When did White Paws leave?

"Stone, what wisdom do you have for me?"

Spears in the sky flashed far away in bright white and yellow. He waited to hear rumbling. None came. Crickets chirped, and he found himself lost in their sound. His whole life he had heard the heartbeat in their rhythm—every dance, drumbeat, song, even in the crackling in campfires. The beat of all living.

He stood with arms raised and swayed to the night music and sang.

"IN THE NIGHT AIR, CRICKET CHIRPS THE SONG OF MY BEATING HEART, FILLING ME WITH INNER KNOWING.

MY BODY SWAYS WITH THE SONG.

I FEEL THE MUSIC GO THROUGH ME, THROUGH THE ROOTS OF MY FEET AND INTO MOTHER'S WOMB, CREATING A BALANCE OF HARMONY.

EVERY LIVING BEING MOVES TO THE MUSIC THAT CREATES THE DANCE OF LIFE I MOVE TO.

SISTER WIND CARRIES THE DANCE, CARESSING EACH BLADE OF GRASS, EACH LEAF OF EVERY PLANT.

SHE GIVES TO ALL THAT IS, AND WILL BE, PASSING ON A PIECE OF ENERGY WITH EACH CARESS... PASSES IT ON.

I AM THIS ENERGY. I AM SO MUCH MORE.

I SWAY TO THIS GENTLE BREEZE OF INNER KNOWING.

I AM CRICKET'S SONG... I AM CRICKET'S SONG."

He placed the stone back, drank from the water bladder, and stretched out on the robe that he moved over.

"Thank you for telling me what I already knew, stone."

***

"Your song, so beautiful. I wish for you to teach it to our people when we get home, man of mine." Speaks crawled next to Shining Light and placed their daughter between them. "The whole camp heard you singing, and the people took your words into their hearts. No one argues, children sleep, and even the dogs no longer cry about their ropes. White Paws walked among their dogs, tail down and greeted each one. That wolf brother of yours offered each dog meat from his mouth! So much I do not understand. Why would a wolf want to make peace with dogs that growled with bared teeth only a sunrise ago? I think we will be a joined people when Father Sun wakes." She laughed and ran her hand through his hair.

Shining Light reached for her hand, held it, and ran his other up and down her arm. "Sweet woman of mine, White Paws saw humans acting silly, being bad to each other, and did what he thought was best—make friends where there were none to show it was possible. Again, animals teach humans another lesson so we do not become split-apart. Perhaps one day, animals will allow us to rejoin their campfire."

Speaks took Dove from the cradleboard, pulled her daughter and herself closer to Shining Light, and snuggled in.

White Paws made a good place for himself beyond the tops on their heads.

Sleep found them while they lay wrapped in each other's arms.

Chapter 44

Speaks and Light headed into camp with mustangs and White Paws following. The wolves sat with and around his band. The Beaver People had moved in closer and sat on shared robes, talking and laughing with the Wolf People. Smoke rose from several campfires, and the smell of food and laughing children filled the air.

Flying Raven, Hawk Soaring, and Wanderer sat with Elk Dreaming, apart from everyone. Shining Light headed for them while Speaks took Dove and sat with the women.

Flying Raven waved his son over. "So, my son has returned. Sit on one of the nice humpback robes Elk Dreaming has given us as gifts. Never before have I felt such comfort." He pointed to his new light brown tunic quilled with designs of flowers along the neckline. He raised his arms to show the finely cut fringe. "His woman has many talents. She also weaves baskets. I know your mother will be happy to have someone to share her talents. We all know of his daughter's gift to paint. Your woman will find her good company when we all get home. And food! His band has made us all food this day that our own women back home will envy. And look, he has also offered beautiful quills as gifts to our women, and brought fine arrow points made from the humpback's bone for us men.

"We are not far from home. Heh, we never did go past a moon away, counting the five sunrises we somehow found ourselves lost." He grinned at Wanderer, who rolled his eyes. The custom of boasting about gifts was expected, as no one wanted to offend another by setting gifts aside.

He looked at Shining Light, his grin no longer showing. "His people are still shy around the wolves, even though their dogs are more relaxed. That is why they stay back. This would be a good day to show the gentleness of White Paws to the families who have children."

Shining Light had never heard his father's mouth so filled with compliments before. His father honored Elk Dreaming. The best way to make things right was by the use of words.

Shining Light turned to Elk Dreaming, who now smiled. "I know we have many gifts to offer your people as well. Perhaps not as nice, but we will show your people a beautiful place where they will have their choice of land." He turned and watched the new people. "I see your women have great beauty, as well as talents. Your daughter is good to look at, as is your woman. I hope our men who seek mates from your people will be worthy."

Elk Dreaming stood, reached behind him, and picked up a hide. "Your words do my people great honor. Please accept this gift." He held out a dark tanned deer hide.

Shining Light rubbed the soft hide with his fingers and smiled. "This is the best tanned deer hide I have ever held. My woman will be very happy to make our baby daughter soft things to wear from it. I will give this to her, and will take some of the wolves with me to visit your people, to show them they have nothing to fear, nor do their children."

A familiar loud laughter rose and he glanced toward Smiling Warrior. "I see the hairy-face I call Brother and his wolf pup. He has many children of his own and loves them much. He would never allow any harm to come to any child."

He nodded to the Beaver People's Holy Man, then turned and took the hide to Speaks. She sat under trees with Gentle Wisdom and Falling Rainbow, playing with Dove and Sparkling Star's babies.

"Speaks, make big eyes to show how pleased you are. Elk Dreaming is watching."

She spread her biggest smile across her face and held the hide up to show the other women. "Does he still look?"

He shifted his head so he could look, but not so much that he drew attention. "He is busy eating."

A soft whistle brought White Paws, Moon Face and the youngest pups. He lowered his hand so the others knew to stay. "I am not used to trying to impress so many strangers at once. Speaks, please come with me. My words are true. I would never speak with a dirty tongue. But I... I do not know how to say so many pleasing words!"

"Why, Light, are you as shy as a new woman?" Wisdom chuckled and leaned into Sparkling Star. "I will go with you, my cousin. Let your woman rest. I noticed she left as Father Sun lowered and did not return until you did." She giggled even more.

Falling Rainbow spoke up. "Since they are my people, I will go with you also. Night Hunter talked long into the night with my father. At sunrise, they left together and returned riding side-by-side. I am so happy!"

Speaks fell backwards laughing. "Our faces will be stretched out this day! Go, Light, stretch out your face also." She hid her laughter in the new robe, her shoulders shaking.

"I am so happy to have such a good woman who does *not* pick on her man! Thank you, Wisdom, my cousin who worries for me, and the very kind Falling Rainbow, who does not tease me."

They made their way through the packs, campfires, and staring people.

"We can sit next to Smiling Warrior. Children already sit next to him and his pup. Perhaps my face can have a rest."

Wisdom giggled next to him.

"Wisdom, keep a smile on your face, but stop the laughing! You make me feel... feel—"

"Bested, Cousin?" She snorted, but quickly cleared her throat and scooped up a little boy who ran to her. "I wonder if these new people have heard the word bested."

Shining Light pinched the back of her thigh and she squealed.

"Now who is bested, Cousin?"

"I think maybe I will turn around and —"

"No! You told me long ago you would be at my side, now stay there!" He nodded and smiled as the people moved away from the wolves.

"I wonder why no one grabs this child from my arms."

Falling Rainbow fell in beside the pair. "Because you hold my aunt's grandchild, and I waved her away when she jumped up."

"Rainbow, thank you for following us." He relaxed his tight shoulders, grinned, and poked Wisdom in her side. "I feel much better knowing I do not have only my mean cousin next to me who needs to be pinched to keep her from snorting laughter."

He shot his cousin a sideways glare that made her poke him back. "We will soon see who is bested, sweet cousin. I see a woman over by Smiling Warrior who smiles your way."

"Light, it is not me she smiles at. I should go back and tell Speaks you have a new woman you wish her to meet."

Rainbow cleared her throat. "If you both would stop teasing each other, you will see that her smiles are for her man who walks their child! I remember Wanderer saying something to me about using your inner eyes to see the truth within." She took the child from Gentle Wisdom, pushed past them both, and greeted the woman.

"Ha! We were both bested this time." He stopped and knelt beside White Paws.

"Falling Rainbow, that child, will she allow you to bring him to us?"

The woman's eyes widened. "I can understand your words. My ears hear well. Who are you that you ask me to give my son to feed that wolf?" She stood, her man beside her.

Falling Rainbow spilled fast words to calm the boy's parents. "He is Shining Light, my cousin, a Holy Man. He is why we all find ourselves here. I have been around the wolves and slept near them. White Paws is a special wolf... his mate is also!" She took in a deep breath. "They all are special, not just White Paws, but he is the most special. I mean he is —" Her words did little to calm anyone close enough to hear.

The little boy slipped past his parents and up to the large wolf. "Father, Mother, he licks my face!"

He giggled and sat in front of him. Half-grown wolf pups crowded in, hiding the boy. His loud giggles attracted other children. Before anyone could grab them, they were all over the wolves, playing and tumbling over them.

Wanderer joined the children. "I think we will be fine now. Shining Light, hold my tunic so my mice do not get crushed." He sat among the crazy mix and laughed as a child might.

Shining Light stood, arms crossed. "Not one dog comes forward to fight. Speaks told me White Paws had actually taken meat to each one! I would have liked to have seen that. I wonder how it is that he made friends with them so easily?"

Wisdom chuckled. "Cousin, have you already forgotten the story about the animals' campfire? White Paws is different from any wolf we had ever encountered as little children. I think he had a grandfather at that campfire. How else could he do what he has done?"

The Beaver People watched as their children and a crazy Elder played and laughed, while wolves chased them through the camp. The children of the Red Clay Clan joined in the chase.

With the tension broken, Shining Light went up to each person and welcomed them, his hand extended. Many arms were clenched in greeting. Tonight they would all dance around one campfire as a joined people, and when Father Sun woke, they would start the journey home where rainbows ran down falling waters and tall trees grew.

Chapter 45

Shining Light and Gentle Wisdom walked among the wolves. The pups chased after each other, and the younger dogs joined in. Many people asked him questions about this strange place that held mystery, the place they called home.

Most watched Smiling Warrior with worry and wondered if they were going to be safe.

"Wisdom, how much do I tell? Many wonder why I call Hawk Soaring my grandfather when he does not look any older than my father, though I do see they both have aged a little since we left. Wanderer assures me all will be well once we enter the forest again."

Eagles called to each other and he glanced up into the clear, soft blue sky. "Grandmother must know we return. I have not seen Eagles for some time."

Wisdom picked up a stick, threw it, and two wolf pups snatched it up and ran with it through the rich green grasses. "Wanderer somehow found his way here long ago, but chose not to stay. I think it was before the hairy-faces came. He does not speak much about what happened to his family, only that his women went to the campfires in the sky as very old women. It was then he maybe found the forest. This makes me wonder why his sons did not follow, but I will not ask. Some things we should never question, Cousin. They make peace for Rainbow, but I think.... We all have secrets we wish not to share. I will share my greatest secrets when we return, but some I will not. I am grown and do not have to explain my choices to anyone."

Night Hunter, Falling Rainbow and Elk Dreaming rode past. Falling Rainbow smiled at Wisdom as she passed.

"Night Hunter still seems tense. He will feel better once he has mustangs to offer her father."

Wanderer grinned at them as he, too, walked. "As soon as the baby is welcomed into the band, her father's heart will melt. Babies do that to people. My mice decided to come with me! I am happy to wake to their whispers. I worried your wolves would not know which were my mice from the others, so White Paws and I agreed on how to do this."

Shining Light stopped midstep as mice ran before him. "You spoke to White Paws?"

"Do not be silly. Wolves do not speak." Wanderer picked up a mouse before she could follow the others. "Look, Rainbow painted their heads white. She will keep painting them for me. I asked the Spirits for help and they said wolves see colors in a way we do not. Maybe they smell them. I do not understand but do not need to." He let the mouse catch up to her companions.

Gentle Wisdom snorted her laughter.

"Will I always have to listen to that... that *mustang* snort, silly Warrior Woman?"

She snorted again. "Perhaps you will, now that I know it bothers you. I am only happy to know Wanderer will come to the forest. I worried he would not come when Falling Rainbow said he missed his family. After Blue Night Sky not wanting to come into the forest, I did wonder."

"Wisdom, when he said babies melt hearts, I knew he also meant his own. He sees Rainbow as a daughter, even though she now follows Night Hunter and her father."

"They have a special connection no one can ever change. Like ours."

"I love you, too, Warrior Woman. We will remain the same, forever and always... even if you do snort."

***

Hawk Soaring rode in silence beside Flying Raven.

Raven's brows scrunched together as he stared at him. "Why do you act sad, Hawk Soaring? Soon we will be home, in maybe only three or four more sunrises."

"Raven, I was not born in the canyons, yet my heart is still there. I had hoped to see them again. Perhaps this time I was not meant to see the beauty of the red and orange canyons. But I make a promise to myself now to see them again."

Flying Raven nodded his understanding. "We cannot see into our own future for a reason. We might make a mistake by trying to change things we are not meant to change. You know your grandson will not stay in the forest. That is not his destiny. He will need help, even if he fights it. I have flown with Raven, and know many Peoples out here will need to come to the forest. If they do not, our Peoples one day will not be as we know them now. My dreams have shown me our people will always remain, but in my dream, they wore masks. They were not themselves."

"Holy Man, what does this mean?" He stopped his mustang and stared deep into Flying Raven's eyes, as if they would show the answer.

"Things will change, ways of life. Only the Mother we walk upon will remain the same." He tapped his mustang forward, leaving Hawk Soaring well behind.

Chapter 46

The Wolf People, Beaver People, and Red Clay Clan shared campfires and stories. Everyone was eager to hear about lands and people they never knew. Wolves and dogs sniffed each other, but remained calm. Pups from both packs played together as they would with other members of their own pack.

Children and many adults gathered around Falling Rainbow as she told of her adventures and showed her painted hides. Her mother and father sat beside her, while Night Hunter was out searching for wild mustangs as a gift to her father.

Sparkling Star and Gentle Wisdom sat among other mothers and talked of babies. Every mother took turns holding Star's babies. No one asked who was first born, but rather if having two at once was hard. Sparkling Star smiled and shared her knowledge. The women stared at her hair and the soft brown of her eyes, but no one asked questions about her appearance.

Animal Speaks Woman had no need to call the animals. Many humpbacks grazed nearby, and after watching the men leave to hunt, she went to be alone. She took a mustang and left the camp, leaving Dove with Gentle Wisdom.

Far enough away that she could no longer feel the animals' emotions, she slid off her mustang to allow her to graze.

Will I ever get used to this? I do not know how to stop feeling what they feel. I must eat to be alive, to give Dove nourishment, but why must I feel, and even see, the animals in my mind as they decide who will come? Their pain is never long, and I feel a tingle go through me as they pass through to the other side. Pure joy for the older and injured ones. I must do as Sparkling Star does.

She sat, took off her footwear, lay them aside and placed her feet pressed to the grass. She wiggled them until she felt the bare ground.

My eyes are closed... feel the bottoms of my feet tingle. That is it... yes.

She set her mind free from all noises around her. Roots began to tickle as they grew from her feet and pushed their way into the Mother.

Deeper... deeper. Let go. Feel the Power, the Energy, come back through my roots and into my body.

She inhaled rapidly. Swirls of color went into her mind and she lay back, her feet still firm on the ground, roots deep into the Mother.

Deeper... deeper. Let go of all worries. True Mother, come into me, guide me and help me to understand —

Pain in her hands, sore from scraping hides, vanished like raindrops on parched ground.

'Understand life, child — living and letting go of life. The body is but a place for

the Soul to live as you learn and grow, child of mine. True freedom is letting go of the worries your mind places in your being.

'I take care of all my children, and all are my children. What you feel is because you wish to feel. Keep the connection open. You become a better Human by allowing this. In this way, you will one day find a need for these emotions. These experiences will guide not only yourself, but also others. You have yet to learn who you are — so much more than a Human mother, Animal Speaks Woman. A mother to many....'

The connection faded and loneliness set in, but the love she had felt made her smile.

I do not yet understand all of this, but I will when the Spirits need me to. I am of Blue Night Sky's blood.

She put her footwear back on and headed to the camp with a lighter mind.

***

"Where have you been, Speaks? I see a different woman approaching me." Shining Light left the other men to greet his woman. "Ah... I see a brighter blue in your eyes. You were connected to the Spirit Land. I seldom see you do this. Or maybe you are sneaky and I caught you!" He played with the fringe on her tunic dress sleeves.

"You smile too much. *You* are the sneaky one. What plans do you make?" She took him away from the other people's eyes and raised a brow while running her hand down his arm. "I see bumps rise on your arm, man of mine. Why is this so? Do you feel me... a need to touch me?" Her fingers crawled like Spider, creeping closer to her prize.

"Oh, Animal Speaks Woman, you make my heart beat faster than Cricket's call." He took her in an embrace meant for inside their lodge, and ran his cheeks up and down hers. "You do not make this easy for a heart as longing as mine. People are everywhere — "

"Speaks! Your daughter cries. She is hungry." Gentle Wisdom stood in the grass, waiting for her to respond. "Where are you? I hear voice — Oh... oops. You use Fox Medicine to hide. I maybe go and see if I can find...."

Shining Light sighed. He was not sure if it was relief or disappointment. "Speaks, we cannot. Dove is so young. What if we made another baby and both need you, one new and one... one.... You smell so — "

"Soon." Speaks gently pushed him away. "Soon we will have no worries about who is around. I know you wait until the baby is no longer nursing. But I have herbs when the time comes that we are alone. Come, I hear people singing."

His woman pulled him toward the sound. "I need to care for our daughter, and I wish to hear new songs."

Her shy smile had him shaking his head. "Sweetness and innocence shows on your face. I know your mind, and you tease!" He pulled her back and ran his fingers up her arm. "Now who has bumps on her arm?"

She turned back his way. "Light — "

"Come, woman, we go to hear singing." He grinned and left her rubbing her arms.

"Who teases now, man of mine?"

Thundering hooves made them turn.

Night Hunter called out as eight mustangs raced by. He turned them toward the tame ones and called out to Elk Dreaming. "Yours, father of my woman!"

Speaks jumped in worry, but Night Hunter's chest puffed out in pride.

Elk Dreaming hurried over, shaking a fist at Night Hunter, whose smile faded. The two stood motionless, then Elk Dreaming slapped Night Hunter's arm and laughed.

Falling Rainbow ran up to the pair and stopped short of her man. Her father waved her over, took her hand, and placed it in Night Hunter's hand. The gift was accepted.

Speaks turned to Shining Light. "You never gave mustangs for me."

"I... wait! *You* wanted *me*. Where are *my* mustangs?"

She smiled, scooped up his hand and drew him close. "I gave you me, and I am worth more than any mustangs given as gifts."

She ran toward camp, and Shining Light chased after her.

Chapter 47

After the sunrise meal, the combined bands—Red Clay Clan, Beaver People, and Wolf People—joined hands, asked for guidance and continued friendship, and offered much in thanks for the new home they would soon have together.

The band began the final journey home.

Gentle Wisdom rode next to Wanderer as his mice all lined up along his shoulders. "I have need to ask you about something that will not leave my mind." She looked forward and played with Brown Dog's neck hair.

"You are young. Yes, a woman of Power, but still you have much learning ahead of you. When you are older and ready, your ancestors will come and guide you. No one can call them to you but you. They will not answer until they see you are in need of them.

"You still wonder who your Spirit Guide is, but you know. A dream showed you. When we are in the forest, I would be honored to help guide you through a Vision Quest. Some women never go through one, never feel the need as a man does. But you, Warrior Woman, you are ready."

"How is it so that you know my questions before I ask?"

"I had no idea what you were going to ask." Mice jumped into their pouch. He turned and grinned at her before racing off on his mustang.

Falling Rainbow trotted up to her. "I love that old Mouse Man! He never makes sense until you stop thinking about what he says." She too raced off to catch up with Wanderer.

Gentle Wisdom scratched her head. "You are all crazy!"

"Wisdom, look up!" Shining Light's voice carried to many people and they stopped, some bumping into the rear ends of mustangs ahead of them. "I see the forest! We will be home long before Father Sun sleeps." He howled and raced off, leaving her behind as the others had.

"Wait, why does everyone leave me behind?" She stretched herself tall. "I do see the forest! Yaha!" She squeezed Brown Dog's sides, and he did his best to catch up to the mustangs ahead of him.

***

After allowing the mustangs to rest from everyone's burst of Energy, they made steady progress, even though Thunder tried to excite the other mustangs into a run. Sparkling Star told her to walk easy, and after the third time of prancing in circles, she settled down.

Star wore the double cradleboard Speaks helped her make. It was a bit awkward, and she swayed on Thunder's back. "Thank you, Thunder. I hope to see you with a baby when the leaves bud again." She caught sight of riders coming their way and her heart beat faster. "Riders!"

Shining Light pulled back on Sandstone and waited for her to catch up. "You will soon meet some of the Peoples from our home. Star, I feel your heart speed up, see it in the way you breathe. I will be at your side. You and your babies are welcome." He reached out, took her hand and squeezed it. "There is no shame here."

Wisdom came up on her other side. "Cousin, I will be at her side. Go find your grandmother and mother. I know you are bursting to do so." She pointed at the wolves. "Ha! They will beat us if we do not slow them down. Go slow your pack, Wolf Man. I am where I belong."

Star lifted her chin and smiled at Wisdom. "So am I."

***

Shining Light watched all the big happenings around him.

Mustangs whinnied to one another as they came closer to the other riders. Smiling Warrior motioned for his pup to join the pack, but he stayed at his mustang's side. Three women and several children stopped short of him and stared, unmoving.

"Your nearly bare face. Ha! You have terrified your family." Shining Light snorted his laughter and motioned Smiling Warrior's family to come closer. He jumped off Sandstone and ran for his grandmother.

"Grandmother, you have not looked so beautiful as you do now." His face beamed with joy and he jumped into her arms. "Squeeze the air out of me until I turn colors!"

"Grandson, you are still my baby, and I *will* squeeze your air out!" Bright Sun Flower wrapped her arms around him and did just that, but then pushed him away and shook her finger at him. "I missed you too much. If you ever leave again, I am going with you."

Hawk Soaring strode up to her. "Oh, my Bright Sun Flower, you will leave, eh? Perhaps then I will stay. I missed our daughter's cooking." He scratched his belly and walked on.

"So you like our daughter's cooking better? I will ask her to feed you while I eat at our grandson's campfire. You have filled yourself up with importance while you were gone." She hurried to reach him, still trying to scold him, and fell into his arms.

Gentle Wisdom pointed toward her mother and father, who raised their arms, waving them to hurry. Her mother held her little brother, Knows Both Sides, and Wisdom nodded. "They will have no trouble understanding." Her sisters ran their way, screaming in joy.

Shining Light stood back as his father took his mother into his arms. He turned around to make sure the new Peoples came. Not one stood alone. The

Wolf People surrounded them, laughing and leading their mustangs forward. There would be no strangers this day.

He stopped at the edge of the Forest of Tall Trees. Eagles above called to each other in a greeting he knew was meant for everyone. With Sandstone, Grey Storm and White Paws beside him, he took his first steps back into the forest, to his home. He laughed as Wanderer ran behind him chasing mice and scolding the tiny animals for not being cautious. He ran his hands across the beads around his neck.

Light smiled and felt at peace. "The next few sunrises will be filled with wonder for the new Peoples, as they explore these vast lands. We have told them nothing of the magic here."

"So my son still speaks to himself?" Makes Baskets untangled herself from Flying Raven.

"Mother!" He reached out and hugged her, and she squeezed him tight enough to make his voice rise. "Moth... er... you... have become very strong!"

"My turn!" Soft Breeze reached up to her big brother while his little brother, Sparrow Hawk, tried to climb his leg.

He scooped up his sister and placed her on his shoulders, so he could lift his brother. "Oh my, you both are so heavy now!" He pretended to stumble from the weight, and both children squealed and giggled.

"I am going with you next time, Brother. I know you will leave one day, and I *am* going with you!" She played with the stone beads around his neck.

Makes Baskets pulled on the braids of her daughter. "Little Daughter, you will never leave the forest as long as I breathe. Besides, your brother is never going to leave again.

She turned, raised her square jaw, and looked into his eyes. "I hear you have brought your cousin, Falling Rainbow, with you. Now I understand my dream." She took Flying Raven by one hand, and Shining Light by the other, as he tried to balance his squirming brother. "Come, let us go greet the new people and help them to understand the magic that lives here."

"Magic works both ways, Mother. To find magic, we must also explore the outside of our forest."

White Paws brushed against Shining Light. *'Human Brother, there is much truth in your words.'*

Many open arms reached out to the new people who stepped forward. They were no longer as strangers, but as people of the Land of Tall Trees.

About the Author

Ruby has been a wanderer, and has seen most of the USA. She's the mother of an amazing son, and the wife of a patient husband who indulges her need for animals. She was also the first woman journeyman newspaper pressman in Colorado.

She spent years rescuing animals and learning from them. They taught her that life does not have to be so hard, if you go with the flow and not against it. Forgive today, because tomorrow may not come.

Her life revolves around writing and her family, which includes, of course, her animals. Two car accidents in the mid-nineties changed her life. She resented it at first, until she understood she had simply been put on another path. It was not an easy one, but she accepted it, and while it continues to be a challenge, she now learns with each step she takes.

She writes because she is compelled to pass on knowledge.

Find out more about Ruby at www.RubyStandingDeer.com, or online at Twitter (@R_StandingDeer) and Facebook (R Standing Deer).

Acknowledgements

Many people helped me to make this book a reality.

Among them is Megan Harris, who is my new editor at Evolved Publishing. I appreciate her patience as she and I work to become of one mind—no simple task, as my writing style is difficult for those who do not grow up in the American Indian culture.

I must again thank Lane Diamond, who is my publisher and chief editor, and who has been my mentor and writing coach for years now. He brought my books into the real world.

To the entire team of talented authors, editors and artists at Evolved Publishing, who support me and make this adventure fun even when it's such a grueling challenge.

I owe much to Aya Walksfar, who helped me shape *Spirals* in its early stages, and who has been a steadfast friend and guide throughout the process.

And of course, my husband Chuck. Goes without saying.

What's Next?

Watch for the release of *Stones*, the third installment in this historical exploration of the Native American Indian culture by Ruby Standing Deer, due in late 2013.

Find some more of Ruby's work in *Evolution: Vol. 1 (A Short Story Collection)*. This anthology, edited by Lane Diamond and D.T. Conklin of Evolved Publishing, boasts 10 Stories by 10 Authors, including Ruby's gripping tale, *Courage through Fear*. The anthology is available as an eBook or softcover.

Recommended Reading from Evolved Publishing:

CHILDREN'S PICTURE BOOKS
THE BIRD BRAIN BOOKS by Emlyn Chand:
    Honey the Hero
    Davey the Detective
    Poppy the Proud
    Tommy Goes Trick-or-Treating
    Courtney Saves Christmas
    Vicky Finds a Valentine
I'd Rather Be Riding My Bike by Eric Pinder
Valentina and the Haunted Mansion by Majanka Verstraete

HISTORICAL FICTION
Circles by Ruby Standing Deer
Spirals by Ruby Standing Deer
Stones by Ruby Standing Deer

LITERARY FICTION
Torn Together by Emlyn Chand
Hannah's Voice by Robb Grindstaff
Jellicle Girl by Stevie Mikayne
Weight of Earth by Stevie Mikayne

LOWER GRADE
THE THREE LOST KIDS – SPECIAL EDITION ILLUSTRATED
by Kimberly Kinrade:
    Lexie World
    Bella World
    Maddie World
THE THREE LOST KIDS – CHAPTER BOOKS by Kimberly Kinrade:
    The Death of the Sugar Fairy
    The Christmas Curse
    Cupid's Capture

MEMOIR
And Then It Rained: Lessons for Life by Megan Morrison

MYSTERY
Hot Sinatra by Axel Howerton

ROMANCE / EROTICA
Skinny-Dipping at Dawn by Darby Davenport
Walk Away with Me by Darby Davenport
Her Twisted Pleasures by Amelia James
His Twisted Lesson by Amelia James
Secret Storm by Amelia James
Tell Me You Want Me by Amelia James
The Devil Made Me Do It by Amelia James
Their Twisted Love by Amelia James

SCI-FI / FANTASY
Eulogy by D.T. Conklin

SHORT STORY ANTHOLOGIES
FROM THE EDITORS AT EVOLVED PUBLISHING:
>   *Evolution: Vol. 1 (A Short Story Collection)*
>   *Evolution: Vol. 2 (A Short Story Collection)*
>   *Pathways (A Young Adult Anthology)*
All Tolkien No Action: Swords, Sorcery & Sci-Fi by Eric Pinder

SUSPENSE / THRILLER
Forgive Me, Alex by Lane Diamond
The Devil's Bane by Lane Diamond

YOUNG ADULT
Dead Embers by T.G. Ayer
Dead Radiance by T.G. Ayer
Farsighted by Emlyn Chand
Open Heart by Emlyn Chand
Pitch by Emlyn Chand
The Silver Sphere by Michael Dadich
Ring Binder by Ranee Dillon
Forbidden Mind by Kimberly Kinrade
Forbidden Fire by Kimberly Kinrade
Forbidden Life by Kimberly Kinrade
Forbidden Trilogy (Special Omnibus Edition) by Kimberly Kinrade
Desert Flower by Angela Scott
Desert Rice by Angela Scott
Survivor Roundup by Angela Scott
Wanted: Dead or Undead by Angela Scott

Visit Evolved Publishing at:
www.EvolvedPub.com

CPSIA information can be obtained
at www.ICGtesting.com
Printed in the USA
LVHW051450130120
643227LV00004B/374/P